William Stephens Hayward

**The Star of the South**

A Sequel to the Black Angel

William Stephens Hayward

**The Star of the South**
*A Sequel to the Black Angel*

ISBN/EAN: 9783337409302

Printed in Europe, USA, Canada, Australia, Japan

Cover: Foto ©Andreas Hilbeck / pixelio.de

More available books at **www.hansebooks.com**

THE STAR OF THE SOUTH

THE

# STAR OF THE SOUTH:

## A Sequel to the Black Angel.

BY THE AUTHOR OF "HUNTED TO DEATH," "BEL DEMONIO,"
ETC. ETC.

# CONTENTS.

# THE STAR OF THE SOUTH.

## CHAPTER I

### DARCY LEIGH'S ADVENTURES.

"SILENCE in the ranks and keep your line, men," thundered forth the colonel of the Seventh South Carolina, as this regiment stood drawn up before him on the parade ground.

"Silence in the ranks!" echoed the captains of companies, the subalterns and sergeants.

But silence was more easily ordered than enforced. The men wavered unsteadily, murmurs and exclamations might be heard, and altogether this hitherto well-behaved regiment conducted itself in an extraordinary manner.

The colonel, with his officers, was on horseback, in front and to the left of the regiment in line before him.

The parade ground, which was an open plain, was crowded with spectators, who were with difficulty kept back by the sentries, and prevented from interfering with the movements of the troops.

The commotion and disturbance was principally observable in the right wing of the regiment. Indeed No. 1 Company had almost entirely broken their formation and seemed greatly excited. The men were gathered in a knot and were shouting and waving their plumed hats. Their attention seemed to be turned towards a group in the crowd to their left.

"Captain Leigh! Captain Leigh!" several voices shouted.

Then some one cried,—" Cheers for Captain Leigh!"

**1**

And instantly, to the amazement of the colonel and officers, a cheer rang forth, which was taken up first by one company, then by another, till it passed all down the line.

"What, in the name of Heaven, is the meaning of this?" cried the colonel, in amazement, to the officers who surrounded him; "are my men in a state of mutiny? This is certainly very extraordinary. Lieutenant Viles, go down the line and see what it is all about."

The men comprising the company on the right were now in the wildest confusion, and while the lieutenant is gone to ascertain its cause we will devote a short space to explanations.

The Seventh South Carolina regiment, or, as they had dubbed themselves, the "Carolina Crashers," although but lately raised, was counted one of the crack regiments in the young army of the rebel States. The privates were all picked men, hardy, and mostly above the middle height, and the officers had all, without exception, distinguished themselves in some way or other.

Colonel Johnson, who had the command, had won many laurels in the Mexican war, and all the other officers, from the major to the youngest subaltern, had seen some service.

The colonel and major were on horseback, and between them, on a splendid black charger, was a young and handsome woman, to whom, as she is to be our heroine, we wish to call the reader's attention.

Her name is Coralie Andrée St. Casse. Fatherless, motherless, and immensely rich, this young Southern lady has, at her own expense, raised and equipped this regiment, the "Carolina Crashers." Of course she could not take an absolute command, but she had again and again expressed her resolve to march North with her men and accompany them into action against the invaders of her country. Those who knew Coralie St. Casse also knew that she would do as she said, and thinking it useless to remonstrate, did not do so; they generally understood among the men and officers that she was to accompany them to the expected battle ground, in

Virginia, for which they had that very day received marching orders.

She sat her horse with ease and grace. Her figure was elegant and well developed, and was set off to the best advantage by the close fitting riding-habit she wore.

None could look on her face without being struck by her great and commanding beauty. Her eyes were large, dark, and sparkling, with ever-varying expression; now lit up with enthusiasm as she gazed on the troops before her, now soft and melting as she exchanged a pleasant word with the officers who crowded around her on all sides. Her nose was straight and thin, her mouth perfect, the lips so curved, as to give a somewhat haughty expression, except when she smiled, and then no bright morning sun could be more glorious and genial. Her hair was dark and profuse, falling over her shoulders in graceful disorder. Her face was oval; her complexion a deep glorious brown, not dark or swarthy, but a brilliant clear brown —infinitely more lovely than the fairest pink and white. A hat with a black ostrich plume was on her head, and from beneath it escaped in wavy masses her rich dark hair.

She wore no ornament of any description, but across her shoulder there was a broad sash or band of light-blue silk. A solitary gold star was embroidered on this, and lay immediately over her left breast.

She held in her hand, drooping over her horse's neck, a light staff, with a richly emblazoned flag or banner. When we say emblazoned, we mean ornamented by a rich silver border. This flag was of the same light-blue silk as the sash she wore, and in the centre there was a solitary gold star.

This flag was to be the regimental colours of the regiment, and the fair bearer was about formally to present them.

The lieutenant, whom Colonel Johnson had sent to inquire respecting the cause of the confusion at the right wing, now returned.

"Well, sir, what is it?" asked the colonel, impatiently. "What say the captains of companies 1 and 2 of the disgraceful insubordination of their men?"

"Their old captain, sir, is on the ground, and they are shouting for him to lead them—Captain Darcy Leigh, who disappeared so suddenly a short time back."

"What! Darcy Leigh come back? Why we thought him dead, or that he had gone over to the enemy. He is marked down as a deserter, and his company given to another."

"No deserter, colonel; no deserter," said a clear voice beside him.

The colonel turned, and Darcy Leigh himself saluted him.

Coralie St. Casse, when the name Darcy Leigh was pronounced, turned first red and then pale. Next succeeded an angry flush, and her bright eyes flashed apparently with anger.

At the sound of his voice she wheeled her horse sharply round and looked him in the face with a proud scornful glance.

The young officer raised his cap, but the lady responded only with a slight inclination, and, touching her horse with the whip, again wheeled him round, and appearing to take no further interest in the new comer, she entered into conversation with the major.

"Well, sir," said the colonel to the new comer, "this is very extraordinary conduct. First, you vanish without a word to your commanding officer, and then, on the very day we have received orders to march north, you as suddenly return. What does it mean?"

"I can satisfactorily explain everything, colonel. Not now, but after parade, when I pledge my honour to give ample and good reason for my absence."

The colonel deliberated for a few minutes, and then said,—

"Well, Captain Leigh, I will not doubt you; you have rendered too good service to our cause, and given too great proofs of your loyalty and bravery for me to do so. I accept your word. You can resume command of your company."

Darcy Leigh coloured, but hesitated to accept the offer.

"Well, sir," said the colonel, "do you hesitate, or

do you refuse to accept what I cannot but consider my clemency?"

"Not so," said the young man, "but before resuming my command I should wish to speak a few words with Miss St. Casse. She it was who raised this regiment and procured me my command, which I will not resume without her sanction."

The colonel was a man of few words. He merely turned in his saddle, and then said,—

"Miss St. Casse, this gentleman wishes to speak a few words with you privately."

Coralie bowed proudly, though a slight flush came to her cheek.

Darcy Leigh advanced as the other officers drew back, and bowing slightly, but somewhat superciliously (for he had noted the contemptuous greeting the young lady had first given him), at once addressed her,—

"Miss St. Casse, Colonel Johnson has requested me to resume the command of my company. I declined to do so without first knowing your sentiments on the subject."

"Since you did not think it necessary to consult me, sir, when you left your post so unceremoniously, it is strange you think it needful to do so on your return."

"I wrote to you hastily, it is true, for I had received news which required my immediate presence at Washington; but I wrote and told you that my reasons for leaving were imperative."

"Washington! So you have been to Washington, the head-quarters of our enemies?" she replied, scornfully.

"Yes, to Washington, at the imminent risk of my life, and for an object of which I am not ashamed."

"And that object?—To see Miss Stella Gayle, I presume, of whom I have heard so much."

"No; that was not my object," replied Darcy, calmly. "I went to save my brother's life, who was in the hands of the Yankees, and condemned to be shot. I succeeded in that object, and should attempt the same again, though I risked the loss of a general's command, and even your displeasure. Since you doubt me, let it be so. I shall not resume the command of my company. I am not given to boasting, but I have no fear of obtaining a commission elsewhere. Miss St. Casse, I wish you goodday."

He raised his hat slightly, and was about to leave, when she stopped him.

"Stay, sir, one moment; you say you left thus suddenly in order to rescue your brother who was at Washington, condemned to death?"

"I did. I started half-an-hour after receiving the news."

"And you succeeded?"

"I succeeded."

She was silent for a short time, and then said, pettishly,—

"You might have written and explained that to me, I think, instead of sending such a brief, abrupt note."

Darcy Leigh looked up, and saw that anger had given place to pique.

"I ask your pardon, but I was so stunned by the news, so flurried, that I scarcely knew what I did."

"And you have but just arrived in Charleston?"

"Not more than an hour. First I called on you, feeling that some apology was due to you for my abrupt departure, especially after your kindness in procuring me this commission; next I went to the barracks, learned there that the regiment had gone to the parade ground, and I came on at once."

"Will you give me a full account of your adventures, and how you rescued your brother, after parade?"

"Willingly," he replied, and drawing closer, placed his hand on the horse's neck, then looking up in her face, from which all displeasure had vanished, he added,—

"Am I to consider myself cashiered, or am 1 to resign?"

"No, sir, resume your command, and —— consider yourself horsewhipped."

So saying, she tapped him lightly on the shoulder with her whip.

Thus the interview which began so threateningly,

terminated in sunshine, and Darcy, making his way to Colonel Johnson, said,—

" I am ready to resume my command after parade, colonel."

The news was soon spread abroad, and the men of his company, the officers scarcely endeavouring to prevent them, broke their ranks, and crowded around their captain.

" Glory to yez, me noble captin," cried a brawny Irishman ; " you're the boy for blood and thunder ! Hoorooh, for his honour, the captin !"

Then another shout broke forth, and was taken up all along the line. It was some minutes before the men could be re-formed, nor would No. 1 company do so before Darcy took his place at their head.

It was in vain he pleaded he was not in uniform—and had not even a sword. His faithful body servant Darby Kelly, who returned with him, had been to his room in the barracks, and now produced a bundle.

" Here yez are, captin ; here are yer military togs."

" Why, you confounded ass, do you suppose I'm going to dress and undress on the parade ground ?"

" Arrah ! what matters ? sure some of the boys will stand before yez, an' I'll make a tint of yer honner's cloak, so as the lady wont see."

This offer, however, was declined, Darcy preferring rather to march at their head in *mufti*.

The men were re-formed in line, and the ceremony gone through of presenting the regiment with colours. Then, when the shouting and cheering had somewhat subsided they were marched off the ground. Darcy in front of No. 1, the leading company, the colonel, major, and Coralie St. Casse on horseback, the band playing, the spectators cheering. Thus, with bayonets gleaming, the "lone star" in the centre of the new colours, flashing in the sunlight, eyes glittering, and hearts beating, the "Carolina Crashers" returned to Charleston.

On arriving at the barracks the regiment was again drawn up in line and dismissed, each man being allowed to dispose of the rest of the day as seemed to him fit.

Darcy Leigh repaired to his quarters in the barracks, the key of which his servant, Darby Kelly, the Irishman, had already procured.

He found this individual busily engaged in putting the scantily furnished room into what he considered a fitting condition. The table consisted of a rough slab of wood, and the principal seat Darby had cunningly arranged by a slab of wood, supported by two barrels placed on end. Swords, bayonets, and guns were hung around on three of the walls, while the fourth was ornamented by Darby's *chef d'œuvre*, the battle of Waterloo, drawn in glaring colours, with an utter disregard to probability and perspective.

Darcy Leigh hastened to change his clothes, which were by no means in the most presentable order. The uniform of the Carolina Crashers consisted of a dark-grey tunic and trousers, with black braiding across the chest, black hat, and plume. The officers wore a light-blue sash across the left shoulder, with a single star in the centre.

This was probably adopted in compliment to Coralie St. Casse, who had been named, from her great beauty and zeal for the Confederate cause, the "Star of the South."

Several generals of high rank were at that time in Charleston, among whom was General Longstreet, who occupied the post of honour on her right hand. General Beauregard had gone north, to take command of the army of Virginia, as also had many other officers, who used to be frequently her guests.

Coralie had changed her grey riding-habit for a dress of white muslin, which offered a striking contrast to her dark hair and eyes and brilliant brown complexion, enhancing the beauty of the whole. She still wore across her shoulders and bosom the blue scarf, with the gold star in the centre, as did all the officers of her regiment.

Indeed, Coralie was looked on as sort of Amazon soldier—a lady officer. She had a guard of honour allotted to her, and two sentries were posted in the portico of the villa, and one at the door of the saloon.

The luncheon was over, and the jingling of glasses and buzzing of conversation succeeded as the wine went round, warming the blood and loosening the tongues of the guests. Coralie was just about to rise and withdraw, when the attention of all was called to a disturbance at the door of the saloon. The negro servants were crowded together in a knot, and appeared to be opposing the admission of some one.

"Come out ov me way, ye blaggards, come out of that, will ye? or I'll make short work ov some ov ye; clear out, ye blak imps, and let me get to the lady!"

The confusion now became greater, and the voice of the sentry was heard ordering the intruder to stand back.

"Stand back yerself, ye spalpeen, sure I'm a kernel—corprel I mane, and you're only a paltry private, an' by all the powers I'll make ye salute me—salute, will ye, ye vagabone—look at the stripes on me arms and salute, ye scoundrel."

But the sentry ignoring the stripes on Darby Kelly's arm—for it was that worthy himself who, in full uniform, was endeavouring to force a passage—only repeated the order to "stand back."

"An' that's it, is it; yez wont salute, an' yez wont let me by, wont yez? Hoorooh, here goes."

Then there was a din and confusion. The negro servants were scattered on all sides, some sprawling on the ground, as the high Irishman burst into the room, followed by the sentry. Indeed, the latter could hardly help it, for Darby, to prevent injury to himself, had grasped his bayonet with his left hand, and, exerting his great strength, was dragging him after him, while with his other hand he beat off and utterly discomfited the negroes who endeavoured to stop his way.

On seeing his gigantic and uncouth figure burst into the room, Coralie started to her feet in alarm. Most of the officers were already on their feet, and a dozen swords flashed simultaneously from their scabbards.

"What means this intrusion? Who are you, fellow?

And how dare you thus force your way into my house ?"
said Coralie, in clear, ringing accents.

" Leave this room, sir, or I'll spit you like a lark," said
an officer in the uniform of the 4th Carolina, advancing
sword in hand.

" It's Darcy Leigh's Irish servant," said Lieutenant
Wharncliffe, who was near Coralie.  " He used to be a
fireman on board the Spitfire."

" Darcy Leigh's servant?" said Coralie.  " Ah ! perhaps he brings a message or a note."

Then, darting from her seat, she placed herself between
the officers who were advancing in a body to expel the
intruder by force.

" Stay, gentlemen, one moment; let me see what he
wants."   Then turning to the Irishman, she asked,—

" What is it, my man—and what means this violence?"

" Sure his honner gave me a note to give your lady-
ship—says I to his honner, ' Will I give it to the lady's
own self?' ' Av course,' says he ; ' then,' says I, ' Devil
a soul else gits it from me.'   These vagabones have wanted
to git it from me ; but divil a bit did I mane to part with
it till I hands it to yer own self.   An' here it is."

" Who is it from ?" asked Coralie, before she took it ;
"who do you call his honour ?"

" Why, his honner, the captin."

" What captain ?"

" Ah, now you'd be after poking fun at me.   Whose
servant and *valo de shum* am I—why Captain Darcy
Leigh's, ov course, and more power to him, though for
the matter ov that, he had plinty whin he hit me on the
head this morning with the bootjack."

" Come, sir, give me the letter," said Coralie, unable to
repress a smile.

After some delay in feeling for it, Darby found it and
handed it to her, terribly crumpled and not over clean.

As she was unfolding and deciphering it, various
remarks were made by the guests.

" Like his confounded impudence," said one young
officer, who was not acquainted with him, and who was
smitten by the charms of Coralie.

" Just like these young sparks," growled an old colonel
of fifty, who was also led captive at Coralie's chariot
wheels—" they think they ride rough shod over all the
girls of the South. If I were she, I'd send the dirty
scrawl back without reading it. Like his impudence to
send a note at all, let alone by such a messenger. Like
his impudence."

Thus some growled their disapprobation, while Wharncliffe and those who knew Darcy Leigh and his uncouth
servant only laughed.

Coralie had now read the note.

" Where is your master ?" she asked.

" He told me he'd walk gently on behind me, your
ladyship, an' meet me coming back."

" Yes ; well, go back and tell him to return with
you—that I await him."

Darby, making a clumsy bow, took his departure,
stalking out as he came in, like a conqueror.

" Ah ! ye villin," he said, as he passed the sentry ; "ye
wouldn't salute, wouldn't ye ? I'll take it out of ye, ye
lazy skulk, at drill, as soon as I'm sergeant. I'll give
ye the ' double quick' and the 'round about face,' I
will."

Coralie resumed her seat, and, as in politeness bound,
her guests followed her example. After the lapse of
about five minutes, however, she rose, and bowing gracefully, begged them not to disturb themselves, and swept
out of the room, followed by many a glance of admiration,
and even more. A few cast significant looks at one
another, for they had heard the message she gave to the
Irishman, and guessed she had left in order to see his
master.

None, however, were so rude as to hazard a single word
on the subject, though, doubtless, many felt sorely cha-
grined at the readiness and obvious pleasure with which
she received the note of Darcy Leigh.

Coralie, on leaving her guests, put on her hat and
shawl, and strolled leisurely out in the direction in which
she expected her friend Darcy, for such at least he was,
even if there were no chance of his being more. She

soon descried him approaching, with Darby Kelly following close behind.

As they approached she could scarcely forbear laughing at the contrast between master and man. The latter was six feet four in height, with broad shoulders, and brawny limbs like oak saplings, rough, uncouth, and clumsy, he was not a bad personation of Orson, the wild man of the woods —while Darcy Leigh, rather below than above the middle height, with small hands, slight form and handsome face, might well have passed for a somewhat feminine Valentine. His features, indeed, would have better become a woman than a man; and, strange to say, bore a striking if vague resemblance to those of the fair Coralie, although they were not related in the remotest degree.

Many were disposed to predict, from the slight form and girlish, beardless face of the young officer, an effeminate disposition, but never could a greater mistake have been made.

Had Darcy Leigh been insensible to the warm greeting bestowed upon him by the beautiful Coralie, he would have been more than human. Such, however, was not the case, and his looks plainly showed the admiration he felt for her.

Coralie led him through the villa and out into the garden at the back, where, she said, they could talk without fear of interruption. Seated on a rough bench, under the overhanging shade of a cluster of magnolias, while orange trees, limes, and the pride of India waved around them in the breeze, Darcy Leigh commenced his promised recital.

The dark eyes of the young lady were fixed on his face during the whole time, in as rapt attention as ever Desdemona paid to the strange tales of adventure and daring poured into her ear by the Moor of Venice.

" You do not wish me to begin at the beginning, and repeat the whole particulars of the seizure of the Spitfire? You know that I was second lieutenant on board, and that on the breaking out of this so-called rebellion I was placed under arrest by the admiral for refusing to drink a Union toast at a fête on board the flag ship; you also

know that I, with some other officers like myself,
Southerners, seized the sloop and ran her out to sea,
right through the fleet, before they had sufficient time
seriously to injure us ; you also know that I was struck
by a splinter while at the wheel, just as we passed the
flag ship, and that when I fell it was supposed that I was
killed, and many still believe that I have been sent to
my last account. Several vessels were despatched in
search of us. The Wabash we once eluded by a strata-
gem ; on the second occasion of our falling in with her
we captured her. As you know, also, we hoisted Yankee
colours, and attempted to run into Charleston harbour,
but were discovered and forced to make a running fight
of it. With the greatest difficulty we accomplished this,
the Wabash going down, and the Spitfire in a sinking
state from the terrible fire of the enemy as we anchored
under the shelter of the shore batteries. Then, the Spitfire being utterly disabled, and requiring great repairs
before she would be ready for sea, my occupation was
gone, and I had to look around for employment on land.
The general in command gave me a captain's commission,
but there was not a vacant post in any regiment. You
then announced your intention of raising a regiment at
your own expense, and generously gave me the command
of a company. The regiment was just equipped and
organized, when news came to me which demanded my
immediate presence elsewhere. My brother Gerald, with
a friend of his, one Captain George, an Englishman, left
Washington, and attempted to cross the Potomac and
join the Confederates. They were betrayed, and inter-
cepted by a party of United States dragoons. There
was a fight, in which they were both desperately
wounded, and two dragoons killed ; on their recovery
they were tried, condemned, and sentenced to death.
The instant I heard the news I started for Washington,
accompanied only by Darby Kelly and Jupiter, the
negro, resolved to rescue my brother or perish in the
attempt. I succeeded, as I have already told you, and
at once started back to Charleston with my brother and
his friend.'

Darcy here paused, and Coralie said,—-

"Yes; you succeeded, I know, for you are here safe; but how did you accomplish this? Do not imagine I am going to let you off with such a brief account. Come now, tell me all. How did you find out where they were confined? and, above all, how did you compass their escape?"

"Well, fair Coralie, I will briefly relate to you my adventures. I sent the negro on to Washington to make inquiries, while I and Darby Kelly lay hidden on the southern bank of the river, waiting an opportunity to cross. When night came we made the attempt in a boat, but were discovered, fired at, and forced to take to the water and swim. We safely got across, and made our way within the enemy's lines before daybreak. All the day we remained concealed in the branches of a tree, and at night I sallied out. First I went to the house of Webster Gayle; I climbed the balcony, and discovered Stella Gayle, his daughter, there alone."

"Ah!" interrupted Coralie; "then your first visit was to Stella Gayle. I have heard much of her; is she very handsome?"

"Handsome, yes; I was almost about to say as handsome as yourself."

"A truce to your compliments; keep them for Miss Gayle; doubtless she is accustomed to them, and will prize them more than I."

There was an angry flash in her eye, and a tone of pique in her voice, which plainly told that the subject, for some reason or other, was by no means a pleasant one.

"Compliments to Stella Gayle, indeed!" replied Darcy, quickly, and with evident annoyance. "I reckon I shall not trouble her with more than she bestows on me. Stella Gayle is a staunch Unionist, and hates me for being a rebel. She would rejoice to hear I was shot to-morrow."

Coralie looked hard in his face, as if to read his thoughts; but she could only discover in his features a feeling of wounded pride and annoyance.

"So, so," she said, with a slight smile ; "you and the young lady are not the best of friends at present. What, is it a lovers' quarrel ? You know the saying, *Amantium iræ amoris integratio est.* Is it so in this case ?— for certainly, if report speaks truly, you were at one time by no means indifferent to this Northern *belle*, and——"

"I never cared for her, interrupted Darcy, hastily ; I might have been fascinated and struck by her great beauty, as—as—as——"

"As you have been many times by other ladies, you would say."

Darcy coloured, for his words would bear that interpretation, and indeed he was in that very predicament when under the influence of the flashing eyes and glorious beauty of the "Star of the South" herself.

But it was only admiration. Darcy persuaded himself fully to that ; and each moment as he basked in her smiles, and ever and anon caught her large liquid eyes fixed on him with by no means a displeased expression— he felt himself being drawn yet deeper into the maelstrom of her beauty.

Perhaps this result was unintentional on her part— perhaps not.

"Well," continued Darcy, "Stella Gayle, on seeing me, believing I was dead, fainted, or nearly so. On regaining her senses she gave me curtly enough the information I required, not forgetting to insult me before I left her. It appears that she informed her cousin Lupus Rock of my visit, and of its object."

"Lupus Rock—ah ! I have met him, I think."

"Yes; last year at Saratoga. He appeared smitten with you. Do you like him ?"

"I scarcely know whether I like or dislike him ; I cannot understand him ; sometimes I actually felt afraid of him."

"Well, to resume. Stella told her cousin that I was determined on an attempt to rescue my brother. Lupus knew the guard-room where they were confined, and took two bottles of drugged wine to the officers on guard. I, with Darby Kelly and Jupiter, overpowered and gagged the sentry, and advanced to the guard-house where the prisoners were confined. Imagine our astonishment when we discovered both the officers, Lieutenant Vavasour and Captain James, in a deep sleep or stupor. We expected a desperate struggle, during which an alarm would probably be given. To our agreeable surprise our course was easy. We bound the sleeping officers, released my brother and his friend, and in half-an-hour were far away from the Yankee lines. After some further adventures we safely crossed the river, and made our way first to Richmond, then on here."

Coralie remained silent for a moment, as if in deep thought.

"Are you sure it was Lupus Rock who drugged the wine which was taken by the two officers?"

"Lupus himself fetched it, and my brother Gerald, who was a prisoner in the back room of the guard-house, distinctly heard him tell James and Vavasour, that he himself fetched it from the cellar."

"Might he not have been sent with the wine, which was previously drugged by some one else?"

"By whom could he have been sent, and who could or would have drugged the wine but he?"

"Stella Gayle," replied Coralie.

"Stella Gayle! ha! ha!" and Darcy laughed scornfully. "I tell you she would gladly see me shot."

"Perhaps so," replied Coralie, sadly, "but I have a feeling, a presentiment, and I think you wrong her. Come, let us have done speculating on the past, and look forward to the future. To-morrow we leave Charleston, and, perhaps, in the course of a week many of us may be numbered among the slain."

So saying Coralie rose, and taking the arm of Darcy Leigh, walked slowly with downcast eyes towards the house.

She paused on the threshold, and raising her eyes, now liquid and melting, to his, said,—

"Darcy, do you know, I think I shall fall by the hand of the enemy. I think I shall die on the field of battle."

"Coralie!" exclaimed Darcy, vehemently, "of what

are you speaking? Do you imagine that we will suffer you to expose yourself? I, for one, can never allow such a thing."

"But I tell you I will," cried Coralie, passionately; "do you think I will suffer my brave men and officers to go into action and battle for their rights, while I remain at a safe distance? No, no; it is useless attempting to dissuade me. Others have tried and failed. Once again, I will go where the flag I this day presented shall be borne."

"Then I, for one, will have none of it. Your presence would unnerve my arm, and make me a coward. I will carry my sword elsewhere."

"As you please," she replied, mournfully. "We have known each other since we were children; and I was foolish enough to think at one time that for old acquaintance sake, Darcy Leigh would be near me in the hour of danger."

She said no more, but was passing slowly into the villa, when Darcy seized her hand——

"Coralie, dear Coralie,"—how her eyes glittered at the word—"a thousand pardons. Where you go, there will I go. I spoke but to dissuade you from this foolish resolve. But if it must be, I will never be away from your side, and, if possible, will be both your shield and sword."

"Thanks, Darcy; I thought you did not mean those cruel words;" and then, with beaming eyes, she held out her hand, which Darcy seized and passionately kissed. Her eyes flashed with a proud joy. Darcy drew her towards him unresistingly.

"Coralie," he began; but at that moment footsteps were heard approaching, and she released her hand and darted away, casting back a parting glance full of significance.

"To-morrow, at eight, to breakfast; we start *en route* for Richmond at ten."

She was gone, and though he knew not why, Darcy, with a feeling of sadness and oppression, walked slowly back to the barracks.

2

In spite of himself, the image of a fair Northern girl would intrude, and Stella Gayle, with her proud classic features, scornful eyes, and commanding carriage, stood ever and anon in fancy before him.

"Pshaw!" he thought, and strove to drive the image away; "she is bad and vindictive—as bad as she is beautiful."

## CHAPTER II.

### NINA THE OCTOROON.

DARCY LEIGH, on leaving the fair Coralie, strolled leisurely back towards his quarters in the barracks, where his brother Gerald and friend Captain George had preceded him.

The thoughts which occupied his mind were of no pleasant nature, if his face could be taken as their index. Notwithstanding the harsh verdict he had just passed on the absent Stella Gayle, still he could not entirely drive her image from his mind's eye. There was no more wretched feature in this war, than the complete rupture and severance which it caused between those who hitherto fast friends, now found themselves ranged on opposite sides.

This was the case with Darcy and Gerald Leigh, and their earliest and hitherto fastest of friends, the sisters, Stella and Angela Gayle. Stella especially had been on the best and most intimate terms with Darcy Leigh, and there were not wanting those who insinuated that the Northern belle took more than a mere friendly interest in the young Southerner. Be this as it might, the outbreak of the rebellion put an abrupt stop both to the intimacy and friendship. Whatever might have been the feelings of Stella, her pride and patriotism both constrained her to treat Darcy with contempt and indignation. He, for his part, believing Stella Gale to be both treacherous and vindictive, felt no less embittered; and if ever he had thought more seriously of her than as a friend, the brilliant beauty of Coralie, the Star of the South, was fast producing its effect.

On arriving at his quarters, he found there assembled his brother Gerald and Captain George, the Englishman, both in cavalry uniform, booted and spurred. Darby Kelly, too, in all the glory of his new uniform, with the corporal's stripes on his arms, was busy pointing out to General Leigh and the Englishman the beauties of the celebrated cartoon, with which he had embellished the wall of his master's room.

" The Duke at Waterloo."

Jupiter, the big negro, was employed in packing valises, polishing scabbards and sword belts, and generally making preparations for to-morrow's journey north. Apparently he was delighted at the prospect of the march, as though it were capital fun, and not the commencement of a series of bloody battles and disasters to both sides. He kept showing his rows of white teeth as he chuckled and talked to himself, all the while polishing away at the accoutrements.

As for Captain George, he had seated himself on the window sill, and was puffing his cigar, and gazing out into the barrack yard with his usual listless indifference ; while Gerald and Darcy were busy in making a few final arrangements for departure.

" Here's a girl coming across the barrack-yard, Darcy," said George, listlessly : "do you know her? She seems as if she were coming here."

Both Gerald and Darcy approached the window and looked out, but neither knew the face or figure of the stranger.

" Can't be coming here," said Darcy ; " I don't know her—must be going to some other fellows' quarters. A storekeeper's daughter sent with her father's bill, I dare say."

And with this, Darcy turned away, and commenced taking the locks of his revolvers to pieces.

The next minute, however, there came a light tap a the door.

" Darby, go and see who is there."

2—2

" It's a famale, your honner," he said, from the outside, when he had cautiously opened the door, taking care to plant himself right in the passage—" will I let her in ?"

On receiving the order to do so, Darby stood aside, and allowed the stranger to enter.

It was a young girl, apparently not more than twenty years of age, tall, slender, and graceful, with that faint brown tinge in the skin and slight wave in the hair which proclaimed the taint, however slight, of African blood. Her eyes were large, dark, and liquid, and her features handsome. Her dress was plain and tasteful, but evidently not that of a lady. The rich outlines of her figure were shown off to advantage rather than concealed by the loose skirt and shirt-like body of plain white ; while her black wavy hair was simply gathered in a knot, and fastened by a horn comb.

" Is either of you gentlemen Captain Gerald Leigh ?" asked the girl, in a low, sweet voice, at the same time glancing inquiringly from one to the other.

" I am Gerald Leigh, young lady."

" Then I have a note for you."

At the same time she produced one from her bosom, and handed it to him. He hastily broke the seal, read the contents, and exclaimed,—

" From Miss Gayle !—then you come from Washington, I suppose, as there is no address on the letter."

" No, sir, not from Washington, but from Yancey Estate, in Virginia."

" Yancey Estate, in Virginia !" interrupted Darcy ; " but all that district is at present held by our troops, and the Gayles are Unionists. What can they be doing there ? Who is with them ?"

The girl hesitated, coloured up, and her eyes glittered with an angry light.

" Their relative, the owner of the estate," she said, with an effort.

" What, Webster Gayle, their father ?" said Darcy, in still greater surprise.

" No, not Webster Gayle."

" Not Webster Gayle ?—but he is the owner of the

estate. Has he sold it? And who, then, is with the young ladies?"

"The estate belongs now to their cousin. It is he who is with them."

"Their cousin—the estate belongs to Lupus Rock! This is news indeed."

At the mention of Lupus Rock's name the girl turned first red, then white, and once more the angry flash came to her dark eyes.

The keen glance of Captain George, who was still seated on the window-sill, noticed this, which escaped the two brothers.

"You mean to say, then, that the estate now belongs to Lupus Rock? How do you know such to be the fact?" asked Darcy.

"He showed the deed of conveyance to the overseer, and he is formally recognised as the owner by the officer of the detachment of soldiers quartered on the estate. Besides, he gave myself and my brother our free papers, which he could not have done had he not been the owner."

Although the girl spoke in calm, passionless accents, Captain George, who watched her keenly, felt assured that she was powerfully affected.

"Then you were slaves—you and your brother?" said Gerald, gazing wonderingly on the graceful girl before him; "and you say Lupus Rock gave you your freedom! It is the first time I ever heard of Lupus Rock giving anything; he does not bear a character for liberality."

"He gave me and my brother our freedom because he could not help it; but think not we accepted it at his hands. We paid the full sum, short of one hundred dollars, which Senator Gayle long ago fixed as the price. I flung the money at his feet; the thirteen hundred dollars which my brother and I had saved—as for the remaining hundred, that shall soon be paid also—I will not be indebted to Lupus Rock even for my freedom."

As she spoke, the girl drew up her slender form, and looked quite queen-like in her anger—her cheeks flushing, eyes glittering; while the way in which she clenched

her hands and teeth told of the passion which she endeavoured in vain to suppress.

"I can't understand this," said Darcy, in a puzzled
tone. "First you say Lupus Rock gave you your freedom ; then that you refused to accept it."

"Refused to accept it as a gift—yes, indeed," interrupted the girl, passionately. "I would rather accept
poison than a gift from his hands."

"Why, then, did Lupus Rock offer you your freedom ?"
asked Darcy, in increasing astonishment.

"Why, because he dared not refuse—because, if I so
chose, I could *hang him !* the base ruffian," she cried
vehemently.

"This is all Greek to me ; I cannot understand it.
The plantation belongs to Lupus Rock ; he gives this girl
and her brother their freedom ; they refuse to accept it
as a gift, call him a base ruffian, and say they could
hang him." Then turning to the girl, he said, "Since,
then, you so hate him, why did you not exercise your
power ?"

"For many reasons—for the sake of the young ladies,
Miss Stella and Angela, who have been to me like sisters ;
and because I have promised I will not."

All this while Captain George, who had said nothing,
was intently regarding the girl from his seat at the
window. There was a half-pitying, half-admiring expression on his face as he looked on the dark slave
beauty. Suddenly turning her head she met his glance,
and blushing to the very temples, curtseyed, and was
about to withdraw, when Gerald Leigh stopped her.

"Stay one moment. This letter is from Miss Angela
Gayle—are you returning again ? and if so, will you
take back an answer ?"

"No, sir, I am not going back—Heaven forbid."

"You are a strange girl," said Darcy ; "what is your
name ?"

"Nina."

"And where are you going ?"

"Perhaps, sir, you can tell me where a lady, Ma'mselle
Coralie St. Casse, lives ?   I am going there."

" Coralie St. Casse ! you are going there ?—for what purpose ?——But I beg your pardon ; I had no right to ask."

"I am not ashamed to own why I go there, sir. It is first to, put the lady on her guard against a conspiracy ; and secondly to seek service under her. The Misses Gayle will answer, if necessary, for my skill as a tire-woman."

"A conspiracy ?" asked Darcy, with interest—"of what nature ? "

"I scarcely know—but Lupus Rock is at the bottom of it, and he is as cunning and wicked as the serpent."

"Come, come, Gerald," said Darcy, "let us show this girl the house of Miss St. Casse ; we may as well walk that way as any other."

Nina expressed her gratitude, and drew on one side to let the young men pass out before her. It so happened that Captain George, the Englishman, was last, and instead of going out, he politely bowed and motioned Nina to precede him.

The girl coloured again and went first, George following her to the bottom of the stone staircase, where he joined her and entered into conversation.

Thus it happened that Gerald and Darcy walked on in front, while the Englishman and the ex-slave girl strolled slowly on behind.

The prejudice in America is very strong against a white man holding any familiar intercourse with those who have African blood in their veins, much more so with regard to a slave or freed slave as was the girl Nina. Darcy or Gerald Leigh, notwithstanding their kindness and delicacy towards the girl, would perhaps have shrunk from walking openly with her in the street on terms of perfect equality. But Captain George had none of these prejudices. His companion was eminently beautiful, notwithstanding the tell-tale tinge and wavy hair. He soon found also to his surprise, that she was far from being uneducated ; her voice was soft and sweet, her bearing dignified and modest.

It was evident that the poor girl had been used to

little kindness, at least *respectful* kindness, froɪa white
men, for many times on their road towards the villa of
Miss St. Casse, she would, when her companion's head
was turned, quickly raise her lustrous eyes and gaze ou
him for a second or so with a look of wondering gratitude.
More than once, too, her eyes filled with tears. It was
so strange, so utterly new to Nina to be treated as an
equal by a white man, and Captain George was as
respectful and polite as he could have been to any West-
end beauty in his own island metropolis.

"But do you know, Nina," he said, in the course of conversation, "that this dashing young lady whom they call
the Star of the South is going North with the regiment
she has raised to fight against the Yankees. On the
battle-fields of Virginia a lady's maid will be somewhat
out of place. What think you of accepting the post
of *vivandière* to the Carolina Crashers, as they call
themselves?"

"Are you going with them?" she asked, lifting her
eyes for an instant to his face.

"Am I going with them?" replied Captain George,
laughing; "well, I hardly know yet, but I shall accompany my friend Gerald. He serves in a cavalry regiment,
while that of Darcy, his brother, and which Miss
St. Casse raised, is infantry, so that it will all depend
on chance whether we serve together. But here we are
at the house of Miss St. Casse. You need fear no rude
reception, for I hear she is as condescending as she
is beautiful and rich."

Nina expressed her thanks gratefully to the Englishman, smiling as she did so for the first time, bowed to
Darcy and Gerald, and then ran lightly up the steps.

"Why, George, old fellow, you have been having
quite a flirtation with that octoroon slave girl," said
Gerald, as he joined them; "what do you think
of her?"

"There is some mystery about the girl I can't make
out. She is educated far beyond her station, and there is
none of that careless levity which distinguishes all the
mulattoes, quadroons, and octoroons I have hitherto met."

" You have seen Coralie St. Casse, have you not?" asked Darcy, sharply.

" Yes ; I saw her for the first time on the parade-ground to-day," replied the Englishman. " Is she not gloriously handsome ?"

" Did you observe in this girl—any, even the slightest likeness ?"

" By Jupiter ! now you mention it, I did. Wonderful! now I call to mind the features of the two, they are almost identically the same. This slave girl is a shade or two darker, and there is a wave in her hair which the glossy tresses of the other are free from."

"Strange, very strange," muttered Darcy. " I did not observe the likeness until she smiled in thanking you. Then it burst upon me like a gleam of light. There is no accounting for these vagaries of nature, but had they been sisters they could not have borne each other a greater resemblance."

" Oh, bother you two sentimental fellows, with your likenesses. Let's come down to the hotel and dine. It will be our last dinner in Charleston for many a long day, perhaps for ever. To-morrow we take the field, in this the first campaign of the army of the Confederate States. So come along."

Then Gerald, taking an arm of each, dragged them off, humming the " Bonnie Blue Flag."

Coralie St. Casse was engaged in writing, when informed by one of the negro servants that a young girl craved an interview with her.

"Show the girl in, Peter," she said, and then continued her writing, on which she was so intent as not to perceive at first the entrance of Nina, who stood patiently at the door, immediately under a portrait of Colonel St. Casse, the father of the heiress.

It was now evening, and the room was by no means light, the jalousies, which had been drawn to exclude the sun, not having been raised.

Coralie gazed for a moment on the face of the girl, as she stood in the shadow, and then, starting to her feet, exclaimed—

"Great heavens! who are you?

"My name is Nina, miss. I am a free girl, and my intention in seeking you is just to put you on your guard against the designs of bad men; and next to seek service with you. I have been with the Misses Gayle, Senator Gayle's daughters, on the Yancey estate, as ladies' maid for a short time; before that I was only a house hand. I have my free papers all duly signed. My brother, too, who was a slave with me, is now also free, and would wish to work in your service. We have heard so much of your goodness and generosity, that I felt emboldened to ask you, more especially as I have overheard bad men talking of you, scheming and plotting."

While Nina was speaking, Coralie stood gazing alternately at her and the picture of Colonel St. Casse overhead.

Though, of course, the features in the girl were smaller and more delicate, the resemblance was most remarkable.

Coralie, who was confused, almost frightened at this unexpected likeness, and with the memories it awakened, now regained her composure.

"My girl," she said, kindly, "this is a strange tale you tell me. Plots, schemes—and against me! What is their nature?"

"I scarcely—know—except that they relate—go back —to your mother; lady, who was your mother?"

"Who was my mother, you ask girl? *Who was your father?*"

"Alas, lady, I know not. My mother died when I was fourteen years old. She used to tell me my father had been dead many years."

"To what part did she say your father belonged?" asked Coralie.

"To this city, miss—Charleston."

"How old are you?"

"Twenty-one, next month, miss."

"Ah! exactly two years older than I am."

"And you know nothing of your father; did your mother never talk of him?"

"No, miss, my mother could only weep when his name was mentioned."

"And your mother, who was she?"

"She was a slave on a plantation some few miles from this, miss. She was sold to a New Orleans planter before I was born. Then, a year after her death, I was bought by Senator Gayle, and have lived since on his estate of Yancey."

"And that is all you know?"

"That is all, miss, except that bad men are plotting to get you in their power."

"To get me in their power—how?"

"They wish to prove you are a slave, and belong to them."

Coralie, who had again seated herself, bounded to her feet. The shawl which she had wrapped around her fell off her shoulders, her hair broke its fastenings and fell dishevelled over her neck and bosom. Her eyes gleamed in the gloom like those of an angry tigress; and her sweet, soft voice sounded quite harsh, as she exclaimed, in passionate accents,—

"A slave! I—Coralie St. Cass a slave!"

"Such it is the design of bad men to prove."

"And those men—who are those who thus dare——"

"One is dead," replied Nina, solemnly, "but the other is a desperate villain, and to be feared. His name is Lupus Rock."

"Lupus Rock? I have heard of him. I think, even have met and been introduced to him. And this is no fancy—no wild dream on your part?"

"No fancy, but truth. Of their power I know nothing. All I know is, that they wish to prove you their slave for their own purposes."

"Their slave! the slave of Lupus Rock? How can it be possible?"

"I think they say they have bought you, or are going to buy you."

"This is to me incomprehensible," said Coralie, reseating herself, and leaning her head on her hand. "Nina, I thank you. I feel—I know you are not deceiving me.

I will be on my guard. Now leave me. If you wish to stay with me you can. To-morrow, I go with our brave soldiers. Will you come, or will you remain here ?"

" I will come. And my brother, miss ?"

" Let him remain here. I will leave him with orders for my agent to see to his welfare."

And so it was settled, that Nina should accompany the Star of the South to Virginia.

When Coralie was again alone, she clasped her hands, and gazing at her father's picture, exclaimed to herself,—

" Great heavens! it must be so. That girl is my sister—my half sister, and till a short time back a slave. I have heard vague rumours about an early love of my father's, before he saw my mother ; but none have spoken openly. It is a mystery. But of this I feel sure, that yonder girl is my father's child. Should I tell her ? would it make her happier ? I think not. Best as it is. My sister a slave—and now they wish to prove me one also. Ha! ha ! I, the heiress, whom people call beautiful, a slave !"

And Coralie, shaking her hair about her shoulders, gazed at herself in a large mirror. She saw shat she was beautiful, and knew that when men told her so they did not flatter.

" And Darcy Leigh," she muttered. " I wonder would he spurn me if he thought me a slave." She repeated the word again and again, as if it gave her a sort of pleasing pain.

" My sister is, and why not I, a *slave ?*"

---

# CHAPTER III.

### CORALIE ST. CASSE'S PROPHECY.

It may seem strange to the reader that Coralie should feel so positive that the girl Nina was her half-sister, with apparently no better reason than a resemblance which might have been accidental. But Coralie had other and better reasons than the likeness for her belief. Although none ventured to speak to her openly on the subject, she could not help hearing certain vague reports of her father's younger days.

One tale was often repeated, and this was, how, when a young man of some five-and-twenty, her father was desperately enamoured of a quadroon girl, the slave of a planter some twenty miles distant from Charleston.

The story ran that, being on terms of deadly enmity with this planter, Colonel St. Casse (then only a captain) was unable to purchase or liberate the girl from her master, who, with vindictive malice, refused to take for the beautiful slave her weight in gold. George St. Casse, however, was not a man to be so easily baffled. He contrived the escape of the girl, whose name was Nina, and carried her off to a small place he had taken in Pennsylvania, where he hoped she would remain undiscovered by her relentless master. For a long time his hopes were realized, and by the exercise of great caution he kept secret the retreat of his mistress. But with impunity he got careless. He was in the habit of frequently visiting Washington, Charleston, and the North, on which occasions he left Nina under the charge of an old negro, whom he could trust, and the servants of the villa.

On his return to Charleston, however, after an absence longer than usual, he neglected his usual precautions, and was followed by his ever-watchful enemy, who knew full well that he had a hand in the flight of his slave. Had he been wise enough to have crossed the boundary line between Canada and the United States into British territory, his mistress would have been safe. But it was not so ; and that law, which is at once the curse and the eternal disgrace of the hypocritical dollar-worshipping Yankees, was put in force, and Nina re-consigned to her implacable master and her Southern prison. The law we allude to is the Fugitive Slave Law, by which the truckling Northerners bound themselves to return to their masters any slaves who might escape and cross the free States.

By virtue of this God-accursed and man-condemned law, the young mother (alas! no wife) was torn with her children from the man she loved, and who loved her as deeply as his somewhat gay, selfish nature would permit, and carried back to her cruel master. It is not our province to narrate here the fury of St. Casse, when he returned, after a short absence, and found that his mistress and his children had been torn away. The two children being born of a slave mother were themselves slaves ; and he had the satisfaction of knowing that they would perhaps be compelled to pick cotton, or perform menial offices for his most deadly enemy. This thought drove him to fury. Collecting all his friends, he started for the plantation, overpowered the overseers and all the white men, determined to seize his mistress and children by force. But they were not to be found. Their implacable master had removed them far from the place, and not all St. Casse's vigilance could discover their retreat. The reader knows more than he could ever discover. The poor girl was so terribly, inhumanly flogged by her master, that she never recovered. Body and spirit alike broke down under the terrible ordeal. Then weak— almost dying, he took her to New Orleans, and sold her with her children for what she would fetch, and returned to his plantation satisfied with his work. He had foiled his enemy, and revenged himself on the girl. He cared now but little whether St. Casse ever discovered her or not. He had broken her constitution by his ferocious cruelty, and knew she would not live long.

" If St. Casse ever does get her back," he used to say to himself, with a bitter laugh, " I wish him joy. He will find a few whip-marks on what was once her smooth skin, I reckon. I wish him joy of his gal. Guess I've paid back with interest the slash with his riding-whip he gave me four years ago."

St. Casse found out this man, horsewhipped him again, then made him fight him, threatened to shoot him like a dog if he would not come out like a man.

They met, each armed with a revolver. St. Casse's first shot smashed his adversary's knee-pan ; the second broke and carried away a part of his jaw, disfiguring him dreadfully, and his last passed through his lungs, lodging on and injuring the spine.

The victor has put up his smoking pistol, smiled a grim smile, and his eyes gleam with savage joy; then glancing at the form of his enemy writhing in agony on the ground,—

"Nina," he muttered between his teeth, "I know you are lost to me now, but, at least, I have avenged you."

He was right, for the wounded man lingered on for nearly two years, paralysed, with but one leg, and hideous to behold from the loss of his jawbone, and then died in great agony.

Nina never again saw or heard from St. Casse, and when she died her two children—the boy Pedro and the girl Nina—neither knowing even the name of their father, were left alone in the world to the mercy of her master and God.

We have said that he never again saw or heard of his lost ones. The vengeance he had taken seemed to have calmed his mind; by degrees he forgot his first love, and married the mother of our heroine, the daughter of a French planter and merchant in New Orleans.

Such was the romance of Colonel St. Casse's early love.

Coralie, as we have said, knew sufficient of this tale to feel assured that it was her father's lost daughter who had thus unexpectedly turned up. She knew that it was so, but determined, for the girl's own sake, to keep her in ignorance of the fact, for of what advantage would it ave been to h ave told the poor girl she was born of a ich man's par amo ur—a child of shame?

It was in the beginning of July that the "Carolina Crashers" received the orders to march for Richmond. There was railroad communication the whole distance, so that they arrived at the Southern capital fresh and unwearied, their uniforms clean, and their arms bright and glistening. Loud were the cheers from the assembled crowds as this splendid body of men, eleven hundred strong, marched out from the railway station.

Coralie St. Casse and the colonel and quartermaster had preceded them in a special train for general officers and their staff, so that she arrived in Richmond nearly a day in advance of her gallant followers.

She had taken up her quarters in the Nebraska Hotel, and was listening to an animated discussion by a group of officers who surrounded her in the saloon. Many of these were of high rank, and among them the opinion prevailed that the Yankees would not attempt an advance into Virginia, at least, for some considerable time.

" It seems to me," said a quiet, middle-aged man, in a general's uniform, " that the Yankees know when they're well off. They know they have got the best of us at sea, and I fancy will be content with that. If they do mean to try conclusions with us on dry land, I reckon they'll ' see snakes.' "

" They'd better bring their coffins with them if they come down our way—eh, colonel ?" said a young aide-de-camp to the afterwards celebrated Stonewall Jackson.

" The less boasting the better, young man," was the sober reply ; " if they come my way, I know my men will do their duty. Let that suffice ; the issue rests with the God of battles, and mayhap we ourselves may sleep our last sleep on the battle-field."

" I don't believe they intend to invade Virginia at all. I believe their great army at Washington and above the Potomac is only there from their fear for their capital."

Many other opinions were delivered to the same effect, a few dissenting.

" Not so," replied a cavalry officer. " I know these Yankees well ; they are so vain-glorious, that they think they can whip creation. They fancy that all they have got to do is to put their army in motion, and walk over us from Washington to New Orleans."

" By thunder !" cried another officer, " if ever they start to march South they'll have a rough journey. They'll want a bigger army than they would have if every man in the North turned soldier, and had better pluck than ever was yet in a Yankee's breast. But they'll never try it. It's all bounce and bunkum."

Coralie listened to these and a great many other opinions, her dark eyes glancing to each as he spoke, When there was somewhat of a lull in the conversation she spoke quietly and firmly, with an air as if she knew what she was saying. At the first sound of her voice all turned respectfully towards her.

"Gentlemen, I have heard a great many opinions, may I be permitted to give mine?"

"We must crave pardon, young lady, for not taking yours first. 'Twas, to say the least of it, impolite."

A dozen voices begged her to speak, and they pressed yet closer around to hear what she had to say.

One or two of the elder officers could not suppress a smile. It seemed so absurd, this young girl of nineteen offering an opinion on military affairs. Coralie caught a smile on the face of one, and smiling in return, said,—

"General Burgess, you are laughing at me. Well, laugh on; I am only a girl, but remember, a girl once headed the French armies, and did what has never been done before or since—defeated the English, and drove them headlong from her country. Her name was Joan of Arc, and I have never heard that she studied the science of war at West Point or any other academy."

"Bravo, Miss St. Casse. Had you there, General, I think," cried several, laughing.

"Who knows our country may not find a second Joan of Arc in this young lady."

"Who knows, indeed? They say that Joan of Arc was very beautiful, and I am sure that Miss St. Casse "——

"There, that will do, sir; I know what you are going to say, and don't want any compliments. If Joan of Arc had been foolish enough to listen to them, she would never have raised the siege of Orleans. Please let me say what I have to say. It appears to be a general opinion among you that the Yankees will not advance into Virginia. You are wrong. I have reason to believe that they will advance, and that soon. I even venture to predict the point they will choose for forcing our lines."

3

All listened with attention; some wondering, some inclined to believe the words of this extraordinary girl.

"They will advance by way of Centreville and Manassas Junction to Manassas Gap, with the rail on their left flank, the road on their right."

"What! endeavour to force the passage of Bull Run stream, surrounded as it is by ravines and wooded hills, which render a large concerted movement by an attacking force almost impossible, but where artillery would play with murderous effect? Impossible."

"Nevertheless, that is the present plan of the enemy, and I fully believe they will endeavour to carry it out. If successful it will give them the command of the Valley of the Shenandoah and a clear road to Richmond."

Great astonishment prevailed generally at this prediction of the fair Coralie, as it was generally believed that the army assembled on the Potomac was only for the defence of Washington, and that the Federal generals would never attempt an advance with their raw undisciplined troops. It was true that the Confederate forces were also raw, and but half disciplined; but it must be remembered that they were on the defensive, and young troops have frequently fought as well as veterans under these circumstances.

A murmur of surprise went round at Coralie's words which, strange as they seemed, nevertheless were deemed worthy of attention. But if the surprise of the officers assembled was great at the confident manner in which she predicted the designs of the enemy, what was their amazement when she went on to say,—

"Yes, gentlemen, not only do I prophesy that the Yankees will advance by way of Manassas Junction, but that the movement will take place at once. To-day is Thursday, the 18th July. Before next Sunday night an attack will have been made—a battle fought and won."

The astonishment at this confident prediction was great, more from the manner in which it was spoken, than from any probability it bore on the face of it.

General Johnston, who commanded a division of some 20,000 men, all in barracks at Richmond or encamped close by, asked,—

"Miss St. Casse, have you any reason for your strange assertion, or is it only a fanciful idea of your own?"

"It is no fanciful idea, General," she replied, gravely. "I have good reasons for believing that it will prove a stern reality."

"And may I ask the source of the information on which you speak?"

"You may, General. My informant is Captain Darcy Leigh."

Several of the officers smiled slightly at the name, for it was well known he was a great favourite with the beautiful Coralie.

"Darcy Leigh; and what are his means of knowledge? Has he been playing the dangerous part of spy?"

"Not exactly; but I will explain. You know, General, that his brother, Gerald Leigh, then an officer in the United States 2nd Cavalry, was taken by the Yankees in the act of attempting to cross the river and join our forces. For that he was tried and condemned to death. His brother, Darcy Leigh, was in Charleston, when the news of his brother's capture and sentence reached him. At once he resolved to liberate him, and started for Washington disguised, and attended only by his Irish servant and a negro. He nobly accomplished his mission, and, after passing through many desperate perils, freed his brother and a friend condemned with him, one Captain George, an Englishman. While within the Yankee lines, he gained the information I now give to you. First he heard it from Miss Stella Gayle."

"Stella Gayle! the daughter of Senator Gayle?"

"The same."

"Then, indeed, the information is likely to be true, if given in good faith, for Senator Gayle is posted as to all the Government plans, to my certain knowledge."

" How, General ?" asked Coralie.

" Why, at this present moment we are receiving the most valuable information from the senator. He is playing a desperately dangerous game, and if discovered by the Yankees, will certainly be hanged for his treason. Nevertheless, all intelligence of importance should be received with caution from such a source. It may be the tactics of the senator to win our confidence by good information of but little import, and then to betray us when a great battle is concerned. Who knows? He who will play the spy and traitor to his own side, would as readily betray the other."

" What you say is true, General, but besides. Senator Gayle's daughter, who let fall the information accidentally, is a staunch Unionist."

" A staunch Unionist?" interrupted a young aide-de-camp of General Johnston ; " what, then, is she and her sister doing in Richmond ?"

" In Richmond?" asked Coralie, with unconcealed surprise, and colouring up ; " is Miss Gayle in Richmond ?"

" Yes, with her sister and cousin, Lupus Rock, who is raising a regiment at his own expense."

At the mention of Lupus Rock's name Coralie suddenly remembered the strange warning as to his deep designs given her by the girl Nina. A feeling of inquietude and vague dread took possession of her, and for some time she was silent and troubled.

Many noticed the perplexed, anxious look on her face, and knew not to what to attribute it.

The silence was broken by another young officer.

" I can answer for it that Miss Gayle, who was last year considered the handsomest girl at Saratoga, is in this town, for I myself have seen and spoken with her. She and her sister will be at the ball to-morrow night."

" What were you about to say, Miss St. Casse, when you were interrupted ?" asked General Johnston.

" I was about to say that I have another source from which I derived the same information as to the projected movements of the enemy. Gerald Leigh when a prisoner overheard a conversation between Captain Vavasour and the nephew of General Scott, the commander-in-chief, in which the same plan of action was spoken of, and even the day for the advance mentioned."

"Then there is indeed some probability that the fools will be audacious enough to make the mad attempt. They must fail, utterly and ignominiously."

"They will, I hope, fail, as you say, General; still I hope no precaution will be neglected, for the attack will be made with desperate determination, and with their whole army."

At this moment a commotion, cheering and shouting in the street, attracted the attention of all, and hurrying to the window, an immense crowd was seen following and surrounding a regiment just arrived. A pale blue flag, with a single gold star, was borne in the centre, and Coralie at once recognised her own men, the 7th Carolinas.

"Nina, Nina!" she called, going to the door of the saloon.

Nina quickly appeared, and a buzz of admiration and surprise greeted her.

The ex-slave girl was attired in a red tunic reaching to the knee, with blue sash and canteen slung across the back. A hat and plume, grey trousers and belt, in which was inserted a small revolver, completed the attire of the *vivandière* of the 7th Carolinas.

"Nina, run quickly, and order my horse, and bring it round. I will ride to the barracks at the head of my brave men."

In less than a minute the horse was brought round to the hotel steps by Nina, who was at once lady's maid to Coralie, *vivandière* to the regiment, and now held the stirrup leather as the Star of the South sprang into the saddle.

Coralie at once started off at a trot to overtake the troops, who were now some few hundred yards ahead, and Nina ran by her side, holding still by her stirrup leather. Great was the sensation Coralie created as she rode along the street, attended by Nina. The crowd respectfully gave way, even the rowdies offering no insult to the fair Southerner. The gentlemen assembled on the various balconies and at the windows along the street cheered lustily as she passed—and thus amid the acclamations of thousands she put herself at the head of her regiment.

Darcy Leigh was in command of No. 1, the leading company, and on seeing him, she beckoned him to her.

"Darcy, who are those people on the first floor balcony of the Washington Hotel, who are staring so hard at us?"

Darcy looked up, and coloured as he recognised them.

"Those are Angela and Stella Gayle, and the gentleman is Lupus Rock, their cousin. I did not know they were in Richmond, and cannot understand it."

Coralie, when she heard who they were, gave one haughty scrutinizing glance, and then turned her attention to the colonel, who was on horseback by her side.

Darcy rejoined his company ; the word was given to march, and amid the cheers of assembled thousands, the regiment marched through the town to their barracks on the outskirts.

It was a real ovation, and among all the men composing the regiment, there was not a heart that did not beat high with pride and hope. As for Coralie, she was thoroughly infected with the enthusiasm of the scene. The inspiriting strains of the band, the measured tramp of the soldiers' feet keeping time to the march, the waving of flags and handkerchiefs, the loud cheers of the crowd, and the glistening array of bayonets, all ready to dash into the thick of battle at her word, made her eye sparkle and her cheek glow with pardonable pride. Nor could she be insensible to the admiration she herself excited. The close-fitting grey riding-habit, with the skirt almost sweeping the ground, displayed her graceful figure to the best advantage ; while her large dark eyes gleamed like black diamonds from beneath the shade of her plumed hat.

# CHAPTER IV.

## THE BALL BEFORE THE BATTLE.

IT must not be supposed that the inhabitants of Richmond and the south were generally depressed or dispirited in face of the tremendous struggle for independence upon which they were entering. Such was far from the fact. On all sides might be heard the most confident predictions of victory, and the utmost contempt for the Yankee invaders was freely expressed. Richmond, at the time of which we speak, was crowded not only with troops and officers, but with Southern ladies and families, who, forced by the war to leave Washington, Maryland, and the Northern States, had congregated at Richmond, the capital of their country. All, or nearly all the young men of good family in the Southern States had taken service, or were waiting for commissions; while the ladies, in every way in their power, encouraged their husbands, brothers, and lovers to prove themselves gallant knights in the coming struggle.

     \*     \*     \*     \*     \*     \*

There is a grand ball in Richmond, given by the officers of the troops there assembled. It is the night of the 20th of July, 1861, and all, or nearly all, the beauty and wealth of the city are assembled to do honour to those about to do battle for independence.

There may be seen assembled officers of every grade and branch of the service. The dashing cavalry officers, spurs jingling, sabres clashing; the quiet, blunt, naval men, with their blue frock coats and brass buttons; the infantry officers, in grey tunics and "butternut" trousers; artillery engineers, surgeons, commissariat officers, members of the government, surveyors, contractors, and irregular officers—or, as the Yankees called them, "guerillas;" each had some representative at the brilliant assembly.

Lovely ladies, too, were there in numbers—dark and fair, tall and short, in all variety of ball dresses.

Glorious beauties in rustling silks, glistening satins, and gauzy muslins, floated like fairies about the room, casting bright glances on all, and glances of deeper meaning still on those loved ones—husbands, brothers, and lovers who so soon might be stretched lifeless on the plain of battle.

Coralie was there, resplendent in her dark beauty. She wore a rich dress of white silk, with no other ornament than the blue scarf over her shoulder, and a single white flower in her hair.

Darcy Leigh, Gerald, and Captain George, the Englishman, stood together near the door of the ball-room, watching the dancers as they whirled by to the music of the band.

Gerald Leigh was in undress cavalry uniform, and his tall figure appeared to still greater advantage, contrasting as it did with his brother and Captain George, who were neither above the middle height. Gerald Leigh was in high good humour—his handsome face was radiant with smiles, his blue eyes sparkling with enthusiasm.

Not so, however, his brother, who, since his entry into the room, appeared wrapped in thought of no pleasant description.

While they stood thus, Darcy leaning with folded arms against the door-post, two young ladies ascended the stairs, and approached them from behind. At the same moment Coralie St. Casse advanced towards them, leaning on the arm of an elderly officer, whom she thanked with a bow when within a few yards of our friends, and then left. Her eyes met those of Darcy Leigh, who, of course, could not help advancing and offering his arm, which the lady evidently expected.

At that very moment, however, he heard a low female voice behind him say,—

" Will you allow me to pass, sir ?"

The words were addressed to his brother Gerald, and the voice was that of Angela Gayle.

Gerald started, coloured up, and, after apologising, off red his arm to the lady, who seemed no less confused than himself. Darcy turned at the same moment, and found himself face to face with Stella Gayle—standing before him, cold, proud, haughty-looking; but, as he thought, more grandly handsome than ever. A slight flush came to the lady's cheek as their eyes met, which, however, instantly disappeared, and was succeeded by the old proud look and glance for which the northern belle was so celebrated.

Darcy bowed, and Stella returned the salutation, bending her head low, but keeping her eyes fixed on his with a somewhat scornful expression, while a slight smile played on her lips.

Darcy, somewhat piqued, turned at once towards Coralie, who was curiously watching the scene, and offered her his arm.

"Miss St. Casse, let me offer you my arm. Will you walk round the room?"

"Yes; but who is that lady to whom you have just bowed? She is very beautiful."

"That—that is Miss Stella Gayle."

"Stella Gayle—ah!"

That was all Coralie said; but as her eyes again sought her out, and she observed her great beauty and commanding queen-like carriage, she felt a sudden pang, and the colour rushed to her face.

"Who is that dark lady in the white silk, with the rose in her hair, Gerald? She is very beautiful."

"What, do you mean her who is walking with Darcy?"

"Yes."

"That is Coralie St. Casse, the 'Star of the South,' the 'Black Angel,' and the handsomest girl in all the Confederate States."

"Coralie St. Casse—ah!" and Stella also felt a pang, as she heard the rival beauty praised.

On all sides it was conceded that the palm of beauty lay between the queen-like Stella, with her classic head and Grecian features, and Coralie with her glorious dark beauty. Stella's complexion was fair, her hair a rich brown, and her eyes of a dark hazel.

Coralie's complexion, on the other hand, was a rich

brown, her hair black as a raven's wings, her eyes large, dark, and melting, with long lashes, which, when closed, drooped far down on her cheeks. Both were about the same height, though Stella, from the commanding way in which she carried her head, appeared slightly the taller. The figure of each was perfect; Stella more slender, though not more graceful than the Southern beauty. It was a debatable point in the ball-room as to which was the belle. But perhaps the majority of the gentlemen, partly out of gallantry to a Northern visitor in the Southern capital, ranged themselves on the side of Stella Gayle.

Gerald Leigh was in deep conversation with Angela, who, by her beaming smiles and soft glances, seemed well pleased with her company; and Captain George, having found an acquaintance, had strolled off, so that Stella was left for a moment or so standing alone. It is wonderful that, accustomed as she had been to so much homage and attention, her proud spirit should feel chafed at even this momentary neglect.

Glancing around the room, she saw standing at a little distance her cousin, Lupus Rock, engaged in conversation with a lady. He was one of the few gentlemen present not in uniform, and was somewhat conspicuous for that reason. Tall, dark, with handsome features and saturnine smile continually playing on his mouth—dressed in plain black—his keen eyes attentively following every movement of Coralie and Darcy Leigh, he seemed an impersonation of the Spirit of Evil in the halls of light. Stella watched him for a short time, and, in spite of herself, a vague feeling of fear and dislike took possession of her. Conquering it, however, she caught his eye, and by an imperious motion of the head, beckoned him to her. Lupus, much wondering at this sudden condescension of his proud and beautiful cousin, with whom lately he had not been on good terms, hastened to obey.

" Pardon me, Stella," he said, " I did not observe you were alone."

" No matter—give me your arm, and take me round the room."

It was now about one o'clock; supper was announced, and while some of the guests had left for that purpose, others promenaded up and down the room, the tables below being too crowded to accommodate all.

"Darcy," said Coralie, suddenly, as they approached Stella Gayle, leaning on the arm of Lupus Rock, "introduce me to Miss Gayle; I think I have already met the gentleman."

Darcy's confusion was great at this request, but of course he could not refuse to comply with it.

As the two couple approached each other in the promenade round the room, Stella quietly led her companion on one side, so as not to pass close to Darcy and Coralie; but the latter also guided her partner to one side, so that they stood face to face with Lupus and Miss Gayle.

Darcy relinquished the arm of Coralie, and shook hands with Lupus Rock.

"Mr. Rock," he said, "I am glad to meet you—I think I am indebted to you for a great service." Then, turning to Stella, he said,—

"Miss Gayle, allow me to introduce to you Miss Coralie St. Casse."

The two girls regarded each other steadfastly for a moment, but Coralie was the first to lower her eyes before the calm, eagle-like glance of Stella.

Each bowed without a word, and Lupus addressed Coralie,—

"Miss St. Casse," he said, in his most insinuating tones, "I think I have had the pleasure of meeting you before, so I am not quite a stranger. Since I have been in Charleston I have heard so much of the splendid regiment you have raised, as to inflame my curiosity. When and where do they next parade? I ask not solely from curiosity, but also with the hope that I may learn something; for I, also, am about raising a regiment."

"But I thought you were a Northerner,—a Yankee?"

"Only by birth—my sympathies are with your brave countrymen, Miss St. Casse, in their approaching struggle for independence."

Stella snatched her hand angrily from her cousin's

arm. She darted on him an indignant glance, and said,—

"My cousin, Mr. Rock, is, I am sorry to say, not a solitary example of a Northern gentleman who has deserted the cause of his country. For such Southerners who, untrammelled by duty or honour, feel themselves bound to espouse the rebel cause, there is some excuse. But what excuse can there be, Miss St. Casse, for those who, in the hour of danger, desert their country, and the flag under which they serve ? I allude to those officers of the United States Navy and Army—who have gone over like traitors to the rebels."

As she spoke her eye rested with unmistakeable meaning on Darcy Leigh.

Darcy knowing that Stella's rude and angry speech was aimed at him—felt painfully embarrassed and annoyed.

Coralie, however, came to his aid.

"On the contrary, Miss Gayle, I think that those brave men who throw up their commissions in the United States Army and Navy, and by the declaration of independence of their country, refuse any longer to serve under the flag of the would-be tyrants, are deserving of all honour."

Darcy, unwilling to prolong a scene which was becoming more than unpleasant, again offered his arm, and led his partner away. Coralie, looking back, caught the dark eyes of Lupus Rock fixed on her with an expression which almost made her tremble, and called back to her memory the strange words of Nina, the *vivandière*.

"Here comes my cousin, my poor father's heir-at-law, and also mine, if I should happen to be killed. I had no idea he was in Richmond. You must leave me with him for half-an-hour, for we have many things to talk about, and some business to arrange. Now, you won't be angry, will you, my gallant captain ?"

"Angry !" said Darcy, smiling ; "what right have I to be angry ?"

Coralie looked as though she would not have been ill-pleased, if he had shown a little annoyance.

" Well, cousin," she said, greeting the new comer—a slight, dark, pale young man, cordially, " what brings you to Richmond ? I thought you were ordered by your physicians to keep very quiet, and by no means to risk any excitement."

" If I were to do all my physicians ordered me, Coralie, I should lead a wretched life. You ask me what I am doing in Richmond ; I will tell you. You know that my uncle—your lamented father—left me a small estate down South, with some twenty slaves ; you know, also, that I always have disliked being a slave-holder. Well, I have this day sold the whole of my slaves for an exceedingly high price. I, this afternoon, signed the deed and received the money."

" Indeed," said Coralie, carelessly ; " and who is the purchaser ?"

" Yonder he stands. His name is Lupus Rock, and he has oceans of money."

" Lupus Rock ! He then has bought up all your slaves ?" cried Coralie, in surprise. " For what reason— with what purpose ?"

" That is exactly what I cannot understand. He could have obtained plenty in Richmond without buying slaves on a Louisiana plantation, and incurring all the expense of their journey to his estate, which is on the Rappahannock. I hear, too, the deed is very strangely drawn. My lawyer was quite puzzled by it. It specially stipulates, that in consideration of a certain sum of money all slaves whatever in which I have a property are sold to him, and even slaves which I may own without knowing it."

Coralie looked troubled and uneasy.

" Without your knowing it ! But how can you own slaves without knowing it ?"

" That is exactly what I cannot understand."

" Supposing my father owned other slaves than those mentioned in his will, to whom would they belong ?"

" They would come to you first as his heir."

" But supposing I were out of the question ?"

" Then they would revert to me."

" Then if I were a slave, for instance, I should belong to you ?" asked Coralie, with a forced laugh.

" What on earth are you talking of, Coralie ?" asked her cousin in surprise; " are you taking leave of your senses ? If you were a slave—I might as well say if I were a slave——"

" Well, never mind. I have a fancy to know who would be my owner if I were my father's slave."

" Supposing such a thing could be, Lupus Rock would be your owner. But I really can't see what you are driving at."

" Come, take me down to supper; it was only my nonsense."

Shortly before two o'clock several officers in cloaks, equipped for travelling, entered the scene of gaiety. They first spoke to the superior officers present, and then hurried about the room as if delivering news of importance. Soon a considerable bustle and confusion might be observed. Officers gathered in groups, and earnestly discussed the news just arrived.

" Be in readiness to join your regiments and mount at a moment's notice." Such was the order the telegraph wires flashed from head-quarters. The news rapidly spread, and fresh arrivals rapidly added to the confusion, which was incomprehensible to the ladies, whose partners, before all attention, had now not a word or glance to spare. General Johnston, who was in command of all the troops in and around Richmond, was present, and aides-de-camp kept arriving every few minutes with fresh news or orders. Minute by minute his brow grew more clouded, his look more serious. The aides-de-camp as fast as they came were dispatched with orders, and many officers hastened at once to take their leave. On all sides could be heard the jingling of spurs and of swords and accoutrements as the owners buckled them on.

Darcy, Gerald, and Captain George had disappeared,. as had many others. The band in the ball-room still played, however, and dancing was kept up, many not knowing the cause of the confusion.

General Johnston beckoned towards him a young officer who was whispering soft words in his partner's ear.

" Go to the railway-station, take with you a sergeant's guard, and order the steam to be got up on all the engines, and see that cars are in readiness for the whole division. Telegraph up the line for more engines and cars—if I am not mistaken we shall want all—let this be your authority."

On saying which the general wrote a line in his pocket-book, and tearing out the leaf, handed it to the officer.

Darcy Leigh had hurried to his hotel and prepared for instant marching; thence he went to the barracks, got the 7th Carolinas under arms, and now hurried back, doubtful whether or not all this was but a false alarm.

As he ran up the ball-room stairs he trod on the dress of a lady before him. He stopped to apologise, and saw that it was Stella Gayle.

Darcy was about to pass on, but on second thoughts decided it would be unmannerly and rude so to do. Besides, there was a sort of triumph in forgiving her insulting speech, returning good for evil.

" You are alone, Miss Gayle—are you looking for your sister ?"

" Yes, I saw her with your brother Gerald a few minutes back ; now I cannot find her."

" May I offer my arm ?"

Stella took it without a word, and Darcy led her through the room.

" Yonder is your sister ; now I will bid you farewell," he said. " You have heard the news, I suppose ?"

" The news—what news ?" asked Stella, in surprise.

" The enemy is advancing, and we expect every moment to receive the order to march. All the troops are under arms, and the streets are lined with them."

" Then there will be a battle ?"

" A desperate battle if they continue to advance."

The band at this moment was playing an inspiriting waltz, and the dancers, many of them quite unconscious of the momentous news just arrived, were gaily whirling around, when suddenly General Johnston, who stood at the end of the room, held up his hand.

Instantly the band stopped, and there was a dead silence. General Johnston stood out in the room as if about to speak, and all the officers deserted their partners and crowded around him. He held in his hand a telegram from the Commander-in-Chief of the army of Virginia.

An instant before the band stopped, Stella Gayle, addressing Darcy, said :—

"You then expect to be ordered with your rebel troops to the front ?"

"Undoubtedly."

"You may fall"—her voice faltered slightly.

"I may fall—it is the fortune of war."

For one moment she struggled with her pride; memories of happy days long gone by, when, as children, she and her sister played with him and Gerald. She thought of the quiet kindness of Darcy, the bountiful hospitality of Colonel Leigh, the rollicking gaiety of Gerald, and of the many happy hours they had spent together before this wretched civil war broke out. She thought of all this—looked in Darcy's pale face, on which sat that look of determination she had so often admired, and her heart softened.

"Darcy," she said, with a look of tenderness in her beautiful grey eyes, which, had he seen, would have purchased her pardon for an offence a thousand times as heinous as a few angry words—"Darcy, I spoke rudely, unkindly to you just now——"

"Pardon me," she was about to say, but at that instant the band gave a final crash which drowned her words, and then ceased.

Darcy turning, saw General Johnston holding a slip of paper in one hand, with the other held aloft as if requesting silence.

All gazed towards the general, and listened.

"Officers, gentlemen, and ladies,—I have just received a telegram from our army in the face of the enemy. It runs thus :—

"'The enemy is advancing—our pickets are driven in. To the front at once with all your forces.'"

There was a buzzing for a moment, which quickly swelled louder and louder, till a cheer made the room ring. Then was heard the booming of signal guns in rapid succession. Next came the shrill blasts of the bugles as cavalry and infantry trumpeters blew the assembly. All was noise and confusion. The streets resounded with the clatter of horses' hoofs, the rumble of artillery, the measured tramp of infantry, as the troops marched on to the railway.

Coralie St. Casse now re-appeared in her riding-habit and hat, with the uniform sash across her breast. Nina was in attendance on her in her *vivandière* dress. No sooner was her figure seen at the door than a young officer, lifting his hat, cried—

' A cheer for the 'Star of the South.'"

And again a shout rang forth, which, for a moment, drowned the booming of the guns, the bugle blasts, and the tramping of the passing regiments.

Now came hurried adieus, in many cases, alas! final ones. Husbands, brothers, fathers, lovers—all hurried away to their posts. Darcy Leigh bade Stella good-bye, and, without a pressure of the hand or a kind look, was gone.

For a few moments she stood motionless, her large grey eyes filling with tears; then she moved slowly to the window of the room which looked out on the street.

The day was just beginning to dawn. Away down the street towards the railway station, as far as she could see, was a long line of troops formed four deep, and marching slowly on, the soldiers making the morning air ring out with songs of defiance and enthusiasm.

She could hear the shrieks of the railway whistle as train after train rumbled away with its heavy load.

Regiment after regiment, squadron after squadron, passed the window, all shouting, singing, apparently drunk with joy at the prospect of a fight with the hated enemy.

4

She waited until the 7th Carolinas passed. Coralie rode at the head, the morning dew spangling her rich hair, which hung in disorder down her back. On one side of her horse walked Nina, the *vivandière*. On the other, occasionally giving a brief word of command to his men, was Darcy Leigh.

Stella gazed after them till they disappeared through the gates leading to the railway. She heard the loud shout with which they took their places in the cars ; then the shrill whistle of the engine as the train moved off, and they were gone.

In an hour's time the last regiment had left, and a silence as of the grave reigned in Richmond. With heavy hearts, the ladies in their light ball dresses wrapt their shawls around them, and sought their homes alone ; those who had conducted them there were not to escort them back—many they were never to behold again.

As the day advanced a deep gloom seemed to settle on the city. All knew that a desperate conflict was going on, but none knew which way the fight was going.

At one o'clock the news came by telegraph that the Confederates were retiring before overwhelming numbers. After that the wires spoke no more, and the gloom deepened, for many thought it meant that they were in the hands of the enemy.

Crowds besieged the telegraph offices, anxious for news, but no news came.

Three—four—five o'clock. Still no welcome words of victory were flashed along the wires.

And now on the wings of fancy we will transport ourselves to the battle-field.

## CHAPTER V.

### THE BATTLE OF BULL RUN.

THE rapid means of transport afforded by railways and steamships have effected almost as complete a change in modern warfare and tactics as have the discovery of

THE BATTLE OF BULL RUN.     51

gunpowder and the perfection to which artillery has been brought.

In the short but bloody campaign by France and Sardinia against Austria, for the first time in the history of war, troops were brought up by train, and landed actually on the battle-field.

On the American continent, however, in consequence of the vast distances to be traversed, railways have, in the present war, played a still more important part.

At daylight on the morning of the 21st of July the Federal army advanced, full of confidence, against the scanty force of rebels opposed to them.

The latter had erected breastworks and posted guns on commanding situations, although an attack at that point was by no means expected. It was generally thought in the Confederate councils, that the Army of the Potomac, as the Yankees designated their force in and around Washington, was so posted in order to defend the capital from a sudden assault.

The Southern leaders anticipated that the advance, if an advance were contemplated, would not be made on the lines at the rear of Bull Run and Manassas Junction ; and thus impressed, the force there was very weak, while strong bodies of troops were posted at various points along the railroad south, ready to be thrown at once on any threatened point. At Fredericksburg and Richmond, too, there were whole divisions of troops, infantry and cavalry, which, but for the telegraph and railway, could never have taken any part in the battle.

Long before the grey mists of morning had risen from the valleys and ravines about Manassas and Bull Run stream, a sputtering fire on the rebel front announced the advance of the enemy's troops. Slowly but steadily this fire increased, till, all along the line for the distance of more than a mile, the constant rattle of musketry might be heard.

The outlying sentries, such as were not shot down at their posts, sought shelter with the pickets, which, in turn, were driven in on their supports, not without great loss. So rapid and determined was the advance of the enemy,

4—2

that in many cases the dead and wounded of the pickets
and outposts had to be abandoned.

When the Federals had advanced as far as the first
line, there was a short pause in the firing on both sides.

The Yankees awaited fresh troops, which constantly
arrived and debouched into line for the attack.

In the Confederate camp all was hurry and excitement.
The hastily-lit camp-fires and the unfinished breakfasts
were deserted, and rough, rugged men flocked to the ban-
ners of their respective regiments, buckling on belts and
accoutrements as they ran, in response to the blasts of
many bugles blowing the "alarm" and the "assembly."

The country was wooded and hilly, and the assailants
would have to mount the hills to carry the positions of
the rebels.

The second or inner line of the rebels is strengthened
by means of low breastworks—batteries and guns posted
on commanding positions. Minute by minute the sharp
rattle of musketry grows louder and fiercer in the front,
and occasionally may be heard the shouts and yells of the
combatants, as the rebels slowly retreated before overwhelming numbers, and the enemy as steadily advance.

And now the pickets have fallen back on their supports in the first line. There is a pause of a few minutes,
then a rapid fire, spreading from the right along the
centre to the extreme left, till all is blended in one long
crashing volley. Shouts rend the air, a rising breeze dis-
perses the morning mist, the cannon from the hills and
batteries belch forth a storm of shot and shell, and the
sun streams forth, revealing to the rebels a vast host
advancing—infantry, cavalry, artillery—against them ;
while the assailants on their part perceive an unbroken
front before them, protected by guns and batteries, of
whose existence they were in ignorance.

Still the Federals have an enormous advantage in
numbers, and bravely led by their officers, press steadily
on. Each moment the roar of battle swells louder. The
cannon shot howl and the shells hiss through the air,
while the sharp "ping" of the bullets, those wasps of war,
make up a chorus only to be heard on a battle-field.

Bravely the outnumbered Confederates hold their ground. Aides-de-camp and mounted staff officers gallop about, apparently in wild confusion. Nearer and nearer are heard the rattling volleys of musketry, the wild shouts, and the bugle blasts, plainly telling the tale that the first line is being beaten back. Still, however, it is but step by step, every yard of ground disputed and strewn with slain, that the Yankees make good their advance.

Meantime, while the regiments in front are slowly retiring, and keeping the enemy in check, every effort is used by the Confederate generals to strengthen their position behind. More breastworks are thrown up, and fresh guns mounted on every available point, till it seems almost impossible that anything can live within that circle of fire. Still, however, the Yankee hordes, confident in their numbers and the *prestige* of the Union, press bravely on, no less bravely led. By noon they have driven back the troops opposed to them nearly a mile, and are still steadily advancing. The Confederates retire slowly and sullenly within the shelter of the woods skirting the hills, which the Yankees are determined to take.

Again there is a comparative lull in the fight as the Northern chiefs marshal their forces to the final dash, the assault, and victory ; while the rebels, bringing every gun to bear, conceal their force in the woods and behind breastworks, and prepare to give the foe a desperate reception.

The bugles sound the advance. The shouts of thousands of armed men as they rush forward on the enemy's position, are followed by a crash of musketry, a booming of guns, and whistling of shot overhead and through their ranks, which make the bravest regiments falter and pause. Now the field artillery, in which the Yankees are greatly superior, is brought into play with terrible effect, and great havoc is made in the enemy's ranks by these well-served guns. For two hours more a series of desperate assaults are bloodily repulsed ; the guns of the rebels on the hills, and the light artillery of the Federals pounding away with might and main.

Fresh troops continually take up the assault; no sooner is a Massachusetts or Pennsylvania regiment repulsed, than a New York or Ohio brigade takes its place, only in its turn to be hurled back from the strong position held by the outnumbered but determined foe. Then comes a desperate charge of the New York Fire Zouaves. They charge right up to the breastwork, to the muzzles of the guns, and are only driven back when half their force is down from the crushing volleys poured in on them. Notwithstanding the obstinate resistance of the rebels, the enemy, continually bringing up fresh troops, slowly but steadily advances. Several guns, roughly mounted behind a hastily thrown up mound of earth are taken, and the attack on the whole position becomes fiercer and more sustained. On the extreme left of the rebel lines especially, a continuous and steady advance is made, while at that particular point the defenders are in numbers weakest. Still hitherto they have held their own and bravely stood their ground. After several desperate but unsuccessful attacks, the assailants retired, or rather halted, to re-form and receive reinforcements. The pause was but of short duration. Once more they press on towards the thinned ranks of the rebels. The position which the Yankees here strove so desperately to gain, was the key of the whole. It was a hill with a low breastwork running round the summit, and two guns in position. The hill was not steep; the guns were light, and the breastwork, which was only some three feet high, was defended along its whole length of a quarter of a mile by no more than two Virginia regiments, numbering only some 1100 men.

It was in vain that the officers in command sent to head-quarters for reinforcements. The invariable answer was—

" None can be spared ; the hill must be defended to the death."

No wonder that the Yankees struggled desperately for this position. It commanded and flanked the whole rebel line. From its summit could be seen the railroad from Fredericksburg, with here and there an occasional train with tardy and insufficient reinforcements, and troops or guns posted there might enfilade and cut up the rear of the Confederate right, while they resisted the desperate attacks on the front.

Frequently a Confederate officer would dash up that hill on horseback, and rising in the stirrups, would gaze out southward with straining eyes for the expected reinforcements, and with a gloomy glance towards the ever-increasing masses of the enemy, would gallop down again the bearer of no good tidings.

At last, loud and prolonged cheers from the rebel right, and a Union flag floating where it was not before, told that the enemy had taken a battery.

They did not long hold it, however, for a desperate charge of the 4th Alabama drove them from their vantage ground, leaving many dead behind them. But this momentary success inspires the centre of the enemy and their extreme right to fresh and desperate exertions to take the hill defended by the Virginia regiments. A whole division, numbering at least 10,000 men, advanced in close column to within 200 yards of the breastworks, and then, deploying into line, advanced rapidly up the hill, keeping up a scattering fire as they did so.

A close and deadly volley, however, when within a hundred yards, caused them to stagger, and the next moment the tramp of horse was heard, and a body of cavalry trotted out of the woods to the right.

## CHAPTER VI.

### THE CAVALRY CHARGE.

An attempt was made to form square, but before the manœuvre could be effected—

" Charge !" was shouted by the officer in command, and in half a minute the horsemen were upon them—among them, cutting, slashing, and shouting.

It was the cavalry raised by Gerald Leigh, and only about three hundred in number, who effected this sea-

sonable charge. Gerald, by whose side rode Captain
George, the Englishman, had been slightly wounded by a
splinter on the forehead ; his cap had been struck off,
and his fair hair was dabbled with blood, a stream of
which ran down his face.

He cut and slashed about him with reckless fury and
energy, spurring his horse with desperate bravery into
the thickest groups of the enemy he could see. It was
in vain they sought to form rallying squares. No sooner
had some dozen men formed around an officer, than
Gerald, shouting to others to follow him, would dash
into their midst and clean through them. Captain
George rode close beside him, but kept himself cooler,
and on more than one occasion presented his revolver and
pistoled an adversary who was aiming at Gerald. In
one case nothing but his steady hand and unerring eye
could have saved his friend's life, for a wounded Yankee,
furious with rage and pain, suddenly rose from the
ground, and presented his rifle at Gerald's back at not
five paces' distance. Before, however, he could pull the
trigger, a shot through the brain from the Englishman's
pistol put an end to his mortal career.

Gerald, borne away by excitement, led his little force
in pursuit of the enemy full half a mile from his supports, and when he turned he found himself followed
only by Captain George and some twenty men ; while
between him and their own troops there were two
squadrons of cavalry and a regiment of infantry in
square.

Making a slight detour to avoid the fire of the infantry,
Gerald led his little force round the foot of the hill, and
then turning sharp round dashed straight up at a canter.
The enemy's cavalry rode to intercept, but a deadly volley
from the breastwork brought down several horses, and
sent others galloping riderless away ; and Gerald with
his few brave companions rode through and over the
rest, and regained the shelter of the infantry amidst
deafening cheers of triumph. Those cheers were taken
up by the whole line, and when they faded away, and
before the musketry fire again opened, an answering

cheer was heard from the rear—faint from the distance, but distinct.

Gerald and Captain George, who were on the very summit of the hill, looking back towards the railroad saw a sight which gladdened their heart and assured them of victory.

" Courage ! my brave boys," cried Gerald, " the day is ours. General Johnston's reinforcements have arrived. Yonder they come, horse, foot, and artillery ; 30,000, if there is a man."

Every possible eminence was instantly mounted, and hundreds of eyes looking out on the plain behind saw that Gerald was right, and that heavy reinforcements had arrived.

On the railway, at distances of about a quarter of a mile, could be plainly discerned long trains of cars crowded with troops. The engines, overloaded as they were, laboured along but slowly, otherwise the welcome reinforcements would have arrived long since.

Now the musketry fire broke out again with renewed violence. The cannon boomed, and the Yankee bugles once more blew the advance. But above the din of war might plainly be heard the wild shouts of the fresh troops as they leaped from the trains, formed, and advanced rapidly in close columns to the battle-field.

Gerald Lee and Captain George had by great good fortune secured a passage in a light train, which carried only General Johnston's staff and some few troops. This train had arrived at Manassas Junction early in the afternoon, and Gerald, to his joy, found his regiment, from which he had a few days' leave of absence, awaiting there for orders.

Thus it was, that, perceiving the perilous position of the defenders of the hill, and the importance of the position, he had sought for and obtained leave to execute a diversion on the enemy's flank, which was carried out, as the reader knows, with the most brilliant success.

It is now three o'clock in the afternoon. The sultry heat of the day, the scarcity of water, and the desperate fatigue of fighting for some nine hours without rest or relief, have told a fearful tale on the Southern troops. There is not a man among the two regiments who has not expended at least seventy rounds of ammunition of the eighty served out.

The rifles are all so hot from the rapid firing as to render it dangerous to load, and the men are compelled to cool the barrels by pouring some of the scanty stock of water from their canteens over them.

Now once again the fierce tide of attack rolls on. Once more on the rebel right two batteries are taken after a bloody resistance, and the guns turned on their former owners.

Desperate attempts are made to recover them, and an assault on a prodigious scale is in progress against that tenacious little hill on the extreme left. This time the attacking force of infantry advance, supported by cavalry and artillery, the cavalry on one flank, artillery on the other.

Arrived within about three hundred yards, the light guns unlimber, and commence pouring a deadly and accurate fire of shot and shell into the low breastwork, above which may be descried the powder-grimed faces of the defenders.

The cavalry take up ground on the right flank, watching the wood from which Gerald Leigh's force dashed out so opportunely on the previous assault. A constant though desultory fire was kept up by the Virginian regiments, each man loading and firing as fast as possible as the enemy moved up to the assault.

Then, and not till then it was, that the ammunition began to fail. While the enemy were yet at least three hundred yards off, fully one-half of the Southern soldiers defending the hill were without cartridges. The officers ran hither and thither beseeching the men to spare their ammunition—to reserve their fire till the enemy were at point blank range—then to deliver one last volley, and to charge with the bayonet.

Encouraged by the taking of the batteries on the extreme right, the Yankees now moved up large bodies of fresh troops to the assault; and on the rebel left especially, dense masses of infantry advanced in column, and deployed into line.

Onwards they came, the bugles sounding the " charge," soldiers cheering, and the light artillery, thundering away from their flank, causing terrible destruction to the breastwork and its defenders. Notwithstanding the destructive fire kept up by the Virginia regiments, the Yankees came up the slope at a run. The cavalry on their flank relieved them from the fear of another charge, and they pressed forward vigorously, though in some disorder.

Arrived within a hundred yards of the rebels, the withering fire kept up from the breastwork suddenly slackened, and, as they approached yet nearer, ceased altogether. This caused some astonishment, and though they still pressed on, a deadly volley was momentarily expected by the officers.

And now above the roar of musketry and cannon is heard the voice of a Yankee captain,—

" Lash into them, lads !—they've got no more powder !"

A shout from the soldiers followed this welcome announcement, and they came on at a run. A few scattering shots are fired from the breastwork, answered by a rattling fire from the Yankees, which scatters dismay among the scant defenders, ammunitionless, and hopeless of resisting so desperate an assault by such overwhelming numbers.

The hill is mounted—the breastwork gained ! The Stars and Stripes, borne bravely on, wave where the rebel flag had been. The Yankees, with wild shouts and one last volley, press forward with the bayonet, and the wearied and dispirited rebels are borne helplessly back by the mere force of numbers, leaving more than half their number dead and wounded on the ground they had so long held.

## CHAPTER VII.

CORALIE LEADS HER OWN REGIMENT.

EVER since the battle began at early dawn, troops kept pouring in by road and rail in response to the urgent despatches sent in all directions for aid. Unfortunately, the division under General Johnston was unable to reach Manassas Junction till near three o'clock in the afternoon, and at that time the Yankees were forcing the outnumbered rebels back all along the line, and had taken two batteries.

For miles before the train came in view of the smoke of battle, the dull boom of the artillery and rattle of musketry could be heard telling what a desperate battle was progressing.

A high rate of speed was impossible with the trains overloaded with troops and ammunition, so that the roar of battle could be distinctly heard from the cars for more than an hour before the trains even approached within view of the struggle. The first ten trains on the line were filled with infantry—some twelve regiments, numbering in all about 10,000 men. These arrived at Manassas Gap about a quarter past three, and with loud cheers leaped from the cars, and forming close columns, ran on towards the battle-field, distant about a mile and a half.

The third regiment which arrived was the Seventh, or Carolina Crashers, and as soon as formed they received an order from an aide-de-camp sent to meet them, to hasten to the support of the hill and breastwork held by the Virginian regiments. They had not marched a quarter of a mile up the slope in the rear of the Virginian troops they were to succour, when a lady on horseback, with the uniform blue sash across her shoulder, galloped by. She bowed to the cheers which saluted her, and pulled up her horse at the head of the regiment, riding by the side of the colonel and major.

Colonel Johnson, with an exclamation of surprise and anger, turned in his saddle.

"Young lady, this is no place for you.   Go to the rear."

Coralie's eyes flashed, and she turned crimson.

"I shall not go to the rear.   I shall go to the front."

"This is madness.   You shall not thus endanger yourself.   I will order your horse to be led back."

Coralie touched with her gloved hand a small revolver she wore in her belt.

"I will shoot the first man who dares to lay a hand on my horse's bridle," she said, quietly.

"I will not suffer this.   I will return.   I will lead my men back."

"Lead them back, if you choose," replied Coralie, scornfully.   "I shall go on.   Is this a time to talk of going back?   Look up the hill; see how our brave troops are pressed—see how the shot and shell are tearing around them, while they are too weak to charge into and drive back the enemy.   Lead back the men, Colonel, if they will follow you, which I doubt.   I will see whether or not they will follow me."

Then wheeling her horse, she addressed the troops:

"Forward, my brave lads, forward.   I will lead you on."

The thundering shout and the quick forward rush of the men in answer to these words, convinced the colonel that the wilful girl must have her way.   As to leading his men back, he never meant it, and if he had, he could not have done it, for every man would have followed the "Star of the South," no matter where she led.

Darcy Leigh, quitting his company for a moment, ran up, and walked by the side of Coralie's horse.

"Coralie," he said, out of breath, "promise me you will halt when we arrive on the scene of battle. Already I can hear the bullets whistling overhead. Promise, when the head of our column arrives to the support of the troops now so hard pressed, that you will fall back to the rear."

" I promise."

"That is right ; now I shall fight with an easy mind."

He was about returning to his company, when she stopped him.

" Stay a minute, Darcy ; just examine my revolver, and load it."

" Your revolver ! what on earth do you want with a revolver ? keep in the rear, and you will be safe."

" No matter, who knows ? We may be defeated, and have to fly. I may have to defend my life and liberty. See that it is right."

Darcy took it, and placing it in his belt, handed his own.

" Here is mine, it is loaded. I will answer for it. It never yet missed fire. Adieu. I shall see you after the battle if I am spared."

" Darcy, Darcy ! take back your revolver ; you have more need of it than I. Mine is not loaded, and a mere toy."

But he was gone ; and with a sigh she placed his pistol in her belt.

A bright flush came on her cheek, and her eyes glistened with pleasure, in spite of the thought of his danger.

" Noble fellow ! he thinks not of himself."

Her thoughts were interrupted by a deafening crash of musketry in front, followed by a shout and an irregular fire in reply.

They were yet five hundred yards from the rear of the breastwork, and each moment wounded men were borne by on stretchers.

Coralie, whose first experience this was of war, sickened as she saw the pale, ghastly faces distorted with agony, and noticed the stretchers dripping with blood. It was a horrible sight, as they were borne by, pale, fainting, bleeding to the rear.

There was no groaning, no crying ; some lay still, with closed eyes and lips moving, as if silently praying for death ; others, as they passed the fresh troops coming to the rescue, raised themselves feebly on their elbows, and with bloody hands waving soiled and gory hats, cheered the 7th Carolinas on.

Others lay still—motionless, glaring upwards into the sky with glassy, filmy eyes. They were dead—had breathed their last—and the bearers were unknowingly carrying corpses.

The men of the Carolina Crashers quicken their pace, and strive to drown their thoughts by shouts of impatience and fury.

The din in front is now deafening. The Virginias fall back in confusion, and amid fire and smoke, cheers and yells, the Yankee flag, the Stars and Stripes, is seen on the breastwork in front.

" Halt !—form line !" is now the word of command, and the troops rapidly, but somewhat confusedly, deploy into line. Darcy Leigh spares one moment, and running up to Coralie, seizes her horse's bridle.

" Your promise—remember your promise. Come to the rear."

He notices her flashing eyes and the wild state of excitement in which she is, and fears she will refuse. But instead of so doing she suffers him to lead her to the rear of the line unresistingly. He has not one moment to spare, for he hears the order,

" Quick ! march !" followed by the rapid advance of his regiment.

" Farewell, Coralie. We shall meet after the fight, please God."

Then he hastily runs to his post at the head of his company.

When within about fifty yards of the breastwork, the colonel, waving his sword, gives the word,—

" Charge !"

And with a yell of defiance the Carolina Crashers rush on.

They cannot fire, for many of the broken and discomfited Virginia regiments are between them and the enemy ; but they, at the welcome sight of friends, fall back into the ranks of the Carolinas, or make for the flanks, so as to make the space in front clear.

The Stars and Stripes do not float long over that bloodily contested mound. Ere the Yankees can recover from the confusion consequent on taking the position, the foe is upon them.

For a moment they try to stand their ground, thinking this to be but a desperate rally of the defeated enemy. But the Carolinas, fresh and furious, dash savagely on with the bayonet, and the Yankees scatter like chaff before the wind.

Back over the breastwork the Yankee flags are forced ; back—still back, the triumphant rebels pouring in a deadly volley as the enemy retreat.

Back they go headlong—pell-mell, till, half-way down the hill, they are met by fresh troops coming to their support. Falling behind these they re-form, and, exhorted by their officers, prepare once more to mount that deadly mound. The supports which have come up are large, and nearly all fresh troops.

At least twenty thousand men are now ready again to assault the position which they have won and lost.

At this moment two batteries of field artillery open on the rebels, and checking their advance, the Yankees reform behind their supports, and seem as if again to mount the hill.

Now along the whole line, and especially towards the rebel right, the assailants waver and fall back. Each moment fresh regiments of Confederates are marched to the field, and their wild shouts can be plainly heard as they arrive by train and hurry forward.

. General Beauregard, accompanied by his staff, galloped up the hill so long defended by the Virginia regiments, and surveyed the field.

On the extreme right Stonewall Jackson's troops, after holding their own against great odds, reinforced by General Johnston, now in turn press on the wavering foe, who, exhausted and dispirited by a prolonged and futile attack of so many hours' duration, seem disposed to seek the rear. But if, on the right, the enemy are disposed to waver, on the left they are collecting all their fresh troops for an assault on the hill.

This, if once carried and held, would decide the day.

And now some twenty-five thousand men are marshalling for the attack. The defenders number only the 7th Carolinas and the remnants of the two Virginia regiments, in all less than two thousand men.

Coralie St. Casse, on the very summit of the hill, saw from her saddle the progress of the fight, the charge of the 7th Carolinas, the rout of the enemy, and again their halt and re-formation behind their supports. General Beauregard at a few paces' distance watched the gathering storm, the dense masses of the Yankees, and the havoc made by the artillery in the ranks of the rebels.

" Three regiments of infantry to the wood on the left, and one of cavalry," he said to an aide-de-camp. " Take the order to General Johnston at once. Let him get well on the enemy's flank before debouching from the cover."

And now the Carolina Crashers fall slowly back before the heavy musketry and field artillery they are exposed to.

" Your men fight splendidly," said Beauregard, turning to Coralie; " but they are falling back. Think you they can hold this breastwork for half an hour, to give time for Johnston's flank march through the woods ? No help can be spared ; they must hold this hill to the last gasp. If they resist till those troops yonder get on the enemy's flank all will be well."

The general pointed to the left, where a column of troops might be seen making for the woods which lined the battle field.

" Pray Heaven they may haste !" cried Coralie, gazing anxiously on her men, who now were retreating in some confusion, bringing in, however, their dead and wounded with them.

" What say you to a final charge, general ?" asked Coralie, as the triumphant shouts of the advancing foe became clearer and louder above the din of battle.

" A charge ! your men will not charge five times their numbers."

" They will—they will—they will follow me. Shall I gallop to the front and give the word ? Quick ! see how

5

the foe press on.   In ten minutes more they will drive
our men back over the breastwork."

Grape shot and bullets now flew freely around, ploughing up the ground on all sides.   More than one of the
general's staff was hurled bleeding from the saddle.   But
Beauregard, scarcely observing the danger, still looked
anxiously through his field-glass on the fight.   Coralie,
too, sat her horse unmoved amidst the storm of death
which whistled by on all sides.

"There they come from the woods ; now is the time.
No, that is the cavalry—patience, patience !   Oh, that
these fellows stand their ground for ten minutes more !"

"They will, they will, general.   Give the word,
and they will drive back the enemy at the bayonet's
point."

At that moment the head of a column of infantry
might be seen issuing from the wood half a mile to the
left, and a little in the enemy's rear.

"Captain Scott," said the general, all the time intently
watching the flanking troop through his glass, "take
word to the colonel of the Carolina Crashers to rally his
men and charge desperately forward.   An attack will be
made immediately on the flank.   If successful, the day
is ours, for the foe are broken, and retreating before
Jackson's men on the right.   The hour is come."

But no answer came from the aide-de-camp, and
turning his head, Beauregard saw the young officer
stretched lifeless, his horse standing riderless some distance off.

Coralie was nearer the general than any of his staff,
and heard the order.

"The hour is come," repeated Coralie, and without
another word, she struck her horse with her whip, and
galloped down the hill towards the 7th Carolinas, who
were staggering slowly back under the crushing fire of
the foe.

The colonel was on horseback, in the centre of the
regiment close to the colours, which showed many a
ragged hole and rent.

"General Beauregard's orders are to charge the foe,"
cried Coralie, in a loud, clear voice, distinctly audible

by all the men of the centre. "An attack is to be made at the same time on their flank."

A cheer broke from the men as they recognised "the Black Angel" in their midst. The bugle blew the "charge." and at the same time a sharp fire in the rear and flank of the Yankees told that there also they were attacked. Two men immediately in front of Coralie's horse fell, mown down by grape shot. Without a moment's hesitation, she dashed through the gap, and galloped along the left of the line in full view of both friends and foes.

For a moment the enemy gazed in amazement at this strange sight. The Crashers gave vent to a yell of enthusiasm, and pressed on. Coralie passed close to Darcy Leigh at the head of his company, and as she did so, he attempted to seize her bridle.

"Coralie!—Coralie!—go to the rear. Remember your promise!"

"I was sent by the general—his *aide* is killed! Lead on your men!"

Then slashing her horse across the shoulder with her whip, she caused him to swerve, and evading Darcy Leigh, she galloped right towards the foe; pointing and calling to the troops to come on. Onwards, still on, she rode, followed at a run by the soldiers. Carried away by excitement, it almost seemed as if she were about to ride right into the enemy's crowded ranks, bristling as they were with steel and jets of fire and smoke.

Suddenly a wild cry burst from the soldiers—a cry of rage and grief. The horse of Coralie is seen to plunge fearfully for a second or two, rear up, and then, with a great bound, fall headlong to the earth, throwing his rider to some distance.

Coralie lay motionless, and several of the enemy ra . out from the ranks as if to secure her; but a scattering volley soon laid these rash men low. The next moment the "Star of the South" started to her feet, her hair in disorder—her hat off. She gazed wildly around for a moment, as if the shock of the fall had confused friend and foe.

5—2

Then, when she distinguished the Yankee flags, she pointed with her whip, and shouted, in clear, ringing tones, the one word—

"Forward!"

And forward the Carolina Crashers went with a vengeance—with a terrible yell of fury they charged on at a run. Their rifles were empty, but they did not pause to reload, trusting to the bright and deadly bayonet. When within twenty yards, the enemy, appalled by that fierce rush, faltered, broke, and fled. At the same moment a whole regiment of cavalry burst on their flank, and the infantry despatched by Beauregard coming up, also opened fire with deadly effect.

Fire and sword!—the gleaming bayonet and flashing sabre—are in their midst. All along the line the advance is general and impetuous. The artillery thunders forth from the hills, hailing shot and shell into the dense masses of the flying Yankees.

Onwards, still onwards, with deafening shouts, the rebels press—back, still back fly the enemy, the officers in vain trying to rally them.

It is four o'clock P.M. on the 21st of July, 1861, and the great Yankee army is flying in hopeless confusion from the foe they so confidently assaulted in the morning.

The retreat becomes a panic—a rout. The ground for miles is strewn with arms, accoutrements, and uniforms; while the dead, wounded, and exhausted soldiers lining the road of retreat tells how complete has been the defeat.

Thus was fought and lost the battle of Bull Run.

---

# CHAPTER VIII.

### AFTER THE BATTLE.—THE CAMP BY NIGHT.

IT was long after nightfall before the pursuit of the flying Yankees was ended.

Towards nine o'clock the various regiments engaged in the battle returned to camp, weary, faint, and footsore from the fatigues of the fight and the pursuit.

The rebel camp at the rear of Manassas seemed in inextricable confusion. Stragglers abounded by hundreds, strolling about in search of their regiments, which they had by some means or another lost.

The wounded were now being brought in, and as soon as discipline was restored, extra fatigue parties were told off to bury the dead and clear the field of wounded and dying men, whether friends or foes.

The tents and rough huts of the rebel camp were arranged in parallel lines to the number of some five or six, intersected at intervals by rows of huts running across.   The infantry regiments occupied the centre rows, of huts, which stretched for nearly a mile from east to west; while the cavalry and artillery were quartered on the outer edges.

The head quarters of General Beauregard were nearly in the centre of the principal street in the camp city.   A rough hut, somewhat larger than the others, with a shed, in which were tied up some horses and a flag flying from a staff on the roof, alone distinguished the quarters of the general from those of the private soldiers.

Gerald Leigh, who has passed safely through the perils of the day, is standing with Captain George and a group of cavalry officers in front of a large tent in one of the outer and narrow camp streets.   Horses tethered two and three together at every tent, and the piles of saddles, trusses of hay, and stable belongings, sufficiently announced that this part was devoted to the cavalry.

Here and there outside the tents lay wounded troopers, gasping for breath in the hot, sultry summer air, while horses lamed, blood-stained, and utterly worn out, showed how fierce had been the pursuit from which they had just returned.

Each minute troopers would come in one by one, walking their horses slowly, wearily, and arriving at their quarters, would throw themselves from the saddle and throw themselves exhausted on the soil, while those of their comrades who had rested would unsaddle and water the weary steeds.

"How many men have we lost?" asked Gerald Leigh of a sergeant who now came up. "I do not see more than half our fellows in camp."

"I don't think that we've lost more than forty men and horses, sir; I believe there are many wounded not yet returned from the pursuit, besides those who are so much hurt as not yet to have been able to return; there was no stopping them; some of them seemed mad, they paid no attention to the bugle calls, 'Halt.' I saw quite thirty or forty of our men a mile in advance of the infantry and close to Fairfax Court House."

"Have any of you seen anything of my brother Darcy or his regiment, the 7th Carolinas?" asked Gerald of those about him.

"I haven't seen anything of Darcy since the very beginning of the Yankee rout; then he was at the head of his company, well and unwounded."

It was Lieutenant Waiston who spoke. No sooner had he ceased than Irving, another young officer, said,—

"I did not see anything of your brother, Gerald; but about half-an-hour before dusk I had, from the top of Gumtree Hill, a clear view both of the Yankee hordes in hopeless rout and our troops in pursuit. Fully half a mile ahead of any other infantry regiment I distinguished the colours of the 7th Carolinas, and further ahead still, seemingly close upon the fugitives, I could see that strange, mad girl, the Black Angel, mounted and gallop- ing hither and thither on the field, as if encouraging the troops to press on."

"Mounted! why her horse was killed in the last charge," said Gerald. "I, myself, saw her on foot."

"Well, if her horse was killed she got another one, that's all I have to say, for I am certain I saw her."

Now an officer, with his head bound up and his arm in a sling, rode up and dismounting, painfully gave his horse's bridle to a trooper who stood near.

"Water him and feed him, my man."

"Hallo! Trent, is that you, old fellow?" exclaimed

some one. Why, I didn't know you with that towel round your head. Are you much hurt?"

"Pretty considerably. I got hit by a splinter of shell on the head and was thrown, my horse killed and falling on me. I believe my left arm is broken; I didn't suppose I should have been alive now, but some fellows of the 7th Carolinas lifted the dead horse off me, and I caught one galloping about riderless."

"The 7th Carolinas! Have you seen them in camp?"

"Yes, they are mustering to the roll call about five tents from head-quarters. Their colours are planted there, and when I passed I guessed there were about four hundred of them lying and standing about."

"Four hundred! why they were over a thousand strong this morning."

"Treskar, you must look in the hospital and on the field for the rest, for there can't be many unwounded stragglers out now; it must be ten o'clock."

Fires now flashed and glittered from the front of hundreds of tents, as the wearied soldiers cooked their evening meal, and talked over the glories and dangers of the day.

Sometimes, as an old familiar name was mentioned, the voice of the speaker would be hushed to a solemn whisper. He who was spoken of was numbered with the slain.

Orders had now gone out from head-quarters, and the bugles of every regiment sounded the assembly for the muster roll, that the losses in the battle might be estimated.

It was a solemn and gloomy scene as an officer of each regiment read out the names. Sometimes it would run thus,—

"Roberts?"

"Here."

"Phillips?"

"Here."

"Williams?"

A dead silence, and after a moment's pause a cross would be made in the muster book, opposite the name.

Williams was among the slain.

"Fergusson?"

Silence—no voice responded. Another cross was made in the book, and the officer went on.

"Corporal Smith?"

"Wounded—both legs broken, and a ball through the shoulder."

It was a comrade who replied for him.

"Maxwell?"

"Dead. I saw him shot through the head."

"Marsh?"

Silence.

"Jones?"

"Here."

"O'Brien?"

No answer.

And so on, through the dreary list the frequent ominous silences, followed by the officer's pencil marking the cross opposite the name, telling how terrible was the loss in killed, wounded, and missing.

Of the Carolina Crashers, six hundred only answered to their names; more than four hundred were killed or wounded.

Darcy Leigh and Coralie were both missing—none knew their fate—they might be dead or weltering in their blood on the ghastly plain of battle.

By degrees the camp subsided into quiet, the bugles ceased to blow, and but few stragglers came in. The wounded men were placed on stretchers and carried off to the hospital, there to undergo the ordeal of the surgeon's knife and probe.

Strong parties, both of infantry and cavalry, were told off for picket and outpost duty, and by eleven o'clock the weary victors of the day were asleep in their tents or around their camp fires. Not all, however, were permitted to recruit exhausted nature by repose; for, in addition to the outposts, pickets and sentries, numerous fatigue parties were told off to bring in the wounded from the field and to dig pits for the slain.

Gerald Leigh was ordered to the command of a distant

cavalry outpost, and after a hasty meal and a draught of brandy was on the point of mounting his horse, full of gloomy fears for his missing brother, when his attention was attracted by an exclamation which broke from his friend Irving.

"Whom have we here?—ladies, by Jove!"

And surely enough, casting his eye along the avenue of tents and camp fires, two female forms were seen advancing towards them.

Gerald paused ere he mounted, and gazed curiously towards the fresh arrival.

"Ladies!" he exclaimed, "as I live. Who can they be, and what can they do wandering about the camp by night?"

As they approached yet nearer an expression of doubt came over his features, which quickly changed to unbounded wonder.

Throwing the reins to an orderly, he advanced to meet them, and in half a minute stood face to face with the sisters, Stella and Angela Gayle.

"Stella, Angela! can I believe my eyes?" exclaimed Gerald. "Is it indeed you? Why, last night I left you at Richmond, and now you are here in camp. What does it mean?"

"You are safe, then, Gerald—safe and unwounded," cried Angela, darting forward and timidly taking his hand, while her gentle eyes, filled with tears of relief, "we inquired for you a dozen times, and were told you were missing."

"Yes, Angela, I am safe and unwounded, it is my brother Darcy who is missing. I fear he must be wounded or killed, or he would have been back in camp with his regiment."

"His regiment, then, has returned without him?" asked Stella, breathlessly, her pale cheek growing yet paler.

"Yes, the regiment has returned to camp, with four hundred killed, wounded, or missing; and in the list is Darcy Leigh," said Gerald, mournfully.

"Is it not possible that he may have strayed or lost himself?"

"I fear not; he must be either killed or wounded, for it is certain the Yankees, in their headlong flight took no prisoners."

"Is it, then, true that our troops have been defeated?"

"Our troops!—do you mean the Yankee troops?"

"Yes, of course; I am not a rebel—I speak of the Union army."

"The Union army?" said Gerald, laughing scornfully, —"the grand army of the Potomac—they called themselves, I think. Well, Miss Stella, if you could have seen them a few hours back, flying in utter rout, throwing away everything—arms, accoutrements—even uniforms, you would hardly speak so proudly of the Union army. A more cowardly rabble it is impossible to conceive. You ask if they have been defeated. Defeated is not the word—they have been utterly routed—driven headlong from the field, screaming with terror as our troops pursued. But for the over-caution of our generals, we might with ease have followed the mob of fugitives across the Potomac, and hoisted the Stars and Bars on the Capitol."

"Is it possible?" said Stella, mournfully; "we heard rumours all along the line that the Union troops had been beaten back, but I scarcely believed them. But now I see they must be true, for you occupy the same ground you did in the morning."

"The same ground, Stella," said Gerald, pointing with his finger. "You see yonder dark hollow to the right— that was the battle-field. In the morning the Yankees advanced some eighty thousand strong—now not a Yankee soldier can be found within twenty miles. They have fled, nor paused till they put the Potomac between themselves and the despised 'rebels,' whom they thought to chaw up."

"And what has become of that mad girl—this Miss St. Casse—who flaunts about on horseback at the head of a regiment, as if she were a man?"

"Mad, you call her, Stella; if the North could boast of many such mad women, and a few thousand of the brave spirits willing to face death at her bidding, they might hope to succeed. You ask where she is? She also, is missing. And now, having answered your questions, let me ask how and why you are here?"

"My father is a prisoner somewhere in your camp. We received a telegram to that effect in Richmond."

"Your father, Webster Gayle, a prisoner! I had not heard of it. How did it happen? When, and where was he captured?"

"I do not know the particulars. I imagine he must have attempted to pass on to Richmond and was captured."

"But why should he wish to go to Richmond? if he is a Unionist, what business has he there?"

"Alas!" replied Stella, "you know, Gerald, that with our father business is ever uppermost. He has estates and slaves near Fredericksburg, the Yancey plantation. He has entrusted Lupus Rock, our cousin, with the management of them, and I fancy was not satisfied with his stewardship, but wished to see for himself."

"But why has he been captured, and why this alarm concerning his safety? He will not be harmed."

"I fear," replied Stella, gloomily, "that at the time of his capture he had some papers on him which seriously compromise him."

"In what way?"

"Can you not guess? Papers relating to the rebel movements, and correspondence from his own Government in which his expedition South is spoken of."

"Still this is incomprehensible to me," replied Gerald; "I have good reason for believing, nay, am certain, that Webster Gayle has furnished our generals with valuable information as to the Federal movements, and has besides undertaken and fulfilled contracts for the supply of arms and ammunition to our troops. How then should he be a prisoner in our hands? I could understand that the Yankees might arrest him for treason ; but it is certainly beyond me why he should be arrested by the Confederates, to whom he is supplying information."

"Nevertheless, Gerald," replied Stella, "he is in danger—in imminent danger, if, indeed, he is in the hands of the rebel authorities."

"There was something strange in Stella's manner which puzzled Gerald. By degrees, however, a light began to dawn on him. Was it possible, he thought, that Webster Gayle had been enacting the part of spy? It really seemed, from Stella's alarm and strange manner, that she knew more than she chose to say.

After a short pause, he said,—

"I will go to head-quarters and inquire for you if it be true that your father is a prisoner, and if so, where he is confined. But first I must provide you with a shelter. Come with me. I and three other officers share a tent, but they must give place to you ladies."

"Gerald, you are too kind," said Angela, with a grateful look. "We cannot deprive you of your tent. After such a terrible day you must require repose."

"I am very unlikely to get it then," he replied, "for I am ordered on outpost duty with half a troop, and it is doubtful if I shall be relieved till long past daylight."

They had now arrived opposite the tent, and the appearance of two young ladies created some consternation and surprise. Some of the officers had thrown off their uniform jackets, and were lounging about the fire in front of the tents, while three others were within, fast asleep.

"Now then, you fellows," shouted Gerald, lifting up the piece of canvas that served for a door, "turn out here; these quarters are wanted."

But the weary men within were not to be so easily roused; they slept a sleep only to be earned by many hours of intense fatigue.

Gerald espying a bugler passing by with his bugle slung behind him, called him,—

"Here, my man, just put your head inside that tent and blow the alarm, not too loud, or you will have all the camp under arms."

The man obeyed, and scarcely had he sounded the first notes of the well-known call, than the sleepers rushed tumultuously from the tent, half-dressed as they were.

"Where's my horse, my orderly, boots and saddle,"

shouted one, but half-awake. "What the deuce is the row ? Are the enemy upon us ?"

"Hillo there, Jackson!—Jackson, send my orderly with my horse," cried another, running out with his jack boots in his hand ; ain't the fight over yet, or have we got to begin again ? Never say die, I'm ready, for one. Hurrah for the 'Bonnie Blue Flag !' "

"Quietly, gentlemen, quietly," said Gerald, smiling, "and please to dress yourselves before you come out; there are ladies present, and there is nothing the matter."

"Nothing the matter, then what the deuce was the alarm blown for ? Ladies, eh ! how the devil can there be any ladies here ? Hillo, by Jove ! "

At this moment the speaker's eye took in the two girls as they stood by the fire, and conscious of his defects in the way of dress, he hurried back into the tent.

"It's all right, old fellow, there's nothing wrong," said Gerald, following him ; " only these ladies want the tent ; they are friends of mine, and have unexpectedly arrived."

" What, more Amazons prancing about on horseback, Thunder ! that Black Angel girl has turned my head and made half the fellows in the regiment in love with her, and now it seems we're to have an addition. Why couldn't you call a fellow quietly, without kicking up such an infernal din with the bugle, as if the enemy were upon us ? "

"Why, simply because there was no other way of rousing you. So bundle out, and leave a rug or two for the ladies. They must for once content themselves with a trooper's pillow—a saddle."

In five minutes the tent was vacated, and Gerald led the ladies in, in spite of their unwillingness to deprive the tired officers of their sleep.

" Come, Miss Gayle and Angela. If you are Unionists and call us rebels, there is no reason you should not seek shelter under our canvas. Rebels or no rebels, you'll find our fellows gentlemen."

And in spite of their reluctance the girls were half-forced into the tent, and, placing a sentry over the door, Gerald left them to make inquiries as to their father.

It was a strange shelter for two young and delicate girls. Angela especially gazed around in timid wonder at all the martial trappings lying about. Half a dozen saddles cumbered the ground, while hung up on hooks in the canvas were bridles, forage bags, valises, sabres, and pistols.

Close by each of the saddles was a coarse horse-cloth ; this served the dragoon officers both as bed and covering.

Stella looking around could not but be powerfully affected. Here was none of the pomp and panoply of war, but all stern reality, and she could not but admire the stedfast purpose which all this rugged simplicity displayed on the part of the rebel officers, any more than her woman's nature could help being touched by the ready and good-humoured gallantry with which these tired warriors turned out of their tent to accommodate them.

" What a pity they are rebels !" thought Stella, " such fine, noble fellows—I wonder if all the rebel officers are like these ?    If they are—and if they fight as they have fought to-day—alas, for the poor old Union !"

In a very few minutes Gerald Leigh returned, and both the girls remarked even by the dim light of the oil lamp suspended in the centre that his look was troubled and gloomy.

" Well, have you any news, Gerald ?" asked Stella, anxiously, and gazing earnestly in his face with her large grey eyes.

" No good news, Stella."

" Then our father is a prisoner—it is true."

" He was a prisoner."

" And is now free ?" cried Stella, joyfully.

" He was a prisoner in the charge of the Provost Marshal's guard, but during the confusion of the battle managed to escape, and was seen running towards the Yankee lines.    He even succeeded in taking his papers with him—the papers which had been seized on his person, but were carelessly left in his reach before his escape."

" He has escaped then," cried Stella, " and is by this time doubtless safe in Washington."

" I fear not, Stella," answered Gerald, gravely.

" Oh ! Gerald—how serious you look—do pray tell us what has happened," said Angela, approaching him with clasped hands.

" I fear some accident has befallen your father."

" Some accident—of what nature ?"

" I told you he was seen after his escape from his guard, running in the direction of the Yankees." ·

" Yes, yes," cried both girls—" did he not escape ?"

"In his course he had to pass under the brow of a little hill which was swept by a cross fire from several batteries."

" Ah !" cried Stella, in agonized tones, "and was he shot dead."

" It is not known. He was seen to fall. That is all the information I have."

" Who saw him fall ?"

" Jupiter, my brother's black valet."

" Then Jupiter can guide me to the place. Where is he, Gerald—where is this negro ? Send him to me. I will reward him liberally. Perhaps at this very moment our poor father is lying wounded, dying, while we waste time here. Angela, come, come, let us go seek for our father."

But Angela had sunk on the ground half-fainting ; her nature was not so strong as that of her sister, and on hearing that her father (of whom despite his failings, both girls were passionately fond), had been seen to fall, she gave way to torrents of tears, and, burying her face in her hands, crouched down and refused to be comforted.

Gerald, as in duty bound, did all he could to console her and buoy up her spirits.

" Gerald, call this negro. Angela do not be such a child. I must go search on the battle-field."

" Jupiter !" Gerald called.

" Yes, massa."

And the next moment Jupiter's ebony head was protruded into the tent, followed by his huge frame.

" Jupiter," said Gerald, " you saw Senator Gayle fall when running across the field to escape ?"

" Yes, massa, I see him run.  Golly ! how he did run ;
he run an' run, an' shook an' shook, an' at last a big
cannon-ball hits him—*whoppo*—right in de middle, an'
down he go.  Golly ! how he did run, till dat d—n big
bullet slap into him."

" A cannon-ball ?" almost shrieked Stella.  " Did you
say, man, he was struck by a cannon-ball ?  Are you
sure it was a cannon-ball ?"

" No, missa, dis chile ain't sure, but he kinder reckons
it war a cannon-ball."

" Why ?—why ?"

" 'Cos dere was lots of 'em a flyin' about jist den,
an' 'cos he went down such a buster, an' nebber try to
get up again."

" Don't pay any attention to what he says, Stella,"
remarked Gerald, unable to suppress a smile ; " you see
by what process of reasoning he arrived at the fact of its
being a cannon-ball.  Look here, you Jupiter : this lady
wishes you to accompany her, and show her where you
saw Senator Gayle fall.  Do you hear ?"

" Yes, massa—I hear."

" Well, will you take her ?"

" No, massa."

" The devil !  And why not, pray ?" asked Gerald,
angrily.

" 'Cos I'se gwine to look for de gub'ner, Massa Darcy
Leigh.  He ain't come in yet, an' his supper 's been ready
in his tent dis two hours, an' most spoiled by dis time.
'Specs he's bin and got cannon-balled too."

" Where's Darby Kelly ?"

" De Irisher ?—on sentry duty."

" Well, then, you must go with this lady."

" Can't do it nohow, massa.  De cap'n's supper 's
waitin', and dis chile's gwine to find him."

" Why, you confounded ass, can't you look for him,
and take this lady over the field with you.  For all you
know, my brother may be lying wounded close to where
you saw Senator Gayle fall."

" By golly ! I nebber tought of dat, Massa Gerald.

I'se ready—come along, Missa Gayle. Dis chicken 'll trot you ober de field of glory. I reckon we gub de Yankees some pepper dis time, Massa Gerald. 'We're de boys for blood an' tunder,' as the big Irisher say."

"Yes, you had a great deal to do with it, certainly, my ebony hero," said Gerald.

"I see all de fight, massa—ebery bit of it. Nebber took my eyes off the scrimmage till we'd licked 'em."

"Well, just hurry up your cakes, and get a lantern; then come back here."

Jupiter promptly vanished.

"Stella, I cannot come with you. I am ordered on outpost duty at twelve o'clock—it is now eleven. I will, however, ask for a sergeant's guard for you."

"No, no, Gerald; let me go alone with the negro. If a sergeant's guard accompanied us, it would be their duty to recapture my unfortunate father; and you said he had the papers with him. I tremble to think what those papers might be."

"You are right, Stella; I had forgotten. Your father may be only slightly wounded; in that case his best course will be to seek the Yankee lines, for if he has any papers which would show him to be a spy, he would meet but little mercy at the hands of our generals. I wish I could accompany you, but it is impossible."

Jupiter at this moment reappeared, bearing a lantern, and a basket of wine and cordials in case of need.

"Come," said Stella, "I am ready."

"Stay," interrupted Gerald; "what of Angela? She is not in a fit state to accompany you. See, she is quite weak and faint."

Stella looked embarrassed. Angela reclined languidly on Gerald, who was seated beside her on a rude bench. Her fair head reposed on his shoulder, her eyes were closed, and altogether she appeared worn out and quite incapable of any exertion.

"Gerald, I can trust my sister with you, but when you are compelled to leave who will watch over her?"

"Where's Captain George the Englishman?" asked Gerald of Jupiter.

6

" He's gone out on de fiel of glory wid de fig leaf of
de regiment," replied Jupiter, grandiloquently.

" Gone out with what?" asked Gerald, totally unable
to restrain his laughter.

" Wid de fig leaf of de regiment," repeated Jupiter,
with imperturbable gravity—" the daughter of de regiment, de veevandeary.    Dey two's gone togedder hunting
after dat Black Angel.   She's—she's been an' got a
cannon-ball too," he added, sententiously ; " dere's been a
rare lot a flyin' about to-day."

" Stella," said Gerald, " I will remain here as long as I
can with Angela, and when I am forced to go I will
place a guard I can trust over the tent, with orders to
blow out any man's brains who attempts to enter."

" Gerald, I know I can trust you," said Stella, rising,
and giving him her hand.

" What, rebel as I am ?"

" Yes, rebel as you are," she replied, with a faint
smile.

It is possible that, though the fire of patriotism might
burn as fiercely as ever in the breast of the proud
Northern beauty, she began to look with less hatred and
more respect on those hitherto despised rebels who had
just given such terrible evidence of their power and resolution.   Motioning Jupiter to precede her, she pressed
Gerald's hand, and wrapping her shawl closely round her,
went out into the night.

" Stay one moment," Gerald called after her.   " In
case you are stopped the password is ——"

He lowered his voice—

" ' Nashville.'   I trust in your honour not to use it
against our cause."

Stella's eyes flashed as she proudly replied,—

" Gerald, I am an Unionist, but I am not a spy or a
traitor."

The next moment she was gone, and Gerald was left
alone with Angela, who, utterly worn out, had gone to
sleep on his shoulder.

Jupiter led the way at a pace with which Stella Gayle
could hardly keep up.   To her surprise, however, he did

not make towards where Gerald had told her the battle-field lay, but in a nearly opposite direction. Not under-standing this, she asked her guide where he was taking her.

" Me gwine to Massa Darcy's tent, missa; mebbe he's come back."

Stella pulled up dead.

" But I do not wish to go to Captain Darcy Leigh's tent," she said.

" Well, now, look yar, missa; you just wait one minute, an' I'll make tracks for de booth, and take de pot off de fire, or all de chicken fixens 'ill be clean spoiled. 'Cause why, Missa Gayle, Massa Darcy's eifer killed or else he ain't killed; an' if he ain't killed, de chances are he's al-mighty hungry. Fact, missa, dis chile knows de gub'nor, and dere'd be a row in de house if he come back from de field ob glory an' no stew ready."

" Well, well, make haste and return," said Stella, impatiently.

Jupiter started off, and presently returned, but not alone; Darby Kelly, the Irishman, was with him; and on his behalf Jupiter spoke.

" Missa, dis Irisher wants to come too. Massa Darcy ain't come back—de stew's a spilin, and dis chile's 'clined to be ob opinion dat he's stretched dead or mortially wounded on de field ob glory."

" An' if I wouldn't be intrudin' on yer honour's lady-ship," said Darby, " it's meself would like to come along wid ye an' de nayger. For supposin' we found his honner lying kilt or hurted, the pair of us could bring him in better nor one. I've got a blanket with me, an' if we have the good luck to find the masther, we're the boys that will walk him off to the docther."

" Lead the way with the lantern," said Stella, im-patiently; "and you (turning to Darby Kelly) walk behind."

Jupiter started off at a long shambling walk, Stella following him, while the Irishman brought up the rear.

" Strange," thought Stella, as she walked moodily behind her black guide, " that this Darcy Leigh, quiet,

6—2

reserved, almost cynical in his manner, should inspire all
who come in contact with him with such respect and
love.   These two faithful fellows would both peril their
lives for him ; and yet—and yet, I hate him—I hate
him ; at least " (she half checked the thought, and men-
tally added), " I ought to hate him, certainly, and I
think I do, the desperate rebel.   Then there is that mad
Southern girl, ' the Black Angel,' they call her—is he
smitten with her, or is she with him ?—which is it ?
Perhaps both.   Well, and why not ? they would be
a pretty pair of rebels, well met and well matched.
What is it to me ?   I care not."

But though thinking she cared not, Stella in truth
did care.

Strange fact, which all thinkers must have observed,
that whereas in affairs of the heart women sometimes
deceive others, they almost invariably deceive themselves.

Half an hour's sharp walking brought them to a
rising ground, from which they commanded a view of
the valley, or rather series of valleys and gullies ; intersected by the stream, where the battle was fought.

After a momentary pause Jupiter again led the way,
and in a few minutes they struck into a road which led
from Bull Run Stream.   Along this road marched in
solemn silence parties of four, bearing stretchers covered
over with blankets, and on these stretchers Stella knew,
from the occasional groans wrung forth by agony, that
wounded men were being carried to the hospital to
undergo the fresh tortures of the surgeon's knife.

Presently they descended into a hollow which a few
hours back rang with the wild shouts of the combatants,
the rattle of musketry, and the thunder of artillery.
Now all was silent as the grave.   The dull sounds of the
pick-axe and harsh grating of the spade were heard, and
the next minute they stood by the side of a vast pit
which was being dug in solemn silence.

Around this pit were laid many motionless forms,
some covered over with blankets, others staring vacantly
up at the heavens with their sightless eyes.   Each moment fresh bodies were carried to the edge of the pit in

blankets or on stretchers, and roughly tumbled down to await the time when their unhewn and common grave should be dug deep enough.

It was a dismal, a dreadful sight.

At each corner of the pit a lantern was fixed on a stake, casting a dull lurid glare on the upturned corpse-faces which every moment increased in number as fresh victims of the day's strife were brought up and carelessly tumbled down ; for familiarity and weariness had made the bearers rather callous.

Even as Stella gazed in horror on the dreadful scene the pit was finished, the diggers clambered up, and now commenced a carnival of horrors.

Federals and Confederates, young and old, were seized by the head and legs and roughly tumbled in. The ghastly blood and dirt-grimed corpses jostled and thumped each other as they were flung down.

The heap in the pit grew higher and higher, till it rose within a few feet of the brink. Legs and arms, heads and trunks, all mingled together in one horrible mass. Ghastly faces, with wide-staring eyes, glared dreadfully upwards, the dim light of the lanterns shining dismally on the lifeless forms, the sightless eyes, the pulseless limbs. More, still more, the heap of dead rises to the pit's mouth, and the cry is still they come.

Spell-bound to the spot, Stella remained till the work-men, when the pit could hold no more, began to shovel the earth on the pile of dead ; then, sick and faint with horror, she motioned Jupiter to lead on.

"And this is war," she thought, "glorious war."

As they pass on down into the valley towards the stream, the ground is strewn yet thicker and thicker with the dead and dying.

For hours parties told off for the purpose have been clearing the field, and yet there seem to be hundreds and hundreds of poor wounded wretches groaning their lives away.

Jupiter again led the way ; the sight he had just beheld had silenced even his voluble tongue, while Darby Kelly in vain tried to whistle " Garry Owen."

They came to the spot where the negro saw Senator Gaylo fall, as he endeavoured to escape. Several dead lay about, but he was not one of the number.

Stella asked in low, muttered tones, which way a man, seeking to cross to the Federal lines, would go ; and Jupiter having pointed across the stream, she motioned him to lead on. They crossed the stream, Jupiter and Darby wading, and carrying Stella—searching the banks up and down where the struggle had been fiercest, but Stella found not her father, nor did Jupiter discover his master. For hours they wandered about, the negro holding the lantern down to many strange dead faces, but not finding what he sought.

A faint hope now arose in Stella's breast.

" After all, perhaps," she thought, "he may not have been killed—perhaps only slightly wounded, and succeeded in making his escape."

It was near four o'clock, and a faint gleam in the east proclaimed the approach of dawn.

Wearily they wended their way back ; Jupiter, who knew the ground well, leading as before.

Oftentimes the fatigue parties—the bearers of the dead and wounded—would pause, set down their burdens, and gaze in astonishment at the strange trio. A negro, a big Irishman, a young, delicate, and handsome girl in company in such a scene.

On their way back to the rebel camp, they had occasion to pass the foot of a wooded hillock. A quantity of low brushwood ran out into the open ground, and at the edge of this was a dismounted field-piece and several dead horses.

The field-piece had evidently been taken from the Yankees in their flight, for the horses were harnessed to the carriage, and their heads were away from the rebel position.

The artillerymen lay dead around, and more than one grey-coated corpse told that the Yankees had not yielded the gun without a fight.

They were passing on, when a cry from Stella caused both Darby and Jupiter to come to a dead halt.

The next moment they saw her kneeling by the side of a body which lay under the gun-carriage ; the face was to the sky.

Jupiter approached with the lantern.

It was the face of a young man in a captain's uniform, deadly pale, with the eyes wide open, and fixed in a stony stare.

A howl of grief burst from the negro.

Darby Kelly said not a word, uttered not a sound, but crouched down in the darkness and hid his face.

Stella Gayle sank down on her knees, raised the head, and gazed in the white face and staring eyes, gazed with desperate longing, hoping against hope, trying vainly to persuade herself there was life in the lifeless body, light in the blind eyes.

A wail of despair burst from her in spite of herself.

"Oh, Darcy Leigh!—Darcy Leigh!—I never knew till now how I loved you ! Is it thus we meet ? Speak to me—awake—say you forgive me the bitter insults I have put upon you! Speak, if but one word."

But no answer came from those livid lips, no light from those dim eyes, no pressure from the cold hand she held.

The challenge of the distant sentinel, the dismal sound of the pick and shovel digging fresh pits, and the faint cries of the wounded, alone broke the stillness of the night.

Otherwise the silence of death reigned around.

## CHAPTER IX.

### LOVE ON THE BATTLE-FIELD.

STELLA GAYLE was not a girl to give way to vain despair while any hope remained. She had with her a bottle of *sal volatile*, with which she endeavoured to revive, as she hoped, the spark of life.

But in vain. Darcy Leigh's head still lay insensible in her lap, the eyes open, and gazing vacantly upwards.

"Jupiter, Jupiter !" she cried, to the negro, "bring water here ; perhaps your master has only fainted."

Jupiter obeyed, and water was copiously dashed over the face and shoulders of the wounded man.

Stella unbuttoned the tight collar of his tunic, thinking it might tend to revive him, and then perceived a large bruise, extending from the left shoulder to the neck. Otherwise there was no wound to be seen, except the cut on the forehead, received on board the Spitfire, and which had again been torn open and bled slightly.

It was evident that he had been struck by a large splinter of the gun carriage, and not by a bullet or shot.

Water in profusion not having the desired effect, Stella next tried brandy, and forcing the flask between his teeth, poured a large draught down his throat.

To her intense joy, this powerful dose of spirit caused the wounded man to give utterance to a sound—half gasp, half groan.

" He lives ! he lives !" she cried ; "come here, Jupiter—Darby—and raise this broken wheel from his legs ; that alone is sufficient to cause death."

Jupiter and the Irishman, when they heard the welcome news, worked with a will, and soon extricated the still insensible form of Darcy Leigh from the *debris* among and under which he lay.

Then they carefully raised him, and laid him on the blanket, Stella still supporting his head in her lap.

Another dose of brandy caused the wounded man first to give a choking gasp, then a deep sigh, and the next moment the blood began to flow from the old wound on the forehead.

Stella hastily tore her cambric handkerchief, and bound it over the wound, first saturating it with cold water. Then she tore a small silk scarf from her shoulders, and tied this also around his head.

In a few minutes Darcy Leigh began to breathe painfully and laboriously, and the eyes, before wide opened, now closed. A faint colour came on the pale face, and they knew that he was slowly recovering from his swoon.

Stella now, with no false modesty or prudishness, looked to the hurt on his shoulder and breast. A very slight examination convinced her that at least one rib was broken, if not the collar bone.

The immediate cause of the deadly faint in which they found him, she rightly conjectured to have been the terrible shock to the system—a shock from which, but for her ministering care, he would never have recovered.

To the bruised shoulder and broken rib of course nothing could be done, and all that remained was to restore the sufferer to consciousness.

Slowly, and by degrees, under the influence of the strong brandy, the breathing became more regular, and the colour deepened on the hitherto pale face. With returning sense pain also came back, and the deep sighs—half groans which he uttered, told how intense was the agony.

Stella, however, had, with rare forethought, provided herself with a small casket of medicines, and quickly mixing a powerful opiate, poured it down the wounded man's throat. Its effects were rapid and salutary.

He shortly opened his eyes, gazed wearily round, too confused and weak to know where he was, or on whose lap his head reclined, and then again closing them, in a few minutes he sank to sleep.

Stella, her hat thrown off, bent over him, and gazed tearfully, hopefully in his face, like a mother bending over a sick child.

Old feelings of tenderness, long since crushed back by pride, now found place in her heart ; and the utter helplessness and weak state of the sufferer enlisted all her woman's sympathies in his behalf.

It was a strange scene. Jupiter and Darby sat respectfully at a little distance on the dismounted gun, apparently content to leave their master to Stella's care.

The red glare of the lantern gleamed on the face of the wounded man, as his head lay placidly in her lap, while her fair young face bent over his in anxious tenderness.

Stella, with her hat off, her shawl thrown back, looked lovelier than ever. Could Darcy have seen the expression on the classically-chiselled features—the fond glance of the large grey eyes, as she stooped her head close to his till her breath fanned his cheek, he would have forgiven all the taunts, the scornful speeches, to which the Northern beauty had subjected him. His head lay on her knees—one hand supported the wounded arm, while with the other she continually sprinkled cold water on the inflamed and bruised shoulder.

Now he begins to murmur in his sleep, but Stella cannot catch the words, they are so faint and indistinct.

The dawn began to break, and Stella thought it time to remove him to the camp, as from the effect of the opiate, he was in a sweet and peaceful sleep. She was just about to give the order to Darby and the negro, when voices are heard and a lantern is seen approaching.

Stella distinguished the low, soft tones of a woman, and then the stronger voice of a man. The stillness of the night made every sound more distinct, and she could hear what was said, although she could not distinguish the persons of the speakers.

"See, yonder is a light," said the man's voice ; " let us make for it—perhaps we may hear something of those we seek ; if not, it is now near dawn, and we had best relinquish the search."

" No, sir ; oh no—I cannot relinquish the search—I cannot relinquish the search for my mistress; and how can you give up that for your friend ?"

The voice was low and sweet, but strange to Stella.

But when the man's voice replied, she felt sure she had heard it before. So, too, did Darby and Jupiter, for both pricked up their ears and listened. " Why do I give up the search? Because, Nina, it is useless. If you, however, are determined to wander about this dismal battle-field till broad daylight, I will remain with you. There are hosts of camp-followers and rowdies about, and it would neither be fit nor safe for a young girl to stroll about alone. But, my poor girl, you must

be fatigued ; this is the second night you have had no rest.
Have you any quarters—any tent ?"

" No, sir ; Miss Coralie said she would see for quarters
in the evening, when the fight was over ; but the evening
came, and she has not returned."

" Then you have nowhere to go ?"

The girl was silent.

" My poor child, this must not be—you must come and
take possession of my tent."

" No, sir—no ; you do not know me.   Why—why do
you insult me ?   I did not expect this from you, who
have hitherto been so kind."

" Insult you !   On my honour, Nina, I did not mean to
insult you.   When I said come to my tent, I did not mean
share my tent ; I meant, and do mean, to give it to you till
you find quarters.   As for me, I can rough it.   A horse-
cloth and a saddle will serve me for bed, covering, and
pillow."

They were now sufficiently near for Stella to recognise
the figures as those of Captain George, the Englishman,
and Nina, the beautiful *vivandière.*

She saw the latter seize the Englishman's hand, and
heard her exclaim,—

" Ah, sir, pardon me ; I have been so used to insult
that I can scarcely credit my senses when I am addressed
with even moderate respect by a man,   I have heard of
the English gentlemen.   If they are all like you, sir, the
women of that far-off island should be happy."

The words from other lips and in other tones would
have seemed like fulsome flattery ; but Nina was so evidently sincere, and spoke so innocently, that Captain
George could not put that construction upon them.

" Come, come, Nina, you will make me vain.   I do no
more than many an American gentleman would do,
doubtless."

" I have never met one yet, sir, either when I was a
slave, or now that I am free."

" A slave ! By Jove ! Nina, if you were a slave, I think
I should be tempted to buy you.   What would you say ?"

" What should I say ?" exclaimed Nina, pausing ; " I

should say what I now say—that I would willingly be
your slave.  Aye! free as I am now, if you wish it, I
will be your slave."

Nina spoke with all the warmth of her Southern nature.
Strong in her loves and fierce in her hatreds, she felt no
shame in that which her heart told her was no shame.

"Nonsense, Nina, you will make me vain," laughed
Captain George, somewhat embarrassed at the intimation.

"It is not nonsense, it is true.  I will tell you what I
have never yet told living man.  Scorn me—spurn me, if
you will, it will not alter the fact.  Sir Englishman, I
love you!"

Nina made the avowal boldly, almost defiantly; and
Stella, gazing on this singular scene, could see her bosom
rise and fall with wild emotion beneath her scarlet *vivandière* tunic.

"Come, Nina," said George, quietly, but kindly, "this
is no place, no time for love passages—the battle-field by
night strewn with slain and wounded.  Let us return;
take possession of my tent, and seek the repose you need
so much."

He spoke kindly and gently, and Stella saw him take
the girl's hand as if to lead her away.

"No, no!  Let us first inquire at yonder lantern for
any news of those we seek."

Then they both turned, and walked towards the place
where lay the sleeping form of Darcy Leigh watched over
by Stella Gayle.

He was still murmuring in his sleep.

Perhaps the love passage she had just witnessed
softened Stella's heart towards her sick hero.  At all
events, she did what those who knew her would scarcely
have given credit for.

She stooped and imprinted a kiss on the lips of Darcy
Leigh.

The next moment she started to her feet as though a
wasp had stung her.

Darcy seemed to be dreaming pleasant dreams, for the
expression of pain had disappeared, and a smile played
about his mouth.

Scarcely had Stella imprinted this first kiss on his lips, than he softly murmured in his sleep, "Coralie, Coralie!"

It was not to be wondered at that Stella should leap to her feet, her face crimson with mortification and shame, for was not the wounded man dreaming of Coralie, even while she tended him, after having, in all proba- bility, saved his life?

Captain George and Nina were now approaching, and the thought suddenly occurred to Stella that she would not be discovered by the side of Darcy Leigh—she would not give any the opportunity of saying or even thinking she cared for him.

Taking her purse from her pocket, she hastily gave Jupiter and Darby a golden five-dollar piece each, saying as she did so,—

"Jupiter, Darby, promise me you will say nothing of my having been here. You can say that I returned to the camp hours ago—quick!—promise."

"All right, missa—just de same to dis nigger. I've told lots o' lies in my time—one more wont matter."

Darby Kelly also promised, and Stella glided off into the shade of the brushwood, and guided by the distant fires, retraced her steps to the camp.

While Jupiter and the Irishman were placing Darcy Leigh in the blanket preparatory to their carrying him in, the Englishman and the *vivandière* came up.

"Hillo!" cried the former, when a few paces off— "whom have we here?"

And before either answered, he recognised Jupiter, and added—

"What! is it you, Jupiter? Have you found your master? We have been searching for him."

"Yes, massa, we's found him, and awful bad he is, too. One of dem dam cannon balls been and hit him slap bang on de shoulder."

"A round shot!' said George, approaching, and hold- ing his lantern down; "impossible—it would have torn the shoulder off."

Then, after a short examination, he added,—

"This must have been caused by a big splinter or a fall; however, it might have been worse. Why, by Jove, he's asleep. How's this?"

"'Spec's it's de brandy," said Jupiter; "he's had a rare ole dose."

"Was there not some one else here just now?" asked the Englishman, looking round; "I am sure I saw a female dress and form."

"Is it a famale?" said Darby; "arrah, now, capt'n, what do yez take us for—what would we be doing wid famales at all, at all?"

"I am certain, too," cried Nina, "that there was a woman here; I distinctly saw the flutter of a woman's dress."

"Come, who has been here?" asked Captain George; "speak—none of your lies."

"No one, massa, only de Irisher and me."

"No one, yer honour; divil a sowl but the nayger an' meself."

"It must have been a spirit," said Nina, solemnly—"a ghost."

"Dat's it," said Jupiter; "'spec's it must have been a ghost; dere's lots of 'em about."

"Strange," said Captain George, musingly; "I suppose it must have been fancy; but I could have sworn I saw a woman's form bending over Darcy Leigh; I saw her disappear as we approached. Come, lift him carefully, and let's get back to the camp. The sooner he has surgeon's aid, the better his chance of recovery."

So saying, he himself helped to raise the wounded man in the blanket, holding his head while Darby and the negro carried the body and legs.

"Why, here's a woman's scarf and handkerchief tied round his head. How came these here, and why?"

"There's a thrifle of a cut on the forehead, an' we jist took the scarf and muslin handkerchief from the breast pocket of his coat, an' tied it up."

No more was said on the subject, and in half an hour's time they arrived at the camp; and having seen Darcy Leigh to his tent, and sent for a regimental surgeon from the hospital, Captain George conducted Nina to his own tent.

"Here you are, my girl; you will need some sleep. Here are lights, and you will find an oil lamp swinging from the centre pole."

"But I cannot, will not deprive you of your rest."

"Nonsense! I know half-a-dozen fellows who will give me a shakedown. Make yourself at home. I will come round in the morning, and then, if your mistress has not returned, we will see what is to be done."

Nina seized his hand, and, looking in his face, said, "Oh, sir, how can I ever repay you?"

"Repay me, nonsense!" laughed the Englishman; "you will not find me a hard creditor. Just give a kiss on account, and go to rest."

Nina obediently, timidly held her face to his. He bent down and kissed her, and pressing her hand, bade her good-night, and turned carelessly away.

Not so Nina. She hurriedly sought the shelter of the tent, and gave way to a flood of tears—neither all sorrow nor all joy; for his careless manner jarred painfully on the girl's spirits. Hopeless as such a passion must be, Nina, the *vivandière*, loved him with all the force of her warm, passionate nature.

## CHAPTER X.

### CORALIE HORSEWHIPS A COLONEL.

AND now, having found and safely brought to camp one of our characters, it is full time we followed our heroine, the Black Angel.

When last we saw her she was pointing to the enemy with her riding whip, and cheering on the Carolina Crashers to the final charge. Encumbered by the long skirt of her riding habit, she was not able to go forward as fast as she could wish. The 7th Carolinas, who were at first behind her, caught her up, and charged past her at a run. Amid the thick smoke from the rapid volleys she was unnoticed, and left in the rear, making her way forward as well as the nature of the ground and the dead and wounded around her would allow.

Suddenly she espied a riderless horse trotting about the field, snorting and sniffing the air, as if unable to understand it. She instantly resolved, if possible, to catch it, and transfer the side-saddle from her own wounded steed This was easier said than done, for although she succeeded in catching the horse and leading him up to where her own lay dead, still she was unable to disengage the side-saddle.

After several fruitless attempts, she cast her eyes round, hoping to see some one of their own men who would aid her. But the Confederate advance was now general and rapid, and their victorious shouts half a mile in front told their position. At that moment she observed a wounded Yankee rise slowly from the ground. He was bleeding from a sabre cut in the head, and seemed giddy and con·fused. Coralie hastily tied her new-found horse to a neighbouring tree, and, drawing her pistol, made for the man, who gazed half wonderingly, half frightened at the strange apparition of a young and handsome woman amid the smoke and turmoil of battle.

She then drew her revolver, and cocking it, advanced to within a few paces, and said, in imperious tones—

"Come here, you Yankee fellow ; you are my prisoner."

The man looked around for his rifle, which lay at some few paces' distance, and seemed as if he would regain it, and show fight.

"Attempt to arm yourself and you are a dead man !"

The muzzle of the pistol was pointed full at his head, and he saw that the hand which held it, though that of a woman, was firm and steady.

With a muttered oath he resigned himself to his fate, and relinquishing his design on his rifle, proceeded to bind up the wound on his head, all the while keeping his eye fixed on his lady captor.

"When you have tied up your head walk before me to where that horse is tied to the tree," said Coralie, pointing.

The man, a tall raw-boned down-easter, obeyed, and

with slow steps made his way over the intervening space, followed by Coralie, who still kept her revolver in her hand and her eyes fixed on her prisoner.

" Now then, just take the side-saddle off the dead horse, and girt it on the other tied to the tree."

The prisoner obeyed, and without much difficulty loosened the girths and dragged the side-saddle off the dead horse, and removing the dragoon's saddle from the other, girthed it on. There was a large Colt's revolver in the holster of the saddle he removed, of which he pos- sessed himself, unperceived by Coralie.

" Now you Yankee fellow, you can go where you please. I do not wish to make you prisoner; make your way back to your own country, and let this day's work be a lesson to you and all your countrymen."

Coralie then replaced her pistol in her belt, and placing her hand on the pommel, sprang into the saddle.

The Yankee, with the pistol from the holster in his hand, stared doubtfully at her for a moment, as if half- minded to bring his audacious captor down. But feelings of generosity and manhood prevailed.

" Well now, young woman, I reckon you're all there. Darn my skin if I aint half a mind to bring you down."

Coralie, without replying, whipped up the horse and galloped rapidly towards where the smoke and rattle of musketry and the shouts of the pursuers told where the rebel troops were, leaving the Yankee gazing after her in wonder and admiration.

Coralie was a bold horsewoman, and notwithstanding the impediments offered by the nature of the ground, the dead, wounded, and _débris_ of battle strewn about, did not slacken her pace nor draw rein until she was once more among the Confederate troops, moving steadily in pursuit of the enemy.

All the cavalry were far in front, nor could Coralie discover among the many regiments moving forward in line and column, the well-known flag of the 7th Carolinas.

Determined to find her brave troops, after a brief halt and a few inquiries, she again gave her horse rein and

7

dashed forward, followed by the cheers of the soldiers, who, weary as they were, still pressed steadily on.

But unfortunately, in the confusion, Coralie bore too much to the right, and after half an hour's sharp riding, saw before her a wooded hill. Far away on the left she could see the smoke of artillery, and heard the boom of the guns. From the other side of the wood, too, came the sound of shouts and desultory firing. She did not doubt, therefore, but that some of the regiments, perhaps the Crashers themselves, had marched through in pursuit, and were now on the other side. She was forced to walk her horse through the trees, and had an opportunity while so doing to look around.

On all sides the ground was strewn with arms, accoutrements, and baggage—but there were no wounded or dead. This fact, if she had considered, should have caused her to pause, for she might have known that here the pursuit could not have been very close. Anxious, however, to rejoin her friends, she pushed on, sometimes trotting her horse, at others compelled to walk and bend her head low to avoid the overhanging branches of the trees.

She passed over quite a mile of ground in this manner before the light ahead through the trees showed she was nearing the end of the wood. Then she increased her pace, and went ahead at a hard gallop. The shouts and noise in front were each moment becoming louder and plainer, and she could hear the cracking of teamsters' whips. The booming of the artillery was now far away to her left, and what musketry fire she could distinguish, was also in the same direction.

She saw before her, at a distance of only a hundred yards or so, a confused mass of troops enveloped and almost concealed by clouds of dust. More than a mile on her left she distinguished the gleaming of arms as the setting sun shone on them. But a wide ravine separated her from those whom she now decided must be the pursuers.

Suddenly awaking to the danger of her position, alone, and so close to the rear of the enemy, she endeavoured to rein in her horse. But the animal was hard-mouthed, and galloped on towards the cloud of dust and the crowd of fugitives, now not more than a hundred yards ahead. Amid the dust she could discern a body of cavalry drawn up across the road, and by the waving swords and the shouts of the officers, she gathered that they were endeavouring to stop the rout of the infantry.

Pulling at her horse's head with all her strength, she succeeded in arresting his mad career and bringing him to a halt. Then she endeavoured to turn his head, hoping to retreat before she should be discovered.

At that moment was heard the blast of a cavalry bugle. The horse pricked up his ears, prancing and plunging so furiously as to be almost unmanageable.

"So ho—steady, boy !"

She patted his neck and endeavoured to soothe him, but in vain. Another blast on the bugle seemed to drive him frantic, for seizing the bit between his teeth he put his head down and galloped furiously right towards the enemy, for such she knew them to be.

In vain she tugged at the rein, and endeavoured even if she could not stop him, to turn him.

She saw before her, quite close, a confused mass of men, many without arms, waggons, tumbrils, and ambulances, all pressing frantically on in full flight.

But fast as terror urged them, her runaway horse bore her yet faster, and the next moment she was upon them.

"Clear the road, clear the road !" she cried, fearing that the horse would gallop right over them, when, at the pace she was going, a desperate fall must have been the consequence.

With cries of terror and astonishment, the fugitives broke on all sides, running for their lives, and crying—

"Cavalry ! cavalry ! the cavalry are upon us !"

Despite her danger, she could scarcely help smiling at the wild terror which she, a solitary woman on a runaway horse, inspired.

"So much for the Army of the Potomac," she thought, all the while tugging desperately at the reins; for she saw that if she could but turn her horse's head, she

**7—2**

might easily pass through the panic-stricken mob on either side.

She had almost succeeded, and had headed him towards where there was a gap in the string of baggage-waggons on her left, when again that unfortunate bugle-blast resounded; and again, with a violent plunge, the animal turned and dashed straight towards it.

Then the truth burst on her mind,—

"This is a Yankee trooper's horse, and he recognises the bugle calls of his regiment. I am lost!"

Lost, indeed, for her unruly steed galloped head ng straight for the place whence the bugle sounded. She saw the bright sabres of the troopers drawn up in line in the road before her. Onwards galloped the runaway, till when within a dozen yards he halted so abruptly, as almost to throw her from her saddle, and stood trembling in every limb.

The next moment a Yankee officer rode up and seized the bridle-reins.

He gazed admiringly and curiously on the handsome girl before him. Her cheeks were crimson with shame and rage being thus entrapped.

"Who are you, lady?—what is the meaning of this?"

Coralie saw that deception could not avail her long; so, bowing her head, she said, haughtily,—

"Sir, I am what you would doubtless designate a rebel, and, I presume, a prisoner. It is the fortune of war."

Great was the astonishment of her captor at her words.

"What!" he cried, "have the rebels, then, regiments of Amazons fighting against us?"

"Sir, I am your prisoner; let that suffice, unless, indeed, you choose to loose my horse's bridle, and let me return," said Coralie, haughtily.

"Let you return, young madam—that's a pretty tale, certainly. Your horse, too! Why, he's got our brand on his quarter—'U.S.' There are the letters plain enough."

"My own horse was killed in the action, so I caught this, which was galloping riderless about."

Coralie now observed her captor more narrowly.

He was a young man, apparently not more than two-

and-twenty, tall, with sandy hair and light grey eyes; his features were not ill-looking, and she fancied, by a certain indefinable mild expression about the mouth, that if opportunity offered, she might cajole or deceive him into permitting her escape. The glance of evident admiration with which he regarded his beautiful captive confirmed her in this idea, and she resolved, if possible, to conciliate him.

"Sir," she said, in her sweetest accents, "you are an enemy, but I perceive an officer and a gentleman; I am your prisoner—may I rely on your protecting me from insult?"

"Certainly, young woman, certainly. Duty's duty, and honour's honour; and Captain John Squails reckons he knows the value of them both."

"Well, sir, lead on; I will follow you."

"Come, then," he said, turning her horse's head, "come with me; I must report my capture to the colonel."

Accordingly he turned the heads of both horses in the direction of his regiment, which now was slowly retreating, totally unable to resist the overwhelming pressure of the mass of fugitives which increased every moment.

It was a difficult matter to force a passage at all through the confused mob of Yankee soldiers, all branches of the service mixed together. Notwithstanding the panic with which they hastened away from the sound of the rebel artillery thundering in their rear, yet many of the crowd found time to gaze insolently at Coralie.

Rude jests were bandied about, and many an insulting remark fell on the ears of the Southern heroine. But she, with head erect, rode proudly on, not deigning to notice by a look the rabble who, even in their cowardly flight, could insult a lady.

She was resolving in her mind any possible chance of escape. She looked around her—ahead, and then turning, gazed hopelessly back.

On all sides she was hemmed in by a vast multitude of fugitives; while in the rear and on either side were hundreds of baggage waggons. For the present, then, she decided that escape was hopeless.

She resolved to see what could be made of her captor, so she addressed him in her sweetest tones.

"Do you know, sir, where I shall be taken? what they will do with me?"

"Can't say, young miss; reckon yu'll hev to go to Washington."

"To Washington?—what, to-night?"

"Well, I can't 'xactly say about to-night, but I rayther guess we'll camp out to-night. If so, I reckon yu'll be under my care, as I captured you; guess you might do wuss than that, young Miss Reb——. If you like to give your parole not to escape, I'll speak to the colonel—then I sha'n't be hard on you."

"My parole not to escape! How can I possibly escape?" replied Coralie, in a very mournful tone. "I am completely hemmed in by your brave troops."

Anybody with less vanity than the gallant Captain Squails, must have been struck by the absurdity of men, disgracefully beaten, and flying, panic-stricken from the field, being called "brave troops."

"Reckon that's neither here nor there; if you can't skedaddle now, you may get a chance by and by. So just give your parole not to attempt an escape, and I'll leave go your rein."

Coralie was in a bit of a fix; she was fully determined to escape should opportunity offer, and yet did not wish to excite his suspicions by refusing her parole.

Her ready wit, however, helped her out of the difficulty.

"For how long a time do you wish me to give my parole?"

"How long? why till to-morrow, when I shall have to take or send you into Washington, I reckon."

"Till to-morrow; good. It is now eight o'clock. I will give you my parole till to-morrow morning—for twelve hours."

"For twelve hours!" he broke in, but she interrupted him hastily.

"Now, sir, leave go my rein; see, there is the colonel

of your regiment ; let us ride up and report ourselves—
prisoner and captor."

"Snakes !" muttered the gallant captain to himself, "if
this aint a queer girl ! Reckon she means to have her
own way, somehow. Handsome as a pictor, may I peel
pumpkins all my days if she aint !"

Coralie well knew he was devouring her face and form
with his eyes, but she wisely pretended not to be aware
of the fact, riding on in apparent unconsciousness.

" A prisoner, colonel," said Coralie's captor, when at
last they had forced a passage through the yelling, swearing crowd, and arrived at the head of the few troops of
cavalry which had vainly endeavoured to check the rout ;
" a she rebel; horse bolted with her right into our
lines."

The colonel, who before this rebellion had never seen a
sword—he was a lawyer from Massachusetts—took a good
look at her.

" A prisoner—eh ? Well, young woman, what have
you got to say for yourself ? Are you prepared to take
the oath of allegiance to the Union ? "

" I'll see you hanged in your boots first, colonel," replied Coralie, coolly—adding, under her breath, "and no
great loss would it be to the service either, for you look
more like a sack than a soldier on your horse."

"Stars and Stripes !—an audacious female rebel!
Very well, my lady ; we'll send you on to Washington,
and then, I daresay, our Government will find quarters
in Fort Warren or Lafayette for you. Captain Squails,
I hold you responsible for the safe keeping of this she-
viper. If she attempts to escape, shoot her like a dog or
a—— ! "

" Cowardly old pettifogger ! how dare you ? " cried
Coralie, indignantly. " When I am free I will find a
Southern gentleman to cut your cur's ears off for that in-
sult to a Southern lady ! "

Even Captain Squails felt a tinge of shame at hearing
a helpless lady prisoner thus outraged, and more than one
officer, to the honor of the North, cried " Shame ! " on the

lawyer-colonel, and looked with admiration on the bold
and beautiful girl.

"Captain Squails," again repeated the colonel, now
white with passion, "I hold you responsible for her
safety!"

"Where shall I quarter her, colonel?" asked the captain, helplessly—"what shall I do with her?"

"Oh, take the usual course," said the colonel; "don't
you know your duty, sir, or is it my place to teach
you?"

Now the fact was that neither the colonel nor the
captain had the least idea what their duty was under the
circumstances; so that Coralie, to her great delight,
found herself left to the discretion of Captain Squails.
She did not doubt for a moment that if there was a possibility of escape Squails was just the man to be gulled.

Coralie, having resolved for her own purposes to fasci-
nate her captor, put forth all her arts, and used unscrupu-
lously those weapons which women know so well how to
wield. She flattered his vanity, and led him insensibly
to believe that his company was very agreeable to her.

With arch hypocrisy, she spoke of the rough boorish
manners of the rebel officers, and praised the style, high-
breeding, and gentlemanly ease of the Northerners in
general, and by implication the peculiar fascination of
manner possessed by the gallant Squails. She also artfully
led him to believe that her heart was not really with the
rebellion, but that while staying in the South, she had
conceived the idea of following the army to the field
more from a girlish frolic than aught else. She spoke of
her friends in the North, and inquired anxiously when he
thought she would be allowed to go on to New York,
for, of course, she added, with charming naïveté, they
would never think of sending a young lady to prison for
a frolic.

"I should hope not," replied the pleased officer,
"indeed if such a thing were to happen, I flatter myself
I could soon bring sufficient influence to bear to liberate
you, young lady. My father is Governor of the States of
Massachusetts; and my uncle, Captain Squails, is in com-

mand of the United States sloop Spitfire; at least," he added, correcting himself, "he was in command, but a confounded rebel ran off with her."

"Oh! I think I heard of the affair," said Coralie, innocently, "it was a Lieutenant Leigh, was it not?"

"Yes—yes—Darcy Leigh!—and we hang him when we catch him. Guess if ever he gets in Uncle Sam's hands he wont have a chance of running off with more sloops!"

Altogether, Coralie played her part so well that not only was the Yankee captain desperately smitten with her, but he also believed her to be simply a gay, frolicsome girl, who, having a bit of fun, and finding it end rather seriously, would be only too glad to go North under his protection, for he thought of asking for a furlough. Then, though Captain Squails, he could inquire as to her family, her character, and perhaps—she was certainly gloriously handsome—he would make her Mrs. Captain Squails.

Little did he think with what utter contempt the Southern beauty in her heart thought of him.

They did not halt until they reached the bank of the Potomac, some few miles above Washington. Tents there were none, so Coralie had allotted to her an empty baggage-waggon, over which Squails placed a sentry whom he could trust.

To do him justice, however, he took this precaution to protect her from insult, not to guard against her escape, for she had given her parole, and Yankee as he was, he was still gentleman enough to believe her word.

Notwithstanding the great fatigue she had undergone, Coralie was up and moving shortly after the break of day. Of course, situated as she was, she had merely snatched a few hours' repose in her riding-habit, and wrapped in a horsecloth which Squails, with many apologies for the want of more luxurious bedding, had provided her. A bucket of clear water was procured from the river. In this she bathed her face and hands, quickly arranged her long luxurious hair with a pocket-comb, and her toilet was complete.

For twelve hours she had given her parole not to

attempt escape, and she would not for worlds be so dishonourable as to break her word.

At eight o'clock she would be free to "make tracks," as the Yankees say, if she could.

If she could! aye, there was the rub, and gazing round on the position, she was forced to own it was not very hopeful. The road where they encamped for the night ran nearly parallel to the river.

On the North was the shelving ground which led to the Potomac; to the east and west the road was blocked up completely by waggons, tumbrils, and the remnants of the army which the previous day had offered battle to the rebels.

There was but one way which offered her even a chance. It is true it was the Southern aspect, the very road she wished to go, but there was a great obstacle. This was a deep and wide ditch, with a fence of strong high posts and rails, at which even an English fox-hunter would look twice ere he rode at it.

Coralie looked at a small watch she carried. A quarter to eight.

The officers were now making a hasty breakfast, and the gallant Squails brought her coffee, with new cake and molasses in a canteen lid. She thanked him graciously, and said,—

" By the way, Captain Squails, you are going to accompany me into Washington, I believe, there to deliver me up to the Philistines."

" I hope to accompany you certainly, if you wish it; but pray do not talk as if you were a felon going to gaol. I think, nay I am sure, I can arrange for your parole being enlarged indefinitely."

"Oh! but I don't want my parole enlarged," she said, quickly. "By the way, what horse am I to ride?"

" Your own, I suppose;" then correcting himself,— " I mean rather, the one that ran away with you."

" Oh, dear—I hate the brute. I wish you could get me another; but for that one, I should not now be a prisoner."

"Another! would you like mine?" said Squails, generously; "he's a beauty—I gave a thousand dollars for him."

Squails really couldn't help it, she looked so piteously handsome in her grey riding-habit—a winning smile on her face—her dark eyes beaming full upon him.

" Can he jump?" asked Coralie.

"Can he jump!—Snakes! I should think he could. Stake my life he'd jump a church."

"Jump a church !" she said, laughing; "I don't believe it; you are trying to impose on my ignorance. Do you think he could jump those posts and rails?"

"Jump those posts and rails!—I should think he could. If he can't, I'll—I'll—I'll let you go free, tarnation seize me if I don't."

Coralie laughed a low musical laugh.

"I'll go free if he can," she thought.

"Dear Captain Squails, how kind of you," she said.

Her eyes dwelt lovingly on his face, and she smiled one of her most ravishing smiles.

The captain was quite intoxicated with her beauty and winning way.

"Come, let us put my saddle on this Bucephalus of yours."

Squails obeyed like a child, fully rewarded by the soft tones of her voice when she spoke to him, and the languishing, melting glances of her large dark eyes.

The side-saddle was on the famous thousand-dollar horse. Coralie stood on one side, ready to mount; Squails on the other, holding the bridle.

Again she looked at her watch.

It was five minutes past eight, and her parole had expired.

But there was one thing more necessary. Even if she got safely away, she would have a ride of some thirty miles before her. She knew that without the countersign, it would be impossible for her to do it. She had heard the countersign given the previous night, but she knew that in war it was an invariable rule to change it every day.

She must get it. Her heart beat wildly at the thought, but there was no help for it—she must ask the captain for the countersign of the day.

She resolved to make a bold dash for it.

"Come, Captain Squails, can't we ride on? I quite long to reach Washington—let us leave at once. Have you got the countersign? if not get it at once. Come, sir, obey. I am not your prisoner? and do you dispute my orders?"

"The countersign? Oh, yes! I have it."

" What is it ? "

She asked the question calmly, smiling, but as she did so her heart beat so violently as to make her feel for a moment almost faint.

" *Pensacola*, young lady, if you must know."

"Thank you, Captain Squails. Be kind enough to look in the waggon where I slept, and see if I have left one of my gloves."

He started off on the errand, and she sprang lightly into the saddle.

The waggon was some thirty yards distant up the road.

She turned the horse's head towards the posts and rails, reining him in tightly, and at the same time pricking him with the silver spur on her heel, for she wished to render him excited, and ready to dash off at a moment's notice.

The ditch, with the posts and rails beyond, was barely twenty yards from where she stood. On the brink of this ditch, with legs hanging over, was a group of officers finishing their breakfast.

Among them, and on the outside, was the attorney colonel who had insulted her.

She saw Captain Squails returning from the waggon, and addressing him, said, coolly,—

" Captain Squails, it is a quarter past eight, my parole has expired. I am going to try if your horse can really jump as you say."

Then, compressing her lips, her black eyes absolutely blazing with excitement, she lashed the horse with her whip.

"Adieu, brave Squails—think of me when far away."

The hoofs of the horse clattered over the hard road. A few bounds brought him to the edge of the ditch. As he rose to the leap she dealt the colonel a slash across the face with her whip.

"Take that, ruffian."

And over the brave steed went, clearing ditch and fence in gallant style, and landing beautifully in tho adjoining field.

A cry of dismay broke from Squails. A shout of fury from the colonel, whose face bore a red wheal where the whip had cut.

"To horse!—to horse!—pursue her!—cut her down!—shoot her!—capture her dead or alive!"

One man, and one man only, obeyed the order and fired his revolver; the great majority were too much struck with astonishment and admiration at the daring feat of the lovely rebel.

In half a minute's time she was out of range, and ere a horse could be saddled, she was no longer visible.

Captain Squails had lost his fair prisoner and his horse to boot.

## CHAPTER XI.

### CORALIE CAPTURES A PRISONER.

WITH feelings of triumphant joy Coralie galloped away from her captors, urging her horse to his utmost speed. She heard the report of the revolver fired at her, and the whistling of the ball overhead.

Fearing that this might be followed by others, she leaned forward till her head touched the horse's neck.

Fortunately this precaution was needless, and in a few moments she knew that she was out of range, and for the present safe.

It was fortunate that Captain Squails's horse was indeed a good one, both in pace and the ease with which

he leaped the fences with which the country was intersected.

Coralie was in high spirits ; the rapid gallop of the
horse, the brisk morning air, and the consciousness of
self-achieved freedom, bringing a bright flush of joy and
pride to her cheek.

After half an hour's rapid riding, she calculated she
must have passed over at least eight miles, and now
thought it safe again to seek the road, which she knew
was only some half-mile to her left. She could now discern in the distance the hilly ground where was fought
the battle on the previous day, and judged rightly that
few Federal soldiers would be found so far from the
defeated army, which was now on the banks of the
Potomac and around Washington.

She met, indeed, as she cantered down the road, one
small body of Federal horsemen, who were out recon-
noitring and driving in stragglers.

As she cantered up to these, she gave the countersign in
a cool, composed manner, and rode swiftly on, merely
acknowledging the presence of the officer at their head
by a bow.

He and his soldiers gazed after her retreating figure,
lost in wonder. They could only conjecture that she
must be the daughter of one of their generals who had
accompanied the army to the field ; but why she galloped
down the road right towards the enemy, bodies of whose
horse were now scouring the country only a mile or so
further on, they could not understand.

Suddenly, at a bend in the road, Coralie perceived,
topping the summit of a hill in front and distant about
half a mile, a considerable force of horsemen.

At that distance she could not tell whether they were
friends or enemies, and as the road here wound about
considerably, she resolved to make a short cut across the
country.

Accordingly she put her horse at the fence, which he
cleared in gallant style, and again she galloped straight
over the fields for the distant camp.

An hour's ride brought her to the verge of the wood,

on issuing from which the Yankee horse she rode the day before had bolted and caused her to be taken prisoner.

She was compelled to make her way slowly through this, and had just reached the outskirts, when suddenly a figure started up from a crouching position, at the foot of a tree close to her horse's head, and ran off.

It is certain, that had the figure remained still, she would not have perceived it, for she was intently gazing ahead, trying to discover the rebel camp on the hills through the trees.

It was the figure of a man, who ran into the open ground, and, turning sharp to the left, seemed as if he wished again to enter the wood at a point further down.

But Coralie was not to be thus baffled. She reasoned justly, that as he ran away from her, he was afraid of her, and that he was not afraid without some reason.

Accordingly she inclined her course to the left also, cutting off his retreat and guiding her horse skilfully between the trees, which here were not so thick as in the interior of the wood.

"Hillo, there! Halt, you sir!" she cried; but the man still kept running; "You wont, wont you?" muttered Coralie, and, in the spirit of mischief, she drew Darcy Leigh's revolver, which had not been taken from her, from her belt, and, cocking it, discharged, or shot towards the fugitive.

The effect was instantaneous, for the running man instantly fell to the earth, uttering a loud cry.

She knew she could not have hit him, for she aimed far above his head. Riding leisurely up, she reined in her horse by the side of the prostrate figure.

"Now then, you sir, get up out of that, and answer for yourself. Who and what are you? Yankee or rebel?"

The man rose and looked at her with speechless wonder. Hearing the sound of horses' hoofs he concluded it to be a mounted trooper, his terror not allowing him sufficient time to look.

He was a handsome, elderly man, tall, and rather stout. His clothes, though stained with mud, and torn in divers places, were yet of fine material. A gold chain which hung around his neck, and a diamond which sparkled on his finger, bespoke him a man of some substance.

"Speak, sir; don't stand there gaping as if you never saw a lady on horseback before. Who and what are you? Yankee or rebel?"

Coralie at the same time pointed her pistol threateningly.

"Don't shoot me—please put down your pistol. I am no rebel, but a loyal Unionist, and have just escaped from the rebels. I thought first, young lady, you were one of the rebel troopers; but now I see it is all right." ·

"Is it all right? We'll see about that, Mr. Yankee. I've just escaped from captivity myself."

"Ah! then," said the elderly gentleman, joyfully, "we can hide in the woods till dark, and then make our way to the Federal lines together. Doubtless you know the country better than I."

"Yes; we'll journey on together, old gentleman," said Coralie ; "but not the way you think. I have just made my escape from the Yankees; you, you say, from the rebels. I have the honour to inform you, you must return with me to the camp."

The man looked wildly around, as if he meditated a bolt. But Coralie significantly raised her pistol.

"Spare me ! spare me ! Pray let me escape."

"Let you escape! why should I? They did not let me go, and by this time, had I not outwitted them, I should have been on my road to Fort Lafayette, doubtless. So now, old gentleman, make up your mind, and come with me quietly. Ah! a capital thought."

Coiled around the horse's neck and linched on to the saddle bow were some twenty yards of thin rope. This had been used to tether the horse, and when Squails saddled him for Coralie, he had not taken it off. She now nimbly uncoiled it, and fastening one end to the crutch of her saddle, threw the other to her prisoner.

"Here, you sir, take that."

" What am I to do with it ?" he said, dismally.

" Tie it round your neck."

" Tie it round my neck!"

" Yes ; and be quick about it, or——"

" Again she pointed her revolver threateningly, and her prisoner, with many lamentations and appeals for pity, was forced to obey.

" Now march on before me, sir, that way, in the direction of those white tents on the hill. And remember, if you attempt to escape I'll see if my pistol wont stop your flight."

Coralie felt absolutely merry with triumph. It was was such a glorious adventure. First she cajoled the gallant Squails out of his horse and heart, lashed her insulter across the face, made her escape, and now had actually herself taken a real live prisoner, who, by his appearance, was a man at all events of wealth if not of importance. On this latter point she soon had conclusive evidence.

After going a little distance quietly enough her prisoner suddenly halted.

" Miss, young lady, I want to speak a few words."

" Speak on, but be quick."

" Allow me to escape, for pity's sake. You cannot know what will be the consequences to me."

" Ah ! ah ! then you have been up to some desperate treachery. A spy, perhaps. If so, my friend, I fear they'll hang you. A long rope and a short shrift."

The prisoner turned ashy pale at these words, and Coralie, though she spoke in jest, now seriously thought she might be right. This all the more hardened her against the man's entreaties.

" No ! Once more, I intend to take you into camp."

" I will give a thousand dollars if you will let me free."

" No !" she repeated, more sternly.

" Five thousand dollars ?"

" No !"

" Ten thousand dollars?"

" Once again—No ! March on."

8

" Look here, young lady, I have with me twenty thousand dollars in gold and notes. I will give it all to you if you will permit me to escape."

" No !—no !—no ! Let that be your answer."

" Twenty thousand dollars in ready money, and a draft on a New York banker on account for fifty thousand more."

" I would not accept a million in ready money. So now, my wealthy Yankee, please to resume your march."

With a groan of despair, the prisoner obeyed.

" So ho !" thought our heroine, " it seems I have caught a millicnaire. Some of these fifty thousands of dollars he speaks of so deftly will be welcome enough to the Confederate treasury. Now then, you Yankee, trot on ; we shall not get into camp before dark at this rate."

Then she put her horse into a trot, and forced her unfortunate prisoner to run also, laughing at his panting and groaning.

" I wonder what he is—a spy? Scarcely possible either that a man of his wealth would play such a paltry part. I have it ! I do believe he is a member of the Washington Cabinet ; come out to view the rout of the ragged rebels ; got taken prisoner in the confusion of the rout ; managed to escape again in the same confusion ; and is ultimately captured by me. Isn't it glorious ! I really think the Government ought to give me a medal, or an order, or a star, for my brilliant achievement."

Thus musing, and in high spirits, Coralie rode on, now walking, now trotting across the battle-field, and up the slope to the Confederate camp.

On an examination of Darcy Leigh's injuries, the surgeon found that one of his ribs was broken, and his shoulder and chest fearfully contused. Jupiter and Darby Kelly took turns in watching him during the deep sleep into which the opiate administered by Stella Gayle, had thrown him. When he awoke, he found himself lying in the tent which Jupiter had on the previous evening pitched for him ; while by his side stood Gerald and Captain George, who had just looked in to see how he fared.

He was very weak, but suffered no pain, his shoulder and broken rib having been strapped up without his awaking.

" Well, boys, what news ?   I know we won the day, for when I was knocked over we were in full pursuit. Have we utterly destroyed them ?   Have we taken Washington ?"

" No, old fellow," replied Gerald, " we have not taken Washington, though I verily believe, had we so chosen, we might have done so, for surely such a rout was never seen.   Our generals, however, were determined on caution ; so after pursuing the flying enemy some ten miles, the order to return was given.

" Are all our friends well ?   Has my regiment suffered much ?"

" Your regiment has suffered fearfully ; at least, four hundred killed, wounded, and missing.   And worst of all, that noble-hearted girl, the Black Angel, as they call her, is not to be found."

" Is she taken prisoner ?" asked Darcy, anxiously.

" No one knows ; either that or killed, for it is certain that, otherwise, she would have returned long since."

" What other news ?"

" None, except that there is no enemy within miles of us ; and that orders have gone forth to strengthen our position and remain on the defensive.   Yes, by the by," added Gerald, " there is one piece of news.   Webster Gayle, who was taken prisoner a few days back in our lines, with some papers on him, supposed to be of a highly compromising character, has escaped, and Stella and Angela are in camp."

" Stella Gayle here !" exclaimed Darcy, raising himself on his elbow.   " What is she doing here ?"

" She came from Richmond immediately she heard her father was a prisoner.   Last night she went in search of him on the field, fearing he might have been killed or wounded ; but up to now there have been no news of either him or Miss St. Casse."

" Stella Gayle !   Stella Gayle !   Strange that it

8—2

should be my fate to be continually meeting that girl. Gerald, take this handkerchief from my head; it pains me."

His brother carefully removed first the thin silk scarf, next the cambric handkerchief which Stella had with her own fair hands bound on.

" Ullo !" he exclaimed, looking at the latter. " Why here is a lady's handkerchief, and——" examining the mark in the corner, " as I live, it is Stella Gayle's, for here is her name daintily embroidered."

" Stella Gayle's handkerchief bound round my head ?" exclaimed the wounded man, colouring. " Impossible ! Let me see."

Gerald handed it to him, and there, sure enough, was the name embroidered, " Stella Gayle."

" Why, you don't mean to say you don't know how you came by it ?"

" Jupiter—Darby—who carried me in ?"

" I, the negro, and Darby Kelly," said Captain George, answering, " carried you in."

" How did I come by this handkerchief ?"

" You had it tied round your head when I found you. Jupiter and Darby did it between them, I suppose, for they were beside you."

" Jupiter—Darby—how did I come by this ?"

" We tied it round yer honner's cut head," replied the Irishman.

" Where did you get it from ?"

Jupiter looked at Darby Kelly, and Darby Kelly looked in return at Jupiter.

" Spake, you black spalpeen," whispered Darby. " Tell his honner where ye got it. Shure it was you found it."

" In de pocket of de tunic, massa."

" What ! of my tunic ?"

" Yes, massa."

" Impossible ! you are telling me a lie ; I never had Miss Gayle's handkerchief. How could it come in my tunic pocket ?"

" Specs you put it dere, massa, an' forget all about
'em," replied Jupiter, quite innocently.

Both Darby and Jupiter, having received Stella's five-
dollar pieces, felt themselves bound in honour not to say,
and, as Jupiter remarked, " One lie more didn't matter."

" This is beyond my comprehension. I can't understand it. I rever, to my knowledge, had a handkerchief
of Stella Gayle's, and yet I find it bound round my head,
and am told it was taken from my breast pocket."

Both Gerald and Captain George thought that he was
slightly delirious, and forgetful from the shock, and
judged it best to leave him to repose.

" There, there, old fellow, go to sleep again, and don't
worry yourself. You'll be all right again in a day or
two. We'll look over again in the afternoon."

And so they left him, racking his brains till his head
ached, to account for the possession of Stella Gayle's
handkerchief.

" I wonder has she asked after me? Not she ; doubtless she is only too glad to hear of my being wounded,
rebel as I am."

How bitterly he wronged her the reader knows ; but
he must be excused, for all that he had lately experienced
knowingly at her hands, had partaken more of the
nature of thorns than roses.

" Well, Gerald, where are you off to now ?" asked
Captain George, as they strolled away from Darcy's
tent.

" Well, you know, old fellow, I've got visitors at my
elegant establishment ; the Misses Gayle."

" Oh, aye, I forgot ; and that reminds me that my
tent is also occupied by a lady."

" The deuce it is," said Gerald ; " why whom on earth
have you got there ?"

" Whom do you think ?"

" I should never guess ; can't imagine who it is."

" Why, that *vivandière* girl, Nina."

" Pshaw ! that's the state of affairs, is it ? I thought
you seemed rather smitten there. A handsome girl,

aint she ?   But what on earth are you going to do with
her ?  keep her with you ?   It's an awkward thing to get
rid of a woman of that sort, old fellow ; so I advise you
to be on your guard."

" Gerald," interrupted the Englishman, quickly, " you
are mistaken ; the girl is a good and fine girl.   Oblige
me by not speaking lightly of her."

Gerald looked astonished.   He could not understand
his friend's delicacy.   In America, both North and
South, it is to a native an incomprehensible anomaly
to see a girl with even the faintest mulatto tinge treated
as an equal.

Nina certainly was very handsome, as white and fair
as themselves ; but then she *had been* a slave, according
to her own account, and that was sufficient in Gerald
Leigh's opinion to preclude her ever being anything but
a white man's servant or mistress.   However, he said
nothing, thought George was a queer fellow, and the subject dropped.   Shortly afterwards they separated, Gerald
going to the tent where were the sisters Gayle, while
Captain George walked leisurely towards his own.

When he arrived he found Nina had already risen, and
having completed her simple toilet, was awaiting him
outside, conversing with the soldier whom George had
procured as sentry.   Certainly he thought she looked
very beautiful in the bright morning sunlight.   The
close-fitting *vivandière* tunic set off her fine shape, and
became her admirably, while the advocates of bloomerism
might, had they seen her, have drawn powerful argu-
ments from the appearance of the grey trousers, setting
so well on the well-turned leg, and falling over the instep
of a very small foot encased in the daintiest of boots.

She greeted the Englishman warmly, and without embarrassment, which was more than could be said of him,
for Gerald's words still troubled him considerably.

It is usually a dangerous position when a man is
thrown constantly in the society of a young and handsome woman ; but how much more so when the said
young and handsome woman loves and does not disguise
her love.

Now our friend, though he liked the innocent freshness of the girl, admired her beauty, and could not but feel flattered by her regard for him, had not the least idea of entangling himself or sporting with her affections. Therefore it was, that with Gerald's words still ringing in his ears, the meeting on his part was constrained and embarrassed.

Nina, with woman's quick penetration, at once saw that something was the matter.

"Sir, you," she said, lifting her bright eyes to his— "you look sad and troubled; has anything vexed you, or are you offended with me?"

"Offended with you, Nina? nonsense; come, let us take a stroll to the top of Gumtree Hill, and see the battery the enemy yesterday so desperately and unsuccessfully assaulted. Come."

Scarcely thinking what he was doing, he offered Nina his arm.

The girl looked at him comically for a moment, and then bust into a peal of laughter.

George coloured up, and looked annoyed, utterly unconscious of the cause of her merriment.

"Pardon me, sir—a thousand pardons. I really could not help it. Did you really mean me to take your arm, and walk thus through the camp?"

George now laughed himself, and Nina's merry peal again rang out.

It certainly would have been sufficiently conspicuous, if not ridiculous to see a cavalry officer parading through the camp with a *vivandière* on his arm, as if he were on Broadway, New York, or in Hyde Park, London.

This mutual laugh put George at his ease again, and he walked on by her side, talking in his old, *nonchalant,* careless manner.

Even as it was, the pair attracted quite sufficient attention—indeed, more than was pleasant. The girl was so very handsome, and her dress so becoming and clean.

As for George, he was always a bit of a fop in his way. The ostrich plume in his hat was fresh and glossy, as though it had never seen the dust or smoke of battle.

His jack boots, too, thanks to a liberal appliance of ebony grease by his servant, shone like black diamonds, his accoutrements and scabbard perfectly bright, his gloves and belt white as pipe-clay could make them; altogether the pair looked as if they had just walked out of Nathan's, the costumier's.

On their way they had to pass Gerald Leigh's tent, at the door of which stood Stella and Angela Gayle. Gerald also was there, talking to Angela; and talking to Stella was a tall man, wrapped in a cloak.

His eyes gleamed fiercely as he saw George and Nina approach, and a black frown settled on his face.

Nina, when she saw him, turned very pale.

"Heavens! there is that dreadful man, Lupus Rock. See how he scowls at us."

"Dreadful—why dreadful?" asked Captain George. "I must say I don't like the man, but I don't see anything to be frightened of in him."

So saying he lifted his hat to the ladies, and returned the fixed look of Lupus, gazing haughtily in return, nor taking off his gaze until the other's eyes dropped.

"For Heaven's sake!" cried Nina, in accents of terror, "never quarrel with that man—never cross his path."

"I don't want to quarrel with the man," replied George, angrily, "but I advise him not to scowl at me as he did just now; and as to crossing his path, I shall please myself about that."

"Ah, sir, you do not know him as well as I do, he is as cunning and wicked as the serpent."

"Why, what do you know so dreadful about him, Nina?" he asked, wonderingly.

"I know much more than I dare say, I know some of his deep plots against Miss St. Casse. I almost think that if her disappearance is caused by her having been captured by the enemy, it is fortunate for her; for then at least she will be beyond that man's power."

"Plots against Miss St. Casse? Does Miss St. Casse know of them?"

"I warned her before we left Charleston, but she seemed to treat the matter lightly; like you, she does not ear him, though, God knows, she has reason so to do."

"What, then, is the nature of these plots, if I am not presuming too much in asking?"

"He wishes to prove that Miss St. Casse is a slave. Why, I know not. I can only guess."

Captain George laughed aloud.

"A slave! what, Miss St. Casse? Certainly the wealthiest single lady in the South. A slave! Nina, you are losing your senses."

"I am not—I am not!—I heard him plotting with another man—as great a ruffian as himself—who is now dead. How do you think he died?" she asked, suddenly, looking solemnly in the Englishman's face.

"Indeed, I can't say," replied George, now thoroughly interested, in spite of his careless manner.

"He was murdered. Lupus Rock murdered him."

"Surely you don't mean that this man who mixes with ladies and gentlemen is a murderer?"

"I do."

"Are you certain? How do you know it?"

"I am certain, and I know it because I saw him."

"You saw him? Good God! Do you seriously mean to say that you saw him murder a man?"

Nina answered slowly and deliberately.

"I saw him tie a bag of dollars round a sleeping man's neck, then I saw him drag that sleeping man down to the river and throw him in. Was that murder?"

"Murder most foul and horrible. How, then, Nina, that, knowing this, you do not denounce him?"

"You ask me why. I have answered every question you have asked me truthfully. I will tell you why. Because that knowledge procured me my freedom."

"But I thought you purchased your freedom?"

"I threw the price at his feet; but ten thousand dollars would not have purchased it from that bad, bold man, had I not possessed that knowledge. Perhaps I was wrong. I now think I was; but I promised never to reveal what I saw. To you alone have I broken that promise. I cannot help it; you have a strange power

over me.   You ask me, and I tell you what torture
could not bring from me."

"Nina, such a promise as the one you made is not
only wrong, it is more—it is void.   You should reveal
all you know.   Such a cold-blooded murderer and
schemer should hang as high as Haman."

"I cannot help it; the day will come, perhaps, when I
may speak.   Pray do not compel me to tell you more.
Pray do not ask me now."

As she spoke, George saw the tears rise in her eyes.

He thought it would be unmanly to use his power and
compel her to speak against her wish, so he pressed no
further.   A silence of some time was broken by him.

"And you say that he is now plotting to prove Miss
St. Casse a slave?   Can you guess his object?"

"I think it is first to get her wealth; next to get herself."

"Ha! I begin to understand.   Have you any idea how
he intends to prove her a slave?"

"Yes; I know vaguely; it is through her mother,
who was the daughter of a New Orleans merchant, one
Louis Crevasse, who——"

"Louis Crevasse!" interrupted Captain George.   "Stay,
I picked up some papers in Baltimore some time back.
They were dropped by a man whom I saw issuing from
Lupus Rock's room.   I have repeatedly and vainly puzzled over those papers without being able to understand
them, though I had a strange presentiment that they
were of importance; I have them here.   Let us rest
ourselves and look them over."

They were now at the summit of that memorable little
hill crowned by the two-gun battery, which the two
Virginia regiments had so bravely defended against the
desperate and repeated attacks of the foe.

Captain George seated himself on one of the light guns
which had hurled such deadly showers of grape into the
enemy's ranks, and Nina seated herself by his side.

They together unfolded the papers and carefully scruti-
nized each.

When all had been examined, he said—

"Well, Nina, what do you make of them?"

"They are plain enough to anyone who understands the laws of the Slave States, which I presume you do not."

"You are right."

"These papers prove," said Nina,—"that is always supposing they are genuine—first, that Louis Crevasse married his own slave—not, however, until he had lived with her for years without so doing. The only child of Louis Crevasse and his slave wife was Coralie's mother, who was also by the laws of the South a slave—the property of her own father. Colonel St. Casse married this girl, not knowing she was her father's slave. Well, then, Louis Crevasse makes over all his slaves to Colonel St. Casse—his own daughter, of course, among the number—though neither St. Casse nor Crevasse seemed to be aware of the fact. Thus we have Coralie's mother a slave and the property of her own husband. By the same laws of the South, the daughter of this union was also a slave —her own father's slave. That is all plain enough, and now I see with what serpent cunning and stenth-hound perseverance Lupus Rock has followed up the track."

"Then it seems that Coralie was her own father's slave, although he knew it not?"

"Yes."

"Well, since Colonel St. Casse left her his property, slaves and all, she would be now, were such a thing possible, *her own slave?*"

"Not so fast. You forget, or are in ignorance of one thing. *A slave can neither inherit nor own property, so that at the present moment Coralie is the property of her father's heir-at-law, her own cousin.* Lupus Rock knows this, depend upon it, and his object will be to purchase her of this cousin. It is as plain as day."

George saw it all now, and was struck by the singular acuteness of Nina.

"What, then, is to be done? Such a ruffian shall certainly never claim property in that noble girl if I can prevent it. What say you, Nina?"

The girl mused for a short time, and then replied,—

"I have heard of this cousin; he is a kind-hearted

young gentleman, in very bad health. He would laugh to scorn the idea of enforcing his accidental claims on Miss St. Casse, and would immediately, as a mere matter of form. present her with her free papers."

- "Where is he?"

"In Richmond, I believe. Miss St. Casse told me she saw him on the night of the ball."

"What say you, then, Nina? shall we go to Richmond together and see him, telling him what we have discovered?"

"You forget that at this moment we do not know the fate of Miss St. Casse; we do not even know if she lives."

At that instant they heard voices behind them, and also the sound of a horse's hoofs ascending the hill.

"Now, then, old gentleman, hurry up, hurry up. We shall get to camp just in time for lunch—and I am hungry after my morning's ride."

It was the voice of Coralie.

Both rose to their feet, and saw the Star of the South riding towards them, a figure with a rope round its neck, preceding; the other end of the cord being attached to her saddle. At the same moment Stella Gayle, Angela, Gerald Leigh, and Lupus Rock came behind, from the direction of the camp.

## CHAPTER XII.

### CORALIE FINDS HERSELF A SLAVE.

"Good morning, Sir Englishman," said Coralie, gaily, as she rode up; "Good morning, Nina. Safe back, you see, after no end of adventures : been taken prisoner, escaped again, and now, in turn, I have taken a prisoner. Behold him!"

Nina did behold him, and gazed with the utmost astonishment.

"Webster Gayle! Senator Gayle!" she ejaculated.

Almost at the same moment Stella Gayle ran forward and over the low breastwork.

CAPTAIN GEORGE AND NINA.

P. 124.

" Father !" she cried, throwing herself into the prisoner's arms. "I thought you were killed."

Then Angela joined her, and, with nimble fingers, began undoing the rope from around his neck.

Gerald Leigh now came up.

" Mr. Gayle," he said, seriously, "this is a most painful position I find you in. What is the meaning of it ?"

" This young woman forced me to come thus a prisoner," he stammered. "I was concealed in the woods, hoping at night to make my way to the Federal lines."

" I thank you, Miss St. Casse," said Stella, bitterly, and glancing angrily at our heroine, "for this indignity you have put upon my father."

" Indeed, young lady, I did not know he was your father. I, myself, had but just escaped from the Yankees, when this gentleman started up in my path, and ran. I considered it my duty to the Confederacy to make him prisoner."

" It is scarcely wonderful," said Stella, scornfully turning away ; "when a woman forgets her sex there is no outrage, no crime she is not capable of committing."

Coralie coloured up at this insulting speech, and was about to retort angrily, but stopped herself.

She remembered, now that she knew it was Stella's father whom she had captured, that there was some excuse for her anger.

It was a painful and embarrassing position for all. Gerald Leigh had often been a guest of Webster Gayle, but his duty as an officer in the Confederate army was clearly to see the escaped prisoner safe back in custody.

Captain George, alone, knowing nothing of Webster Gayle, was cool and unconcerned.

" I tell you what," he said to Gerald, " Miss St. Casse, when she made a prisoner, knew not that he was a personal friend of any of her friends. She knew not that he was the father of these young ladies."

" No ! no ! certainly not ! I had not the most remote idea such was the fact," said Coralie.

" Well then," continued the Englishman, " it seems to me that the best way out of the difficulty will be to put things *in statu quo*, as they were before. No one but ourselves knows of your capture, young lady, and I think it would be a pleasant solution of the difficulty if this gentleman, Mr. Gayle, be allowed to depart again."

" Yes, yes, by all means !" said Coralie, who was now eager to repair the injury she had done.

The prisoner stood in the centre of a group composed of Gerald, Nina, Stella, and Angela ; Captain George standing by the side of Coralie's horse, distant a few paces.

Gerald thought for a moment, and then, addressing Mr. Gayle, said—

" Yes, a good suggestion ! You must conceal yourself till nightfall, and then escape to the Federal lines."

" And my daughters," asked Webster, " what of them ?"

" It is impossible they can accompany you—utterly impossible. You must leave them in the care of myself and Darcy."

" But Lupus Rock—where is he ?"

Then Stella and Angela suddenly remembered that Lupus Rock had been with them. He had disappeared.

" I wish to see Lupus Rock," said Webster Gayle, anxiously. " I must see Lupus Rock. It is of the utmost importance that I see him. It was for that purpose I came South, and I cannot return without seeing him."

" You risk imprisonment, if not worse, by remaining," said Gerald.

" Can no one find Lupus Rock for me before night, and send him to me ? Where am I to conceal myself ?"

" In the wood to your left. No time is to be lost."

During this time Captain George and Coralie were together examining a packet of papers, which the latter produced.

" My papers, my papers, young woman !" cried Webster Gayle, " give me back those papers ; they are useless to you."

" Useless to me, perhaps, but very useful to the enemy," said Coralie, continuing her examination.

" Give my father the papers," said Stella, angrily; " would you rob him in addition to all ?"

Coralie coloured with anger, but answered calmly—
" No, I cannot give you the papers."

Stella was about to give vent to a burst of passion,
when an exclamation from Captain George, who was
looking towards the camp, attracted the attention of all.

" The Provost Marshal !"

And then all saw cantering towards them a mounted
officer, followed at some little distance by two soldiers on
foot.

The next moment he reined up his horse.

" Ha !" he exclaimed, " my escaped prisoner ! In the
name of the Confederacy I arrest this man, and require
you, gentlemen, whom I see are officers, to assist me in
conveying him to head quarters."

Great was the consternation which the arrival of the
dreaded Provost Marshal caused.

To this functionary, always a commissioned officer, and
his subordinates, is intrusted the custody of prisoners, as
well as the punishment of offenders against military
discipline.

It is the Provost Marshal who carries out the dreadful
sentence of death when a heinous crime causes that
penalty to be incurred.

Altogether, the Provost Marshal is to evil-doers the
most dreaded of functionaries.

The two soldiers who followed him on foot were two of
his subordinates—provost sergeants.

When they arrived on the spot he turned to them.

" Search the prisoner, and take from him all papers;
then convey him to head quarters. If he again endeavours to escape, shoot him."

Webster Gayle was quickly searched, but nothing found
on him, save a large sum of money in notes and gold.
Stella had reason now to be thankful that Coralie had not
complied with her demands.

The search concluded, Webster Gayle was marched off
in custody of the two sergeants, looking the picture of
despair. Stella would have followed him, but Gerald
stopped her.

" Stella, it is useless to accompany your father. It

would only attract attention uselessly, and you will be
permitted to see him on applying to the general."

Coralie now rode up to Stella, and with the papers in
her hand addressed her.

" Miss Gayle, you used some bitter words just now with
respect to me. I have no wish to rob your father, but
did not feel justified in giving him the papers. It was
fortunate for him I did not. I have examined them—
here they are, take them. And let me tell you, that had
those papers been found on the prisoner, he would most
certainly be condemned to death as a spy. Take them ;
I advise you to destroy them."

Stella eagerly took these silent witnesses, and coloured
with shame at the generous revenge the Star of the South
took for her insulting speech.

She murmured a few words of apology, but Coralie
proudly turned away, and rejoined Captain George and
Nina, who were walking behind in earnest conversation.

" Here comes Lupus Rock," said Gerald, as they approached the camp. " I wonder does he know of your
father's re-capture ?"

Stella said nothing, but when they met Lupus, although
Gerald treated him with marked coldness and suspicion,
she by no means followed suit.

" Lupus, have you heard ?" Stella asked.

" Heard what ?"

" My father is again a prisoner."

" Again a prisoner !—When was he taken ?"

" You were with us a moment before, Mr. Rock," said
Gerald, looking in his face suspiciously ; " strange that
you should disappear, and the Provost Marshal ride up a
few minutes afterwards."

" Not at all strange," said Lupus ; " I had occasion to
return, and met him on the road. He was riding straight
for the hill where I left you. How was he retaken ?"

Stella was silent. She did not trust herself to speak
again of Miss St. Casse. She felt strangely bitter against
the Southern girl ; she hardly knew why, and after the
generosity she had shown in giving her those dangerous
papers Stella was too honourable to say a word against

her. And she feared if she *did* speak that her feelings would get the better of her judgment and sense of right.

"He was captured by Miss St. Casse," said Angela, angrily; "the bold, forward girl, it appears, does man's duty, riding about on horseback, and——"

"Angela, it is unkind of you—you have no right to speak thus! Please to remember that Miss St. Casse is my friend, and more especially the friend of my brother Darcy."

"And more especially the friend of my brother Darcy!" How the words jarred on Stella's ears!

"It is very well you talking, Gerald," answered Angela, somewhat angrily; "but do you think you would be quite so calm and good-tempered if it was your father who was captured?"

"My father," replied Gerald, "would never place himself in the position where he could ever be accused as a spy."

"A spy! Gracious Heavens, Gerald! but our father is not a spy. Say, oh, say he is not!"

"I cannot say he is or is not," replied Gerald; "but such is the accusation."

"A spy—a spy—it cannot be true," exclaimed both Stella and Angela; "it is the vile invention of an enemy."

"Examine those papers you have, Stella, those which Miss St. Casse gave you; she told me but five minutes ago that they contained a complete map of our positions and lines, as well as information concerning our councils of war and intended movements. The bearer of those papers, addressed as they are to the Yankee Government, spy or not, would assuredly be executed on suspicion; it is exceedingly fortunate that they were not on your father's person when searched by order of the Provost Marshal."

It may well be imagined that these words did not tend to raise the spirits of the sisters. As for Lupus Rock, he walked by their side in silence; several times he had addressed Stella, and, receiving no reply, desisted. As for Stella, her pride had received a desperate blow, and

9

she felt quite crushed in spirit. Her father a spy, in the hands of the despised rebels, and his life, in all probability, only saved through the generosity of Miss St. Casse, the Black Angel, as she was called, and as Stella sometimes spoke of her in scorn.

"Lupus, my father wishes to see you," said Stella, when once again they had arrived at the tent of Gerald Leigh. "He is most anxious."

"I doubt if I can do any good at present," was the reply. "However, I will go." Then Lupus strode off sullen and moody. Stella, who knew him well, felt certain that he was disappointed and savage from the failure of some scheme or other, and by degrees she grew more and more convinced that Lupus was thus sullen and gloomy because the fatal papers had not been found on Webster Gayle.

Captain George walked slowly on by the side of Coralie's horse. Briefly and deliberately as possible he explained the singular discovery they had made. The young girl was almost overwhelmed, and could scarcely believe the terrible fact. The very idea was, to her proud nature, a bitter humiliation.

"A slave, a slave!" she thought to herself, and rode on in silence. Pale, drooping, and spiritless, she seemed utterly prostrated.

George strove to reassure her.

"I do not think, Miss St. Casse, there is any occasion for despair; the matter can be easily arranged. Will you leave it in my hands?"

"Alas! you know not what you say. Easily arranged! when you say that Lupus Rock has the proof complete?"

"Yes; but the proofs are useless to him if your cousin Edward St. Casse chooses to waive his claim, and give you as a mere matter of form nominal free papers; there is no doubt he will do this."

"Yes, sir," replied Coralie, raising her eyes and gazing despairingly in his face; "but suppose he has already placed it beyond his power—suppose he has sold all his slaves and signed a deed—what then?"

"That will complicate matters, certainly; but no matter who the purchaser, I feel convinced it could be easily arranged. No Southern gentleman would enforce an accidental claim of the kind; he would be scouted by every honourable man."

"My cousin Edward St. Casse has sold all his slaves, and if I also was one of his slaves he has sold me."

"To whom?" asked Captain George.

"To Lupus Rock," said Coralie, in tones of deep despair.

"Lupus Rock!" gasped Nina—"then all is lost. I know his ruffian nature; a million dollars would not buy him off—he will have his pound of flesh. Fly, Miss St. Casse, while there is yet time. Escape to the Canadas, where the glorious British flag flies; take shelter under its folds, and all the world cannot tear you away. Fly at once—for from Lupus Rock you may expect no mercy."

Nina's terror of Lupus Rock seemed intense, unaccountable even to Captain George, to whom she had confided so much. Coralie seemed to have lost all her energy, and to be quite prostrated at the terrible truth she had just learned.

"Miss St. Casse, do not give way to despair; there is little to fear; this Lupus Rock, I know, is a coward; leave him to me; I may have a little trouble, but I am certain I can force him to do justice."

"Ah, sir, you do not know what you say," said Coralie, sadly.

"No, no, do not you attempt to thwart Lupus Rock—it would be of no avail, and he would surely sweep you from his path," said Nina.

"Would he?" said Captain George, scornfully; "that remains to be proved. Miss St. Casse, leave this to me; take my word for it, that ugly as the affair looks I will pull you through."

There was something at once so quiet and withal so confident in his tone as to inspire her with hope.

"Can you indeed aid me, and without endangering yourself?" she asked.

"I can and will. If I do not bring this Lupus Rock to bay, and force him to relinquish his intended prey, my name is not—is not——"

"By the way, what is your name?" asked Coralie, now smiling.

"My name—Captain George," he also replied with a smile.

"Ah, yes; but that is not your real name."

"It is at least sufficient for both friends and enemies," he replied. "I wish Darcy Leigh were well—Gerald is a good fellow, but he has not the brains of Darcy."

"Ah—Darcy Leigh," exclaimed Coralie, quickly and anxiously; "is he then ill—wounded?"

"Yes; badly, but not dangerously."

"Poor fellow! and I had very nearly forgotten him; how selfish my own troubles have made me; where is he? I must see him."

George smiled at her eagerness, and replied—

"Yonder is his tent, and there is Gerald, standing outside."

"I will dismount. Nina, will you take my horse?"

"Shall I let my man attend to him?" asked George; "he seems a splendid animal. What did you pay for him, if I may ask?"

"Nothing," she replied, now laughing; "I stole him. I have not time now, but will relate the whole adventure some day."

The Englishman assisted her to dismount, and gathering up her habit, she hastened towards where Gerald stood, outside Darcy's tent.

"Jump up, Nina; I will walk by your side, and we can talk over our plan of action."

He held his hand, and Nina, placing her foot in it, sprang lightly into the saddle.

"Now, my fair ally," he said, "we have undertaken this business, and must carry it through. Have you anything to propose?"

"You will then. You are determined to brave this man's vengeance."

"Aye, that I am, were he ten times as terrible. You shall see how soon I will pull his house of cards about his head when I commence. But you, Nina—do not let me influence you. You seem to have so strange a fear of this man; perhaps you had better——"

"Fear! fear!" she interrupted, passionately; "it is not for myself, but for you I fear. If you would only consent to let me brave all the danger I should not care; but I know you will get hurt, killed, or something dreadful will happen. What can I do?"

Nina seemed half inclined to cry.

"There he is—there is Lupus Rock," suddenly exclaimed Captain George. "See, he is mounted, and giving some directions to his groom. I will go up to him at once, and break the ice. I rather fancy I shall astonish my gentleman a trifle when he hears what I have to say. Wait here, Nina. I will go over and speak to him."

Accordingly the Englishman walked quickly towards him; but whether Lupus guessed he was about to accost him, and wished to avoid an interview, or not, when George was within about twenty yards he galloped off.

"Where has your master gone?" he demanded of the groom, who was walking away.

"Brentville," replied the man, laconically.

"I see he has a valise strapped on his saddle. When does he return?"

"Not for a week. Head recruiting quarters at Brentville. Major Rock's gwine to raise a regiment."

"Major Rock! How long has he been a major? He knows as much of soldiering as he does of Chinese."

"Don't know, and don't care anything about it," said the man, sullenly.

And George, seeing there was no hope of getting further information, walked back to Nina.

"Nina," he said, "Lupus Rock has gone to Brentville, distant about fourteen miles. I can get away—no outpost or picket duty for two days, thank Heaven. Gerald Leigh knows every yard of the country. I will go and get information from him as to the shortest cut. Then, what say you? let us ride and be there before our arch conspirator. That alone will astonish him not a little, seeing that he left us here behind him.   What do you say ?   Will you come, my fair ally ?"

"But Miss St. Casse ?"

"Oh, she will excuse you."

"But then I have no horse."

"Take the one you are on."

"But it belongs to Miss St. Casse."

"Well, are we not going on the business of Miss St. Casse ?   Do not fear, I will take all blame."

Nina wanted but little persuasion.   It was too much in unison with the dictates of her heart to accompany him for her to offer any serious opposition.

Captain George started off, found Gerald Leigh, and got from him directions for a short cut across country, by which he might save at least three miles out of the fourteen.

In ten minutes he was back by Nina's side on horse-back, and the pair started off across the fields at a rattling gallop.   He was astonished at the ease and grace with which she rode.   Certainly no costume could be at once more picturesque and convenient for the saddle than the tunic descending to the knee and grey trousers the *vivandière* wore.

But if George was surprised at the grace with which the girl rode, he was still more surprised at the ease with which she conversed.   Of course she was not highly educated : that, from the very nature of things, was an impossibility ; but he heard enough to convince him that a very little time and trouble, judiciously bestowed, would put Nina on a par with many a fine lady.

George had never been in such a position before.   The easy self-possession of the girl quite flabbergasted him. She had made no secret that she loved him, and yet she was willing to go with him, alone and unquestioning, wherever he bid her.   " She must either be the most art-ful or the most innocent girl in the world," he thought.

We will now leave them galloping across the country, and follow the fortunes of Lupus Rock, whose house of cards the Englishman had sworn to pull about his ears.

# CHAPTER XIII.

Mr. Lupus Rock did not think it wise or necessary to refuse seeing his uncle, Webster Gayle, although his plans were not yet quite ripe. Accordingly he went, and easily obtained admission to the hut where the New York merchant and senator was confined under strict guard.

" Well, sir," said the uncle to the nephew, "you have got me into a pretty scrape : what have you to say for yourself?"

" It was all your own folly," said Lupus, sullenly ; "you would come South before it was safe for you to do so."

" Come South ?" was the angry reply ; "and about time ! Again and again I wrote, urging explanations and a full statement of affairs, but you continually put me off with one excuse and another. Was it not enough that you had full command and sway over large sums of money and my estates in the South, but you must also deprive me of my daughters ? For what devilish purpose have you been taking them thus about the country ; from Washington to Jersey, thence to Richmond, and now actually to the rebel camp ?"

" To what purpose ? for the best of purposes. I gave out that you were for the Confederate cause, and their presence with me in the seceded States proved it. Besides, had Stella been in the North, among her Union friends, hosts of whom, in her enthusiasm, she would gather round her, your dealings with the rebels would infallibly have been discovered. Besides, why should not at least Stella remain with me ? Am I not her cousin, and is she not to be my wife ? I believe that was arranged between us, uncle Webster."

" I will never force my daughter's inclinations. If

she chooses to accept you I shall throw no obstacle in the way."

"But that is not sufficient, Senator Gayle," said Lupus, sternly; "you must, if necessary, use your influence with her. I demand the fulfilment of your promise."

"Demand ?"

"Aye, demand! I am not a man to be trifled with, so I warn you; even now your life is in danger. You will be tried by court-martial, and if found guilty will be certainly shot as a spy."

Webster Gayle grew deadly pale.

"Shot—shot !"

"Aye, shot as a spy. A few words from me would easily turn the scale; remember, I am supposed to be a fervid secessionist; I know the contents of those papers which the Black Angel gave your daughter. I know many other facts also."

Webster Gayle seemed prostrated with terror; and seeing this, Lupus was satisfied.

"Mind, unclo," he said, in softer tones, "I do not threaten; I only wish to show you my power. Not for worlds would I injure you, but the worm will turn when trodden on; and I, were my honest affections trifled with, could not answer for the consequences. There is but one step between love and hate. However, let us to business. You must be cleared of this charge; it will go hard with you."

"But how ?"

"Leave it to me, I can clear you; but we must have Stella's co-operation. Write a note for her to come to you at once, and I will send it."

Webster Gayle did as requested, and Lupus despatched it by his servant, who was holding his horse without.

"Stella will be here in a few minutes," said Lupus; "she is at the tent of Gerald Leigh. It is now necessary that we distinctly understand each other. I pledge myself to clear you of this charge, that is to say, if my directions are implicitly followed; your daughter Stella must take on herself some part of the blame—her youth, her sex, her beauty will protect her."

"My daughter—my beautiful Stella!" cried the father; "my dear loving girl—I cannot, will not drag her into it."

"Listen to me, Webster Gayle. Your life is in my hands; if you hesitate or falter, either from foolish scruples or obstinacy, you will assuredly be shot. Your trial by court-martial will come on to-morrow; if found guilty the sentence will be death, and it will be carried into execution before sundown—so choose."

"Do as you will," groaned Webster Gayle, "I am in your hands; only spare poor Stella."

"Fear not, sir; my love for Stella, as my future wife, is as great as your own. There is one other point. I wish Stella, in your and my presence, to consent to receive me as her future husband, that is to say, when I have succeeded in clearing you of this charge."

"But supposing she refuses—I cannot coerce her."

Lupus set his teeth, and smiled a bitter smile.

"She will not refuse when she knows her father's life is at stake."

At this moment Stella Gayle was ushered in.

"Stella, I have sent for you," said her father. "You know the danger I am in."

"Oh, father, father," she said, kneeling at his feet, "I have just heard such terrible news. They tell me you will be tried by a court-martial and condemned—that is almost certain; and that no mercy will be shown. Oh, these rebels are terrible in their vengeance—why, why did you run such a terrible risk?"

Webster Gayle grew yet paler as he heard these words, confirming what his nephew had stated.

Lupus Rock's eyes gleamed with savage joy. All was going well. No time could be more opportune to wring from father and daughter that which he wished.

"Stella, there is yet one means whereby I can be saved," he faltered.

Stella raised her head, and looked anxiously in his face.

"But, my dear girl, it is—it may be dangerous—that is, inconvenient to you."

Stella Gayle leaped to her feet.

"What are those means of escape? Danger to me? Don't let that influence you. Father, I will do anything! risk anything to save you, save honour. Speak, father, Fear not I will refuse."

But the father, in presence of his daughter's noble self-devotion, could not find words. Again and again he tried to express himself, but the sentences seemed to choke him.

"Lupus, you tell her," he said at last; "God help me, I cannot."

"Stella," said Lupus, soothingly, "in order to clear your father, you and I must both take some risk, some blame. For my part, I am willing—I 'shrink not; do you?"

"No, no—a thousand times no. Lupus, speak."

"There is one other subject on which I wish to come to an understanding. I am about to place myself in a damaging, even dangerous position, in order to save your father; sure I deserve some return. I have spoken to my uncle, and he coincides with my views; is it not so, sir?"

Webster Gayle bowed his head in silence.

"Stella," said Lupus, "you know, you must know, my deep love for you."

"Ah," she gasped, fearing what was coming, "do not go on, Lupus—this is no time."

"But, Stella, I must and will go on. I said you could not fail to know my deep love for you; all I ask is a return of that love—a promise that you will be my wife if I succeed at my own peril in clearing your father of the charge against him, which, as you know, is that of being a spy, and the penalty, *death!*—a certain and igno-minious death."

Lupus laid cruel stress on the crime and its conse-quences. Webster Gayle bent his head and felt sick with terror, while poor Stella stood the picture of despair, gazing first in wild alarm at her father, then in dislike, almost loathing, at Lupus Rock. A terrible conflict was going on in her mind. Spite of herself, the image of

Darcy Leigh rose before her ; she thought how different would have been his conduct, how gladly he would have served her, and how proudly he would have disdained reward ; but then another picture appears before her eyes—a terrible picture. She saw in fancy her father kneeling blindfolded before a file of soldiers with presented rifles, and in fancy, heard the dreadful word " Fire !" given.

" Father, what shall I do ?" she asked, distractedly.

"Daughter, let me not influence you ; but remember that my life is in your cousin's hands."

The old man buried his face in his hands, and for a long space there was a solemn silence in that prison hut.

Lupus stood with folded arms. On his face might have been discerned an expression of bitter satisfaction. He felt sure of ultimate triumph, but the evident repugnance of Stella galled him bitterly.

She, pale and beautiful, with clasped hands, gazed on the figure of her father seated at the rough table with head bowed down. Her bosom rose and fell, her breath came gaspingly and thick, her brain reeled, and a dizzy feeling came over her as she thought on the sacrifice she was called on to make.

At last she broke the stillness ; her voice was low and deep, but without terror.

" I would be alone with my father for a few minutes," she said, turning to Lupus.

He left the hut sullenly and muttering to himself. He did not enjoy his triumph, sweet as he had pictured it. The repugnance and shrinking horror of Stella revived the memory of the scorn he had suffered at her hands. He remembered how she had spurned him when it suited her, and again how she had first used him and then laughed at him, when she made him the instrument in drugging the two officers and saving the lives of Gerald and Captain George. He walked moodily up and down outside the hut, scowling at the ground and grinding his teeth, as he called to mind instances of Stella's haughty hatred and contempt for himself.

"Father," said she, when they were alone together, "is this necessary? Cannot you be saved without—without the aid of Lupus? Can I not sacrifice myself without his hateful aid?"

"It would be useless, Stella—I fear him. He knows the contents of those papers."

"But surely he would not—dare not betray you. Such perfidy is impossible. A fiend from hell could not be guilty of such black ingratitude."

"Stella," replied Webster Gayle, "I cannot say. All I know is, that for the present I am in the power of Lupus Rock. Whether he would use the power I know not. Are you so bitterly averse to him?"

"Averse to him!" she cried, for the first time speaking excitedly, and raising her voice, "I hate and despise him."

The walls of the hut were thin, and Lupus, stalking up and down outside, heard the words of his cousin. They did not tend to conciliate him. The scowl deepened on his brow, and he stamped on the ground with fury.

"And I also," he muttered, "begin to hate. Nevertheless, proud Stella, you shall be mine. Then shall you feel the bitter humiliation of being a wife with a mistress nearer the throne. Ha! ha! my proud beauty, how it will make your haughty spirit writhe to find another in the first place—you with the name of wife, but a toy—a plaything!"

His savage thoughts were interrupted. Stella appeared at the door of the hut, and beckoned him in.

No sooner was he inside than she said, calmly—

"Lupus, I consent to what you ask; now you can go."

He was taken by surprise at her ready acquiescence, when he expected strong and bitter resistance.

Stella held the door open for him, and he slunk away, unable to find words, so completely had her calm, proud manner discomfited him.

"What is the meaning of this? Does her ready consent disguise some desperate purpose?"

He walked slowly on to his own quarters, the cloud by

degrees vanishing from his face, and the old triumphant look replacing it. He had known Stella and studied her, and felt sure that, having once given her word, she would keep it. Nor did he wrong her, for when once again alone with her father, she knelt by the side of the small table, and burying her face in her hands, sobbed bitterly.

"Stella, Stella," said Webster Gayle, his voice faltering and tears trickling down his face, "I cannot suffer this. Call your cousin back, and tell him you cannot marry him. Tell him you do not love him."

"He knows it, father," she interrupted.

"Tell him you dislike him."

"It is useless ; he knows it."

"Tell him, then, that you will not marry him. He cannot, dare not injure me."

"He can, and dare. Father, I have said the word, and so it must be. I have promised to marry him, and I will; but I will leave him at the church door. No power short of force shall compel me to cross his threshold. Before he shall hold me in his arms, I will kill—my God! I will murder him."

Her eyes blazed fiercely, and her voice shook with passion.

"Stella, Stella, do not talk so dreadfully," groaned the wretched father. There was a wild scared look in the girl's eyes that made him fear for her reason.

When she left the hut her eyes were red with weeping, and her cheeks flushed and hot. Nevertheless she carried her head erect, and her foot trod the ground as firmly as though she was a victor, instead of vanquished, and when she appeared before her sister and Gerald Leigh, but for the red eyes and flushed cheek, she was calm and quiet as ever.

"Stella, dear, you have been crying," said Angela, anxiously.

"I have been to see our father," she replied. And Angela took that as a sufficient reason for the red eyes.

"Will he be liberated, Stella?"

"Yes, Angela, dear, to-morrow."

But Angela knew not what desperate str
of her father's freedom had caused her siste

Lupus Rock gradually regained his equar
interview with his cousin and uncle, in '
himself could not but see he had, thoug
victor, appeared in a very unfavourable l
thought of this, though for a moment u
soon dismissed by the desperate scheme
feeling of present, and confidence in future
ceeded. Hitherto he had been far too caut
himself fully to the rebel cause. He all al
the rebels would make a desperate effort, bu
it possible they might be crushed by the f
slaught of the North.

But the battle of Bull Run decided
with a natural acuteness that the power wi
terribly repulse the first advance of the in
vance being made under the most favo
stances, would offer successful resistance t
Yankees could bring against them. In h
it had only been a question whether the i
would fight. He knew the difficulties opp
vader by the climate and the vast area of t
seeing the Yankees hurled bleeding back v
miles from their own capital, he concludee
conquest of such a vast country defended
was an impossibility.

From that day Lupus Rock determined
tire adherence to the Confederacy. The ;
Yancey was his, and his he intended it
Convinced as he was, that in the struggle
commenced, the Confederates would preva
far as holding their own was concerned—
that the best way to retain his nefar
property—a property of which he had
robbed his uncle—was by actively aiding t
Yancey plantation was near the border, a
true, be seized and held by the Yankees ;
of the struggle, he knew full well, that i
stored to the South, compensation would

him by the Confederate Government. He had sold all the slaves, cattle and crops, and had thereby realized nearly 70,000 dollars.

There were yet other reasons why he should espouse the Southern cause. These were his deep designs on the person and property of Coralie St. Casse.

Once having made the accidental discovery that she was a *slave*, he had never taken his nose from the track until he had obtained ample and decisive proof—proof which no court of law could possibly resist—on the subject of slavery. The very basis of Southern institutions, he knew that the law was clear, and also that it must be inflexibly administered. If once the right of a man in his *slave*, legally acquired, were overruled or successfully disputed, there would virtually be an end to the system. He knew that if he could establish his case, however painful the decision might be to all men of honour, or however popular the victim might be herself, that the decision must be in his favour. If, then, he could prove that Coralie was a slave, and had been legally purchased by him, he felt assured that he could successfully claim both her person and property. Lupus thus thought he had good reason to feel triumphant.

Coralie was undoubtedly the handsomest girl south of the Potomac, and well deserved the title "Star of the South." Then her wealth ; for, in addition to being the greatest beauty, she became, on her father's death, the greatest heiress ; that alone would make him a very rich man.

At times he almost thought of making her his wife, but then, there Stella stood in the way. He had sworn to possess her, and knew his cousin sufficiently well to feel certain that in no other way could he obtain her than as his wife. She would suffer first a hundred deaths.

But there were two reasons why he was resolved on making Stella his wife—one was because of the scorns and slights with which she had treated him : the other was his avariciousness. With the addition of Stella's fortune, his wealth would be enormous—princely.

And Lupus had desperately ambitious dreams. Who

could tell, he thought, what might be the future of the
Southern Confederacy—why might he not some day be
President—and who could say that his future should stop
even at that elevation ?   History told of more than one
chief of a republic who had assumed almost unquestioned,
irresponsible power.

He had resolved at once, then, on assuming a military
command, and in prospect of such a resolve, had been for
weeks reading up drill, tactics, and fortification.   To obtain a command, he thought the easiest—in fact the only
way—was to follow the example of the " Black Angel,"
and raise a regiment, equipping them at his own expense,
and obtaining arms from the Government.

That very morning he had sent his agent to Brentville,
there to establish his head-quarters ; and by placards and
liberal treating, at once to form the nucleus of a regiment.

It was about three in the afternoon when he mounted
his horse to ride to Brentville, which he expected to reach
in a couple of hours.   The more he thought of it, the more
satisfied he felt with the thought of having at his own
command a force of men, all of whom he would be able
personally to select, and whom he could depend upon.
He saw no bounds to the power such a force as he could
raise would bestow on him.   He well knew that he could
find, with ease, hundreds of " rowdies " and " loafers,"
who would be ripe for any villany, if paid accordingly ;
and with a force of eight hundred or a thousand men at
his command, what might he not do ?   Woe, then, to any
rash enough to cross his path !

There was but one drop of bitter in this his pictured
cup of sweets.   There was one who, from the bottom
of his soul, he both feared and hated—one by whom
he had been repulsed and foiled, and who held sole
possession of a terrible secret.   That one was Nina,
the Octaroon.   In spite of his fury and scowls, he
could not meet that girl's eyes.   He felt that she feared
him, but also that she defied him ; and, spite of himself,
he trembled.

But he quickly dispelled these unwelcome fears.  Nina

would not cross his path ; if she did, he would find means to remove her.

And so he rode on, building castles in the air, and gloating over the idea of his future greatness—the gratification of all his desires, and the accomplishment of his vengeance on all those who dared to thwart him.

Thus he rode on to Brentville, building his house of cards ; but at the same time, Captain George and Nina were riding by a cross country cut to the same place.

And Captain George had said he would pull his house of cards about his head.

Let us see how he fared in the attempt.

## CHAPTER XIV.

### THE RIDE TO BRENTVILLE.

Of course Lupus Rock had no idea, as he rode somewhat leisurely towards the town, or rather village of Brentville, that Captain George and Nina were also bound there, and would arrive before him. But, as the reader knows, such was the fact.

The short cut which Gerald had directed his friend to take led again into the main road, about half way to their destination. Determined to be there, if possible, before him, although he had fully twenty minutes' start, they rode at an increased pace for a couple of miles, and then, thinking that if he had been in front they must have overtaken him, George pulled rein, and Nina following his example, they walked their horses.

From the pace at which they had been riding conversation was all but impossible, so Nina took advantage of the occasion.

"Now I want you to tell me," she said, "what you undertake to do ?"

The word undertake, be it understood, in Yankee phraseology means—what do you intend to do ?

"What do I undertake to do ? Well, I undertake to do what I said—pull this Lupus Rock's house of cards
10

down—a very pretty little fabric it would make, no doubt, but my idea is that it's doomed to destruction."

"But how are you going to do it?" she asked, anxiously. "I know you are brave, but what will bravery avail against cunning, and such cunning as that man possesses."

"Are you afraid, Nina? Do you wish to give this up? Perhaps I am wrong in leading you yet further on to what may be to you desperately dangerous ground. You say that Lupus Rock hates you: you fear him. Then why venture to cross him? Come, let us go back. I will ride with you to the camp, and then follow up this affair myself."

So saying, he reined in his horse, and came to a dead halt.

Nina did likewise.

"Yes, I will go back," she said, quickly, an angry ring in the tone of her voice ; "I will go back."

"Very well," said the Englishman, in a not very amiable tone, "let us go back."

"Us—us—us !" said the girl. "No, not us, but I. I will go back alone. I shall keep to the road, and so cannot miss my way."

George was savage at the girl's petulance ; he could not understand it. She seemed afraid to accompany him ; then when he proposed to go back with her, she refused his company almost rudely.

"Very well," said he, "as you please."

Without a word, Nina lashed her horse with the riding-whip, and galloped off back.

As Captain George looked after her, half vexed, half wondering, he pulled out his case and lighted a cigar. Then the thought struck him, that as she rode back she must meet Lupus Rock, unless, as was very improbable, he had ridden so fast as to be ahead. He remembered her undisguised terror of the man, and thought that there must be some ground for it. So he at once turned his horse's head, and galloped after her.

Perhaps he thought he had shown a little want of courtesy in taking her so readily at her word. Be that

"WITHOUT A WORD, NINA GALLOPED OFF BACK."

as it may, in less than five minutes he overtook her, and was again riding by her side. She was quietly walking her horse, and as he rode up on the off-side, her face was turned from him.

" I suddenly remembered," he said, " that on your road back you would probably meet this *bête noire* of yours, Mr. Rock."

" I am not afraid for myself, thank you," she replied, carefully keeping her face turned from him.

Her horse suddenly shying at some object by the road-side, darted ahead, and when she reined him in, it was on the other side of her companion.

She could not then conceal her face from him, and he saw she was in tears. Then it dawned upon him that he must have done or said something unkind.

Few men can stand woman's tears—and he was at once quite melted.

"Nina, my dear Nina, what on earth is the matter with you? I am sure if I have said anything unkind I am very sorry. I rode back to tell you that you must meet this Mr. Rock, whom you fear so much ; and—"

" I do not fear him," she said, suddenly turning her eyes, glistening with tears, full upon him ; " at least I do not fear him for myself. It was for you I feared."

What man could resist that? Not Captain George, certainly. The very abrupt artlessness with which she said it carried an indescribable charm.

" Nina, my dear Nina, I beg your pardon ; come, turn back with me."

" No—no, you do not want me."

" I do not want you to run any risk," he said, seriously ; "and you seem so terrified at this Lupus Rock, that I thought I should be doing wrong——"

Again she interrupted him.

"I am not afraid of Lupus Rock for myself; do you want me to repeat my reason for being afraid of him ? "

" Well, Nina," he said, " if you are not afraid, I am sure I am not. Let us go on together."

With his right hand he took her left, which held the

bridle, and gently turned her horse's head with his. "Come, Nina, are we friends?"

She raised her eyes for one moment to his, and then put her horse into a canter on the road to Brentville.

"Strange girl!—extraordinary girl!" he thought; "for, as the Yankees say, guess I'm making a fool of myself."

After less than an hour's ride they cantered into the village together, he wondering how he could have been such a brute as to grieve her, she blaming herself for her own presumption and ill-temper.

"So you mean to say, that on your own account you do not fear this Lupus Rock one bit?"

"No," said Nina.

"Well, I am sure I do not fear him for myself, so we ought to make brave allies—each without fear."

"Will you never learn," she exclaimed, "that if there is no danger for me, there is for you?"

George, lifting his eyes, caught hers fixed on his face. There was a strange expression in them, he fancied. A dreamy, anxious, weary look, whose meaning he could not decipher.

She moved her head slightly till her profile was towards him, and as he noted the clear, classically cut outlines and the graceful form, he thought, "Danger for me,—danger for you—aye, danger for both."

And he almost regretted he had started on that Quixotic errand, at least, in company with Nina the *vivandière.*

There was but one street worthy of the name in Brentville, and in that were situate all the stores and liquor bars and inns. They had not gone far down the street, gazing about on each side, when Captain George descried a great canvas placard hung up outside a building which, from the wide open doors and crowds of loafers, was evidently a place where liquor was sold. The placard was hauled close up to the shingle roof, and reached down as low as the entrance door. One glance satisfied him that this was the head-quarters of Mr. Rock, for in large letters his name was there.

It set forth various inducements for enlistment. First, ten dollars bounty, the chance of promotion, and free kit and uniform. Then there was a long paragraph about "glory," another inimical to the Yankees, and it wound up by holding forth the hope—in fact, as it was stated, almost the certainty of the plunder of Washington, Baltimore, Philadelphia, and all Yankee towns near the border line.

At the foot, in flaming capitals, appeared the name of "Lupus Rock, Yancey Estate, Virginia;" and beneath, in smaller type, "Aaron Smith, Recruiting Agent. All applications to be made at the bar."

There was a considerable crowd of men assembled in front of the door, many of whom had already enrolled their names and taken the ten dollars, which they were now spending in drink, which their glittering bloodshot eyes and boisterous talk sufficiently testified.

Nina and Captain George were greatly stared at, but no insulting remarks were made, for the Englishman was in the uniform of a rebel cavalry officer, and looked around him on the men standing about with an expression which seemed to say, "This girl is under my protection—so insult her at your peril."

Riding round to the back of the inn, George leading the way, they passed through an open gate, with a paddock, on the side of which was a long shed with a manger, where were tied up several horses. Rightly conjecturing this to be the stable, he dismounted, and having assisted Nina to do likewise, he tied up the horses, and gave them a feed from a sack of Indian corn which stood in one corner.

Then he looked round for the landlord or some of the men. Espying a negro standing at the back door engaged in plucking a fowl, he called to him—

"Hi, you Sambo, where's the landlord?"

"De boss is in de bar, massa."

"Well, just put down that fowl, and go and tell the boss a gentleman wants him."

The landlord soon appeared in his shirt sleeves from the bar, where he had been compounding sundry drinks, smashes, and juleps for the crowd of rowdies who thronged the place.

"Got any accommodation?"

"Reckon I hev; best board and private room. Only one in the house, and the gentleman raisin' this 'ere battalion hev engaged that."

"Lupus Rock?" inquired Captain George.

"Yes, sirree; you're right this time—seem to know. Guess you're a secesh officer by the cut of yer ——"

"Yes. Well, Mr. Rock's room must do. I know him, and have ridden here to meet him. Just show me and this young woman up into the private room, will you?"

The "boss" hesitated for a moment, but thinking from George's confident manner that all was right, he obeyed.

George ordered busk and wine, and while this was being brought he looked around. The house was only of one story, and immediately above them were the bare slanting shingles of the roof. One window faced the front, while the other commanded a view of the back. The front window was completely taken up by the great placard, so that the room was entirely lighted up by the back.

After hastily partaking of some corn cake and cold meat, George made up his mind to descend and wait for Lupus outside.

"Look here, Nina. I am going out to wait for this fellow. So you'd best lock the door when I am gone, and let no one in without asking who and what they are."

Captain George from the back window, had noticed a large summer-house at the end of the paddock, distant about eighty yards.

"Here, landlord," he said, going into the bar, "just send me a 'stone-fence' and some cigars out to the summer-house at the bottom of the paddock, and when Mr. Rock comes, tell him a gentleman's awaiting him there. My friend the young woman has locked herself in upstairs. I see you have got rather a rowdy lot about. Just see no one attempts to go into the room. If any man is fool enough or drunk enough, it'll be bad for him."

And George significantly tapped the revolver he wore in his belt.

" Right you are, cap'n. Guess you know yer way about,' said the landlord, who was impressed by the cool determined manner of our friend. " No one will interfere with yer lady. I'll send Major Rock to ye as soon as he comes ; the agent's here now—do you want him ?"

" No, my business is with Mr. Rock."

The "stone-fence" and the cigars were duly brought, and George threw himself at full length on the rude bench and commenced alternately smoking and sipping, all the while, however, keeping his eye on the gate into the paddock and the window of the room where he had left Nina. The room was so dark, however, from the big placard in front, that he could not see her, although, of course, as the evening sun shone on the summer-house, she could see him.

He had not lighted his cigar five minutes when a horseman rode into the paddock, dismounted, and tied up his horse in the stable. He at once recognised Lupus Rock, and rising, walked at once towards him.

But Lupus turned, and walked quickly through the back entrance into the bar, where his appearance was enthusiastically welcomed, to judge by the shouts and din which arose.

## CHAPTER XV.

### GEORGE BUYS A PRETTY SLAVE.

CAPTAIN GEORGE carefully examined his revolver, and finding all right, replaced it in his belt.

"I am not afraid of the fellow," he thought, " but I mean to be on my guard. He's a desperate villain, and when he finds I know so much, he will be glad of the chance of putting me out of the way, if he can do so safely."

Thus thinking, he was about to follow him to the house, when the window was suddenly thrown open.

Nina's quick eyes had seen the arrival of Lupus Rock. She had seen Captain George look to his pistol, and had also, with woman's quick perception, observed something else. She knew, from the care with which the Englishman examined his pistol, that he anticipated danger.

"Quick!" she cried, through the open window, "look in his holster—he has left his revolver!"

Captain George at once caught her meaning, and was quickly by the side of Lupus's horse.

He drew out the revolver—a large six-shot Colt—and producing a sharp instrument he carried for the purpose, carefully and quickly picked out the conical bullets one by one, and held them in his hand. Then he shook the powder from each chamber, and again carefully replaced the bullets. This done, he walked leisurely back to the summer-house, resolved to await him there.

He had not been seated more than a minute, when Lupus strode hastily from the house and into the stable.

George, although he could not see, guessed that he had gone for his revolver. Then Lupus walked quickly towards the summer-house.

There was an angry scowl on his brow.

"Who the devil is this that has taken possession of the room I ordered?" were his thoughts. "It's like his d——d impudence, whoever it is?"

A row of apple trees, the branches of which swept the ground, prevented him seeing into the summer-house till he arrived on the threshold.

He glanced angrily around, and seeing Captain George, started in surprise—for he had last seen him in the camp on foot, and talking to Nina.

He nodded superciliously, and said at once—

"The landlord told me that some one had taken possession of my room. Is it you, sir?"

"Yes," replied the Englishman, deliberately, and lighting a fresh cigar.

"May I ask you on what grounds you have taken such a liberty? I know very little of you—certainly not enough for you so far to presume."

"Yes, that is quite true; you know very little of me, but you shall know more presently—just sit down."

"What the h—l do you mean?" shouted Lupus, fu-riously—"are you drunk? By G—d! I will order my fellows to kick you out of the place."

"Will you? There will be a free fight then before they do it. You don't think I should be such a fool as to come here and say what I mean to say alone. I rather fancy the few fellows with me of Gerald Leigh's regiment will make short work of you and your drunken rowdies."

This pricked Lupus Rock a little, for he fully believed it. Judging from himself, he thought it extremely un-likely the Englishman would be so cool and defiant unless he were well supported.

"Well, sir, what is it you have to say? I have business to attend to, and am in a hurry."

"So much the worse for you; when you hear what I have to say, you will not be in quite such a hurry—sit down."

Lupus, with a muttered oath, took a seat. As he did so, George saw him feel in the breast pocket of his coat for his revolver. There was something in the English-man's manner which Lupus by no means liked—he could not imagine what he wanted with him, though he felt rather than thought that this was not an affair from which he could escape by bullying.

Captain George threw his cigar away. "Confounded bad weeds these—how are yours? Just hand me one."

This was too much; there was a provoking smile on the other's face which drove Lupus frantic with rage.

"D—n!" he shouted furiously. "Did you send for me to beg a cigar? If so, you are mistaken. I have had enough of this folly. Now, if you have anything to say, speak."

"As you please, my dear fellow," was the quiet reply of the Englishman, who at the same time raised his glass to his lips, and sipped the "stone-fence."

"Capital liquor this! The landlord knows how to brew! let me offer you some."

Then raising his voice, he shouted to a negro that he saw at the back door—

'Here, boy, bring another glass, and some more 'stone-fence.' You'd better take a little to steady your nerves, sir. You'll want it by the time I've done with you."

Lupus tried to pull out his revolver and make deadly use of it, but the other's eye was upon him, and Lupus saw that George, having his revolver in his belt, would be able to fire first.

The liquor and another glass were brought. George politely poured out a glass for Lupus, and pushed it over to him.

"Now, suppose you tell me your business," said the latter.

"Certainly. My business is to buy some slaves of you."

"Indeed!" sneered Lupus; "is it your ambition to become a slave owner—is that all?" Lupus asked with apparent carelessness, but with secret misgiving.

"That is all."

"And supposing I refuse."

"You will not refuse—you dare not."

Lupus grew gradually paler and paler.

"I dare not? I don't understand you."

"Listen, and I will explain. What price do you put upon the slaves you purchased from Mr. Edward St. Casse?"

At these words Lupus turned livid with passion.

"He knows—he knows—curse him! he knows!"

Then he replied, "I am not a slave dealer."

"No matter; I wish to buy those slaves, and you shall sell them to me."

"It's a lie—you cannot force me to sell property."

"But I will force you. I know you, Lupus Rock; you would not sell those slaves if you could help it—*especially one.* But you would rather sell them than be hanged, and that is your alternative."

"Hanged!"

"Yes; hanged! or shot, at my option.'

"You lie!" said Lupus, savagely. "I defy you."

"Name a price," said Captain George.

"I'll see you in hell first!"

"You refuse?"

" Yes, d—n you !"

" What an obstinate fellow it is," said George, smiling in affected pity ; " I wish my friend Malpas Thong were here, perhaps he could bring you to reason."

At the name of Malpas Thong, Lupus started to his feet—his face was hideously white, and for a moment he glanced around him in terror.

" Malpas Thong !" he faltered—" Malpas Thong—he is——"

" Not dead, I hope. Such a loss he would be to society. I hope nothing has happened to him. If he were to get shot, for instance."

" What the devil are you talking about ? What do I care or know about Malpas Thong ?"

" Or drowned," continued George, not heeding him. " The Rappahannock is a deep river; very deep at places; if he were to fall in he would most likely be drowned."

Then he paused, and looked smilingly in the dark face of Lupus, which was now bathed in a cold sweat.

Lupus took a big drink of " stone-fence," then shouted for brandy.

" Well," said Captain George, after a short pause, " will you sell me the slaves ?"

" Look here, Mr. Englishman," said Lupus, " you have got hold of some d——d lie or other about me, and think you're going to frighten me. But you're just wrong this time."

" You wont ?"

" I'll see you d——d first."

" Well, my friend, keep your temper—don't excite yourself, and I will tell you a little anecdote. Here comes your brandy, take a good drink. You'll want all the Dutch courage you can muster."

Lupus did take a stiff dose, and dashing down the glass violently on the table, prepared to listen.

" About a month ago," commenced Captain George, " I had business on the Rappahannock. The said business brought me in the neighbourhood of the Yancey estate, which I believe is now your property, my friend"——

" What of it?—Go on."

" Well, this business of mine brought me frequently on the river. I was stopping for a few days at a log hut some two miles above the Yancey estate, and in the furtherance of my plans I hired a boat for the use of myself and friend. One use for this boat was principally in the evening and by night. One evening I was out in the boat on this business. You don't feel curious to know the nature of it, Mr. Rock, do you? because if you do, I have no objection to tell you."

" No, not I. Some d——d smuggling game or another, I suppose."

Lupus Rock had a presentiment which amounted almost to certainty of what was coming. Then he longed to feel for his revolver ; but he felt that the eyes of the Englishman never left him for an instant. He, however, changed his position, and placed himself right up in the corner of the summer-house, and leaned against the stakes of which it was built. He was now some feet further from his unwelcome companion, and being comparatively in the shade, he thought he stood a better chance.

" Well, as I was saying, on the evening in question I had occasion to go down the river and pass the Yancey estate, which, as you know, lies along the Northern bank. Now, curiously enough, as it turned out, I had also occasion to fasten up my boat and land on this estate of Yancey——"

" Like your cursed impudence trespassing on my property. Well for you my overseer did not catch you."

" Yes, exactly ; so I thought myself, and to avoid such a contingency, which was quite foreign to my views, I crept along under the shelter of trees by the bank, till I came to a hut about fifty or sixty yards from the river. Now, if I had gone along by the bank I must have been seen by any person looking out from the hut, as the ground was there clear. I did not think it likely there would be any one in the hut, but, as I am remarkable for caution, I did not choose to risk it, so I made a detour round by the back of the hut. Now, strange to say, the hut, although no one lived there, *was* occupied. Two men were sitting there at a table, on which were bottles, glasses, and a box of cigars. By the way, just pass me a light, they are by you. Talking of cigars always makes me want to smoke. I am a great smoker—are you, Mr. Rock?"

"Go on with what you are saying. I am deeply interested," said Lupus, in a voice which now trembled with fear and rage.

George could see his eyes glare like those of a wild beast in the deepening twilight.

"There was a window in this hut, and to this window I cautiously crept, placing myself in such a position as to be able to see everything that passed. Papers were produced, Mr. Rock, and liquor was drunk in abundance. Presently one of the two men, having probably drunk too much, fell into a deep sleep.—— Pass the brandy, please, Mr. Rock. Talking always makes my throat dry."

George mixed himself a glass, never, however, taking his eyes off Lupus Rock, as he sat smoking in the corner, on the opposite side of the table.

"Now comes the exciting part of my narrative, Mr. Rock. It is well worthy of your attention. The man who was awake, first made himself certain that his companion was in so deep a sleep that nothing could rouse him. Then he proceeded to rifle the sleeper's pockets. Sharp practice, Mr. Rock, was it not? Shall I go on, or will you sell me the slaves?"

"Go on, sir—go on. You are playing a desperate game, but you have not won yet."

"I have the cards in my hands, however, my friend, as you well know. Well, as you wish me to go on; having rifled the sleeper of his papers, the other man, muttering something to himself which I could not quite catch, produced a bag, containing, as I guessed by the chink, silver dollars or half-dollars. This bag he tied round the sleeper's neck, and then he dragged him from the chair and out through the door of the hut."

George paused here to watch the effect on Lupus Rock. He could see his eyes glaring in the dark corner of the summer-house, and knew that now the wolf was indeed brought to bay.

He was careful never to remove his eyes, and kept his hand beneath the table on his revolver. He was by no means sure that Lupus did not carry another pistol besides the one whose charge he had drawn.

" The rest is soon told. The *murderer*—for such he was, Mr. Rock—dragged his sleeping friend down the sloping bank, and plunged him in. The body sank at once. I was struck with horror, but could render no aid to the wretched sleeper. The deed was done before I could imagine what was about to happen. The murdered man's name, Mr. Rock, was Malpas Thong. The murderer was Lupus Rock !"

There was a deep silence after these last words of Captain George. He could see the glaring eyes and hear the hard breathing of the man in the corner.

" Now will you comply with my demands ?" asked the Englishman, still calmly, but with every faculty strained to the utmost, for he could see the right hand of Lupus Rock slowly stealing upwards to the breast pocket of his coat.

" Hands down, Mr. Rock, if you please. I am not asleep if Malpas Thong was."

At that moment a rustling of the branches of one of the apple trees without drew the Englishman's attention. For one moment he turned his head, but saw nothing. When he looked back, Lupus Rock sat apparently as before, with one hand on the other under the table ; but in that moment of time he had drawn his revolver, and was now feeling the caps and bullets to make sure all was right. He felt the caps and the conical points of the bullets.

All right ! His eyes gleamed more savagely than ever, and his breath came rapidly. George could hear his deep pantings and the grinding of his teeth.

" Well, Mr. Rock, I have told my tale. Have you any question to ask ?"

" Yes—one."

" What is it ?"

" Who was with you?"

" No one."

" In the boat?"

" No one."

" At the hut?"

" No one."

" You, then, were the sole witness of this affair according to your account?"

" Yes."

Lupus thought thus : " It was, then, this Englishman who saw what happened, and not Nina. If he speaks truth, he must have told her. If she spoke the truth when she demanded her free papers, it must have been she who told him. But I am inclined to believe that it was he—not she. He instructed her what to do. It is my belief he was slinking about the plantation after her. He is sweet on her, and having seen what he saw he put her up to this. Then it is only him whom I need fear."

" And there was no witness with you when you saw this. How could you prove your words?"

" The proof lies at the bottom of the Rappahannock. The bag of dollars was heavy, and the handkerchief a stout one. The body would only float away when the head came off, and there has not yet been time for that."

Again Captain George heard a rustling in the branches.

Fearing treachery, he hastily looked round, and saw Nina the *vivandière* standing at scarcely a dozen paces distance.

He saw that she held a gun or rifle in her hand.

That momentary look round gave Lupus Rock his chance.

Quick as lightning he presented his revolver at the Englishman's head.

Crack !

The cap snapped, and Captain George sat unmoved before him.

Crack ! crack !

" Fire away, my friend," said Captain George, coolly. " It pleases you and doesn't hurt me. I've taken the trouble to draw the charge."

This bit of bravado was unfortunate.

Lupus, with a furious oath, threw down the pistol, and, quick as thought, produced another and smaller one.

Captain George, aware of the danger, leaped on one side, and at the same moment seized the heavy bottle in which was the brandy.

Lupus fired, and the bullet grazed his cheek. He made a furious blow with the decanter, but missed.

Again Lupus Rock's pistol covered him, his finger was on the trigger; when suddenly a sharp report is heard outside; and, with a cry of pain, Lupus let fall the pistol from his hand.

At the same instant Captain George leaped on the table, and dealt him a desperate blow with the decanter. Had it taken full effect, it must have smashed his skull, but striking obliquely it merely cut a deep gash across the forehead and glanced off. He fell to the ground, the blood streaming both from this gash and from his right fore-arm.

Then George looked around to see whence came this timely shot, and perceived Nina standing some few paces distant, with a small rifle, still smoking, in her hands.

Lupus Rock, who was not stunned, staggered to his feet and with his left hand felt for his pistol, which lay on the table.

He was half blinded with blood from the cut on his forehead, so that George, who had now drawn his revolver, might easily have shot him.

He contented himself, however, by giving Lupus a left-hander full in the face, which again sent him staggering back in the corner.

"You murdering cur!" cried Captain George, "what have you to say that I should not blow your brains out?"

Lupus sullenly took out his handkerchief with his left hand, first wiped the blood from his face, then attempted to bind up his right wrist, from which a stream of dark blood flowed.

"It is your turn now," he said, savagely; "but do not fear, mine will come."

"Yes, I know it—on the gallows," was the scornful reply.

MORTAL STRUGGLE BETWEEN CAPTAIN GEORGE AND LUPAS ROCK.

P. 160.

Now, the landlord of the place, followed by half-a-dozen rowdies and several negroes, came running up, having heard the pistol-shot.

"Snakes! what's up?" cried the worthy proprietor; "a fight, a free fight. Darned if it ain't Mr. Rock and the stranger."

"Seize him!" cried Lupus, seeing some of his new raised men. "Seize him and hang him! He attempted to murder me. He's a cursed Britisher!"

"Lynch him! string him up to an apple tree. At him, boys; here's a d——d Britisher been muzzling Major Rock."

Several advanced towards Captain George, armed with knives and slug shot, for they could not raise a revolver among them.

"Stand back! Listen to me. The first that attempts to lay a hand on me is a dead man."

George's pistol was raised, and pointed full at the foremost of the rowdies.

This gave him time to look around, and he discerned a tall man in the uniform of an officer approaching from the house.

"Lupus Rock," he said, without, however, turning his head or lowering his revolver, "your fate is in your own hands. Say this was a free fight—a fair fight, or by G—d I will arrest you for murder!"

The crowd around the summer-house increased each minute, and the Englishman saw several quiet-looking men, and one or two officers in uniform.

"Is the mayor of this town present, or the town marshal?"

"I am the town-marshal; by name, Jabez Jones. Here I am if I'm wanted."

The speaker pushed through the crowd to the front.

"I am an officer in the Confederate service," said Captain George, "a lieutenant in the Second Virginia Cavalry. Stand forth, Lupus Rock."

Lupus obeyed, he scarcely knew why.

"Mr. Town-Marshal, I charge you to arrest that man for ——"

11

" *Murder !*" Captain George was about to, say, but
Lupus, seeing the turn affairs had taken, now spoke,
sullenly and doggedly, but hastily ; knowing well that if
once the Englishman accused him of this crime, there
would be no retreat.

"Stop !" said Lupus, "it was a free fight—a fair
fight, and I got the worst."

" Ah, well, as the gentleman is content to acknowledge
it was a fair fight, we shall not trouble you, Mr. Town-
Marshal. Now, one of you fellows, just get a surgeon.
My friend here, and I, have had a slight quarrel, and
he's slightly wounded. And landlord, send some more
brandy ; this got spilled in the mess. Cigars, too, a light,
and pens, ink, and paper. By the by, gentlemen, I am
afraid we disturbed you, brought you away from your
liquor at the bar. Landlord, here's a twenty dollar bill ;
let these good fellows drink it out."

" Hurrah ! — bravo, Capt'n ! — Rally for the Britisher," was now the cry, and in half a minute the mob
of rowdies who just now wanted to Lynch him, were
drinking his health at the bar.

The landlord was the last to retire, which he did after
a puzzled look at the two.

The boy came with an oil-lamp, some sheets of paper,
and pen and ink.

Nina was unnoticed in the confusion, and when she
saw matters likely to end satisfactorily, she made her
way back to the house, regained the room, and locked
the door. A feeling of fear for the safety of the
Englishman had possessed her from the moment she saw
them seated together in the arbour ; so finding a small-
bore rifle, with bullets, caps, and powder, in one corner
of the room, she loaded it, and silently made her way
down stairs, and gained a position behind one of the
apple trees, where she could see and hear all that passed.

This was the history of Nina's unexpected and opportune aid to her friend.

Captain George paid not the slightest attention to the
wounded man's groans of pain. He was himself in a
savage temper, for the tingling of his cheek where the

bullet had grazed it, reminded him how narrow had been his escape.

" Aye, groan away, you cur," he said. " If you had your rights, you would be past all groaning. Now will you do what I demand ? Yes or no ? If you refuse, it's the toss up of a cent whether I pistol you myself, or hand you over to the town-marshal. *Will you sell those slaves ?*"

" Yes—yes ; d——n you. You've won this time, but my name is not Lupus Rock if I don't ——"

" Silence with your threats and curses, or I'll ram them down your throat with the butt-end of my pistol."

George now commenced carefully drawing up a deed of sale. It set forth in very few words that Lupus Rock had sold to him, Captain George, all the slaves, he, Lupus, had purchased of Mr. Edward St. Casse.

It was so worded as to leave no possible loophole ; and Lupus Rock, when the Englishman read it over to him, ground his teeth with impotent rage.

" And now the price. What price do you put on them ?"

" Thirteen slaves, male and female," said Lupus, sullenly—" worth at least five hundred dollars apiece."

" Five hundred dollars apiece," said Captain George, quickly filling up the blank he had left—" that makes six thousand five hundred dollars. So far so good. Now then, to make assurance doubly sure, I will add a little memorandum—codicil I will call it."

He then wrote a few more lines, and when finished, slowly read them out to Lupus Rock.

" And whereas I, Lupus Rock, have reason to believe that by some means a lady named Miss Coralie Andrée St. Casse is not free according to the strict laws of the Confederate States, and that by reason of my purchase of Mr. Edward St. Casse, the said lady is now, by the law of the Confederate States, my sole and absolute property, I hereby relinquish all claim upon the said Miss St. Casse utterly and for ever, in consideration of a sum of one thousand dollars over and above the six thousand five hundred dollars aforesaid.

" Signed     " Lupus Rock."

While Captain George was writing this the surgeon arrived, and dressed Lupus Rock's wound.

Captain George then produced a roll of English bank notes, counted out the value of seven thousand five hundred dollars, and obtained Mr. Rock's signature.

The surgeon having also affixed his signature as witness, the Englishman carefully folded up the papers and placed them in his pocket.

## CHAPTER XVI.

### A FORCED CONVOY.

" I suppose, sir," said Captain George to the surgeon, " the slight wound my friend received in our little quarrel need not prevent his riding ?"

" It would be well to keep the arm as quiet as possible, otherwise inflammation and fever might intervene."

" Ah !—that must be guarded against as far as possible. I should be inconsolable if I thought I were instrumental in increasing this gentleman's pain—to say nothing of endangering his valuable life. Unfortunately it is absolutely necessary that the gentleman should ride with me a short distance to-night."

" I am going to remain here to-night," said Lupus, in surprise and anger.

" Possibly, my good friend, but you will first ride a short distance with me."

" Hell and fury ! do you think I am a slave, to be thus ordered ?" exclaimed Lupus, furiously.

" Practically, my dear sir, on this particular occasion, you are a slave—my slave, I may say, for the next hour or so."

He spoke in the most provokingly gentle and urbane manner, which nearly drove Lupus Rock frantic with impotent rage. If ever a man's eyes looked murder, those of the defeated villain did as he glared on his victor.

The surgeon, who was a quiet, elderly gentleman from one of the Western States, was lost in wonder at this strange scene. There had been evidently a desperate fight, and yet now he saw one of the combatants quietly handing over a large sum of money, and talking with the most perfect good-humour. He was almost inclined to believe at one time that the pistol-shot was an accident, and that there had been no fight, but the gash cut by the decanter negatived such an idea; so altogether, the man of the knife took his leave in a state of utter bewilderment.

" Landlord," he said, as he passed out at the bar, " guess you've got a couple of lunatics down there?"

" Guess I can't quite make it out myself," said that worthy. " Shouldn't wonder if the fight wasn't about the gal upstairs."

" Oh! there's a girl in the case? That's enough to account for any amount of lunacy."

" Now look here, Mr. Lupus Rock," said Captain George. " I never do things by halves. I've got these papers, and, by Jupiter! I mean to keep them. We've played our game out—I've trumped your last card and won; I should be a fool to give you another chance. Now, I mean what I say—you must ride with me half way to the camp—as far as the cross roads, seven miles from this, at least. It's no good hesitating or turning sulky, because you must and shall do it; and if I could make you do what you have done, I can make you do more."

There was no gainsaying this.

" How do I know you don't intend to murder me?"

" My dear sir, you don't know at all; perhaps I do intend to murder you. That, however, is my business. What you *do* know is that you have got to come with me as far as the cross roads."

The matchless coolness with which this was said quite took Lupus Rock's breath away. He well knew why the Englishman insisted on his accompanying him a part of the road. He saw he had his match, and that for the present all was lost. However, he asked—

" For what object am I to accompany you ?"

" My good Mr. Rock, I will tell you. I am almost a stranger in these parts ; you are well known. I saw, when I first came here, a crowd of as ruffianly rowdies and blacklegs as ever cursed and drank at the bar ; they are your recruits, I believe. Allow me to congratulate you—you are well matched. Well, you must know it struck me that if I were to ride on and leave you here, you might get talking matters over with your amiable friends. They might think you ill-used—you would gladly pay ten times the seven thousand five hundred dollars if you could regain those papers I now have, and also be assured that I should trouble you no further. A very simple thing. Some of your friends, out of pure love for you, might be tempted to ride after me. They might overtake me, argue the point, and finally we might quarrel—who knows ? When gentlemen quarrel, they sometimes fight ; and when they fight they sometimes kill each other. I might be killed, than which nothing in the world could be to you more pleasing. Now you understand why you are to accompany me. In the first place, I will see you do not exchange a word with any soul as we ride away from this together ; and, in the second place, supposing you could elude my vigilance, and by any means—say by dropping a note, communicate your wishes—on the very first signs of an attack I should open the ball by blowing your brains out. So now you see I know you, and you may as well accept your fate quietly."

Captain George now shouted for the landlord. When that worthy arrived, he paid the reckoning, and said—

" Have the horses brought round here—mine, Mr. Rock's, and the lady's. Just tell her I am ready to start.'

" What lady ?" asked Lupus Rock, a vague suspicion that it was Coralie herself flashing across his mind.

" What is that to you ? Don't ask questions, but speak when you are spoken to." He seemed determined to make him feel his utter helplessness, and drink to the dregs the bitter cup of disgraceful defeat.

Lupus felt it was useless resisting; he saw that, for the present at least, he had got his master.

Now Lupus had not seen Nina at all—did not know it was she who had shot him through the arm, but imagined that his antagonist had himself fired with his left hand.

This was quite natural, for Nina's bullet and George's blow with the decanter took effect within less than a second of each other, and the latter was quite sufficient to confuse any ordinary mortal's brains.

When, therefore, two negro boys appeared, leading the three horses, and Nina with a lantern, his rage, shame, and mortification were bitter indeed.

Nina glanced at him contemptuously for one moment, and then turned to Captain George.

" Is he coming with us ?" she asked.

" Yes, part of the way ; it is necessary."

With this she seemed perfectly satisfied, and mounted her horse.

Captain George carefully reloaded his own revolver, and also the one he had dashed from the hands of Lupus Rock.

" Mount !" he said, laconically.

Then he also mounted, and, handing one revolver to Nina, said—" Take this pistol. If that man attempts to escape, or if you see anything suspicious in his behaviour which may possibly escape me, shoot him. It is necessary for our safety, or rather for my safety."

" I will shoot him like a dog," she replied.

And Lupus noted by the lantern light that her eyes gleamed in a manner which convinced him she meant it.

" Now then we are ready. Nina, you lead the way, he shall ride next, and I will follow behind him. And now, Mr. Rock, just listen to my words. If you attempt to communicate with any of your vagabond rowdy friends, you die. That is all."

They passed out, and Lupus did not attempt to infringe this order. For the time he was utterly subdued. Neither force nor cunning could avail him now.

He fully realized that the Englishman was wide awake, and would infallibly keep his word. So he was forced to ride by within half a dozen yards of men who would have taken his enemy's life for fifty dollars, and yet he dared make no sign.

As soon as they were in the street, Captain George brought his horse up on one side, while Nina took up her post on the other.

" Come, let us push on."

They struck into a canter, and rode on at a steady pace for some seven miles, when, at a word from Captain George, they halted at the cross roads.

" Now, Mr. Lupus Rock, you may ride back. You're bound to be hanged some day, you white-livered, cowardly scoundrel that you are ! But if you wish particularly to hurry that day, just cross my path again."

So without a word the baffled Lupus turned his horse's head, dug the spurs in, and galloped back at headlong speed.

The moon was now shining brightly, and Captain George, looking in the beautiful face of his companion, took her hand.

" Nina," he said, " I believe you saved my life. How shall I repay you ?"

He pressed her hand warmly as he spoke.

" I am repaid," she murmured ; " thank God you are safe. That man is terrible ; but it was glorious the way in which we beat him."

"As you say, glorious, Nina. May equal success attend everything we undertake in common."

Then they struck into a gallop, and in less than an hour their steaming horses stood in front of the Englishman's tent. It was about nine o'clock—the night clear and beautiful.

" Now, Nina," he said, " you must occupy my tent again to-night. To-morrow we must get you proper quarters, if you remain in the camp, which, by the way, is no fit place for a young girl. I must find Gerald, and give him an account of our adventure and its successful issue. A very nice little scheme this of Lupus Rock's— and very cleverly demolished; eh, Nina ? Good night, my brave girl, and pleasant dreams."

" Good night, sir."
" Don't dream of Lupus Rock."
" No."
" Nor of me."
" I can't promise."
Then she retired into the tent.  Captain George
mounted his horse, and, leading the other by the bridle,
walked slowly towards the cavalry quarters.

" A brave, noble girl," he thought; " I believe she
saved my life by that shot of hers.  A pity she is not a
lady.  Ah, well, it's no use talking."
Whatever is is right ; so say some philosophers.

CHAPTER XVII.

A STRANGE PRESENT TO DARCY LEIGH.

THE fears of Stella Gayle for her father's safety were by
no means groundless.  It was well known to the rebel
authorities that many Yankee spies were in the South,
and that valuable information had been furnished to the
enemy.

Great exasperation was felt on the point, and it was
resolved to make a summary example of the first spy
they caught.

Circumstances were strongly against Webster Gayle.
Previous to his capture he had been proved to be in
communication with men in Richmond suspected of being
Yankees at heart—traitors to the cause they pretended
to serve.

He was taken suspiciously prowling about the lines, as
if taking accurate notice of the strong and weak points
of the position.

Then again the brief glance which the officer who
captured him bestowed on the papers, led to the conclusion that a careful examination of them would convict
the prisoner of being a spy by indisputable evidence.

The papers were addressed to Yankee generals, and

members of the government. Great blame was bestowed
on the officer who not only allowed his prisoner to escape
in the confusion, but also to regain his papers.

It was generally known, however, that the papers had
been taken from him by Miss St. Casse, and it was supposed she still had them, and would, on the forthcoming
trial, produce them.

At eleven o'clock on the morning of the 23rd of July,
the day but one after the battle, Webster Gayle was
taken, guarded by two soldiers, to the large tent where
he was to be tried for his life.

Of course the members of the court-martial were all
military men, and had but little time to waste. The proceeding was likely to be summary enough, and it was
confidently predicted that the accused would be condemned and shot before sundown.

Darcy Leigh was sufficiently recovered to be able to
walk with assistance, and, leaning on his brother Gerald's
arm, walked through the camp towards the tent where
the trial was to be held.

Stella and Angela Gayle were in attendance on their
father, and accompanied him even when under the
guard of a file of soldiers. With fixed arms he was
marched before the court.

Angela wore in her sweet face a look of helpless
terror quite pitiful. Even the rough soldiers were
softened as they looked in her pale face and tearful eyes.

Stella also was very pale, but there was a look of
confidence on her features which her gentle sister wanted.
Angela could only weep, and gaze helplessly around.
Stella, through the whole of that terrible passage of the
camp to the head-quarters tent, which was right at the
other end, did not cease to encourage and buoy up her
father's spirit by every means in her power.

Bands of soldiers of all regiments lined the road to
see the Yankee spy led to trial. Some few gave vent to
hisses and hooting, but on these occasions Stella stopped,
and with her proud glance seemed to ask, "What! are
you men? Would you condemn an accused before
trial?"

The feeling of hatred for the supposed Yankee spy was soon changed for one of pity and admiration of those two fair girls, who did not desert their father in his desperate danger, but walked bravely by his side.  Stella, with head erect, and defiant look ; Angela, with bowed down face, and in tears.

More than once remarks were made and hopes expressed to the effect that, for the girls' sakes, the Yankee would not be shot.  Pity for them counterbalanced hatred of the supposed spy.

When the file of soldiers with their prisoner arrived at the tent where the dreadful issue was to be tried, the sisters were perforce separated from their father.  He was placed at the foot of the table round which his judges were to sit, while they had to remain outside a light barrier, which had been erected to separate the few privileged spectators from the witnesses, the officers, the prisoner, and guard.

Angela and Stella were the first of the spectators, and as the officers composing the court-martial had not yet taken their seats, the silence and desolation of the great tent had a dreadful chilling effect on their feelings.  The files of soldiers stood motionless and silent by the side of their prisoner.  Presently an orderly sergeant came from behind a screen at the back of the tent, and laid on the table, opposite each chair, pens and paper.  Opposite the chair at the head of the table he also placed a large sheet with the rebel government arms at the head, and a blank space with a row of wafers at the bottom.

On this sheet the verdict was to be recorded, and, if adverse to the prisoner, the sentence.  Opposite the red wafers each officer composing the court would sign his name, and if, as every one believed, the sentence were death, the prisoner would be immediately condemned and marched to execution.

Captain George sought Coralie St. Casse the first thing in the morning, and gave her the welcome intelligence that he had confronted Lupus Rock, beaten him at his own weapons, and wrung from him a total abnegation of his nefarious claims.

"Here," said Captain George, producing the deed he had compelled Lupus to sign, "is the paper by which he has sold to me all the slaves he purchased of Edward St. Casse, your cousin, and yourself specially mentioned. So that now, young lady, in consideration of a sum of money paid, you are my absolute property. I really hardly know what to do with my purchase. I feel like the man to whom the Eastern Emperor sent the 'white elephant.' I am fully conscious of the honour of my proprietorship, but don't know what to do with my 'white elephant.'"

"It's like your impudence, sir, to compare me to a white elephant, I'm sure. But seriously, what money did you pay him, this Mr. Rock?"

"For the thirteen slaves I paid six thousand five hundred dollars—an exorbitant price, of course, but I did not think it worth haggling about, as so much more was at stake. Then in addition, I paid a sum of a thousand dollars, and made him sign a sort of codicil, in which he entirely and for ever gave up all claim and interest in you, real or fancied."

"You have paid this sum of money?"

"Yes, undoubtedly. I thought it best. I hope I did not do wrong?"

"Heavens! no. How can I ever show my gratitude?"

"You have Nina to thank as much as me."

"Nina—dear Nina—she is a good loving girl. I will see that she is provided for as long as I live, and afterwards."

"Afterwards?" said Captain George, smiling, "why, I believe you. I have understood that you are a year younger than she, and you talk as if you were old, and about to leave this bright world first."

"Ah, well—there's no saying—life is uncertain ; and I sometimes think—— No matter. Do you require this money at once, sir, or can you wait without inconvenience until I go to Richmond—to-morrow or the next day? You can, if you please, accompany me. What more fitting than that a master should go with his slave— for am I not your property?"

She spoke jestingly, and her dark eyes sparkled with pleasure. A great load had been taken from her mind, for her proud spirit had been bitterly wounded by the intelligence that Lupus Rock would attempt to claim her as his slave. With Captain George it was different; he was a friend of Gerald and Darcy, and she had heard so much of him from them that she knew him to be an honourable gentleman.

"By Jove !" said the Englishman, suddenly, "there go Gerald and Darcy—a splendid idea—a capital idea ! I know what I will do, Miss St. Casse."

" What ?"

" I will get rid of my ' white elephant.' "

" How ?"

" I will make you a present to Darcy Leigh."

A deep blush suffused Coralie's face at these words— a blush that spoke much.

" As you please," she said, laughing, and turning her head away—" but please don't do it in my presence ; it would be too embarrassing."

" No, not in your presence—I will call him aside, and inform him of my purchase and how I intend to dispose of it. Come, let us overtake them."

" They quickened their pace, and George shouting to the two brothers, they stopped and waited.

Gerald shook Coralie warmly by the hand, and Darcy also greeted her, though in a somewhat embarrassed manner ; for he could tell by her looks and those of Captain George that there was something between them, and that it related to himself.

" Well, and how are you, Darcy ?—is your wound painful ?" she asked anxiously, noticing how haggard and pale he looked.

" No ; it is more weakness than anything now—I shall be perfectly right in a day or two. And you—how are you, after your adventures and escape from the Philistines ?"

" Philistines, indeed," said Coralie. " I wonder how poor Squails feels, after having lost his prisoner, and his boasted thousand-guinea horse to boot."

"Do tell us your adventure in full," said Darcy; "I have merely heard a vague account from Gerald, and he is an abominable story-teller; his memory is so atrocious, he forgets half."

"Thank you, Darcy," said Gerald. "My memory is bad, but not so utterly feeble as yours. I think I can mention one instance unparalleled for forgetfulness in all history."

There was a quiet smile on Gerald's face, which caused Coralie to ask—

"Oh, do tell us, Gerald."

"Yes, Gerald, out with it," said George, who, however, well knew what was coming.

So did Darcy, for he coloured up and said—

"What nonsense! let us hurry on and get to the tent."

"Nonsense or not, let us hear it, Gerald."

"Aye, Gerald, tell us," said the Englishman.

"Well, it is this," said Gerald, disregarding all Darcy's attempts to stop him. "My brother was carried in from the battle-field, his head bound up with a lady's cambric handkerchief and part of a lady's scarf. He declares he does not know how they came into his possession, although Jupiter and Darby Kelly both say they took them from his inside breast pocket—right over the heart, is it not, Darcy?"

"A lady's handkerchief!" said Coralie, glancing inquiringly at Darcy, who, however, coloured up, and did not answer.

"A lady's handkerchief!" she repeated, turning to Gerald.

"Yes, a lady's handkerchief, and that lady Miss Stella Gayle. He actually has the effrontery to declare he does not know how he came by it. Talk about my memory after that."

Coralie now coloured up in turn, and a close observer might have noted a flash, certainly not of pleasure, in her dark eyes.

"And he actually pretends he does not know how it

came into his pocket?" said Coralie, forcing a laugh to hide her annoyance.

"Nor do I," said Darcy, hastily; "I have not the most remote idea."

Coralie looked at him first in surprise, and then, seeing he spoke seriously, with undisguised anger, almost contempt; she lowered her eyes, and with a heightened colour passed ahead, motioning Gerald to join her.

Darcy was now left behind with Captain George, and the mute anger of Coralie was not lost on him.

The Englishman now at once began the history of the discovery he and Nina had made of Lupus Rock's claims and designs on Coralie, and how he and the girl together had compelled him to relinquish both.

It was with feelings of astonishment and indignation Darcy listened, but these were soon changed into admiration at the skilful way in which the wolf had been brought to bay, and forced to relinquish the prey he thought he had so securely in his grasp.

"And now," said Captain George, at the end of his recital, "to whom do you think the fair Coralie belongs?"

"To whom? Why to no one now, I should hope."

"Ah, but she does; and to me."

"To you?"

"Yes—here are the papers; and now, my friend, I hand them over to you, and make you a free present of the handsomest and wealthiest girl in all the South. That's what I call generosity, and no mistake; it's a long time since you had such a present, Darcy."

Darcy Leigh remained silent, and George watched with amusement the changes on his face—first doubt, then surprise, next perplexity, probably at the novelty of his situation, and lastly pleasure.

"Well, what will you do with your present?" he asked.

"Can you doubt? Of course I shall give her the papers. I should be dishonourable indeed were I to repay all her kindness by any other course."

They were now at the tent where the court-martial on Webster Gayle was to be held. The officers composing it had just taken their seats, and a solemn silence prevailed. They awaited but the presence of the officer who was to act as president of the military tribunal.

*

---

# CHAPTER XVIII.

## THE COURT-MARTIAL.

A LITTLE distance from and on one side of the table stood the prisoner, guarded by two soldiers.

Facing the prisoner on the opposite side of the tent, seated on a low bench, were Stella and Angela Gayle. Near them stood Lupus Rock, while Darcy Leigh, Nina, Captain George, Gerald, and Coralie were nearer the entrance of the tent, having come in later. The remainder of the space was filled by a group of officers assembled to hear the trial and verdict on the Yankee spy.

The President spoke, and after referring to some notes said—

"Bring forward the prisoner."

Webster Gayle was brought forward a few paces, and stood facing the court.

"Webster Gayle," said the President, in a calm, firm voice, "the articles of accusation against you are—

"First, treason against the Confederate Government.

"The second is that of being a Yankee spy.

"You will have a fair trial, though a strict one. declared innocent so much the better for yourself—guilty——"

"Captain Edwards," said the President, raising his voice, "have ready a file of soldiers."

No threat could have been more terrible than this order. A thrill went through all present. Stella Gayle felt her heart almost stand still. Angela buried her face in her hands and moaned piteously.

"Silence in the tent!" cried the stern President. "Justice must be done, however painful to the prisoner and his friends."

Webster Gayle was ghastly white. The order for the file of soldiers to be in readiness struck a chill of mortal terror to his heart. His appearance was abject, and excited contempt, but there was scarely an officer present whose eyes were not moist at the bitter grief of the two girls—Stella pale, almost as pale as her father, with a strange wild look in her large grey eyes ; Angela sobbing as if her heart would break.

Nevertheless, *justice must be done !*

"What say you, prisoner—guilty or not guilty ?"

"Not guilty," faltered Webster Gayle.

"The prisoner pleads not guilty," said the President, calmly. "The trial will proceed. Let the witnesses stand forth."

The first witness was the officer who found Webster Gayle prowling about the lines in a suspicious manner, and made him prisoner.

Examined by the President :

"Did you search the prisoner ?"

"I did."

"What did you find ?"

"A large sum of money, in notes and gold, and some papers, which I detained."

"To whose custody did you commit the prisoner ?"

"To that of the Provost-Marshal."

"What did you with the papers ?"

"I laid them on a shelf in the hut where the prisoner was confined."

"So, sir, and that you think was doing your duty ? You should have placed the papers in the most secure custody, or brought them to head-quarters. Consider yourself under arrest, sir, so soon as this trial is concluded. You will have to stand a court-martial yourself for failing in your duty."

The officer, without a word, unbuckled his sword, and laid it on the table.

The President merely bowed, and continued,—

12

"Of those papers, I believe the prisoner afterwards re-possessed himself and escaped?"

"Yes."

"Did you examine them?"

"I did, but not thoroughly."

"What was their nature, so far as you saw?"

"*Treasonous!* They were addressed, many of them, to Yankee generals and officials, and were hostile in their tone to the Confederates."

"Did any one else examine them with you?"

"Yes; Sergeant Smith looked over them with me."

"Stand down, sir."

Sergeant Smith was then examined, and gave evidence similar to that of the officer.

He said, also, that the prisoner, in the confusion caused by the battle raging so near the camp, escaped, and succeeded in taking his papers with him.

The next witness called was Miss St. Casse.

She related how she recaptured the prisoner, and was highly complimented by the President on her heroism and devotion to the cause.

A murmur of assent and admiration of the Southern beauty went around the tent as she gave her evidence; but Coralie looked sad and grieved, knowing that the prisoner—Yankee though he might be—was still a friend of her friends.

"Did you take any papers from the prisoner?"

"I did."

"Did you examine those papers?"

"I did, but only in a casual manner. What I saw convinced me they were written by no friend of our cause."

"Ah! what did you do with those papers?"

"I gave them to my *friend*, Miss Stella Gayle. I knew not, when I captured the prisoner, who he was; and when I found out, I was determined, knowing his danger, not wilfully to injure him further, Yankee though he be."

"Young lady," said the President, "I have no right to blame you—your loyalty and well-known patriotism might excuse more than this."

EXAMINATION OF MISS ST. CASSE.

A murmur of assent went round at these words, for Coralie was highly popular. No more witnesses were called, and the President and officers consulted together for a short time.

"Prisoner, have you any statement to make—any witnesses to call?"

Webster Gayle replied not a word; and he appeared utterly prostrated.

Then again there was a consultation among the officers, and it was decided that the evidence against the prisoner was ample. Three witnesses spoke to their being of a compromising character; then his movements had been so suspicious, that that alone might suffice for his being taken as a spy.

The silence was only broken by the low mutterings of the officers composing the Court as they spoke together. One by one it was noticed that they nodded their heads in token of acquiescence with the President.

Then the latter spoke. His tone was solemn, calm, and dignified, as became such an occasion.

"Prisoner, you have been captured under suspicious circumstances wandering about our lines. Your object is best known to yourself. We have a right to presume, taking all the evidence into consideration, that it was to exercise the detestable trade of spy! Papers are found on you addressed to Northern generals and officials, you all the time pretending to be our friend. The contents of those papers are proved by evidence to be treasonable. Miss St. Casse, who is inclined to shield you from the consequences of your treason, does not deny the compromising character of the papers. You are unable or refuse to give any account of them, either as to their contents or as to how you came possessed of them."

Here the President paused, as if wishing to give the prisoner an opportunity to speak. But Webster Gayle uttered not a word. He had been instructed to say that the papers were written by his daughter, and that he knew nothing of the contents. Either, however, he was too terrified, or now, in this moment of dreadful peril his feelings as a father would not allow him to accuse his daughter. Perhaps it was so, for, with all his faults, Webster Gayle loved his children.

After a pause, the President went on. This time his voice was more solemn, his utterance more slow.

" Prisoner, you refuse, or, as is more probable, you are unable to refute the damning evidence against you. This Court is satisfied with that evidence, and speaking through me, the President, unanimously finds you guilty."

An unexpected interruption here took place.

Stella Gayle advanced to the foot of the table. She held up her hand to demand attention.

There was something terribly beautiful in her appearance. Pale and lovely as a statue, her eyes blazed, and her whole frame trembled with excitement. Her hands were clenched, her left foot defiantly planted in front, her head thrown back ; she gazed scornfully, almost defiantly, at the President and the Court.

It seemed as if she would defend her father by her *very* beauty, and many of the officers composing the Court would, could they have done so with honour, have declared the prisoner not guilty on the spot.

Grandly defiant, beautiful as a statue, she stood thus for some moments. Then, in loud, passionate tones, she cried—

"THE LETTERS WERE MINE ! I WROTE THEM ! ! SHOOT ME, YE REBELS ! ! !"

These words of Stella Gayle, uttered in tones clear, almost shrill with defiance, caused great astonishment. Her impassioned utterance, pale, handsome face, and queen-like defiant carriage, produced a great effect upon all ; and even the stern President gazed with admiration and respect on the beautiful Northerner, who so willingly and fearlessly accused herself to save her father.

For the space of full half a minute Stella Gayle stood bareheaded, dauntlessly gazing round on the members of the court, pale but fearless, trembling, but with excitement ; her bosom heaving, her breath coming in short pants.

Then the President spoke.

" You say, young lady, these papers were written by you ?"

" Yes."

" Did your father know of their contents ?"

" He did not. I charged him not to open the packet."

" To whom did you address those papers ?"

" To friends of mine, loyal and true gentlemen in the North."

" Some to Northern generals, I believe ?"

" Yes."

" And these, I believe, were counselling and urging a course which, if carried out, would be most disastrous to our cause ?"

" No ! they counselled a course the most beneficial to you rebels. They advised the strongest and most rigorous measures by which this wicked and insane rebellion might be quickly crushed out. It is by such measures only that you misguided men can be brought back to a sense of your duty, and compelled by the strong arm of the United States to return to your allegiance. The longer and more mild the process, the more blood and treasure it will cost, and the greater the ultimate loss to you rebels in men and money. For this rebellion must be crushed. Therefore, I say the quicker the better, for you and all."

" Ha ! a fervent Yankee, indeed," said the President. " Now I will put a few questions to you."

" Can you produce these papers, which you say were written by yourself ? If it was as you say, it can be easily proved."

Stella hesitated, and for the first time looked embarrassed.

" Will you produce them ?"

" I cannot."

There was a consultation for a few minutes among the Court, during which time Stella stood at the foot of the table, motionless, pale, anxious.

" This story is clever, young lady," said the President, sternly ; " but it will not suffice. You seek to save your father by accusing yourself. It does honour to your filial affection, but it would be weak on our part, who have a solemn duty to perform, to be influenced by it.   It is not credible, nor do we, for a moment, believe it.   If you have no evidence to produce in support of your statement, you may stand back.   The Court will pronounce verdict and sentence."

Stella glanced wildly around.   She saw the officer told off in command of the file of soldiers leave the tent, and then she heard the rattle of the steel ramrods outside, as the rifles were loaded.

Great God! in five minutes her father would be sentenced ; in ten more he would be shot.

Was there no help—no hope ?

She remembered the promise of Lupus Rock.   She glanced to him appealingly, and the next moment he stood by her side.

He bent low, and whispered,—

"Stella, I can save your father.   Will you keep your promise ?"

All eyes were upon them.   Stella gazed wildly around. Her eyes fell on Darcy Leigh, who was intently regarding her, as though he divined what Lupus was saying. She coloured up violently.   Her heart throbbed violently. It was, indeed, a terrible sacrifice.

Now, again, the President's voice is heard.

"Prisoner, the Court will now, again, proceed to pass verdict and sentence."

"Quick, there is no time," whispered Lupus Rock. "Will you be my wife ?"

One more glance around, seeking for hope and help. But there was neither hope nor help.

"I will," replied Stella ; "only save my father."

Then she darted from the table, and crouched at her father's feet, burying her face in her hands, and for the first time sobbing bitterly.   Many sympathizing tears were shed, and even the rough soldiers guarding the prisoner turned away, and tears trickled down their cheeks.

Mayhap they had sisters and daughters.

"My daughter, oh ! my daughter," said Webster Gayle, in a choking voice ; "my own, my beautiful Stella, this must not be.   Leave me to my fate."

The fatal word " Guilty" was for the second time about to be pronounced, when Lupus Rock spoke.

" General," he said to the President, "suspend your verdict—I have some evidence to give."

" Is it important?" asked an officer, impatiently, for the scene was so harassing, that all would feel glad when it was over, and the dreadful duty done.

" It is important. I believe it will cause the acquittal of the prisoner."

A movement, too, of attention and interest was observed among the members of the Court. For the sake of the two girls, there was not one who would not joyfully hail a chance for a favourable verdict consistent with duty.

Lupus Rock was now sworn.

Stella Gayle had not been sworn, and she was thus spared the dreadful dilemma between perjury and her father's condemnation.

But Lupus Rock took the oath and kissed the Bible with the utmost coolness, although he knew he was about to swear to deliberate falsehoods.

He was dressed in the uniform of the new regiment he was raising, and wore a sword. His head was bound up, and his right arm was in a sling. This was from the joint handiwork of Captain George and Nina.

Examined by the President.

" Your name is Lupus Rock?"

" Yes."

" You have offered to raise a regiment for the Confederate service, and have been granted an officer's commission, with the promise of being created colonel so soon as your military knowledge shall appear sufficient?"

" Yes."

" What do you know on this subject?"

" Miss Stella Gayle gave me the letters and papers in question. They were in her handwriting, with which I am well acquainted, and their contents were much as she said—violently hostile to us, and Yankee in their tendency."

" Have you those papers?"

" They are in my possession."

" Produce them."

Lupus Rock paused as if to collect his thoughts, and then said—

" General and officers of the Court : There can be no question of my loyalty. I hope I have sufficiently proved it, and shall do so more. I am willing to give my life and wealth to the Confederate cause. But I will also sacrifice that life and wealth rather than produce those papers. Miss Gayle is my cousin and my affianced wife, and I will neither by word or deed do aught which may by any possibility injure her."

These words of Lupus Rock were cunning and judicious. His loyalty was not doubted, and his refusing to implicate his cousin and affianced wife told in his favour.

There was some surprise among the audience at the news that he was affianced to Stella Gayle. Gerald seemed thunderstruck, Captain George looked indignant, Coralie amazed, while Darcy turned first red and then white. His eyes sought Stella Gayle as she crouched at her father's feet. She also for a moment raised her head, and for an instant their eyes met. She coloured crimson from brow to bosom, and without a word again buried her face in her hands. Darcy Leigh, after gazing at her for a moment wonderingly, sorrowfully turned away, and spoke to Coralie.

Meanwhile the trial went on. There was another brief consultation between the officers composing the Court, and again the President spoke.

" Lieutenant Lupus Rock, you will have yourself to stand a court-martial for refusing to produce the papers when ordered to do so by your superior officer. However, the Court does not doubt your word, so far as it goes. *The prisoner is acquitted.*"

The Court then rose, and, at a signal from the President, the two soldiers fell back, and Webster Gayle was free. Angela Gayle no sooner heard the joyful tidings than she threw herself on her father's neck, and sobbed hysterically.

Stella, usually the stronger-minded, was now utterly prostrated, almost fainting; and Coralie, taking pity on her, raised her and led her into the open air. Webster Gayle and Angela followed them, the old man tottering and weak, Angela smiling through her tears.

Stella and Coralie walked slowly up and down, the latter soothing, ministering like a sister to Stella, for the terrible excitement, and the no less terrible promise she had made, had completely unnerved her, and for once prostrated her proud spirit.

It was such a bitter humiliation for the proud Northern beauty to hear the man she now most hated in the world, declare he was her affianced husband, and to be unable to contradict it.

It was a strange sight to see the two girls, of such different types of beauty and character; the one a fierce Secessionist, the other as devoted to the old Union.

" One touch of nature makes the whole world kin."

In proof thereof, Stella gave vent to her grief in tears and sighs, her head ever and anon resting on the shoulder of Coralie, whom she at one time considered her enemy, and knew to be her rival in the love of Darcy Leigh; for in spite of her pride, in spite of herself, Stella loved him, and felt it the more bitterly at this moment, when she knew that love was hopeless. For had he not heard Lupus Rock claim her unquestioned as his future wife ?

## CHAPTER XIX.

### STELLA GAYLE'S SACRIFICE.

IT was some time ere Stella could regain her composure or talk coherently, so great was the reaction after the terrible excitement. Barely had she dried her eyes and schooled her features till they wore in part the old expression, when Lupus Rock approached them. There was a mocking smile of insolent triumph on his face as he addressed her.

"Let me offer my congratulations, Stella, on the safe termination of this dangerous business."

"Have I not kept my word?" he added, in a lower tone.

Stella bowed slightly, and turned away without attempting to conceal her dislike.

Lupus turned to Coralie, and bowing obsequiously, addressed her.

"Miss St. Casse——"

But she drew herself up, and regarded him with a glance of such utter scorn, that his blood boiled with fury.

"Sir! do not dare to address me."

This was all she said. Then she walked quietly away, ostentatiously drawing away the skirt of her dress, as she passed him, as though the touch would pollute her.

"Miss Gayle," she said to Stella, "I will leave you with this *gentleman*."

Lupus could have ground his teeth with rage. Thoughts of vengeance on this girl, who scorned and defied him, flitted across his mind. But then came another thought, suggested by a man's figure he saw walking slowly in company with two others. It was the figure of Captain George, and he remembered the murderous secret he possessed, and knew he would be the man to use it on occa·sion. Lupus by no means wished to match himself with the Englishman. He had been beaten on his own ground, and had no wish to renew the conflict. So he stifled the thought, at least for the present, and said to Stella, who was walking slowly by his side, gazing straight before her, like one in a dream—

"Stella, I have performed my promise, and saved your father. Are you ready to fulfil yours?"

She started at the sound of his voice, as though she had only that moment become aware of his presence.

"Have I not promised? Is not that enough for you? Do you think I will break my word as easily as you can perjure yourself?"

"It well becomes you to reproach me," he said, sneeringly, "when it was to save your father's life."

" It is false !" she cried, indignantly ; "you did not do it for that reason. It was for your own selfish ends. You would have seen my father, your benefactor, perish before you would lift a finger, were it not for your own schemes."

" At all events," he replied, " what you are pleased to call my perjury had the effect of saving your father, for your bare word would not have been believed."

" I will not discuss the point with you," she replied, wearily, "leave me."

Then she stopped dead, and turned her back, so that Lupus had no choice but to go on alone. When he was some distance ahead, she again walked slowly on, and in her gloomy abstraction was not aware that some one else had joined her, till a voice, which made her heart beat and the blood thrill in her veins said—

" Stella, Miss Gayle ?"

She knew at once whose was the voice, and raising her eyes, saw Darcy Leigh by her side. She made an attempt to smile, but it was a poor one, and the momentary flush on her cheek was quickly replaced by pallor.

" Miss Gayle," he said, " I have something of yours I wish to return to you, which, under other circumstances I might wish to retain."

" Of mine ?" she said, resolutely mastering her voice. " I cannot conceive——" but she suddenly checked herself, for she saw in his hand the handkerchief and scarf with which she had bound up his head in the battle-field. She trembled all over, for she feared he was about to ask her how he became possessed of them, and in her weak, nervous state she felt she must have burst into tears.

Again he spoke. His voice was low and mournful, and painfully recalled to the wretched girl memories of old and happy days.

" Stella," he said, " I assure you I know not how I came by them. My servant, Darby Kelly, tells me he took them from the pocket of my tunic, and bound up my head with them. How they came there I know not."

He paused, thinking, perhaps, she might explain, but

no word fell from her lips. Her bosom rose and fell rapidly, and she felt herself tremble. She dared not trust her voice to speak.

"However," he continued, "I feel I have no right to them, however I came by them, and therefore take this opportunity of returning them to you."

"No right to them?" she said, in a low voice.

Why she spoke she could hardly tell herself. It was partly from impulse, and partly a task she imposed on her voice to say something, lest her silence might be more conclusive than speech. The words, however, were unfortunately chosen.

"No right to them—certainly, I repeat I have no right to them. No right with anything of yours, no right to think of you even in my wildest dreams. If there is one who has that right, it is he who has just left you."

"Do not name that man," she said, with a shudder she could not suppress.

"Is it not then true?" asked Darcy, eagerly. "Was it an audacious assertion?"

"True—what true?" she said, absently.

"That you are betrothed to Lupus Rock—is that true?"

It was long before Stella could trust herself to reply. When she did so, it was in firm though low voice. Even her very lips were white as the hated words issued from them.

"It is quite true."

Whatever were Darcy Leigh's feelings, his face did not betray them.

"Therefore I repeat, Miss Gayle, that I have no right to anything of yours. Take your handkerchief and scarf."

He placed them in her hand, and she mechanically held them. She did not attempt to speak, but turned away her head.

But Darcy saw that she was deeply agitated, that her breath came in pants and sobs, and he even discerned a tear trickle down her cheek. This emotion, however, he misinterpreted. He thought it was from friendship—

from the memory of old times.  He fancied she had divined that he loved her, and regretted she could not return his love.

"Stella," he said, taking her hand, "I do not like to see you thus sad ; I own my madness—my folly in ever daring to love you, for I have been foolish enough to love you, nor could all your scorn and insult kill that love."

Stella had never heard the avowal word from his lips before, and now, when it came, it brought first a flush of fierce joy, then a chill of icy despair shot through her frame.  A whirlwind of passion raged in her breast.  The man whom she, in her wicked pride, had scorned and outraged, now owned he had loved her, and even that scorn and outrage had not been powerful enough to quench all-powerful love.

How gladly would she have thrown herself in his arms, rebel though he were—trampling all pride underfoot, have wept on his shoulder, and sighed her love to him— a love which burned all the fiercer because hopeless— with a fire which the dark waters of death alone could quench.

"But now, Stella, all that folly is past.  I respect myself and you too much to think further of you.  Even though I had been worthy of your love, and you not so scornful, the fact of your being betrothed to your cousin would be sufficient barrier.  All that is past.  Men do not die of love, I assuredly shall not.  I have duty, ambition, honour, all to live for—and, let me hope, Stella, your friendship."

He turned for a moment and then said, abruptly—

"This subject is painful to me—disagreeable to you.  I will never mention it again."

She felt desperately inclined to tell him all—to own her deep love for him, and seek some way of escape from her fatal promise to Lupus Rock.

But, alas ! she thought escape from that impossible.  For a moment she wavered on the balance.  But she thought-

"It is useless, there is no escape, I must marry Lupus Rock ; he will never relinquish his claim on me."

Then pride stepped in and said,—
" Why should I needlessly humble myself before a man,
even though I love him ?"

Alas, for Stella Gayle !   Had she spoken, all might
have been well.   Both laboured under a fatal error,
Darcy Leigh thought her *unwilling* to break the bond
between herself and Lupus Rock.

She thought herself *unable.*

*He* did not know her love for him.

*She* did not know that Darcy could, if he chose, bring
her future husband to his knees, and compel him to beg,
in abject tones, for his life; for Captain George, the Englishman, had related to Darcy Leigh his adventure with
Lupus Rock—how he had brought the wolf to bay, and
forced him to relinquish the fruit of his schemes.

Had Darcy so chosen, it was certain that he and his
friend, the Englishman, together could have dictated
their own terms to Stella's cousin and affianced husband.

But Stella spoke not.   The chance which could have
saved her from misery was missed, and Darcy Leigh bade
her adieu, little dreaming she loved him, and convinced
that her heart as well as her hand was pledged to Lupus
Rock.

Now she was again alone, and wandered listlessly on,
scarcely heeding where she went.

A dull, vague feeling of misery and humiliation pervaded her and crushed all definite thought.

She sought the tent of Gerald Leigh, which had been
given up for the accommodation of herself and sister—
almost mechanically, and remained standing outside,
looking vacantly down the long, straight canvas street,
like one half-bereft of reason.

Indeed, it is doubtful whether her mind was not
slightly weakened by the excitement and agony she had
gone through.   Her face wore that dull, spirit-crushed
look, so often the forerunner of insanity.

Angela had gone with her father to head-quarters, to
endeavour to get the necessary permits across the lines in
order once again to go North, for Senator Gayle was
thoroughly sick of the South, as may well be imagined.

How long Stella would have stood outside the tent, a mark for the rude stare of every passing soldier, it is hard to say, but the sweet voice of Coralie aroused her from her fit of vacancy—it could not be called *reverie*, for she thought of nothing.

"My dear friend," said the Southern girl, kindly, "what is the matter with you? All is well now, surely. You have no cause for unhappiness, I trust. Your father is safe, and he will now, doubtless, be permitted to go North. You will accompany him, and, far from the scene of this desperate struggle, will enjoy peace and comfort in the company of your friends. Why then so sad?"

"Am I sad?" said Stella, wearily; "it is very foolish of me. I ought to be happy—very happy, if only for my father's sake."

She spoke of happiness and strove to smile, but her heart was ready to break. The afternoon sun shone in all his glory, the white tents glistened, and the camp resounded with strains of music—brass bands, drums and fifes, while songs and shouts might be heard in the distance.

The gleam of arms, the occasional clatter of horses' hoofs, and ever and anon the bugle's shrill blast—all were there to brighten and exhilarate both sight and hearing.

But to Stella all was dull and cold.

For her the sun shone not—for her the music was but a funeral dirge—the songs but the wailings of the mourners. Within her heart all was cold, dark, dismal.

No present, no future, no help, no hope, no light, no life, *no love.*

And yet she smiled—a sad, dreary smile, as she answered Coralie; who, not looking closely, was thereby deceived, and fancied Stella only slightly low-spirited.

"Stella," she said, looking down, and speaking in a doubtful, timid manner, as though afraid of the ground she was venturing on, "I should like to ask you a question. May I?"

"Oh, yes," was the listless reply.

"It is about your friend, Darcy Leigh," continued Coralie, blushing deeply.

Stella awoke instantly from her listless apathy.
" About Darcy Leigh ? Has Darcy Leigh sent you to
me ?  If so, it is useless.  What I have said must be."
" No, indeed," replied Coralie, somewhat piqued, " why
should he ?  He knows you are engaged to Mr. Rock,"—
there was a contemptuous tone in her voice as she spoke
the name, which at another time Stella's pride might have
resented.   " Besides—besides, I think——"

Here Coralie stammered, and finally came to a dead
halt.  Stella looked suddenly in her face, and saw in it a
deep blush mantling through the rich brown skin.

" Besides, you mean to say he loves you," said Stella,
who now, by a great effort, had regained her self-possession.

" No, no ; I did not say so.   I did not mean anything
of the kind."

But the blush which yet deepened on her cheek told
Stella was not wrong, so far as this, at least, that Coralie
*hoped* she had Darcy's love.   In affairs of this kind, a
woman may deceive a man, may even deceive herself, but
she can never deceive another woman.

" Well, it matters not," said Stella ; " what is it you
wish to ask me about Darcy Leigh ? I will answer if it is
in my power.   You have been kind to me ; I have found
in you a friend where I least expected one.   Does the
question concern me ? "

" Yes, a little," faltered Coralie ; " but, perhaps, you
will think me rude to ask—will be offended ? "

" No I will not, I promise you."

" Well, I will speak out then, and trust in your
womanly honour.   I despise a man who would descend to
falsehood, and Darcy Leigh has told me a most improbable
story.   He has a handkerchief marked with your name,
and part of a silk scarf——"

" Has he shown them ?   Has he boasted of possessing
them ?—but it is impossible.   I know Darcy Leigh to be
incapable of such meanness," said Stella.

" No, he has not boasted of them, he has not shown
them ; but if I understand you, you *did* give them to
him ? "

" Did he say so ? "

" No ; he did not say so."

" You asked me whether I gave them to him. I did in one sense, for I bound them round his head."

" Then he told me a falsehood. I was deceived."

Stella now fired up. Though lost to her, she would not hear Darcy Leigh ill-spoken of.

" How deceived, Miss St. Casse ? " she said, raising her eyes to the other's face.

" I thought Darcy Leigh to be true ; at least, that he would not lie."

" Lie ! Darcy Leigh lie ! " cried Stella.

" He told me that he knew not how he became possessed of your handkerchief and scarf. I did not ask him —do not think that, pray ; " this she said hastily ; " but his brother, and his friend Captain George, as he is called, were teasing him on the subject. He said, in reply to them, that he knew not how he came possessed of them, and when I asked him if he were serious, he repeated that he knew not how they came to be bound round his head, although his servants who carried him in declare they took them from the breast of his tunic."

" And you think Darcy Leigh could lie ? "

" What else can I think, when you say you yourself bound them round his head ? "

" Yes ; I bound them round his head, but he was insensible and knew it not. I told Darby Kelly, his Irish servant, and the negro not to say that I had been with him. Darcy Leigh at this moment does not dream that it was I who found him faint, insensible on the battlefield, nor do I wish him to know it. And you thought he could lie. Ha ! ha ! you do not know Darcy Leigh, although, perhaps, he may love you, and you love him. Darcy Leigh is as honourable as he is brave, and rebel though he be, as noble a gentleman as ever trod God's earth."

Stella's voice rose as she concluded, and her last words were harsh and almost threatening in their tones. Her cheek flushed, and her large grey eyes sparkled as she

13

defended Darcy *absent*, whom when *present* she had treated with such scorn.

Coralie looked at her in surprise ; her flushed face and glittering eyes and vehement manner were unintelligible to the Southern girl. Strange that she should be so wanting in penetration, but since she had heard that Stella was betrothed to Lupus Rock she had never given her a thought in connection with Darcy Leigh.

For a few moments both the girls were silent. Coralie looking in the other's face, saw the angry flush fade away, and the fire vanish from the large eyes. Then came a look of blank, hopeless despair ; such a look of misery as she had never seen before.

Slowly it dawned on the mind of Coralie that Stella, though betrothed to her cousin, deeply, passionately loved Darcy Leigh. When once the idea presented itself, a thousand little things corroborated it. Her fiery defence of him—her flashing eyes when his truth was assailed— Coralie could read it all now. She turned very pale.

Stella moved slowly inside the tent, as if wishing to be alone, but Coralie quickly followed her.

Placing her arms around Stella's neck, she said, or rather murmured—

" You love Darcy Leigh—perhaps he loves you ? This engagement with Lupus Rock is mere boast on his part. Is it so ? I shall be glad for your sake, for Lupus is a bad, a desperately wicked man. You do not mean to marry him ? "

" You are wrong—I do mean to marry him—I must marry him ! If for no other reason, because my word is pledged, and for my father's safety."

" Then you do not love Darcy Leigh—noble, honourable, as you say he is ? "

A desperate struggle was going on within Stella Gayle's breast. Could she own her love, a hopeless love, a love which perhaps Darcy himself might now scorn since she had plighted herself to another ? She sought to deceive herself, to make a compromise between her heart and the truth.

"I do not love him," she said, in a low voice—"rest easy on that score."

She tried to persuade herself she spoke truth, that since her interview with Darcy Leigh she no longer loved him; had given up in heart as she had in fact.

" You look pale and ill," said Coralie, kindly, " and your eyes glitter as if you were feverish. Sit down and rest for an hour or two ; I will sit by you if you like."

" No, no—I wish to be alone."

To this Coralie could, of course, say nothing, so she bade her adieu, wondering much at her strange manner.

"I think the excitement must have worked on her mind and disordered it a little. Poor girl, she looks quite wild and scared."

No sooner was Stella alone, than she threw herself on a pile of rough horsecloths, which for the last two nights had served the sisters as a bed, and laying her head on a dragoon saddle, covered with a fur rug in place of pillow, and covering her face with her hands, she sobbed as though her heart would break.

Was it not a bitter sacrifice?

In one day she had pledged herself to a man she hated, forsworn for ever the man she loved, and sent her rival to his arms by clearing his honour in her eyes.

She wept till no tears came, and when the fountain of tears was dry, she still sobbed on. She thought now, were she but free, could she but escape from the hateful bond she herself had forged, how gladly would she humble her pride and ask pardon for all her offences.

The day passed on. The sun sank low in the heavens ; —still Stella lay, her head on the saddle, her face covered by her hands. Tears had long since ceased to flow. There remained now a dull aching misery, worse than the most passionate burst of sorrow. The sun set in the west. Still she lay crouching in the tent, nursing her misery.

The twilight deepened into the darkness of night, but Stella moved not.

"Would she could have been annihilated where she lay !" that was her thought, prompted by bitter despair.

She might have lain thus all night, but the voice of Angela fell on her ears,—

"Stella! Stella! where are you?—are you here? It is so dark I cannot see."

"Yes, Angela, I am here."

Her sister started at the voice, so hoarse and husky with weeping, and unutterably miserable. But if the voice caused her surprise, it was as nothing to her consternation when a light being procured she looked in Stella's face.

That she was pale was not to be wondered at, but the terrible expression of misery on her face frightened Angela. Her eyes were surrounded by dark circles, through which they shone with a wild unearthly glitter. There was a restless, scared look, too, in her face, which Angela had never seen before. Her gaze wandered rapidly about, as though she were a prisoner and seeking some means of escape. She did not look either her sister or father, who were with her, in the face, but appeared to shun meeting their eyes.

This, and the expression of utter misery on her wan face, went straight to Webster Gayle's heart. He was proud of and loved his beautiful daughter, his " glorious Stella," as he delighted to call her. Where now was her glory? The lips—those exquisitely cut lips—which used to wear so proud, almost scornful expression—were now bloodless and pressed close together. Her eyes, famous of old for their grand queen-like glance, now wandered restlessly, vaguely around.

"Stella, my dear Stella!" cried the old man, taking her in his arms, "you are ill—the excitement has unnerved you."

She laid her head on his shoulder without replying.

Suddenly she started, and almost tore herself from his arms.

"Hush! hush! he is coming. Oh, save me, father."

She started to the further corner of the tent, and crouched down, staring at the door of the tent with a wild, terrified look.

"Heavens! this is dreadful," groaned Webster Gayle;

"her mind is unsettled. Stella, my dear Stella, there is no one coming—do not look so dreadful."

" Yes, yes,—he is coming—I can hear his step."

Sure enough, Stella's morbidly acute hearing had caught the footfall of Lupus Rock, and the next moment he stood at the tent door.

"I have been seeking you, sir,—your presence is required at head-quarters ; you ———"

Then his eyes fell upon Stella crouched in one corner of the tent.

" Stella ! " he said in surprise, " what is the matter ? "

But she, with a low moan, shrank yet further back, and hid her face.

" Come in, Lupus Rock," said Webster Gayle, removing his pitying glance from his daughter, and looking sternly at his nephew.

Lupus obeyed.

"Stella, my child, look up, and listen to what I have to say."

She raised her head, and glanced timidly—like a frightened child—towards her father and cousin.

" Lupus Rock," said Webster Gayle, quietly and firmly, " you this day obtained a promise from your cousin Stella that she would be your wife. Look now at her— see her pale face—her shrinking from the very sight of you. Is that not enough for you? Do you not see the promise was wrung from her by fears for my safety ? Is not that enough ? If you have any honour or manhood, release her. Do you not see that she detests you ? "

" I see nothing of the kind," said Lupus, sullenly ; " the excitement has been too much for her. She is ill and feverish. Stella, let me feel your hand."

He advanced towards her, but she, with a slight scream, sprang to her feet, and clung to her father as if for protection. It was easy now to see, by the wild glare in her eyes, that her mind was unsettled.

" Lupus Rock, stand back and listen to me," said Webster Gayle, with more firmness and dignity than was usual with him. " You obtained a promise from my poor girl here—you refuse to give it back—I cancel it. You forced her to promise to be your wife—I utterly refuse my consent to the union, and defy you to your worst. Stella, my dear daughter, listen to me."

He took her head in his hand, and looked in her wild eyes.

"Stella, I refuse my consent to your marriage with Lupus Rock. Do you understand? I command you not to marry your cousin. You will not refuse to obey me?"

Stella seemed slowly to gather the meaning of his words. The wild light faded from her grey eyes, and they rested lovingly on her father's face. A sigh of relief escaped from her.

"Ah! then I am not to marry him?" she murmured.

"No, no—a thousand times no! Lupus Rock, leave us—you have heard my words."

Lupus saw that at present he could do nothing. There was a look in the old man's face that told him to contend was useless. Besides, for the present, the schemer had parted with his power, little thinking to be thus checkmated by the weak and irresolute Webster Gayle. He was trembling with passion, but disguised it, and said, in a voice he did his utmost to render calm—

"Very good, sir. For the present I leave you; but you will reconsider your words, I trust."

"May perdition seize me, if I do not make that old greybeard and his scornful daughter pay a bitter price for this. I will gain Stella Gayle—that is my first aim; my next shall be to revenge myself on this insolent old man. First I will gain the daughter, then crush the father."

How fearfully he kept his word the reader will learn.

\* \* \* \* \* \* \*

Webster Gayle kept repeating to his daughter that she should not marry Lupus Rock; that he, her father, would not allow it. It seemed to soothe, and gradually bring her scattered senses back. At first she could hardly realize it, but when she did, a feeling of deep relief possessed her. When she fully understood that her father expressly forbade the hated union, and that Lupus Rock was powerless, she felt raised from the abyss of despair.

True, she had given her word to Lupus Rock, but she had not anticipated her father's direct commands against the marriage. She knew her father, his timid nature, and fancied the dark schemer, Lupus, had gained an entire ascendancy over him. .

Her thoughts were in a whirl, and her dried-up tears again flowed.

"Leave me, father ; leave me, Angela. I should like to be alone and think."

Thinking it best to humour her, her father and Angela left her, first carefully wrapping her in a horsecloth and disposing her pillow somewhat more comfortably.

But a cloud soon overspread the joy caused by the news that she was not to marry the hated Lupus. She remembered Darcy Leigh ; that she had permitted him to tell his love without one encouraging word from her. Then she remembered Coralie's questions to her as to his truth.

"I am free," she thought, with bitter grief, " but he will give his love to another. I, in my accursed pride, have spurned his noble heart, and now this Southern girl will win the love which was mine. Even now, doubtless, she has seen him. Who knows, that, stung by my coldness, he may not even now be holding her in his arms ? "

She shuddered at the thought. Death could not be more unwelcome, yet she *felt* it was but too' probable.

Alas ! Stella Gayle, your evil star pursues you, for at the very moment you hear that, so far as Lupus Rock is concerned, you are free, at that very time Darcy Leigh is whispering soft words of love in the not unwilling ear of Coralie, the Star of the South.

The thought was madness, and again the free blood coursed through her veins ; visions and phantoms rose before her. Incoherent mutterings soon gave place to wild ravings, and when her father and sister returned, they found her in a raging fever. In her wild, delirious ravings the name of Darcy Leigh was ever on her tongue, and then it was her father and sister knew how deep was her passion for the young Southern officer.

# CHAPTER XX.

## LOVE'S YOUNG DREAM.

ALTHOUGH Webster Gayle was, mainly through the devotion of his daughter, acquitted of the charge against him, it by no means followed he was to be allowed to go and come at will.

Immediately on his release he transmitted a request to head-quarters for a pass to cross the lines and return North. This was not complied with, and Webster was ordered to report himself at head-quarters. On his arrival, he was severely questioned, and finally required to give his parole not to endeavour to escape, or even leave the lines, nor to hold any communication whatever with the enemy ; furthermore, he was informed he must report himself at Richmond, and there remain with his daughters during the pleasure of the Confederate Government.

It was significantly hinted to him that the least infraction of these orders, or attempted breach of parole, would be followed by swift punishment, and what that punishment would be, he too well knew.

Under the circumstances, the generals commanding could not have done otherwise, for it was well known in the camp that the position at Manassas was to be cautiously abandoned. Doubtless, Webster Gayle was aware of so patent a fact, and such being the case, it would have been the height of folly to allow him to go North, for if the intended retreat were known to the enemy, the most disastrous consequences might be anticipated.

In obedience to these orders, then, Webster Gayle made preparations to start for Richmond on the following day. When, however, the morning came, it was found impossible. Gerald Leigh, whose tent the sisters again occupied, waited on Webster Gayle, and with grave face informed him that his presence was required, that his daughter Stella was very ill, so ill that Angela was unable to leave her.

When the unhappy old man arrived at the tent, a terrible scene awaited him. Stella, his beautiful Stella, as he was wont to call her, was sitting upright, her hair dishevelled, her dress all in disorder, and with wild and glistening eyes, was talking rapidly and incoherently.

At first, her father thought she was addressing him, but in vain endeavoured to catch the meaning of the rhapsody she poured forth. It scarcely required a second glance at the flushed face and wild wandering eyes to know that, for the time at least, reason had left her — that she was delirious.

A regimental surgeon having been called in, pronounced her to be in a violent fever, which might last many days, and in its terrible course might kill the patient. Certainly removal was out of the question.

Representations to that effect having been made to head-quarters, Webster Gayle was permitted to remain in camp till such time as his daughter could bear removal. Gerald permanently gave up his tent, which was fitted with every possible comfort for the invalid, and the duty of watching by her bedside was shared by Angela and a hired nurse. For many days the fever ran its fierce course, and when, at last, it left her, she was so weak that her friends entertained serious fears for her life. However, youth and careful nursing prevailed ; the grim enemy was beaten off, and in a week's time Stella began slowly but surely to recover.

She was, however, greatly changed. It is doubtful whether even her most intimate friend, suddenly admitted to her presence, would have known her. Not that she was less beautiful. During her delirium the name of Darcy Leigh was ever on her lips. When she recovered her senses, she inquired after him, and being informed that he had gone to Richmond in order to recover from his wounds, she mentioned his name no more. Once it was casually mentioned in her hearing that Miss St. Casse had also left the camp for Richmond. Stella's pale face turned a little paler, and even the first flush of returning health faded away. Her voice, too, faltered slightly, as she asked if Miss St. Casse was well.

Meanwhile Lupus Rock—far too wise to appear obtrusive—merely sent once a day to inquire after his cousin's health, and devoted himself to the pleasing task of again getting his uncle into his toils.

Once again he used all his wit to disarm suspicion, and played his cards so well that, by the time Stella was convalescent, the New York merchant believed that Lupus was not really bad or treacherous, but that his deep love for his cousin and her indifference to him had caused him to act as he had.

Lupus owned his deep dejection and bitter grief that his cousin should be averse to him. He hoped, he said, that some day she might think differently—it should be the aim of his life to induce her so to do.

He did not openly blame Webster Gayle even for refusing his consent to their union in defiance of his promise, but put on an aggrieved and injured manner, which he thought most prudent under the circumstances.

Now Webster Gayle had anticipated difficulties with Lupus Rock relating to money matters, especially with regard to the Yancey Estate. It will be remembered that some months previously, when Webster Gayle was in the North, and had no intention of coming South, he had assigned or made over the Yancey Estate to Lupus Rock in order that, as Lupus was going South, and at least nominally to espouse the Confederate cause, the estate might be secure from confiscation in case of Southern victory.

Lupus, as the reader knows, at once assumed possession, and from many circumstances which had since transpired, Senator Gayle anticipated that his nephew would refuse to give up possession, and claim the estates as his own, according to the strict letter of the deed of assignment.

However, when the subject was mooted Lupus at once declared himself willing to give up possession to his uncle, and immediately commenced to prepare a statement of accounts of his stewardship. The accounts were satisfactory, and Webster could not but own that under the circumstances Lupus had acted prudently and well. The conversation turned upon the sale of the slaves—Lupus explained his reasons for so doing—that the estate being situate so near the borders of Virginia, was quite likely to become a battle-ground. With such a contingency in view, it was clearly the best plan to sell the slaves and remove a constant source of danger.

" By the way," said Lupus, " do you remember a girl named Nina? She is now a sort of *vivandière* or something of the kind, and is with Miss St. Casse. She said you promised her her freedom on your last visit to the estate at a low price. She seemed a good sort of girl, and as Stella and Angela had taken a great fancy to her, I offered to let her have her freedom for nothing. But the jade was so confoundedly proud that she would insist on paying the price you fixed. You will find the money duly entered in the accounts."

" Yes, yes—I remember," said Webster Gayle, " a very good girl, indeed—you did quite right, Lupus—quite right."

Lupus merely bowed acknowledgment, but his quick eye caught an expression of satisfaction in his uncle's face. He could not have played his game better. Webster Gayle now felt certain that he had wronged him. Everything appeared so fair and above board—the accounts satisfactory—prudence and caution in all his dealings. Then Webster remembered what a clever manager and agent he had always found his nephew ; on several occasions—that of a slaver, for instance, in which the merchant once had a share and which was seized, Lupus had been willing to take all the blame on his own shoulders. He remembered all this, and now felt inclined to pity Lupus for his deep passion for Stella. It is questionable whether there did not lurk in the Senator's mind a slight feeling of dissatisfaction and inclination to blame his daughter for her hard-heartedness. But the memory of her weak and suffering state soon quelled this thought.

" And now, sir, what are your plans?" asked Lupus, suddenly.

" I really hardly know. What can you advise ?   At present, it seems I am powerless."

" Your interests—mercantile interests, especially—must be suffering terribly in the North from your prolonged absence."

Webster Gayle sighed deeply.

" Oh, terribly—I don't know how many thousand dollars I lose."

" It would be desirable, if possible, for you to return North," said Lupus, musingly.

" Desirable—certainly ; but how is it to be done ?"

" Supposing you lay the case before the Government, and petition to be allowed to return—I would use all my interest in your favour."

" I fear I should never get permission.   What in case of a refusal ?   It is much to my interest to remain here. In the first place, no one in New York will believe I was really detained against my will."

" True," said Lupus, " quite true : it is an awkward situation."

" Can you suggest nothing ?" said Webster.

" The only thing I can think of is a carefully arranged escape."

Lupus narrowly watched his uncle's face as he made this suggestion, and saw the shuddering terror with which it was received.   Webster Gayle could not forget the terrible court-martial : and the ringing of the steel ramrods as the file of soldiers loaded, yet sounded in his ears."

" I should not advise it," said Lupus, " unless it could be done without danger to yourself."

" Aye, without danger ; but there is such terrible danger—see my last attempt."

" Ah—yes—truly ; but you must allow that in that case the attempt was clumsy in the extreme."

" Yes, yes ; but can you see any way by which I might escape without danger ?"

Lupus pretended to think deeply for some time, and then replied slowly—

" If you could get leave to visit Fredericksburg—it is

less than twenty miles thence to Acquia Creek ; and the Federals have both troops and gunboats there."

" Fredericksburg, yes ; but could I get permission ?— on what grounds ?"

" Why, it is known you own the Yancey estate, near that city. Business in connexion with that would be a sufficient excuse."

" True !" replied Webster, brightening up.

" Lupus, you are fertile in expedients. And you think I could get permission to visit Fredericksburg ?"

" I am sure I could obtain it for you."

" And then ?"

" Then lay your plans well, and make your escape to Acquia Creek—eighteen or twenty miles are soon covered."

" What about Stella and Angela ?" said Gayle.

" They should accompany you ; or stay—perhaps it would be better they followed with a guide. Three riding together would be more liable to interruption than one ; and if they were captured, they stand no danger. Two hours' sharp riding would bring you safe to Acquia Creek."

Webster Gayle hesitated a little, but finally said—

" Well, Lupus, I will risk it. To remain here all the summer would be ruin."

" Well, then, to make all safe, I should go about it in a business-like manner. Take a house in Richmond, and furnish it as though you intended to make a long residence. Spare no expense, and you will disarm all suspicion. Then, in the course of a month, you can obtain leave to visit Fredericksburg with your daughters. In the meantime, I will prepare all the accounts ; and before you start, I will give you the papers relating to the Yancey estate."

" Yes, yes," replied Webster Gayle, eagerly, "that is all right enough. I am glad to see you act so straight-forward and honourably, Lupus. The correctness of your accounts, and what you say about the papers, convince me that I have wronged you in thought, I will own."

Webster Gayle finally agreed with Lupus, and, notwithstanding the danger, determined to make the attempt. Indeed, Lupus so skilfully presented the view he
wished his uncle to take, that the latter believed there
was little or no danger attached to it."

Accordingly, it was arranged that, in pursuance of the
course agreed on, Webster Gayle should, as soon as
Stella was sufficiently recovered, proceed to Richmond,
and there rent and furnish a large house in the best part
of the town.

As for Lupus Rock, the regiment which he had raised,
and to a company of which he was appointed captain, was
ordered to Richmond ; and Lupus, both from inclination
and necessity, was bound to accompany or follow immediately afterwards. He, however, lingered a few days
longer, and did not fail to make the best of the time.
He strove hard and effectually to reinstate himself in his
uncle's opinion, and regain all the influence he had
lost.

He was not without military ambition, nor was he
wanting in ability ; and as he read works on drill, tactics,
and fortification assiduously, it was probable he would
soon be qualified for more than subordinate command ;
indeed, it is hard to say how far his ambition ascended.
There were great prizes looming in the distance, supposing the Secessionists should succeed ; and the keen
eye of Lupus had not failed to mark them. He neglected no opportunity of bringing himself prominently
forward, and was looked upon by the Confederate
generals as, at all events, a zealous young officer, if not a
trained and skilful one.

Shortly after he had been gazetted to his company
there was a supper given by the ladies of Richmond to
such officers who were in the capital.

It took place in the large room of the Vermont
Hotel, a long table being ranged down the centre of the
room. All the windows were thrown wide open, for the
heat was oppressive.

In most houses in the Southern States and the West
Indies, a balcony usually runs right round the first floor ;

in fact, so to speak, the *walls are all windows*. These are closed by jalousies, Venetian blinds, or matting, all glass being frequently dispensed with. Thus it was that the Venetian blinds and mattings being raised all around, on account of the heat of the sultry August night, the brilliantly lighted room was as open to the gaze of the crowd whom the strains of the band and the sounds of merriment had collected, as though it had been out of doors.

The ladies retired immediately after supper, leaving the table to the gentlemen, who proceeded to do ample justice to the iced wines and drinks provided.

Coralie St. Casse returned to Richmond on the very day she had the interview with Stella Gayle, and did not hear of the latter's illness for some days after. Darcy Leigh, who was seeking her in order to give her the papers confided to him by Captain George, learned of her departure, and though somewhat surprised, resolved to wait till his regiment returned to Richmond.

He heard with sorrow the illness of Stella Gayle, and was informed day by day of her state by Angela. On each occasion when he saw this young lady, he noticed that she appeared embarrassed, as if wishing to say something and yet not liking to do so.

On the very morning he was to start for Richmond, whither all troops were being quietly withdrawn, it being resolved to abandon the present position, Angela informed him that Stella had passed a quieter night, and that the fever had almost left her.

" I am truly glad to hear it, Angela. I should have been sorry indeed to have left without the knowledge of your sister being better."

" You are going then?" she asked, looking sadly in his face.

" Yes, I go with the regiment this afternoon. Gerald's regiment is likely to remain a few days yet; so that, Angela, you will not be quite alone."

" It was not of myself I was thinking, Darcy, but——" said Angela, quickly. Then she paused and hesitated.

" Not of yourself ?" he asked in wonderment.

" No," she replied, colouring, and casting down her eyes.

" I don't understand you," he said.

Still she hesitated and seemed unwilling to speak, and yet loth for him to go without her doing so.

Now the fact was that Angela, knowing nothing of the scene which had taken place between her sister and Darcy, yet knew perfectly well that she deeply loved the young officer. She knew it even before this illness, but lately in her delirious ravings, and even the mutterings of her uneasy sleep, the name of Darcy Leigh had ever been on Stella's lips.

" Darcy—dear Darcy, come to me ; let me see you, Darcy !" That was the continual refrain of the sick girl.

Now Angela, fully aware of her sister's overpowering love, thought that Darcy Leigh was unaware of the fact, and that to inform him would be to put all things straight. She never disguised from herself her own affection for the gay and dashing Gerald, who was her *beau-ideal*, both of manly beauty, bravery, and goodness.

How delightful, thought gentle Angela, it would be if Darcy and Stella would only come together. Two brothers and two sisters ! A delightful idea, and delightful little castles in the air did Angela build on it.

She pictured to herself the dreadful war ended, and Darcy and Gerald each inhabiting a delightful little villa within an easy distance of each other. Now all knew that Gerald Leigh and herself were ready and willing to complete their part of this charming plan. Stella, too, she knew, loved Darcy, and all that was wanted was his co-operation.

That he could be indifferent to Stella, so gloriously beautiful, she could not believe, but thought that perhaps diffidence, or his misinterpreting Stella's proud manner, alone kept them apart.

A word, a hint, would put all straight, and however embarrassing, she had made up her mind to speak that word.

Accordingly, when Darcy for the second time said, wonderingly—" I don't understand you," she resolved that he should understand her.

" Darcy," she said, falteringly, but determined to say all she meant, " you know Stella would be deeply grieved if you left without seeing her."

" I don't know anything of the kind," he replied, quickly ; " as a friend I am grieved for Stella's illness, as, doubtless, as a friend she would regret if harm befel me, but more than that there is nothing."

" But there is more than that," she said, impatiently ; " I have often noticed that you are not indifferent to Stella. I know—I feel sure that your feelings towards her are more than those of friendship, and ——"

" Angela, it is useless talking. Whatever may or might have been my feelings towards your sister, I know her feelings towards me. Besides, she is going to marry your cousin Lupus."

" You are wrong, doubly wrong. I see you do not know Stella's feelings towards you, and she is not to marry Lupus Rock—she dislikes him. I believe it was the thought of the promise he had extorted, by working on her fears for our father, that made her ill."

Darcy looked surprised, but replied, quickly—

" Of that I know nothing. I certainly understood Stella was affianced to her cousin. I :she has broken off the engagement, so much the better fo. her, for I believe Lupus to be a bad man, and by no means calculated to make her happy. But as regards her feelings towards me, I do know——"

" You do not—cannot," interrupted Angela.

" But I do ; there can be no mistake. I have the very best authority for speaking."

" The best ?" repeated Angela.

" Yes ; her own words."

" Her own words !" said Angela, in wonder; " but she did not—could not say that. She ——"

" She herself distinctly told me that she had no feeling for me other than friendship. I had long known it, or

14

rather feared it, and was glad when her distinct avowal put the question beyond all doubt."

"Her distinct avowal?" murmured Angela, utterly confounded. "Surely you do not mean to say you told her you loved her, and she replied she was unable to return your love?"

"But I do mean to say so, most distinctly; so my dear Angela, that question is at rest for ever. It is useless and painful for me to discuss the subject further."

"There must be some mistake—some terrible mistake. I cannot conceive it possible."

She remained silent for a few moments, and then said, suddenly—

"Darcy, you are going to Richmond to-day. As soon as Stella is sufficiently recovered we also shall come. Leave it to me. Surely I ought to know my own sister. I will bring you a message from her of very different import."

Darcy, smiling faintly, said, "Nonsense, Angela. You do not know what you are talking of."

"But it is not nonsense, Darcy, and I do know of what I am speaking," she said, earnestly; "trust me."

"I must be going now, Angela," he said, anxious not to prolong the subject. "Adieu until we meet in Richmond."

"Good-bye, Darcy. I will keep my word, trust me."

He made no reply, and the next moment Angela was alone.

On his arrival in Richmond, Darcy Leigh's first visit was to Coralie. There could be no misunderstanding the cordial joy with which she greeted him, and Darcy could not but be sensible of it.

"Miss St. Casse," he said, as soon as they were alone, "here are some papers which were given me by a friend. They relate to you, and it is right you should have them."

The subject was a delicate one, and not wishing to wound her feelings, Darcy merely handed them to her unopened, and wished to drop the subject. She, however, not knowing the nature of these papers, asked—

"Papers relating to me? What is their nature?"

"You know the claim which Mr. Lupus Rock attempted

to set up, but which he was compelled to relinquish by my friend Captain George?"

Coralie coloured up and looked embarrassed. It was not unnatural that it should be painful to her feelings to be reminded of the degrading claim made upon her liberty by Lupus.

"That dreadful man! How can I ever thank your friend the Englishman sufficiently for his noble conduct? Do you think it is true, Darcy? Do you really believe that he could have made good his claim, and that I was indeed a slave?"

"Legally, Miss St. Casse, I believe he could have claimed you; but that he ever would have done so is another matter."

"But he would have done so, else why did he take all this trouble? Why did he purchase the slaves from my cousin?"

"I do not doubt that he would have attempted to enforce his claim; but that he would have been allowed to succeed is quite impossible. Do you think, Miss St. Casse, that you have no friends? Do you think you would find no one to champion you, or that, were you twenty times a slave, you would not be freed? Had not the Englishman forced him to relinquish his claim, there would be many who would do so. Why, half the gentlemen in the South would do battle in such a cause."

"Darcy," said Coralie, looking him in the face, "do you think worse of me on this account? The thought that I am or was a slave is humiliation enough. How much more bitter would be my humiliation were I to lose old friends."

"You cannot think so, Coralie," said Darcy, taking her hand. "I should be ungrateful and base indeed, could I forget all your kindness."

The evening sun shone through the open windows; a soft warm breeze rustled among the magnolia trees in the garden beneath. Darcy felt the warm hand he held tremble slightly in his grasp, and saw in the cast-down eyes and flushed face of the girl that, if he chose to speak, he need fear no refusal. The situation had its charm;

14—2

the calm quiet of the summer evening, the air of refine-
ment and luxury around, and above all, the brilliant
beauty of the young girl whose hand he held, all tended
to one inevitable end.

Coralie stood motionless beside him, nor attempted to
withdraw her hand. Darcy gazed on her in deep admiration, and thought she never appeared to such advantage.
She wore a white muslin dress confined at the waist by a
black velvet band, her black hair falling loosely over her
bare shoulders and neck—for she was in evening dress.
He could see her bosom heave, and noticed the colour
deepen on her face and neck, as she was conscious of his
admiring glances.

Still she gave no sign of displeasure, but remained
motionless, trembling before him. Darcy tried to reason
with himself. "Do I love her, or are my feelings those
of admiration only?" Thus he thought and strove to
master himself.

Perhaps she guessed what was passing in his mind, for
she raised her eyes from the ground and gazed in his face
with, as he thought, a reproachful glance.

To have resisted, with the light of her dark eyes flashing
on his, would have required more strength than he possessed. She made a motion as if to withdraw her hand
and end the embarrassing scene. But he gently detained
it, and drawing her towards him, placed his arm around
her waist. " Coralie," he said, in low tones, " you know,
you can guess what I am about to say. Shall I speak ?"

She made no reply in words, but he felt her nestle
closer to him. The next moment he had clasped her in
his arms.

" Coralie, I love you."

That was all that was said, nor could volumes have
spoken more. He kissed her cheek, her lips ; and she,
laying her head on his shoulder, wept tears of joy.

Her soft yielding form lay in his embrace, her breath
fanned his cheek, and he could feel the wild beating of her
heart against his breast.

This, though pleasant, could not last for ever, so gently
disengaging herself, and permitting him again to kiss her

DARCY AND CORALIE.—LOVE'S YOUNG DREAM.

lips, Coralie, her eyes beaming with the light of love, led Darcy out on the balcony, and, motioning him to take a low chair placed there, seated herself on a stool at his feet. Then she spoke in low, soft tones, breathing love in every accent.

"Darcy, you have made me so happy. I feared you did not care for me, and I loved you so deeply."

"Not care for you, Coralie! What should put such an idea into your head?"

"Do you know, I thought once you loved Miss Gayle; but now I know I was wrong."

Darcy felt a sudden pang at these words, and Stella's image rose involuntarily before him. Her great, grey eyes, he fancied, beamed scornfully on him, but he drove the phantom angrily back. "What am I to her or she to me?" he thought.

Then the soft tones of Coralie's voice, murmuring words of love, brought back his wandering thoughts. His duty and inclination now both prompted him to return the deep love she bore him and make her happy. Even if he had not loved her, it was certainly no painful task to learn, and if at first Darcy had some doubts as to his feelings, it was not long ere he was as desperately infatuated with Coralie—at once — so kind, generous, loving, and gloriously beautiful—as ever was foolish man of fair woman.

He was still weak, and suffered occasionally from low, intermittent fever, brought on by his wound; so Coralie made that an excuse, and insisted on his taking up his abode at her house.

Her cousin, Edward St. Casse, was also a visitor there, so she silenced Darcy's faint resistance, and claimed as a right, the task of nursing him till well. Every afternoon, for many days, she would lead him out on the balcony, and, taking her seat at his feet, would indulge in her sweet dream of love; nor is it strange that with such gentle tending, Darcy was in no hurry to be completely cured.

# CHAPTER XXI.

## A FREE FIGHT.

Thus, for some time, the summer days passed on. There was a lull in the war, the Federals being in no humour to renew the campaign in Virginia, with the shattered and demoralized Army of the Potomac. Darcy Leigh abandoned himself to the pleasing intoxication of Coralie's love, and day by day, in the light of her smiles and bright eyes, he grew more and more deeply in love.

The mornings were spent about the town or on the quiet waters of the James River. Occasionally Coralie would accompany Darcy to the parade ground of her *own* regiment, as she called the 7th Carolina's. Often when Darcy was asked playfully when he intended to be quite recovered and return to duty, Coralie would answer for him, and declare it would take a long time to restore him completely to health and strength. On such occasions her eyes would rest tenderly on the face of Darcy, as though she regretted that the time must come when her care would no longer be necessary.

Nevertheless, Darcy gained strength so rapidly, that, for very shame, he could not remain any longer on the sick-list, and after some faint opposition from Coralie, he sent a note to the colonel of his regiment declaring himself ready to resume duty.

This was on the very day when Webster Gayle and his two daughters arrived in Richmond—Stella being sufficiently recovered.

On the afternoon of the day when the supper given by the ladies of Richmond to the officers in the town was to take place, Darcy was strolling down the principal street with Coralie on his arm. The young lady was bent on shopping, and had already ransacked several stores in search of some articles of luxury or adornment, on which she had set her heart. Darcy not caring to enter with her, usually remained outside the shop while she

went in search of what she wanted. It was after she had
tried several in vain, and was making an unusually long
stay in one, that Darcy, almost tired of sauntering up
and down, was thinking of going in and reclaiming
her from the gay fascinations of dress and ornament
which detained her, when he perceived two ladies and a
gentleman approaching on the same side of the street.
It required not a second glance for him to recognise
Webster Gayle and his daughters. Angela looked well
and blooming, and greeted him with affectionate warmth,
a flush of pleasure mantling her fair cheek. Stella shook
hands and languidly greeted him. Looking in her face,
he felt a pang of grief as he observed how pale and wan
it was.

"I am so glad to see you have recovered, Stella," he
said, in earnest tones; "our Southern climate will, I
trust, soon restore the roses to your cheeks. Richmond
is a healthy town. I doubt not but in a few weeks you
will have recovered all your strength, and bring half the
young men of the city to your feet."

He spoke without embarrassment or hesitation, and
after warmly pressing her hand, he turned and addressed
Webster Gayle.

"You, too, have been ill from the effect of your
wounds, have you not, Captain Leigh?" asked Stella, in
tones she tried to render firm and unconcerned.

"Yes; I have suffered from low fever, but now, thanks
to a good constitution and good nursing, I am quite well
again. I resume duty to-day for the first time."

"And shall you again risk life and health in this terrible conflict?" she asked.

"Assuredly. Do you think so meanly of me, Stella?—
do you imagine I could fail in my duty—or what I con·
sider my duty?"

"No, I do not, Darcy—I know you better; but, nevertheless, I regret it."

There was something in the earnest kindness of the
words which struck strangely on Darcy's ear. He raised
his eyes quickly, and caught hers fixed on his face, with
a glance which, though he could not quite interpret, sent

the colour to his face, and caused a thrill to shoot through his frame. There was a faint tinge of pink, too, on the pale face of Stella. She did not drop her gaze immediately ; her large grey eyes, seeming even more lustrous from the pallor of her complexion, looked earnestly, wistfully in his face for a moment or so ; then she let them fall, and the faint pink on her cheek deepened to crimson.

Darcy Leigh, in spite of himself, felt considerably embarrassed, more especially as he knew that Angela was intently watching him.

The two girls now moved on a little, while Darcy remained standing by Webster Gayle. He noticed that Stella glanced back in a timid manner—her head half-turned over her shoulder. Darcy felt discomposed, and strange doubts possessed him. What was Stella's meaning—was she coquetting with him ? But that was so foreign to her pure, proud nature, that he at once dismissed the thought. For a brief time he hesitated, and then, scarcely knowing why, he joined the two girls and walked by their side.

Stella spoke not a word, but walked slowly on, her eyes on the ground, and nervously playing with the tassel of her sun-shade. Darcy could not but see that she was deeply agitated from some cause or other, and thought possibly she might be unwell.

" Stella," he said, doubtfully, " I fear you are unwell ? Perhaps the heat is too much for you ?—will you cross to the other side, to the shade ?"

" No, I thank you ; I am quite well."

Again, for an instant, she raised her eyes to his ; the look welling up from their depths was unmistakable ;— it was a sorrowful, appealing look—as though, spirit-broken and miserable, she asked for forgiveness.

For a moment Darcy's heart stood still. Was he then mistaken ? Did the proud Stella really care for him ?— and had she so far forgotten her pride as thus mutely to own it ? For the time he forgot everything—he forgot past slights and insults, and he looked on the pale, beautiful girl by his side, and his early love, with all its force, swept over his soul. He saw her pale, contrite, and more beautiful than ever; the old haughty look had fled, and a gentle, beseeching expression had taken its place. For a moment he forgot himself—he forgot his honour, duty—he forgot Coralie, to whom he had pledged himself. But at that instant the Southern beauty issued from the shop, and looked around for her escort. Darcy, whose face was partly turned that way, saw her, and instantly he was recalled to himself. He turned very pale, and the words which were on his lips died away. He halted suddenly, to the great amazement of Angela.

"Excuse me, ladies," he said, hurriedly, "I must leave you now."

Stella said not a word, but turned away her head. Angela, however, returned a few paces to where Darcy stood.

"Papa, will you walk on with Stella?—I wish to speak a few words to Captain Leigh."

Webster Gayle obeyed, and Angela at once began, speaking quickly and nervously.

"Darcy, when I saw you last, we spoke of Stella—I told you you were mistaken, and that——"

"Stop, Angela; for Heaven's sake, stop! You do not know what you are talking of."

"But I will not stop," cried Angela, passionately. "You owned—you told me—you loved my sister. You told herself so."

"Yes; and she replied that she would not return my love—that she was engaged to her cousin Lupus."

"Listen to me, Darcy. Whatever may have been the case with Lupus, it is not so now. Stella is free. It is true that Lupus Rock still hopes; but unless he again succeeds by his wicked scheming in getting our father in his power, his chance is hopeless. Stella loathes—detests him; at the same time, fears him. He is desperately wicked—desperately treacherous—desperately cunning. I tremble for poor Stella. Even now I believe he is plotting and scheming. Darcy, let it be your task to shield and guard her from this man—let yours be the arm interposed between her and the man she hates, but in whose toils she may yet again fall. Let it be at once your pride and pleasure to watch over and protect her."

Angela paused; her blue eyes beamed imploringly in Darcy's face; gentle and timid as a fawn, for herself she could not have said a word, but pleaded passionately for her beloved sister.

Darcy was strangely moved, and knew not what to reply. Time pressed, however, and Coralie, whom Angela had not perceived, impatiently awaited him.

"Angela, it shall be as you say; so far as it lies in my power I will defend her with my life. As for Lupus Rock, I do not fear him. If he does couple her name with his in any way, it shall be my task to make him eat his words. This I will do for 'Auld Lang Syne,' Angela; more I cannot say."

Angela's eyes beamed with pleasure. Knowing her sister's love, she proudly congratulated her on having secured her happiness, for had not Darcy himself owned *his* love.

"And you will speak to Stella, Darcy?"

"Impossible, Angela; it would be folly and worse."

"Darcy, you stupid fellow, will you never understand? Must I tell you in plain words that——"

"Stay! Angela," he interrupted.

"Once again I tell you, Stella is free. You love her, and she——"

"Angela, will you be silent?" said Darcy, vehemently, pale as death, and almost trembling with excitement. "You say Stella is free. I *am not.* Adieu."

Then he pressed her hand, and hastened to rejoin Coralie.

Angela remained speechless from dismay and grief. She saw him rejoin Coralie, who took his arm. In an instant the truth flashed across her mind. Smarting from his haughty rejection by Stella, and thrown into the society of the pretty Southerner, Darcy had become infatuated with her splendid beauty, had declared his love, and had been accepted.

Poor Angela! Thus was the dream and hope of her gentle heart rudely dashed. How she hated Coralie, while she watched her retreating figure as she swept proudly down the street, leaning on Darcy's arm. What stupid dolts, she tried to persuade herself, were the men, who turned back as she passed, and looked after her with undisguised admiration. How foolish were the women, who regarded her with envious glances! She was not handsome—she was a bold, bad, intriguing girl!

This and much more injustice Angela did Coralie in her bitter grief. Her blue eyes filled with tears of rage and shame, and stamping her little foot, she exclaimed passionately to herself—

"It is best so. Darcy Leigh is unworthy of our beautiful Stella. The idea of the fool preferring that dark girl to my sister!"

"He is unworthy of you," she said, indignantly, in reply to Stella's inquiring glance, when she rejoined them. "He is a weak, foolish, mean fellow."

"Weak, foolish, mean!" cried Stella, firing up. "It is not true, Angela, and you know it. It is I who am to blame, it is I who should bear the punishment. Darcy Leigh is all that is good and brave and honourable. What has he done that you should think differently?"

"Done?" said Angela, indignantly, "why, he has engaged himself to that bold, artful girl—Coralie St. Casse."

At these words of Angela, Stella suddenly turned ashy pale, every vestige of colour forsook her face, even to her lips. She grasped Angela's arm, as though fearing to fall.

"Angela," she gasped, while her eyes dilated wildly, "are you sure—do you know this?"

"Angela, alarmed by her deadly pallor and trembling excitement, sought to fence off the question.

"I will tell you all about it presently, Stella. Papa, let us come into an hotel—Stella is faint."

"Answer me, Angela; do not trifle with me. Quick, speak! this suspense is worse than death. Are you sure?"

"Yes, it is too true, Stella; I am sure," said Angela, with bitter anguish. "Now come on; let us come in here, and rest for a few minutes."

Webster Gayle took one arm of his daughter and Angela the other, fearing, from her continued deadly pallor, she would fall. But they were mistaken. Stella recovered herself, and, though still pale as death, she detached her arms from theirs, and walked firmly, proudly on, as though scorning to give way.

Webster Gayle, seriously alarmed, in spite of her forced composure, hurried up the hotel steps, and ordered a negro waiter to show them to a private room.

Stella threw herself on a couch, and lay for a time motionless—as though utterly exhausted.

"It is nothing, papa," she said, presently; "I am not quite strong yet, and fancy the heat and the walk have been too much for me. I should like a glass of wine."

The wine was brought, and in a few minutes Stella, though very pale, seemed to have entirely recovered.

She rose from the couch and carefully re-arranged her bonnet, and the folds of her dress.

"Now I am ready, papa; let us go home. It must be near dinner time. How stupid of me to frighten you so."

None but herself could tell the desperate effort this forced composure and careless words cost her.

\*    \*    \*    \*    \*    \*

"Darcy, dear, how pale you look," said Coralie, when he rejoined her. "You really must be careful, I am afraid you are not really well yet."

"I think it is the heat, Coralie; let us cross to the other side into the shade."

"What a conference you were holding with Miss Angela Gayle. May I be permitted to ask the subject? I declare I feel quite jealous," she said, laughingly.

"You have no reason, Coralie. Angela was speaking to me about her sister and Lupus Rock, of whom she stands in great dread. It seems that he is scheming for the hand of Stella, who detests him.

"But I thought they were engaged."

"Yes, once; but that is all over. Lupus only forced her to listen to his suit by availing himself of her fears for her father's safety, whom, it appears, the cunning scoundrel had, by some means, got into his power."

"Scoundrel, indeed!" cried Coralie, indignantly, "we all knew that long since; but if possible my contempt and loathing for the man is intensified. To think of such meanness! Force himself on the poor girl by trading on her love for her father and her fear of him! I hope, Darcy, you will do all you can to protect her from his schemes."

"I have promised to do so, Coralie," he said, quietly, "and so far as lies in my power I will assuredly keep my word."

"You dear, noble boy, you. But promise me not to endanger yourself in any way. You know I have some little right to you now."

"Every right, Coralie," he replied, with a faint smile, "and, tyrant that you are, you do not fail to exercise it."

"Am I, then, so very tyrannical?" she asked, reproachfully.

"Oh, yes, very; but it is a pleasing bondage, and the slave kisses his chains."

At this moment they passed through a wicket into the garden at the back of Coralie's house. She glanced mischievously in his face at his last words; and the slave did more than kiss his chains—he kissed herself.

Her dark eyes sparkled with pleasure, and she ran hastily up the garden, followed more leisurely by Darcy.

Who shall say that in the midst of his dream of happiness, the sad, pale image of Stella Gayle, his early love, did not arise in fancy before him?

Who shall say that the joys of the present were not slightly dashed by memories of hopes and aspirations of the past—that the cup of nectar was without some drops of bitter?

Gerald Leigh and Captain George were now also in Richmond, and in the evening they called round for Darcy, that he might accompany them to the supper to be given at the Nebraska hotel. Coralie declined to go, declaring that she felt too tired, and she did what she could to dissuade Darcy. But he, restless and uneasy, having not yet got over his interview with Angela Gayle, was bent on going, and not all Coralie's persuasions and assertions that he was not sufficiently recovered, could deter him.

Accordingly the three strolled out together, and entered the hotel where the affair was to take place.

Already the street in front was blocked by carriages, and the balconies and windows were brilliant with gauze, muslin, and the many-coloured dresses of the ladies.

The hotel was the largest in Richmond, but on this occasion every room, every avenue was blocked.

Crowds of officers stood at the large bar, not so much for the sake of drinking as to secure a "stand-point," till the gong should proclaim the repast ready.

Supper it was called, but it should rather have been styled a late dinner, as it was to take place at eight o'clock, and night was but just setting in.

George and Gerald noticed that Darcy appeared restless and distraught, but knew not how to account for it.

"Come, Gerald," said the latter, "let's come to the bar and 'liquor up.' I feel a cup too low, and reckon a brandy smash will do no harm."

"With all my heart," replied his brother, elbowing his way through the crowd.

Darcy called for the liquor and drank his off at a draught, to the no small surprise of Gerald. But Darcy, not content with one, called for another, and yet a third —and it is by no means certain that a fourth would not have followed, had not the great gong boomed forth the summons to supper.

It was a brilliant affair. About three hundred were present, and fully half of them were ladies. Their white dresses, gay ribbons, and sparkling jewels showed to all the more advantage by the side of the plain grey uniforms of the officers. As the repast proceeded, the chill which always pervades the commencement of such assemblies, wore off. The murmur of voices, silvery peals of laughter, the clatter of glasses and popping of corks, all mingled together. Bright eyes sparkled, the fair owners just a *little* exhilarated by the wine the gentlemen assiduously pressed on them, and all was mirth and gaiety.

But the more merry and joyous the company, the more morose and gloomy became Darcy Leigh. It was in vain he tried to arouse himself and drive off the dark fancies which haunted him. Copious draughts of wine made the blood course more rapidly through his veins, and caused his face to flush, but his mood was no merrier. He felt fierce and savage, he could hardly tell why. He reasoned and asked himself what there was to cause so deep a gloom. Was he not beloved by the beautiful Coralie— lovely as the summer night—rich, amiable, and accomplished? Undoubtedly. Did he not in return love this fond girl, whose whole soul was centred in him?

As he asked himself the question, her image rose before him—the graceful figure, the lustrous eyes, and lovely face. He saw in fancy the soft, beaming expression on her features, with which she was wont to regard him. Instantly his heart warmed towards her, and he answered himself that he did love her—deeply, passionately—as such a woman deserved to be loved.

But then in fancy another form flitted before him— that of a tall, fair girl with large grey eyes ; in fancy, he saw his old love, Stella Gayle, with her queenly carriage and swooping crest. Do what he would, he could not drive away the phantom.

As the time passed, the merriment and noise increased, till, in the confounding din of laughter and the rattle of glasses, the ladies had difficulty in making themselves heard even to their immediate neighbours. So uproarious did the revellers become, that ere long the ladies judged it prudent to retire.

This was the signal for increased uproar. Songs and toasts were now the order of the day. The " Bonnie Blue Flag," which may be said to be the Confederate national song, was roared forth again and again, the crowd outside taking up the chorus, and waking up the echoes on the distant Virginian hills.

Darcy Leigh sang and shouted as though his heart were as light, his spirits as high, as any among that company.

Gerald was seated next him, and Captain George some little distance down the table.

Either by accident or design, a great number of the officers of the Seventh Carolinas were seated near Darcy Leigh, on the same side of the table. Nearly opposite Darcy was Lupus Rock, and around him were many of the officers of the regiment which he had raised, and in which he held a commission.

Lupus had contrived, in a great measure, to secure officers whom he thought he might bend to his own purposes. Though of course every appointment was nominally made by government, yet in the case of any one who at his own cost and risk raised a regiment, they were not particularly strict, so long as the officers proposed were sufficiently up in drill. As for the men, Lupus had taken especial care to enrol by choice the greatest rowdies and blackguards to be found in the Confederacy.

Darcy Leigh had not spoken to Lupus Rock, but if looks meant anything, his feelings were the reverse of friendly.

Lupus, flushed with wine, did not fail to return these amiable glances, and the scowling faces of the two were noticed by many, and a quarrel was thought not unlikely.

During the intervals between the songs, toasts were proposed and noisily drunk. Every one who chose proposed some lady, either by name or by some *sobriquet* by which the fair one was known. At least a dozen young men had risen, and having, with due solemnity, demanded order, proceeded to proclaim their own particular lady-love as *belle* of Richmond, and proposed her health accordingly.

Lupus Rock several times set on p... the point of rising, but on each occasion he was forestalled.

Darcy Leigh, who had a vague presentiment that he would propose a toast which it would be his place to ban, felt a fierce joy at the thoughts of an approaching row. Certain it is he was never before in so savage a temper, and weak though he was, warmed by the wine he had taken, he thought himself equal to any encounter, however desperate.

His eyes glared vindictively on Lupus, who, though well aware of it, affected not to see. Both had been drinking freely, Darcy particularly.

Lupus, who at times had a species of desperate courage, by no means felt disposed to shun the encounter on this occasion. He hated Darcy Leigh with the most bitter hatred. He knew that Stella loved him, and on that account he thought she so scorned his own suit. Then it was well known that Darcy was formally engaged to Coralie St. Casse, and there, too, Lupus had been ignominiously worsted by his rival.

Of Coralie he had for the present given up all thoughts. His schemes had been so utterly frustrated by the Englishman that he by no means felt inclined to renew the contest with a man who had in every way shown himself his master.

But he looked on Darcy as a boy, who had achieved his position only by good luck and foolish daring. He had never yet been in collision with him. It is true he had crossed his path, and on more than one occasion had foiled his plans. But when he thought of Stella Gayle, who he knew loved Darcy, he ground his teeth with rage.

At the first pause Lupus Rock rose, and, something like order being restored, he addressed the company.

He was pale enough, though his eyes were bloodshot and inflamed from the deep draughts of wine he had indulged in.

Feeling that the eyes of Darcy Leigh were upon him, he first glanced around him to see by how many of his own adherents he was surrounded, and furtively felt for the hilt of his sword, determined, if there was a row, to be prompt in its use, and so possibly disable his adversary at once.

In America, and especially in the South and West, it is " a word and a blow ;" nor, in a quarrel, is it thought murder among rowdies for one who is readier than the other to draw bowie knife or revolver before his enemy

15

has time to do likewise, and thus settle the affair at once by a shot or a stab.

"Gentlemen," said Lupus, at the top of his voice, "many of you have given toasts and proposed the healths of ladies whom you severally declared peerless in beauty. I now claim my right to propose the health of one to whom all must yield the palm".—(Cheers, shouts, and yells from his own adherents, and cries of "Name! name!") "It is no matter that the lady I am about to propose is not a Southerner, either by birth or sympathies, but a strong Yankee ;—yet, gentlemen, I do not think we make war upon women."—(" Brayvo !" "Cheers for the fair Yankee !"—" Who is she ?"—" Bet a dollar I know !" These and many other cries here interrupted him.) "All in good time, gentlemen. The lady whose health I am about to propose, I have the honour to be related to, and hope that relation will some day be yet closer——"

Darcy Leigh leaped to his feet.

"Mr. Lupus Rock," he said, quietly, "if I am right in my guess as to whom you allude, I warn you not to do it."

"I have yet to learn that I am under your orders, Mr. Darcy Leigh," he replied, insolently ; "and, as I am not a private in the Seventh Carolinas, I shall do as I please." Derisive cheers from his own side greeted this speech.

"At your peril !" shouted Darcy, feeling for his sword. Unfortunately he had not his sword with him, having unbuckled it and laid it on a side table. In his present mood, however, that would not deter him.

Lupus did not fail to notice that Darcy wore no sword, and, with a smile of affected contempt, proceeded, though not without turning somewhat paler.

"The lady, gentlemen, whose health I am now about to propose, is——"

"Once again at your peril !" shouted Darcy.

"Her name is Miss Stella Gayle," said Lupus.

No sooner were the words out of his mouth, than Darcy seized and hurled a bottle full at his head. How-

"DARCY SEIZED THE CHAIR ON WHICH HE HAD BEEN SITTING, AND LEAPED ON THE TABLE."

ever, it struck his breast, and though he staggered back
from the blow, the next instant he drew his sword, and,
amidst terrible uproar, lunged furiously at Darcy's unprotected body.

Fortunately his thrust did not take effect, for a dozen
missiles were instantly aimed at him by Darcy's friends
—tumblers, plates, bottles flew about in glorious style,
and some of these so deranged his aim, that his sword,
instead of running Darcy through the body, passed under
his arm, inflicting merely a slight graze.

Darcy had neither sword nor revolver, but without a
moment's hesitation, he seized the chair on which he
had been sitting and leaped on the table. Frantic
with rage, he seemed possessed with the very demon of
fight.

Smash! crash! the chair came down on Lupus Rock's
head and shoulders. In vain he endeavoured to parry
and run his assailant through the body. His guard was
beaten down at the second blow, at the third his sword
flew from his hands, and the fourth blow descended full
upon his head and shoulders. For a moment he staggered
back and felt in the breast of his tunic for his revolver,
but ere he could draw it, one final smash on the head
sent him prone to the earth, stunned and bleeding.

Loud cheers from Darcy's side of the table hailed this
victory, while yells of rage burst from Lupus Rock's
friends.

Several now drew their swords, and prepared to attack
Darcy as he stood on the table defiantly, swinging his
impromptu weapon ; and his friends crowding to his support, the fight became general.

The numbers on each side were about equal, Lupus
Rock having on his side of the table many of the subalterns of his regiment. These were mostly men without
property or character, having spent the one and lost the
other.

One and all then rallied round him, and while some
raised him from the ground, others commenced a furious
attack on Darcy Leigh and his party. At first the fight
was by missiles only, but as the supply of tumblers and

crockery began to fall short, the chairs and benches were broken up, and many drew their swords.

Lupus Rock, as soon as he was a little recovered, leaped on the table and, sword in hand, slashed and cut furiously about him. "Slay them!—slaughter them!" he shouted, "drive the hounds out of the window."

With loud yells his party leaped on the table, and charged their opponents' ranks. So long as they remained on the table they were on vantage-ground, but when the others retreated, and they, leaping down, followed them, the fight was more equal. Gerald Leigh and Captain George leading a charge, they were driven back, and were glad to scramble over the table again, with many a bleeding head and bruised limb.

The windows were wide open, and the mob in the street could plainly see the scrimmage among the officers. Feeling himself getting worsted, Lupus dashed downstairs, and going out to the porch, shouted, "Come on, my boys—follow me—five dollars a-piece, and lots of liquor!"

This was a very powerful inducement; and when he again ran upstairs, he was followed by a shouting mob of roughs and rowdies, who, arming themselves with bottles, or whatever they could lay their hands on, rushed into the long room, and, with savage yells, backed up their employer.

Finding himself in an overwhelming majority, and knowing the popularity of Darcy Leigh and his friends, Lupus determined to guard against reinforcements coming to the other side. Accordingly, while his new allies mounted the table and savagely attacked the others, he employed himself in locking up and barricading the door. He then joined his ruffians, and, sword in hand, attacked Darcy and his friends, who were slowly retiring before the overwhelming numbers.

The uproar was now deafening—the shouts and yells within the room were echoed by the mob outside, and soon a thundering noise at the door told that an attempt was being made to force it.

And now Gerald and Darcy Leigh have been forced

out on the balcony, notwithstanding a desperate resistance. Gerald's right arm is disabled by a blow from the
leg of a chair ; and Darcy, though unhurt, feels the effect
of his late wound and subsequent illness, for he is quite
faint and weak, and is glad to take a moment's breathing
time. Meanwhile, Captain George, the Englishman, is
fighting desperately at the head of the little band. It is
evidently not the first row of the kind he has been in,
for though many blows are aimed at him, and he seems
to expose himself recklessly, yet his guard is always
ready, and the return both quick and severe, as more
than one bleeding head testifies.

Darcy Leigh, while taking a moment's breathing time
on the balcony, notices in the shouting mob below a
number of the men of the Carolina Crashers—some are
endeavouring to batter in the front doors of the hotel,
which have now been closed and barricaded by the
proprietor. Nearly opposite was an unfinished house—
bricks and mortar, scaffolding, and ladders abounding.
Darcy caught sight of Darby Kelly, who was foremost
in pounding away at the front door.

"Darby, Darby ! he cried ; "up by the balcony—get
a ladder from over the way—quick !"

On hearing his master's voice, Darby gave a peal of
joy. In an instant he caught the words and their
meaning.

"Come along wid me—lave the door ; if we can't
get in that way, by Jabers ! we will by the windy." Then
shouting to the rest to follow him, he fought his way
through the mob to the other side of the street.

A ladder was quickly shouldered by half-a-dozen, and
charging battering-ram fashion across the street, in a jiffy
it was raised to the balcony. Darby Kelly was the first
up, and leaped on the verandah, followed by three or four
more of Darcy Leigh's company.

"Hirroo for the captain ! Tear an' ouns, blood an'
tunder !—here goes for ould Ireland !" And rushing into
the room, he snatched up a bench, and breaking it across .
his knee, he swung the half of it around his head, and
went into the fight.

This welcome reinforcement was not a moment too soon The odds were still greatly against them, for only some six or seven had yet made their way up the ladder, and they were outnumbered fully two to one.

Captain George about this time received a blow in the shoulder, which sent him staggering back out on the balcony, where already three or four had retired disabled. His quick eye caught the piles of bricks and building materials opposite. Several were already swarming up the ladder to the rescue, when a thought struck him.

"Quick, all of you," he shouted, "over the way,—pass up some hodsful of bricks." There were two or three Irish friends of Darby Kelly, at the foot of the ladder, waiting to come up, and they at once took up the idea. Before a brick was thrown, every one on the balcony armed himself with two; and shouting to their friends within to stand back, Captain George gave the word, and a crashing volley was delivered. This was quickly followed by another, and quite changed the state of affairs.

Lupus Rock's party fell back panic-stricken at this un-expected storm. Add to this that each minute fresh men of the Crashers swarmed up the ladder and took part in the fray. Although still superior in numbers, they crowded together in the corner like a flock of sheep. The bricks flew about their heads like hail. Some hastily re-moved the barricade and endeavoured to open the door. This operation was accelerated by a movement origi-nated by Darby Kelly. Running to the front, and followed by four or five others, they lifted a heavy table, and wheeling it round on their shoulders, used it as a battering-ram and charged the enemy. This completed their discomfiture. The door was thrown open, and they fled in panic down the stairs.

"Clear out of this, ye vagabones. We're the boys for blood and tunder, ye thieves of the world. Hirroo! run it at the varmints; and then borne on sturdy shoul-ders, the heavy table would be dragged back and again dashed forward, amidst oaths, screams, and yells from the overpowered, and with shouts of laughter and triumph from the conquerors.

A final shower of bricks followed the last of Lupus Rock's party, and the victors were left in possession of the battle-field. None were seriously hurt, though many had received cuts and bruises. The table was replaced on the settles, more liquor was called for, and the proprietor having been conciliated by the promise of payment for all damage done, the welcome aid of Darby Kelly and his friends was acknowledged by *carte blanche* to order whisky ; and what with singing, shouting, and the general triumph and uproar, the morning was far advanced before the victors broke up, the foe leaving them in peace, nor again attempting an entrance.

There was but little soreness of feeling, at least on the side of Darby and his party, the affair being looked on as a free fight, which had ended gloriously for them. On the other side, however, it was different ; and much ill-blood and many future quarrels arose out of this night's work. Lupus especially, desperately savage and vindictive, swore with a dreadful oath as he passed out of the hotel with his gang, that Darcy Leigh should pay for it with his life.

Meanwhile, not thinking of the consequences to follow, shortly after daylight Gerald, Captain George, and Darcy left the scene of the fight and victory—the former for their quarters, and the latter to the house of Miss St. Casse, where for the present he resided.

## CHAPTER XXII.

### THE DUEL.

DARCY LEIGH did not make his appearance at the usual breakfast hour on the following morning. Indeed it was past noon when he strolled into the room where Coralie and breakfast had been for hours waiting him. A glance at his flushed, feverish face and eyes, told the young lady that the previous night had been passed, to say the least, in a convivial manner.

However, she said nothing; but as he declined to partake of either coffee or the various delicacies spread before him on the table, she compounded him an iced drink to cool his palate and quench the burning thirst.

"There, sir, drink that," she said, handing it to him, "and think yourself better treated than you deserve."

"He drained it off gratefully enough, and then went out on the balcony, and took his old seat in the rocking-chair, Coralie placing herself on a stool at his feet.

"And now tell me all about last night's proceedings," she said, "disgraceful enough, I have no doubt. I begged of you not to go, weak and ill as you are. You would not take my advice—now see the results. Your head aches, your tongue is parched, your hand hot, and altogether you are feverish and ill. What have you to say for yourself?"

"Very little, Coralie," he replied, languidly, "except that I am very sorry. So please don't bully me."

"Bully you!" she said, laughing; "certainly, Darcy, you are the coolest fellow in the world. You go out in the evening against my wish, leaving me all alone—you indulge in what I fear was a terrible debauch—come down to breakfast the next day at one o'clock—cannot touch your coffee, but condescend to let me make you some iced sherbet—and, then, when you are asked to account for your overnight's doings, you say, "don't bully me!" I wont bully you, as you call it, but I insist on your relating the history of the supper and the *finale*."

"Of the supper I know very little, Coralie," he said. "I only know there were hosts of pretty women there—that lots of wine were drunk—songs sung and toasts given. Then when the ladies retired there was more wine, more songs, and more toasts, till all got pretty well flushed. Then to wind up there was a trifle of a row, and then I came home. There, now I have told you."

"Indeed!" she said; "and do you think I am going to be satisfied with that? There was a trifle of a row you say. Between whom, and what was it about?"

"Well, it was between our fellows and some of Lupus Rock's blackguards, headed by himself. I reckon we made it rather hot for them, however," he added, brightening up at the memory of the victory; "we were outnumbered three to one, Coralie, and what do you think we did?"

" Really I can't imagine."

" Why, there was some building going on over the road—ladders, bricks, scaffolding, and all that sort of thing, you know; well, I saw my man, Darby Kelly, in the road, so I shouted to him to get a ladder and carry bricks up. Then I rather imagine we gave them snakes —lay my life some of their ribs ache this morning."

" I know some one whose head aches, at least," she said, smiling ; "but you have not told me what this disgraceful row was about. How did it commence?"

" Oh, it began with myself and Lupus Rock ; and then my fellows took my side, and his rowdies his, and so the fight became general."

" But what was it about? You have not yet told me."

" Oh—ah—you know, Coralie, when fellows get a little too much, any little trifle breeds a quarrel."

" Yes, but what particular trifle bred this quarrel."

" Well, don't you see, Coralie, it was about some song, or toast or —— something ; and then, you know, Lupus's fellows took it up, and then we took it up, and so the fight became general."

" Yes, exactly," she said, laughing at his attempt at evasion, " you said that before ; but you have not told me what was the original cause of the quarrel."

" Well, don't you see," he stammered, and then suddenly started up. " Hilloa, by Jove, here's Chloe with a letter ;" and a female slave advanced, bearing something on a salver. It was not a letter, however, but a card.

" Dere's a gemmen in de hall want to see Massa Capt'n Leigh. He tell me take up dis card."

Darcy took it and read—

" Lieutenant Soames, 8th Virginia Regiment."

" Don't know the fellow," he muttered ; " wonder what the deuce he wants with me. However, I'll go and see. Shan't be a minute, Coralie."

He was not gone more than a minute, and returned looking somewhat troubled.

"What is it, Darcy ?  You look vexed."

" Oh, nothing, nothing ; it's only a little business relating to my brother and his friend.  By-the-bye, I must walk round to their quarters."

" Indeed, you shall do nothing of the kind.  The heat of the sun in your present state would give you a fever.  I will send round ; Nina will not mind going, I am sure.  Who is it you want—your brother ?"

" No, I would rather see Captain George first."

Coralie ran off, and returned accompanied by Nina, who had for the present discarded her *vivandière* costume, and plainly but tastefully dressed, looked more charming than ever.

" By Jove, Nina, you get handsomer every day.  I declare, Coralie, you must look to your laurels."

Nina blushed and laughed, and Coralie said—

" There, don't flatter her, Darcy.  I daresay she has plenty of woman's vanity.  Nina, Captain Leigh will feel obliged if you will run round to the quarters of his brother, and deliver a message to Captain George.  Will you go ?"

" Oh, yes, willingly.  What is the message ?"

" Only to ask him to come round here *alone*.  Bring him back with you, but be sure you do not let Gerald accompany him."

Nina laughed, and ran off on her errand, sooth to say, by no means sorry to have an opportunity of seeing her friend, the young Englishman.

Since the return to Richmond Nina had left off her *vivandière* uniform, and appeared to quite as great advantage in plain dress.  Coralie treated her on terms of perfect equality as a friend, a companion, and insisted on the same respect being shown her by all who visited the house.  She was not so dark as many a Northern brunette, and the faint wave in her hair was but an additional beauty.  It is not wonderful that, with all the advantages which dress and toilette conferred on her already handsome face and form, Nina should attract many admirers.  None, however, could make any way, for she studiously kept herself aloof from all.

In less than half an hour she returned with the Englishman, and said, laughing—

"I caught him! He was just going to mount his horse, and made desperate attempts to escape, but it was hopeless."

"Hopeless indeed, Nina," said Captain George. "Those bright eyes of yours might well hold any one captive. To show, however, that I bear my captor no ill-will, may I offer my escort for a ride presently, Nina?"

The girl's eyes sparkled with pleasure, and she turned inquiringly to Coralie.

"Certainly, Nina. You can order any of the horses you choose. You had better run and put your riding-habit on. Stay! I will come with you. I see these gentlemen want to talk privately."

"Do you know this fellow?" said Darcy, tossing over the card as soon as they were alone.

"Can't say I do. What does he want?"

"Comes with a challenge from Lupus Rock," was the laconic reply.

"Hem! What will you do?"

"Don't know; that's why I sent for you."

Having talked it over for some time, Captain George came to the conclusion that Darcy should fight.

"The fellow's an infernal blackguard, and you might, if you chose, refuse to meet him. Still, under the circumstances, it might give rise to unpleasant remarks. These infernal fellows would be insolent and boastful, and probably other quarrels would arise, and blood be spilt before they could be taught manners."

"Yes, you are quite right, George—I must fight him; and if I rid the world for ever of the scoundrel, it will be, I believe, a good deed. Will you see this fellow Soames about it, and arrange matters as soon as possible. To-morrow, at daybreak, I should think would do."

"Pistols?"

"Yes—one barrel of a revolver."

"You are a good shot?"

"Yes, very. I have no fear, and shall do my best to let daylight through him. When will you call on Soames?"

" I am going for a ride with Nina, and will stop on my
way—I wont take five minutes."

" Let one of the servants brew you a julep ?"

" Don't mind."

Darcy rang a small bell, ordered two iced drinks, and
before they were finished Coralie and Nina reappeared,
the latter in a riding-habit and hat.

" Have you, gentlemen, finished your conference ?"

" Yes, quite ; and George here is impatient to be off.
Look round in the evening, old fellow, and tell me what
arrangements you have made ; and, by the way,"—
calling him back—"don't say anything to Gerald, it
would make him uneasy uselessly."

" Very good," said Captain George.

No sooner were they gone than Coralie asked—

" What would make your brother uneasy uselessly ?"

" Oh, nothing of any importance, Coralie—only a little
business between myself and George."

Coralie seated herself at his feet, and looked full in
his face.

" Darcy," she said, reproachfully, " why will you not
give me your confidence ?  Am I unworthy of it ?"

" Unworthy ?  no, indeed, Coralie !  but there  are
things of which it is best you should be ignorant."

" I do not think so ; you cannot love me, or you
would trust me."

" Not love you, Coralie," he said, soothingly, and
patting her cheek, " how can I help it ?"

" And yet you treat me like a child," she said, pettishly.  " I can only guess and surmise, and that makes
me far more miserable than if I knew the truth.  What
is this business between yourself and Captain George ?
I cannot but fear that——"

" Well, Coralie, I will tell you," he said, all at once ;
" perhaps it is best you should know.  I am sure your
love for me would never cause you to wish me to act
dishonourably.  I told you there was a row at the hotel
last night, in which Lupus Rock got worsted.  Well, he
has challenged me, and I am going to fight him."

Coralie turned a trifle pale, and was silent for some

moments. Then her large bright eyes sought his face.

" And it is the opinion of your friend, Captain George, that you ought to accept this man's challenge ?"

" Yes, Coralie."

" Then far be it from me to dissuade you, Darcy." She rose, and throwing herself on his breast, burst into tears, and murmured—

" Dear Darcy, may God guard and spare you to me !"

Her white arms are around his neck, her soft cheek rests on his, and the tears from her dimmed eyes fall on his shoulder.

" Cheer up, Coralie ; I have passed through greater dangers than this. Do not doubt that I shall yet be spared many a day for my duty and your love."

Darcy, although he had so far acknowledged the truth, thought it better that Coralie should not know that the duel was to take place the next morning. Accordingly he let her imagine it would not be for some days, and hoped himself to bring her the glad news that he was safe.

In the evening, Captain George came round, and calling Darcy aside, informed him that he had arranged with Lupus Rock's second, Lieutenant Soames, for three o'clock in the morning, at a quiet spot, about three miles from the city.

Coralie had no suspicion that the hostile meeting was to take place at daybreak on the following morning, and when the two young men, after partaking of supper, were about to go out together, she asked—

" Shall you be long, Darcy ? Nina and I will wait up for you, if you will not be very late."

" By no means, Coralie," he said, hurriedly ; " I may not be back till past twelve. I am going with Gerald to the quarters of a friend, and may be detained late."

" Well, I will wait up for you till one o'clock. Nina and I can keep each other company, since it seems we are not to have the pleasure of yours."

Darcy, glad to escape, muttered some words and hurried away. Not wishing Gerald to know anything of the affair, they mounted their horses and rode to an inn in the outskirts of the town, to pass away the time till about two o'clock, when they intended to start for the rendezvous.

Darcy declared that sleep was out of the question, so to while away the time, they strolled into the billiard room and commenced playing.

Somewhat to the surprise, and also to the cost of the Englishman—for they bet a dollar a game—Darcy Leigh's hand was perfectly steady, his eye true—he had never played a better game.

At one o'clock Captain George put up his cue, and declared he would play no more.

" By Jove, Darcy, if your pistol practice is as good as your billiards, they may put the shutters up at Lupus Rock's lodgings. Nine games we've played, and you've won eight."

" Yes, my hand is steady enough ; I think I can knock him over. By the night it's past one o'clock ; let us ride back to Richmond. I have left my favourite re- volver in my room at Miss St. Casse's. I must manage to get in and out without being seen. I shouldn't like her to think this affair was to be settled so soon."

" Wont you have mine? it's very true, and doesn't throw high, which nine out of ten do."

" No, I prefer my own ; it has saved my life more than once, and it would be an act of ingratitude to the playful little bulldog not to give it a chance at such game as Lupus Rock."

" Game ! vermin rather !"

" As you say, vermin—but the fox is vermin ; never- theless, in your country, George, he affords excellent sport."

Few would have thought from the light, careless, manner in which the friends spoke of the coming en- counter, that the terrible issue of life or death depended on the accurate pointing of a pistol and a pull on the trigger. Perhaps familiarity with war and death on a large scale had rendered them somewhat callous. They did not, perhaps, pause to think that oftentimes the warrior who has been through a hundred fights is laid low by an obscure hand—by a chance shot.

Darcy dismounted at some little distance from the house, and giving George his horse's rein to hold, let himself in by means of a key through the garden at the back.

He noticed a light burning in the dining-saloon on the first floor, and as he had to pass through this to reach his own room, he felt considerably annoyed, as he conjectured that Coralie was still awaiting his return.

From the balcony of this room steps led down into the garden, and Darcy, not caring to enter by the door, ascended these, and passing through the open window, stood in the room and looked around. An oil lamp burned on the table, but it was all nearly exhausted, and gave a dim flickering light.

Resting on a couch he saw a female figure, and a glance told him it was Coralie. Her slow, regular breathing showed she was asleep, and taking up the lamp he passed noiselessly on to his own room, and having possessed himself of his revolver, he hastened back.

He looked on the sleeping figure of Coralie, and a pang of remorse shot through him. She had watched and waited for his return till she had fallen asleep. And now he was leaving her without one word of adieu, perhaps only to be borne lifeless back. For a moment he felt inclined to awake her, but on second thoughts he remembered in what agony of suspense she would pass the next two hours did she know his mission. Setting the lamp down on the table he bent over her, and softly imprinted a kiss on her forehead, and then, as she moved slightly, as if about to awake, he blew out the lamp and hurried away.

In five minutes he was galloping by the side of his friend to the rendezvous, which they reached some few minutes before three o'clock, and before the least dawn of day could be perceived in the east.

Darcy and Captain George fastened their horses each to a tree, and paced up and down the ground which had been selected. It was fully twenty minutes before Lupus

Rock and his second made their appearance. They were accompanied by another, who proved to be the surgeon.

"You are late," said Captain George, as they came up. "We began to think you had thought better of it, and resolved to keep away altogether."

He spoke sneeringly, and with design, for his experience taught him that on occasions of the kind, whoever lost his temper had by far the worst chance.

"You will find I am quite early enough," muttered Lupus, savagely; and by the dim grey light of dawn, which was just beginning to break, George saw the eyes of Lupus gleam fiercely.

Ten minutes were occupied in measuring and marking out the ground. This done, the men were placed, and Captain George and Lupus Rock's second proceeded carefully to load the pistols, each loading for his own man, and submitting to inspection to show that all was fair.

Six barrels of each revolver were loaded, and the nipples capped. Then the seconds tossed up to decide who should give the word, which was won by Soames, and the pistols were placed in the hands of the two antagonists.

"Aim low, Darcy," whispered George, "you can't do wrong. Disable him the first fire, or it will be bad for you. If ever I saw murder in a man's face I see it now in that of Lupus Rock."

Darcy laughed scornfully.

"Never fear, old boy. I am not to fall this time."

"At the word Fire each is to discharge one barrel of his revolver. I shall give it thus—

"One—two—three. Fire!"

There was a deadly silence of some few seconds. In the dull grey light of morning Darcy Leigh could see the pale, cadavarous face of Lupus, his gleaming eyes, and even the white teeth, as the lips were drawn back. Tiger-like as he looked, Darcy was not a whit dismayed, but kept his eye on a spot in his adversary's body, about six inches above the waist.

"One—two—three. *Fire!*

Both fired together, but the report of Lupus Rock's

"IF HE'S KILLED, BY HEAVENS! IT'S MURDER."

P. 241.

pistol seemed to be a second after that of Darcy, who fancied he heard the ball whistle harmlessly by. The next instant he staggered back and fell.

"Hit, by Heavens!" cried Captain George. But instead of running to his friend, he dashed up to Lupus, and, before he could resist, wrenched the pistol from his hand, and after a rapid glance, shouted—

"*If he's killed, by heavens! it's murder. He fired two barrels!*"

"It's a lie!" shouted Lupus, dashing at him, and endeavouring to regain the pistol; "if I did it, it was an accident."

But George leaped on one side, and levelling the pistol full at his head, cried—

"Stand back, till the surgeon examines him. If he's mortally wounded, by the God of Heaven, you die like a dog. I will pistol you myself, so sure as your name is Lupus Rock. Surgeon, how is my friend? Is he dead, or mortally wounded?"

"I protest against this, sir," said Soames, the other second, now advancing to the aid of his principal.

"Protest as much as you please, sir," replied George, "but keep off till the doctor makes his report—if you move a step nearer you are a dead man."

Soames was unarmed, and saw the advisability of doing as ordered.

"Now, you murdering hound, think yourself lucky if Darcy Leigh is only slightly wounded, for if he is dead or dying you go off this ground a corpse."

George hissed these words through his teeth with savage emphasis, and he saw Lupus turn paler and paler, till his complexion was of a yellowish green. The villain felt there was no escape from that deadly little tube levelled straight at his head. It was his own pistol, and he knew it was as faultless as the hand that held it was steady and the resolution to carry out his threat unflinching.

No wonder that thus, on the very brink of a violent and sudden death, Lupus Rock turned sick with terror. Frantically he cursed his own good aim, frantically he

16

longed to hear the surgeon say Darcy was only slightly wounded. Slowly the doctor rose from the ground ; but, to his intense horror, Lupus saw that the form of Darcy still lay motionless. Each second he expected to hear the fatal word, dead ! issue from the lips of the surgeon, and then—oh, horror, he pictured to his fancy a bullet from his own pistol crashing through his brain. Sick and faint, his knees shook, his heart stood still.

At that moment the surgeon spoke—

"He is not dangerously wounded—not even seriously hurt. The ball struck his neck, near the spine ; and although the skin is scarcely broken, the blow has been sufficient to stun him ; but he is fast recovering. Bring water and dash it in his face."

So terrible was the revulsion of feeling in Lupus Rock on hearing the words of the surgeon, which gave him life instead of instant death, that he tottered forward and fell to the ground, half fainting.

The Englishman smiled scornfully, and lowered his pistol.

"Sir," he said to the other second, "you had better attend to your principal, if such a murderous hound is worthy of attention."

"I do not understand all this. Murderous hound ? why so ?—was it not a fair duel—did they not each fire ?"

George tossed to him the pistol he held.

"Look at that, sir, and then tell me all was fair. Two barrels are empty, and your man fired two shots. It was the second from which my friend fell."

Soames briefly examined the pistol.

"You are right, sir," he said. "I wash my hands of the affair. On my honour, I know nothing of this. Perhaps it was an accident."

"An accident ! Doubtless Mr. Rock will assert so, but who can believe it ? Wait till he recovers, and ask for an explanation."

George now proceeded to where Darcy lay, and found him already recovering. In a few minutes he was able to sit up, and only complained of a feeling of numbness at the back of the neck.

Looking around, he saw Lupus Rock on the ground, and his second, Soames, bending over him.

"Ah! I hit him, then!" he said. "I thought I could not miss."

"No, you have not hit him. In body he is well and unwounded."

"What's the meaning of his being on the ground, then?" asked Darcy.

"Well, I reckon I gave him a bit of a fright, and his nerves couldn't stand it," said George, laughing, and then proceeded to explain.

"But I am sure I hit him—I must have hit him. Besides, before I fell myself, I thought I saw him stagger back."

"By Jove! so did I," said the other. "I could have sworn I heard the thud of your ball, and saw him reel for a moment. But we must both have been mistaken, for certainly he is unhurt."

"Mr. Rock says it was an accident," cried Soames, advancing, while Lupus rose from the ground.

"Indeed!" said George, sarcastically. "I presume, however, your *friend*, Lieutenant Soames, is satisfied; if not, on the part of my principal, I claim a shot. Your man owes mine one, and I now demand that he be placed to receive Captain Leigh's fire without returning it."

This completed the discomfiture of Lupus, who walked quickly to his horse, and, without a word, mounted and rode away.

Darcy was now perfectly recovered, and in half an hour he and George were again in the saddle, and galloping back to Richmond. Just as they were entering the town the Englishman suddenly reined in his horse.

"Darcy, I have it, by heavens!"

"What?"

"You say you feel almost certain you hit Lupus Rock?"

"Yes, the more I think of it the more certain I feel, and yet he is unhurt; the affair is incomprehensible."

"I have it, by heavens! I also feel certain you hit him. I heard the bullet strike and saw him stagger."

"How, then, is he unhurt?"

"I believe he wore a coat of mail beneath his clothes."

"By Jupiter! you are right, George, the murdering scoundrel! It is too late now to prove it, but from the very fact of his having fired twice we will make Richmond too hot to hold him."

Then they again rode on, and as soon as he had put his horse up, Darcy hastened to the house of Coralie.

The sun shone brightly as he walked through the garden and up the balcony steps into the room where some two hours before he had left her peacefully sleeping. She still lay as he had last seen her, and though the morning sun bathed her figure and face in its golden light, she slept peacefully.

Darcy looked on the soft outlines of her graceful form as, unconscious of his presence, she lay in dreamy *abandon* before him. He watched the regular rise and fall of her bosom, and bending down let the breath from her half-parted lips fan his cheek. Then desiring to awake her he kissed her lips, and said softly—"Coralie."

She started up in alarm, but when she saw who was kneeling beside her, she threw her arms around his neck, and said,—"Oh, Darcy, what kept you? I waited and waited till at last I fell asleep, and now I declare it is morning! You will kill yourself, staying out night after night in this manner.

"Come, Coralie, put your hat and shawl on, and let us walk in the garden this splendid morning. I have a great deal to tell you which will, I hope, give you pleasure."

"You don't deserve it, sir. I declare I have a great mind to go to bed and let you walk by yourself. Do you think that I, like you, am made of iron, and can live without sleep?"

"Assuredly, Coralie, I don't think there is much fear of your perishing from that cause. I believe you have been asleep on the sofa ever since I left you first, about ten o'clock last night."

"No thanks to you," she replied, pettishly. "It is really too bad of you."

"There, Coralie, don't be angry. I am sure if you

knew what a narrow escape I have had for my life, you would not."

" For your life, Darcy ?"

" Yes ; you know that I had to meet Lupus Rock."

" Ah ! and it has taken place, and you might have been shot without my ever seeing you or bidding you farewell."

" Do you not think, now that it is all over, that you were happier sleeping than if you had known I was in danger. I looked in about two o'clock, just before I started ; you were in a deep sleep. I had occasion to go for my pistol, and kissed your forehead as I passed through the room on my way out."

" Then it was not all a dream. I thought I dreamed that you stood by my side, but I suppose it was reality. And you have had a narrow escape. Tell me all about it."

" Do you see this little mark, half bruise, half graze, on my neck just behind my right ear ? That was caused by Lupus Rock's bullet."

" Heavens, Darcy !" she cried, clasping her hands, " another half inch, and—and—"

" It would have been all over with me, sweet Coralie. A miss is as good as a mile, however, and you see my good fortune has not yet deserted me."

" Well now, Darcy, tell me all about it. Now that it is over I should like to hear."

Accordingly he commenced at the beginning, and related the whole affair, not forgetting the treachery of Lupus in firing twice.

If it were possible for Coralie to have loathed and despised the man more, she would have done so now, on hearing this last piece of unsuccessful villany.

" At all events, Darcy," she said, " this affair will surely rid us of him. He cannot have the audacity to remain in Richmond, with every one's finger pointed at him as a cowardly attempted murderer. I don't think your friend the Englishman will be likely to let the matter rest, even though you may be careless about it."

" Yes, I think you are right. I do not imagine he will

be able to face the hatred and contempt which will surely follow the knowledge of his baseness."

"Now let us return to the house. I see the servants are about, and just now I caught a glimpse of Nina, so that we may hope for an early cup of coffee. Where is your friend, Captain George? Will he not join us at breakfast?"

"He has gone home, but I do not doubt he will be happy to come. Shall I be the bearer of the invitation?"

"By all means; only make haste and return."

Darcy went on his errand, and in half an hour returned with his friend. They found the breakfast table spread on the balcony, in the slanting rays of the bright morning sun. Nina and Coralie awaited them, and surely no happier party of four sat down to the morning meal that day in all Richmond.

Nina, in her plain white morning dress, her hair gathered loosely in a knot behind, her eyes sparkling, her cheeks glowing with health and happiness, she looked lovelier than ever, the sheen of her white teeth as the dancing smiles played about her mouth, testifying her satisfaction with herself and her company.

Breakfast over, the girls donned their riding-habits, and horses were ordered for four. While these were being saddled they strolled into the garden—Darcy by the side of Coralie, while George and Nina were in deep and pleasant converse at some little distance. As they rode down the streets of Richmond they passed the hotel where Webster Gayle and his daughters resided. Darcy looking up caught sight of the sisters standing at the window, and bowed his acknowledgments. In reply Stella Gayle bowed slowly, but Angela turned angrily away. Behind the girls Darcy saw the figure of a man standing with folded arms. He was in the shadow, nevertheless Darcy recognised the scowling brow and piercing eyes of his late antagonist, Lupus Rock.

"See, George, yonder is our friend Lupus at the window," said Darcy, turning in his saddle.

"Ah, yes—I see. Wait till we return from our ride. I have a pill in store for him."

" What will you do ?"

" Why, I'll post him all over Richmond as an attempted murderer and coward. If he can stand that, he must be thick-skinned indeed."

---

# CHAPTER XXIII.

## PLOT AND COUNTERPLOT.

CAPTAIN GEORGE kept his word, and that very afternoon Lupus Rock, when he went out into the streets, noticed that strange glances were cast on him, for which he could not at first account. At the hotel bar of the Nebraska, there was a group of officers, discussing the latest. Lupus ventured to address them, but, to his rage and mortification, his words were received with a cool stare, and all turned their backs on him. He noticed that more than one of them glanced at a placard on the wall; and following, he saw his own name. Approaching closer, he read this placard, and ground his teeth with rage. The placard was signed by Darcy Leigh and Captain George, and denounced him as a scoundrel and attempted murderer, and a coward, and declared him unfit for the company of gentlemen.

White with passion, he turned and walked away, followed by the scornful look of the officers. At first he thought of resistance, of again defying Darcy and his friend; but in spite of his fury, he knew it was useless. Had it been only Darcy Leigh with whom he had to deal, he might have bullied through it; but the Englishman knew too much, and he felt he was more than a match for him.

He was not long in making up his mind. For the present he was foiled, defeated, and could not even hope for revenge without destruction to himself. He determined, then, to leave Richmond at once, and endeavour to get the regiment in which he held a captain's commission transferred elsewhere—for a time, at least.

Having no idea of relinquishing his schemes on Webster

Gayle, he resolved that the merchant and his daughters should accompany him. This he did not doubt being able to effect, and at once sought his uncle.

"I think I have good news for you, sir."

"How so? Have you got me a pass to return North?"

"No; but I have reason to believe that your application, backed by mine, to proceed to Fredericksburg—of course, on parole—will be favourably received."

"Fredericksburg!—ah! And what then?"

"Why, you will be close to the Potomac and the Northern lines. You must then wait your opportunity, and——"

"Break my parole?" said Webster Gayle.

"Either that or remain in the South till the end of the war, which is very likely to last years."

"·Till the end of the war? Ruin! ruin! ruin!" groaned the merchant. "As it is, my business in the North is suffering fearfully—another year of this will cost me millions of dollars."

"I know it, sir; therefore it is that I have strained every nerve—tried every channel—to get you permission to visit Fredericksburg, alleging as a reason the vicinity of your Yancey estate; and now, at last, I believe my endeavours have met with success."

"Ah!—the Yancey estate. By the way, you have not yet given me the papers relating to them—the papers which re-transfer them to me."

Lupus Rock's eyes lighted up with a sudden gleam.

"No, sir, they are not yet quite prepared; besides, I should like you to go over the estate with me first, and see the various alterations I have ordered."

"Ah, very good, Then you think there is a chance of my being permitted to reside at Fredericksburg on parole?"

"I think it almost a certainty; but I am now going to see about it. In half an hour I shall have an answer, and do not doubt but it will be a favourable one."

"Fredericksburg!" muttered Webster Gayle to himself, when his nephew had left him. "It is only some twenty-five miles from the Potomac, and doubtless some

Union forces are yet nearer. I must get back North. Every week I spend here makes me a poorer man. Thousands and thousands of dollars I lose through being forced to remain in Richmond. What enormous sums are to be made in New York, now, when all is speculation and uncertainty; and here am I, forced not only to forego gain, but actually to lose money."

Webster Gayle thought of the gigantic Government contracts a man of his wealth and standing might get, and the millions of dollars he might make, and finally, halting in his hurried walk up and down the room, he slapped his forehead, and exclaimed—" I must escape at all risks!"

Shortly afterwards Lupus Rock returned, and with affected joy, cried—

" Glorious news, uncle—I have succeeded! I requested that my regiment might be transferred to Fredericksburg in place of a North Carolina regiment just returning, and my request was at once acceded to. Then I pressed that your parole might be enlarged, and that you might take up your abode there also. This, too, after some little discussion, was granted. Here is the order, signed by the commander-in-chief and secretary."

" Capital !—then we are to go to-morrow ?"

" Yes—to-morrow."

" And there is no suspicion ?"

" Not the least. The fact of your taking a house in Richmond, and furnishing it so elaborately, has told in your favour. I represented that you only wished to reside in Fredericksburg for a few weeks to look after your estate near there, and while your house in Richmond was being got in readiness. Had you not better inform the young ladies of your intention ? I dare say they will have numerous preparations in the way of packing, &c."

" Yes, yes," said Webster, " I will do so at once; but wait, I want half an hour's conversation with you on other matters."

He rang the bell, and ordered the waiter to inform his daughters that he desired to see them.

The ladies were not long in answering the summons.

"Stella, my dear, and Angela, I have good news! I cannot exactly say that we are to return home, but, at least, we are to leave the capital of the rebels, and take up our abode close to the Federal lines, where we can, at no distant date, make our escape."

"But, papa," said Stella, "I thought you were paroled? Is your parole returned unconditionally?"

"No, my dear girl—not exactly," replied the merchant, in some confusion, under the searching gaze of his daughter—"only enlarged. We are to be permitted to accompany your cousin Lupus, who goes with his regiment to Fredericksburg."

"But you spoke of escape, papa," said Angela; "how is this possible when you have given your parole not to do so?"

"My dear Angela," broke in Lupus, hurriedly, "you cannot be aware what enormous losses every day's absence from New York subjects your father to. All is fair in love and war, you know; and a parole extorted from your father, almost forced from him, can hardly be binding."

Stella gazed steadfastly at her cousin as he spoke.

"Do you think, Lupus," she said, quietly, "that the rebels—whom you, traitor as you are, serve—would look on it in that light?"

Lupus Rock's aim now was conciliation with his cousin; so he answered, laughing—

"Really, Stella, you use hard words. You do not know all the circumstances. I assure you, what I do now I do for the best."

"I only know," retorted Stella, hotly, "that any way you must be a traitor! If you serve the rebels truly, you are a traitor to your country. If your intention is to betray them, you are a still greater traitor."

"Come, come, Stella," said her father, "do not speak so angrily. Your cousin Lupus is acting from the best motives. Yo do not know him so well as I do."

"Indeed!" said Stella, with bitter scorn. "You wish us then, papa, to prepare to start with you for Fredericksburg?"

"Yes, my dear, to-morrow. It is absolutely necessary, is it not, Lupus?"

"Yes, indeed," he replied, gravely; "I see no other way out of the numerous difficulties which surround you."

"Very good," said Angela, quietly. "Stella, let us come and make our preparations."

No sooner were the sisters in their own room than Angela hastened to put on her bonnet and shawl.

"Stella, I dread and distrust this journey to Fredericksburg. Did you observe how anxious Lupus was we should go, how pleased and self-satisfied he seemed? I feel—I know that our going there is a part of his devilish scheme. God help us. I cannot pretend to fathom that scheme, but I know that he is still plotting—has never ceased plotting. I suspect, Stella, he has not yet given up all hopes of your hand."

Stella laughed bitterly.

"Given up all hopes, Angela? not he. Lupus Rock will never give up until he has gained his point, as he assuredly will gain it."

"Will gain it, Stella! What on earth do you mean?"

"I mean what I say. Lupus Rock wishes me to marry him, and for that he is scheming and plotting, for that he will continue to scheme and plot until he has gained his end."

"And do you think he will gain his end? Surely, Stella, you cannot mean that you will ever marry him?"

"But I do mean it, Angela. Willingly or unwillingly, *I must marry Lupus Rock.* It is my fate. I feel—I know it; I can no more escape from this, my certain destiny, than I can from grim King Death, himself."

"Stella, this is dreadful," cried Angela, piteously, her hand shaking so that she could hardly tie her bonnet strings. "Much as I love you, my dear, my only sister, I would almost rather see you in your grave, than the wife of that bad man."

Stella placed her arm round her sister's neck, and kissing her brow, said—

"Angela, it is my fate. I shall soon be in my grave

afterwards, but nevertheless I am destined to marry Lupus Rock. And now, dear sister, where are you going ?"

" I am going to seek for Gerald and Darcy Leigh. They can prevent this journey to Fredericksburg—they, if any, can save us."

" Ah !" murmured Stella, " Darcy Leigh ; yes, he could save me—he could save me ; but it is not to be. He has not the will."

" Stella, you wrong Darcy. Angry as I am with him, I know he will keep his word. He promised to aid us, *you* in particular, if ever we needed his aid ; and he will keep his word."

" Yes," murmured Stella, speaking half to herself, " Darcy Leigh could save me ; but to him I am lost— forgotten, and wanting his aid. I go to my fate."

Then Angela, promising to return soon, ran off on her errand.

On their return from their ride Darcy and George called on Gerald Leigh to invite him, at the request of Miss. St. Casse, to spend the afternoon at her house. Gerald readily assented, and having partaken of lunch, Gerald, Darcy, and Coralie took their seats on the balcony, while George strolled about the garden with Nina.

" Seems to me, Miss St. Casse," said Gerald, between the puffs of his cigar, " that our friend yonder seems rather smitten with that young woman."

" With Nina," said Coralie, hastily. " She is a dear, good girl, and as good as she is beautiful."

" There's a mystery about her neither I nor any one else can fathom, except perhaps yourself, Miss St. Casse. I thought she was a slave once—people say so ; but then if such were the case, she would not be on the terms of equality she is with you, Miss St. Casse."

" Gerald, do not trouble yourself about Nina. You are right ; I could, if I chose, reveal much. She is not what she seems, although she inherits a great misfortune from her birth. Let it suffice that Nina is neither penniless nor friendless, and that after my death she will be rich."

" After you, Coralie?" said Darcy, laughing. " Why, really, to hear you speak, one would think you were on the shady side of sixty, instead of being a year or a year and a half younger than Miss Nina. By the way, what is her other name? Does any one know?"

" Darcy, I shall be angry if you speak so. Yes, I know what her name should be; and if ever any one should come who would have the right to ask, I could speak. Enough for the present; do not let us pursue the subject."

There was a silence of some minutes, during which Gerald and Darcy lazily puffed their cigars and sipped the delicious iced drink compounded by the fair hands of Nina and Coralie—the latter of whom gazed dreamily out on the broad expanse of fertile country bathed in the light of the summer sun.

" Gerald," she said presently, " you know what we were talking of just now?"

" Yes, of Nina."

" I said that after me she should be well provided for."

" Nonsense, Miss St. Casse! I hope you and Darcy will spend many happy years together."

" Perhaps so—perhaps not. At any rate, I wish you to do me a favour."

" Granted, before it is named."

" I wish you to be one of the executors of my will."

" Good heavens! You don't mean to say you have made your will?" said Gerald, aghast.

" But I do, and I want you to be one executor; my cousin, Edward St. Casse, is the other. Yes or no?"

" Well, if you wish it, yes, of course; but you could not have a worse. I never could keep a secret."

" You need keep no secret. There are only two bequests, and I am ashamed of neither," she said, with a faint smile.

At this moment a negro entered the room, and approaching the balcony, said—

" Missa, dere's a lady called for Massa Cap'n Leigh."

" It is for you, I suppose, Gerald," said Darcy, laughing. " You are the more likely to have a lady call."

"I wonder who it can be," said Gerald, lazily, but not showing any disposition to move.

"Inquire of the lady her name, and whether it is Captain Darcy Leigh, or Captain Gerald Leigh, whom she wishes to see," said Coralie, quickly.

Darcy burst out laughing, for he noticed the slightly displeased accents of Coralie's voice, and knowing she had no cause for jealousy, he could afford to laugh.

"Bravo, Coralie! That's what I call a bold stroke, a dashing manœuvre, and it does you credit."

Coralie coloured up with vexation at being thus detected, but nevertheless laughed good-humouredly.

The servant returned, and said, "De lady's name's Miss Gayle, and she want to see Cap'n Darcy Leigh."

It was now the latter's turn to colour and look confused. Of all persons in the world he least wished at present to see Stella Gayle, and had for some time persistently avoided her. Now, however, there was no help for it, and, rising, he followed the servant to the reception room on the ground floor. A lady arose as he entered, and to his surprise he saw not Stella, but Angela Gayle.

"You will excuse me, Captain Leigh, but I am come to claim the fulfilment of a promise."

"My dear Angela, you can command me."

"You promised to do all in your power to aid and protect my sister Stella."

"And that promise, please God, I will keep. How can I be of any service to you or her?"

"I will tell you," she said, speaking rapidly; "you know my dread and horror of Lupus Rock?"

"I do, and do not blame you."

"Well, it seems he has persuaded papa to obtain leave for his parole to be extended to Fredericksburg. The regiment of Lupus is going there to-morrow to relieve another, and we are to accompany him. I know nothing of his object or his schemes, but I feel certain that he intends again to get our father in his power, and so force Stella to accept him as her husband. I believe he counsels him to break his parole and endeavour to escape."

"And is it possible that Webster Gayle, after the

terrible ordeal he went through, would again venture?" asked Darcy.

"Lupus Rock has gained such complete influence over him, that he can persuade him to anything."

"And how do you wish me to aid you, Angela?"

"I wish you to cause the authorities to forbid our father accompanying Lupus Rock to Fredericksburg."

"Ah, I see; but on what grounds?"

"Could you not say you have reason to believe that he would endeavour to escape, and that he is possessed of too many secrets as to your intended movements and plans for such to be desirable?"

"But that would sadly compromise your father, Angela."

"No matter," she exclaimed, vehemently; "that— anything is better than our going to Fredericksburg, where we should be completely in the power of Lupus Rock."

"Stay here a few moments, Angela. I will call Gerald. He is up-stairs."

As soon as Gerald heard that Angela Gayle was below, he displayed sufficient alacrity, and at once descended with his brother.

Angela, all blushes and smiles, greeted him warmly.

Taking her hand, he drew her towards him, and said—

"Now, Angela, tell me how I can serve you. You know that both Darcy and I would do so with our lives."

Angela then repeated what she had told Darcy.

"We must manage this," said Gerald, when the young lady concluded. "It can be done, I am sure. What do you think?"

"I think with you. But there is no time to be lost. Suppose you accompany Angela home and meet me in half an hour at the Nebraska Hotel."

This arrangement was sufficiently agreeable to all parties; and Gerald left, with Angela on his arm, while Darcy returned up-stairs to make his excuses to Miss St. Casse.

Half an hour later Darcy met Gerald, as appointed, and they at once set about the business in hand.

It was necessary that the order forbidding Webster Gayle to leave the city should emanate from the general commanding; also that all passes granted by the general to Webster Gayle should be revoked. Now there was no doubt that Lupus Rock had duly furnished the merchant with these passes, and it became necessary for them to find the general. They learned that he had gone, with his staff, to visit some works on the river, about three miles from Harrison's Landing, and twelve from the city.

Accordingly, the brothers mounted their horses and galloped off in that direction. In the course of an hour the road wound around a small hill; and, as time pressed, instead of following it, they rode straight across the summit. Here they suddenly came across a horse tethered to a tree, and a man sitting on a camp-stool, and engaged in drawing with rule and compass on a large sheet of paper before him. The man started as the horses clattered over the hill close to him, and the paper he was drawing on was blown away by the wind, which was somewhat high. It was borne within reach of Gerald, who stretched out his hand and caught it.

In doing so, however, a small piece was torn off one corner. They reined in their horses for a minute, and then, for the first time, they saw that the man was none other than Lupus Rock. A glance at the paper told Gerald that it was an elaborate plan of the defences at that point. As soon as he discovered who it was, Gerald contemptuously threw the piece of paper on the ground, retaining, however, the small piece which had been torn off. This Gerald placed in his pocket, saying laughingly to Darcy—

"'Keep a thing for seven years, and you will find a use for it'—so says the proverb, and for that reason I will keep this torn piece of paper. I wonder what our worthy friend is doing, and for what reason he is making plans of the fortifications?"

"Heaven only knows," replied Darcy, carelessly; "perhaps he is going to astonish the world by some new system of fortification."

With this the subject dropped, and in half an hour

more they found the general and his staff. They had little difficulty, on stating their reasons, in obtaining the requisite order for the return of the pass granted to Webster Gayle, and late in the evening they started to ride back.

Gerald at once sent word to Angela Gayle that they had succeeded. A note came back from her thanking them warmly for the trouble they had taken, and recommending that the order should not be delivered to their father until immediately before his intended departure.

Thus Lupus Rock would be obliged to accompany his regiment to Fredericksburg, and would be unable to do or attempt anything to obtain renewed permission for Webster Gayle to leave Richmond.

Then, at all events, reasoned Angela, they would at once be rid of his presence, and defeat his scheme, whatever it might be.

At noon on the following day the regiment which had the distinguished honour of numbering Lupus Rock among its officers and of calling him patron, received marching orders for Fredericksburg, and in the course of an hour, the men, with knapsacks and kits complete in heavy marching order, set out from the barracks they occupied, for the railway station.

Lupus Rock remained behind to hurry the departure of Webster Gayle and his cousins. He saw them into a fly with all their luggage, and left them at the door of the hotel, hurrying on to join his company; for although the regiment had been raised principally at his expense, yet discipline was strictly enforced on all, by the general of the brigade and his staff.

The men were all seated in the cars, and were singing and shouting, as large bodies of men will do no matter under what circumstances, while the officers walked up and down the platform, awaiting only the arrival of the colonel and the quartermaster to start.

Lupus went frequently out into the street in expectation of Webster Gayle and his daughters. When his patience was well-nigh worn out the fly hove in sight and,

17

drawing up, Webster alighted, and proceeded to give orders about his and the ladies' luggage.

Stella was as usual, pale and silent, while Angela, who appeared flushed and excited, looked anxiously around, and up and down the road, as if expecting some one.

But her looks were in vain, for neither Darcy nor Gerald Leigh could be seen, and she began to fear that they had failed or would be late.

While their luggage was being shifted to the platform, the colonel and quartermaster arrived.

The order was given for all to take their places, the captains and subalterns in the respective cars where their companies were; the colonel, major, quartermaster, and some other officers in the last car.

"Come, sir, make haste," said Lupus, hurrying up to Webster Gayle. "Come, young ladies, there is no time to lose."

"Captain Rock!" shouted the major, "take your seat and keep your men in order."

"One moment, major. Now, Stella and Angela, make haste, your luggage is all on the cars."

At that moment a mounted officer trotted up in time to hear the last words of Lupus, followed by two other officers.

"That's a pity, for the ladies' baggage will have to be removed again," said the mounted officer.

Angela looked up with a bright smile of relief. She knew the voice, and the next moment her blue eyes rested with a grateful expression on the handsome face of Gerald Leigh.

Lupus turned with a scowl on the speaker.

"How so, sir? These ladies are going with their father to Fredericksburg. Here is the pass," and so saying he produced a piece of paper duly signed and sealed.

"Captain Rock, take your seat in the car," shouted the colonel.

"Come, sir, come," said Lupus to his uncle.

"Not so," said Gerald, calmly. "Mr. Gayle may have a pass for Fredericksburg; but here is an order for him to deliver up that pass, and expressly forbidding him to leave Richmond. It was duly signed by the general commanding in my presence, and has been placed in my hands to see carried out. Now, some of you fellows," Gerald shouted to the negroes acting as porters, " make haste and unload that luggage you have just put on the cars. Hurry up, or I make some of you see snakes."

Lupus Rock was dumbfounded. There was no time for anything. The colonel again thundered 'to him to take his place, and in face of that order he knew it would be madness for Webster Gayle to accompany him.

There was no help for it, so his mind, all in confusion by this sudden and unlooked-for catastrophe to his little plans, and with the voice of the colonel ringing in his ears, he muttered an oath and took his seat.

The whistle shrieked, and as the train slowly rumbled from the station, the baffled Lupus looking from the window, saw Gerald Leigh triumphantly wave his hat; he saw a smile of joy on the face of Angela, and noticed her give Gerald her hand, as if in thanks. Then he understood it all. He had been outwitted and foiled by this girl and Gerald Leigh.

Darcy and George at this moment joined the group, and Lupus ground his teeth with rage, as he saw them all turn and walk slowly back together.

" Once again I am foiled, and by one of those accursed brothers. This time it is their turn for triumph ; but mine will come—shall come, and then I will take a bitter vengeance."

———

## CHAPTER XXIV.

### DARBY KELLY'S PRISONER.

GREAT was the joy of Angela Gayle at Lupus being forced to leave them. Webster Gayle, on the contrary, had made up his mind, and set his heart on getting permission to go to Fredericksburg preparatory to making his escape North. He knew not by what agency his

pass had been cancelled, but felt aggrieved and angry
with Gerald and Darcy Leigh, the former of whom was
charged with the carrying it out.

He flattered himself, however, that he would be en-
abled yet to obtain permission to leave and join his
nephew, on whom he depended for escape. But the
merchant was disappointed in his anticipations, and every
application met a curt and decisive refusal. Lupus
Rock was similarly foiled, and though he chafed and
fumed under this untoward hitch to his schemes he was
powerless. He well knew that some influence was at
work which caused the military authorities to retain
Webster Gayle a prisoner on parole and in Richmond,
and not suffer him to go North, or even near the Federal
lines.

Things were at a dead lock. Lupus could not leave
his regiment, and, besides, Richmond had been rendered
too hot to hold him after the duel with Darcy Leigh.

Weeks and months passed on, and a change began to
come over the face of affairs. The second invasion
of Virginia and attempt to capture the capital was about
to be made.

General M'Clellan thought the way most open to
success was not from the North, but from the sea, up by
the peninsula formed by the James and York rivers.
Accordingly he transported his army by sea to the aforesaid peninsula, and advancing slowly and cautiously, approached within sight of the rebel capital. But he
found his further progress stopped by powerful works,
which the Confederates were prepared to desperately defend. To resist the invading army troops from all
quarters were massed in Richmond, and among others
Lupus Rock's regiment was recalled from Fredericksburg. This was no time for intestine quarrels ; the foe
was at the gates, and all private animosities were dropped
in view of the common danger.

Thus Lupus was permitted to remain with his regiment
unmolested ; Darcy Leigh, Gerald, and Captain George
treating him with silent contempt. Webster Gayle
eagerly welcomed his coming, for the merchant chafed

bitterly under his forced residence in Richmond, and believed that his nephew alone could extricate him from the dilemma.

Angela Gayle saw the return of her cousin with ill-concealed uneasiness, while Stella treated the matter with haughty indifference. All through the winter the sisters had led a quiet, unobtrusive life, Angela frequently seeing Gerald, although he did not visit the house. As for Darcy, he purposely kept himself aloof ; and Stella and he, when they met, merely acknowledged each other's presence by a bow—polite on his side—cold, almost contemptuous, on hers.

Meanwhile the 7th Carolina regiment, recruited to its full strength, composed of picked men, well drilled and commanded by able officers, who had the confidence of the soldiers, became one of the most efficient in the service. It was constantly told off for severe and dangerous outpost duty, and the men all became deadly shots.

As the spring of 1862 advanced, and the summer heats commenced, the Federal host, slowly and cautiously advancing, laid close siege to Richmond. The sentries of the hostile forces were in view of one another, and it was common for Southern ladies to go out on the ramparts of some of the works, seat themselves, and calmly observe the formidable approaches of the enemy. Though within long rifle shot, they were not fired at, as the war had not then assumed the savage character with which the brutalities of such men as the infamous Butler have since stamped it.

But as the Union forces slowly pushed on, making regular siege approaches, and calling into play the heaviest siege guns, they found at each step unlooked for obstacles.

At all events, whatever might be the result of the struggle, Lupus Rock determined that the time had come for him to carry his point with his cousin Stella by a *coup de main.* He resolved on the same tactics which had before so nearly proved successful. He knew it was hopeless to attempt to influence Stella either by fear or persuasion. Her love for her father and fear for his

safety should again be the lever by which he would bend
her proud spirit to his will. His plans were laid with
the utmost skill and cunning, and when all was in readiness, and he thought the time come, he resolved to
strike. Accordingly he sought an interview with his
uncle. He was immediately assailed with reproaches and
complaints as to the ruin this enforced delay involved the
merchant in. Lupus answered humbly and depre-
catingly, that he was aware of all this, and it was on that
very subject he had come.

"At last I see a chance—more than a chance—by
which this state of affairs may be ended," he said. "To-
morrow night my regiment is ordered on outpost duty.
Our outlying sentries will be actually in sight of the
enemy. Not a day or a night passes but many of the
enemy, tired of the misery, fatigue, and disease in their
camp, desert to us. Our men do not in turn desert to
them, but if they chose they could do so. ·Of course
to-morrow night before going on duty I shall have the
pass-word. I can give it to you ; then all that remains
is for you to steal through the lines in the darkness,
giving the word to any of our men who may challenge
you, and gain the enemy's camp."

"But my daughters—what of them ?"

"They can go with you. Once give the countersign,
and none will oppose you."

"And you are sure you will be on this outpost duty
to-morrow night, and have the pass-word ?"

"Sure," answered Lupus, briefly.

Webster Gayle hesitated only a little. He was natu-
rally timid ; but Lupus was so plausible and confident,
and the scheme seemed so simple, that he determined to
do as advised.

Accordingly he signified his intention to prepare his
daughters, and eight o'clock on the following evening
was appointed for the final arrangements to be made.

Angela received her father's commands to be in readiness to start on foot and without luggage, with consternation and dismay. Gerald Leigh and Captain George

had gone with their cavalry on a foraging expedition, and Darcy was on duty with his regiment, but where she could not discover.

Stella manifested but little interest; she had sunk into a listless, careless apathy, and had given way to a species of fatalism. She had a morbid, wretched belief that her fate was decided—that no struggle on her part could avail. So she merely bowed her head, and said—"As you please, father; only pray run no such terrible risk of danger as you escaped last year."

"There is, there can be no danger. Your cousin Lupus has explained all to me, and the arrangements are so made as to ensure success."

"Then this plan is Lupus Rock's?" said Angela, distractedly; "for Heaven's sake, do pause before you commit yourself to so desperate an attempt. Think how hard it would go with you if captured."

"But there is no danger; and even if such a thing should happen, I should have no compromising papers on me."

This comforted Angela in a measure, and as there was no help for it, she perforce resigned herself to her fate. It was a sore trial, however, and the more she thought on it the more she disliked it. This stealthy midnight flitting—liable any moment to be brought back prisoners. Then, too, perhaps they might have no opportunity of bidding adieu, or seeking counsel of Gerald or his brother. It was a prospect which wrung the gentle girl's heart with anguish; but, ever accustomed to obey, and receiving no aid from Stella, Angela was forced to resign herself to her fate.

All the next day, great movements were observed in the Federal army. The watchful Confederate generals noting this, continually felt and pressed close on the pickets and outposts, so that no important change of position should be effected without their knowing it. Fierce skirmishing was kept up all day, and many wounded were brought into hospital. By night, however, the continual sputtering, irregular fire ceased, and

again all was quiet. But sufficient information had been
obtained by various channels to cause great movements
in the Confederate forces.

It was thought probable that the Yankees might medi-
tate a retreat from a hopeless position, as sickness and
demoralization were known to prevail to a frightful extent in their camp. To prevent a retreat being effected,
without, at least, inflicting terrible loss, was the object,
and in furtherance thereof large bodies of troops were
under orders to march out at a moment's notice, and
attack the enemy, should they attempt to retire. The
most trusted and intrepid troops were ordered to the
front on outpost duty, while whole brigades were held in
hand, ready to be launched on any point.

The sun went down, and, true to his appointment,
Lupus Rock came to Webster Gayle,

"The password for the night is 'Louisiana.' My
regiment is stationed at the head-quarters at Porter's
farm, and some of the companies on extreme outpost
and picket duties. Make straight for Porter's farm,
whence you can penetrate through the last line, and in
ten minutes will be within hail of the Federal sentries.
Allow yourself to be made prisoner and taken within
the lines, when in a few words you can explain who and
what you are, and you will be set at liberty. Be at
Porter's farm by half-past eleven o'clock; at twelve I
will place sentries in front whom I can trust, and then
you can pass through. Here are the title deeds of the
Yancey estate, and some other papers and accounts which
I have prepared. You can always communicate with
me; and perhaps in a few months, or even weeks, I may
join you."

Webster took the papers, and just glancing at them,
placed them in his breast pocket. Lupus watched him
narrowly as he did so, and saw that he had not examined
them. A gleam of satisfaction might have been observed
on his face.

"So far so good," he thought; "the old fool little
thinks there is evidence enough in that pocket to hang a
dozen men for spies."

What then was his scheme?

It was simple enough. Lupus determined that Webster Gayle should be challenged and stopped by certain of his men whom he could trust, and made prisoner in spite of the countersign. He would be searched and the papers examined. Among them was a complete plan of a vital point in the works of defence. Then his uncle's life would be once again in his hands, and he resolved swiftly to use his power. He could throw off the mask and have Webster kept in custody of his own men, until not only Stella should consent to marry him, but until the ceremony was actually performed. He had made all necessary arrangements, and had a clergyman in readiness to tie the knot at half an hour's notice.

His regiment was told off for duty at Porter's farm, and would not be relieved for three days, while one day would suffice for his purpose, during which Webster should be kept in close arrest in the farm-house instead of being sent to head-quarters. He would, if possible, so contrive that the possession of the condemnatory papers should appear to Webster Gayle an accident, and in such case he would declare himself willing to take all the blame and run all the risk, provided Stella would consent to marry him at once.

He felt certain that the prospect of her father being led to a certain and ignominious death would so influence Stella that she would consent to his wishes ; for had she not done so before, and was not the cup snatched from his lips only by the unexpected obstinacy of Webster Gayle when the danger was past? This time, however, the halter should not be taken from around his neck until promise should have been ratified by actual performance.

Shortly after ten o'clock Webster Gayle left his house, his daughters accompanying him, and started to walk on foot to Porter's Farm, which was distant about three miles. Any lingering misgivings he might have were dissipated as he walked on without challenge or molestation. Occasionally small bodies of troops hurrying to the front passed him, but no notice was taken or even inquiry made.

Shortly they were clear of the city, and walked quickly along the smooth hard road, on which might be heard in front and rear the measured tramp of hoofs.

"Hark, Stella !" said Angela, "what is that ?"

They were not long left in doubt, for several squadrons of cavalry thundered up and galloped past without heeding them. Angela thought she distinguished amongst them the uniform of Gerald Leigh's regiment, but it was too dark to tell with any certainty. Shortly afterwards a regiment of infantry passed at the quick march—then another and another, till it became evident that a strong force was being moved to the front, probably in anticipation of some movement of the enemy.

At last the merchant became alarmed. "Come, Stella, Angela, let us quicken our pace. The road is getting quite thronged, and more are coming up behind."

They now moved on at such a pace that no more troops passed them, though both in front and rear might be heard the incessant monotonous tramp of feet. There was no moon, and though the sky was unclouded, the night was still so dark as to preclude their distinguishing objects at a greater distance than a few yards ; hence they came quite close to the farm-house indicated by Lupus Rock before they were aware of it. Crowds of soldiers surrounded it, lying and standing about in all directions. Their arms were stacked, and it was plain that they were held in hand ready to move at a moment's notice. There were many stragglers coming along the road, who had been left behind, and now were hurrying in search of their various regiments. Webster also noticed some civilians, and felt comforted thereby, as it made the presence of himself and daughters less conspicuous among the armed host. Sauntering about with apparent carelessness, he spoke to an officer—

"What is the meaning of all this ? Is a Federal attack expected ?"

"I know nothing about it. We are ordered to the front, with full supply of ammunition, and brigaded with Jackson's division. That is all I know."

At that moment a few scattering shots were heard

about a mile in front. All listened anxiously. The firing became more frequent. Soon the flash of hundreds of rifles might be seen in the distance, and an evident excitement might be noted among the soldiers.

"Ready to fall into your ranks, men—ready. Get your rifles."

The clattering of the arms as they were unstacked was now mingled with the sound of the distant fire, and Webster Gayle's heart began to fail him.

"Shall I be permitted to pass to the front?" he asked of the officer to whom he had before spoken.

"Pass to the front?" was the reply, accompanied by a look of curiosity, "for what reason?"

"Oh, merely curiosity," Webster stammered.

"Not unless you have the password."

"I have it."

"Then you can pass, I suppose."

We must now leave Webster Gayle for a short time, and visit Darcy Leigh in command of No. 1 company of the 7th Carolinas.

At nine o'clock in the evening he was posted with his command on outpost duty, on an eminence commanding a bend in the James River. There was a battery of field artillery and several heavy guns mounted in such a way as to command the road which wound beneath. A mile and a half above the road was held by the enemy, but to pass down it to the river they would have to sustain the fire of several batteries, so strongly posted as to make the task almost impossible.

Darcy Leigh, at ten o'clock, visited all the sentries, and having enjoined vigilance, returned to the battery, where were the remainder of his men. Scarcely had he done so, when an aide-de-camp rode up—

"Captain Leigh—you, and Captain Edwards, will proceed with No. 1 and No. 2 companies to Porter's farm, and there join the rest of your regiment, who have been ordered there to brigade with Jackson's division. This battery will be held by one company until relieved by more."

In five minutes Darcy had formed his men, and was

marching towards Porter's farm.   An hour's sharp march
brought the little force there, where they found the
remaining companies of the regiment.

"Captain Leigh, take your company to the front, and
post a line of sentries close to the enemy's line.   Endeavour to draw fire—press them ; and if they retire,
close upon them.   Constantly feel them, so that their
sentries and outposts cannot be withdrawn."

Such were the orders he received from the colonel.

Cheerfully Darcy's little force of about seventy men
started off on their dangerous mission.

"Captain Leigh," shouted the colonel, calling after
him.   Darcy at once halted his men, and ran back.

"Allow no one to pass—the word is changed from
' Louisiana' to ' Texas.' "

"Very good, sir," said Darcy ; then, rejoining his men,
he hurried to the front.

About the same time, Lupus Rock received orders to
march his men from Porter's farm to a point some two
miles distant.   He received this command with the utmost dismay.   It would upset all his plans, spoil everything.   There was, however, no alternative.   He even
asked for an hour's leave, but was sternly refused by the
general who gave the order.

" No, sir ; take the lead of your company, and march,
as ordered.   An attack is expected."

There was no possible help for it, so Lupus gloomily
moved off with his men.   He cursed his luck again and
again.   Webster had the countersign, and might pass
through the lines, and be for the time out of his power.   It
was desperately vexatious ; and look at it which way he
would, he could see no escape from the dilemma.   If the
merchant passed through, and got out of his power, his
hopes of Stella Gayle would be futile.   If, on the other
hand, he were stopped and searched, the compromising
papers would be found on him, and he would be condemned and hanged as a spy, most assuredly.   Nor could
anything save him, and this Lupus well knew.

There was but one chance, and that was that he might
be challenged, and not allowed to pass the lines, and

would simply return without being searched. This
Lupus thought very probable, and consoled himself
thereby as best he could.

Meanwhile Darcy Leigh dispersed his men at intervals
of about thirty yards, and gradually pushed them on.
No effect followed this for some time, but after advancing cautiously and slowly from tree to tree about a
quarter of a mile, the challenge of a Yankee sentry is
heard, followed by the discharge of his rifle at only some
thirty yards' distance. The fire was returned, then taken
up by several other Yankee sentries, till it became general all along on each side—jets of flame bursting from
behind trees and brushwood, where all before had been
so still and dark. The bullets hissed and sputtered
around and overhead in a most unpleasant way. Several
of Darcy's men were hit and carried to the rear, and at
one time it appeared probable that a brisk action might
ensue.

But the enemy slowly withdrew his sentries, and Darcy
cautiously following up, the firing ceased—first on the
part of the enemy, who evidently were determined not
to betray their positions if possible. Shortly after midnight the rest of the regiment arrived at the post,
whither they had been ordered in consequence of the
smart firing. Darcy was engaged in visiting his line of
sentries nearest to the enemy at this time, and was, in
accordance with his orders, moving them cautiously on a
few yards at a time. On his return to the outpost, where
he had left those men he held in reserve, he found
Colonel Johnstone and the other officers with the rest of
the 7th Carolinas.

"Captain Leigh," said the colonel, "march your men
with me to the line of sentries, and double them. I will
see you are supported by two other companies. I will
accompany you, as I wish to see where the enemy are
posted."

The colonel was on horseback, and rode by the side of
Darcy. They had passed along about half the line of
sentries, and had seen each man at his post, when suddenly Darcy heard the voice of Darby Kelly—

" Who goes there ?"

There is a moment's pause, and then the reply—

" A friend."

" Halt, friend, and give the word ; or be jabers, I'll spit ye like a lark !"

"Louisiana," was the confident reply, and Darcy instantly recognised the voice of Webster Gayle.

Down came Darby's rifle to the charge.

" Come forward, whoever ye are, and let me have a look at ye. Divil a sowl goes back or forward this way without the password ; and by the piper that played before Moses, it ain't yerself wid yer Louisiana."

Webster Gayle advanced as ordered, and was engaged expostulating with the sentry, and trying to convince him that the word was Louisiana, when Darcy Leigh and the colonel came up.

" Who and what are you, sir," said Colonel Johnstone, sternly, to Webster, " who seek to pass our lines without the word ? You may be a spy for all I know !"

Webster faltered out some words which the colonel did not catch.

" Sergeant Smith, take a couple of men. Seize this fellow, and search him. He may be a spy !"

---

# CHAPTER XXV.

## SHOOTING THE PRISONER.

IN obedience to the colonel's order, Webster Gayle was instantly seized and searched. Darcy Leigh, who had recognised the voice of Webster, stood a little aloof, not wishing to take any active part in the affair. An occasional shot along the front told that the enemy's pickets and sentries were near and vigilant.

Webster submitted, without remonstrance or opposition, and declared that he was merely strolling about the lines from curiosity. The packet of papers given him by Lupus Rock was taken from him, and at once submitted to Colonel Johnstone for inspection.

"The lantern, sergeant—this looks like a map."

The lantern was brought, and by its light the colonel examined one by one the papers taken from Webster. A very short scrutiny was sufficient to reveal the treacherous character of the documents. Among the papers in the packet were letters to Federal generals and officials, and also a complete plan of the defensive works along the eastern and southern face of Richmond.

"A spy—as I thought," said the Confederate officer to a lieutenant who was by his side. "See here is a plan of our works. In a few minutes, had not this lusty sentry stopped him, the fellow would have been in the lines of the enemy, and they would have been as well informed of our defences as ourselves. Keep him in secure custody till the relief comes round, then send him to the rear. He will be hanged in the morning without fail."

Great was the dismay of the New York merchant, as the papers taken from him were one by one unfolded, and greater still his terror at the words of the colonel. He protested he knew nothing of the plan of the fortifications or of the letters, but his assertions were received with contemptuous unbelief.

"Captain Leigh, see that this man is safely delivered into the hands of the provost-marshal. If he attempts to escape, shoot him down."

Darcy, without a word, stepped up to the prisoner, who, with clasped hands and terrified look, was begging, explaining, and protesting his innocence. At that moment a brisk fire commenced along the front.

"Shall I take him to the rear at once, sir?" said Darcy.

"No; keep him in safe custody here; not a man can be spared. The enemy must be closely pressed. Keep advancing your line of sentries until daylight or fresh orders."

Then the colonel rode off to the rear, leaving Darcy Leigh in charge of the prisoner.

Darcy Leigh was in total ignorance of the fact that Webster Gayle's daughters had accompanied him.

He had given an order for the prisoner to be conducted

some distance to the rear, when a hand is laid on his shoulder, and he sees Stella Gayle by his side.

Even in the dim uncertain light he notices the deadly pallor of her face, and the unearthly glare of her eyes.

"Stella!"

"Darcy, release my father. I have heard all; his life must pay the forfeit of this mad attempt. I have never before asked you a favour; now I will do so on my knees. Darcy, for Heaven's sake let him go free. You have always behaved as a friend till now. It is life or death; let us pass on."

"My duty. I cannot disobey my positive orders."

"Captain Leigh, I know nothing about the papers found on me. I am innocent of their contents, and do not even know how they came into my possession. Some enemy has done this. I own that I intended to pass the lines to the enemy, but I am guiltless of these papers and plans."

"Darcy, let my father go, and take a daughter's blessing. You well know the terrible issue at stake. I heard the colonel's words, and guilty or not guilty, his fate is certain if taken to the rear. Darcy, for Heaven's sake, for the memory of old times, hear my prayer."

A great conflict was going on in the young man's mind. He was as pale as the suppliant girl before him, and for a moment he seemed to waver.

"My duty, Stella—my duty. I cannot play a traitor's part."

"Darcy, be merciful. Release him; you will never regret it."

While his cause was being thus pleaded, Webster Gayle stood the picture of abject despair. Each moment the firing along the front grew sharper, and one or two wounded sentries were carried past to the rear.

"Stella, I will do all I can. Now go to the rear; this is no place for you. Hark how the bullets hiss around."

"I will not leave my father."

Darcy, without another word to the two girls, called a sergeant, and committed the prisoner to his charge, ordering him to take him some hundred yards or so towards the rear, and seek the shelter of the woods.

Meanwhile, what was at first but a desultory sentry firing, soon became a brisk skirmish, and Darcy pushed his men slowly but steadily on.

After some time the enemy appeared to give way, and the rattle of the musketry ceased.  But this was only a momentary lull, and was shortly succeeded by fresh bursts of flame and the crash of more rifles, as fresh troops were thrown forward as skirmishers.

Now the men under Darcy Leigh's command were sorely pressed, and it took the services of well nigh half to carry the wounded to the rear.

It was evident that the Federals had ceased retiring, and, having brought up fresh troops, were in turn pressing on, keeping up a constant and galling fire.

About an hour before dawn, an aide-de-camp rode to the front bringing orders for the pickets and sentries to be withdrawn, as the position of the Yankees had been sufficiently ascertained, and daylight would soon prevent the possibility of their retreating without notice.

Darcy gave the necessary orders—the sentries were withdrawn and ordered to fall back to the outpost. Webster Gayle, accompanied by his daughters, was marched back towards the rear, Darcy riding by his side.

Stella and Angela saw this with alarm, but in reply to their inquiries and entreaties Darcy said not a word. A faint light in the east told of approaching day, and the enemy's fire being no longer replied to, waxed fainter and fainter, till at last it died away and all was silent.

Webster Gayle was guarded by two soldiers and a sergeant; Darcy also was by his side.  He was well aware of his desperate peril, and did not cease entreating his guards to let him free.  A deaf ear, however, was turned to all his prayers, the soldiers, sergeant, and officers answering not a word to the wretched man's promises and bribes.

The grey dawn was just breaking, and but for the

18

heavy fog which hung all around, objects might have been discerned. A brisk fire now again opened, and once more the bullets hailed around. From a small thicket of brush-wood, about a quarter of a mile on the right, a most galling and irregular discharge was kept up, so that, notwith-standing the darkness and fog, several men were badly wounded. As the light gradually broadened, the mist which hung about also cleared away in a measure, and the jets of smoke from the clump of brushwood told that the enemy's riflemen had established themselves there, and were making the most of the opportunity to annoy the retreat.

Suddenly Darcy gave the word to halt, and disposing his men in skirmishing order gave directions to clear the bush. Scattering on all sides they advanced to do this, firing as they went, from tree to tree, bush to bush, some-times at a run, at others crawling on the ground. In less than ten minutes the fire from the thicket ceased, and in five more it was entered and cleared, amid loud yelling and shouting. At this moment, and as soon as the men had plunged into the thicket and were hid from view, Darcy turned to the sergeant, who, with two soldiers, still guarded Webster Gayle.

"Go after the men, and see that they do not pursue the enemy. Take these men with you, I will guard the prisoner. Bugler, blow the cease firing and the retreat."

The sergeant, wondering somewhat at his officer pre-ferring to guard the prisoner than head his men, started on his errand without remark; and now Darcy is alone with Webster Gayle and the two girls.

"Darcy Leigh, it is now all but daylight. In a quarter of an hour we shall be back at the outpost. If you have any pity—any mercy, let my father free. Now—now is the time."

It was hard indeed to resist the frantic appeal of a daughter who, with clasped hands, pleaded for her father's life.

Darcy looked around him. The retreat had been blown, and from the woods in all directions the sentries and skirmishers were coming in, followed up by the enemy, who, at the well-known bugle call, again pressed on, keeping up a scattering but nearly harmless fire. There were many soldiers and non-commissioned officers in full view of them, so that had Darcy decided to let his prisoner go free, in the first place, it would be seen, and in the second it was all but certain he would be recaptured and brought in by some of the retreating skirmishers.

Without returning any answer whatever to Stella's prayer, he marched Webster to a clump of brushwood about twenty yards distant, and said a few words in a low tone of voice. The merchant started, and hurriedly—excitedly asked Darcy to repeat his words. This he did, but in so low a tone that the girls could not hear the words. Then Darcy looked around until he saw Darby Kelly, who having been relieved from his sentry duty, was retreating with the others. He held up his sword to attract attention, and the Irishman was soon by his side, panting and out of breath.

He spoke a very few words in a low tone of voice, which, however, produced a great impression.

" By jaber ! an' is yer honner in airnest ?"

" Yes, quite—do as I told you, quick !—no hesitation."

Darby muttered a few more expletives expressive of wonder, and then taking up a position about twenty yards off, commenced firing in the direction of the enemy.

" Now, sir—march on," said Darcy, raising his voice so that he could be heard by any stragglers in the vicinity ; " at the slightest attempt to escape, I blow your brains out."

All this was inexplicable to Stella and her sister, and the former felt a pang of anger at the rough, brutal tone in which he spoke.

Darcy Leigh was pale—very pale, almost as much so as the unfortunate he guarded. In the mind of this latter there was evidently a great struggle going on—his whole frame trembled with excitement, as though he were trying to work himself up to some desperate attempt.

Suddenly, and without a moment's warning, he started off with a sudden bound in the opposite direction to which they were going. Stella and Angela, whom this move took by surprise, gave utterance to a faint scream.

But the sudden effort of Webster Gayle was but a futile one. With a spring quick as a tiger cat, Darcy Leigh bounded after him. There was a brief struggle, in which Webster Gayle for a moment seemed to have a chance—but it was but for a moment, and the next Darcy dealt him a blow on the head with the butt end of his pistol which felled him to the ground.

Stella gave vent to a piercing scream at the sight. She saw her father attempt to rise and grapple with Darcy—then, oh, horror!—she saw the latter take deliberate aim with his pistol, placing the muzzle within a foot of the other's head, and fire.

Webster Gayle gave one fearful cry, and then fell back and lay quite still. His forehead and face were covered with blood. So close was the discharge that it seemed he must have been instantly killed.

Scream after scream broke from Angela, who fell on her knees at the dreadful sight, clinging to Stella and hiding her face. At the sound of the discharge and the screams of the girls several soldiers who had seen the struggle ran up. Many were quite close enough to see the whole affair—the brief effort of Webster to escape, the blow on the head from Darcy's pistol, and finally the shot, close and deadly, which for ever laid him low.

" So dies a traitor and a spy," said Darcy, calmly replacing his revolver in his belt.

" Murderer! scoundrel! coward!" cried Stella.

Darcy turned yet paler at these words.

" Seize the girls and drag them to head-quarters. They are as much spies and traitors as their father. Seize them, men, at once, and stop this outcry."

The men who were hurrying up hastened to obey, and Stella and Angela were roughly laid hold of, and dragged away from the scene.

" Darby," said Darcy, in a loud voice, " come here."

The Irishman obeyed, and then Darcy stooped down, and appeared for a moment to be examining the body which lay at his feet.

" Dead—quite dead—he met his just fate. Take up the body on your shoulders, Darby, and carry it into the little thicket ; throw it down and leave it—a fitting burial for a spy. Here, give me your rifle, I will hold it for you while you go. Come, quick !"

Darby gave the young officer his rifle, and then lifted the dead body on his shoulder and marched off with it as though it had been but a feather. Arrived at the clump of brushwood, he threw it carelessly from his shoulders, and rejoined Darcy Leigh.

" If the enemy occupy this ground, and choose to bury the spy they can do so. My men have other work to do than digging graves for spies."

With these words, which were heard by many, he walked quietly on towards the men who, by his orders, had seized and held the girls.

" Fall in, men, fall in. Sergeant, see those two women do not escape ; if they attempt it, shoot them as I did their father."

Even the rough soldiers looked astonished at this un-necessarily severe, even brutal order. For how could two weak girls escape from the custody of strong men ?

"Murderer ! unmanly, cowardly murderer !" said Stella, her whole frame trembling with passion. " Shoot us—shoot me and complete your work, cowardly dog that you are ! "

" Stella, you will regret your words."

" Never, villain, ruffian ! May a daughter's curse and the curse of the Almighty ——"

" Stop her mouth," shouted Darcy, apparently furious; " gag her, one of you fellows, instantly."

A soldier placed his hand on the mouth of the girl, not harshly, but firmly, and she seeing resistance vain, desisted. Her eyes gleamed for a moment on Darcy like an angry tigress, and an expression of desperate hate was on her handsome features.

Darcy turned sadly away, unable or unwilling to en-counter the gaze of the now fatherless daughter.

" At least, she did not curse me," he muttered. " I was

in time to stop that. *That* would, indeed, have been hard to bear—' Scoundrel—coward—murderer ! ' "

By this time it was broad daylight, and the mists of morning were being fast dissipated. After a quarter of an hour's walk Darcy suddenly gave the word to halt, and gazing long through a small telescope towards the enemy, gave orders for the men to remain under arms till his return, and started off back again. He went quickly on, sometimes walking, at others running, till he came in view of the clump of brush where Darby had carried the body of Webster Gayle. He was obliged to use the utmost caution, for in the broad daylight he might at any moment be discovered and fired at by the enemy's sentries and skirmishers, of which he knew there were many in the woods, and who might, even now, be advancing. As soon as he reached the thicket or brush he entered it, and skirting the edge, sought for and found the place where Darby Kelly had deposited his burden.

There was the place undoubtedly—but the body was gone !

Darcy did not seem in the least surprised at this, but having ascertained the fact, he hastened to rejoin his company, which he did in less than a quarter of an hour. The men were somewhat surprised at his absence, but it was generally supposed he had gone forward to endeavour to discover if the enemy's skirmishers were advancing.

The two girls were closely guarded in obedience to his orders. What then was the surprise of the guard when he said, " I have no orders to keep these ladies prisoners. Release them."

The next moment Stella and Angela were free.

" Yonder are the enemy's lines," said Darcy, pointing. " It is now daylight; if you take my advice, you will at once seek to cross over. You will be soon seen ; and the firing has ceased, so there is but little fear of a stray bullet."

"Liberty from your murderous hands, Darcy Leigh, is almost worse than death," said Stella, passionately. " However, to rid ourselves for ever from your sight, and the company of your ruffian soldiers, we go. The day will come when your coward heart will quail—the day of retribution for traitors and murderers. Then, too late, you will repent your bloodthirsty ferocity."

"The day will come, Stella, when you will repent your words," said Darcy, sadly, and then turned away, and gave the word—

"Fall in there—quick—march."

Then the soldiers moved on with measured tramp, and the two girls are left standing alone.

Alone between two armies—alone and unprotected, and with the dreadful memory of their father's violent death fresh in their minds. Angela clung to her sister in helpless misery.

"Oh, Stella, what shall we do? Is not this terrible?"

"Come, Angela, let us cross to the Union lines, if possible, and shake the dust off our feet on leaving these bloodthirsty treacherous rebels."

Then Stella drew her sister's arm within her own, and they walked on—not quickly, for Angela was weak, nervous, and, frequently near fainting. The mist slowly but steadily cleared away, and in less than an hour they could see the white tents of the Union camp, on an eminence ahead of them. They knew it must be the Union camp, for, from one tent, the United States ensign floated in the breeze. Soon after this they could distinguish dark forms flitting about among the trees, and Stella, knowing these to be the Federal skirmishers and sentries, waved her white handkerchief, lest they might possibly be fired at. Nothing of the kind happened, however, and they were permitted to advance unmolested for some distance. Suddenly a sentry challenged,—

"Who goes there?"

"Friends," replied Stella, in loud, clear tones.

"Halt, and give the word."

"We cannot; we are loyal ladies, and have just escaped from the enemy."

The sentry called to another at some distance, and both advanced to the two girls.

"We must make you prisoners, and convey you to head-quarters."

"As you please. We can soon explain to your officers who and what we are."

They were then marched off some little distance, and handed over to a fresh escort, who conducted them along a road through the wood, towards the camp they had seen on the hill. An hour brought them there, and they passed down the street of tents, and halted before the one over which was the flag. An officer walked up and down outside, smoking a cigar.

"Two prisoners, sir," said one of the soldiers, saluting ; "they crossed from the direction of the enemy, and were captured by our outlying sentries."

The officer looked at them curiously for a moment, and then said,—"Who and what are you?"

"We are loyal ladies, and have long been forced to remain South with our father. This morning that father was cruelly murdered, and we were permitted to leave."

"Your names?"

"We are the daughters of Webster Gayle, of New York."

"Webster Gayle!—ha!" cried the officer, in astonishment; "and he was shot this morning, you say?"

Angela burst into tears, but Stella, controlling her emotion, answered,—

"Use the right word, sir,—murdered! Our father was cruelly and brutally murdered!"

"Then, by Jupiter, the fellow inside must be an impostor—a spy! Stay one moment; I will go and announce your capture to the general."

So saying, he passed into the tent.

"An impostor—a spy! Of whom can he be speaking?" thought Angela and Stella, but before they could devote much thought to it the officer re-appeared, and said, "This way, ladies—follow me."

They followed him, and the next moment stood inside the tent. An officer sat at a table, and also a person who appeared to be a clerk, for he was busily employed in writing. The tent was rather dark, so that at first they did not perceive any one else.

"These are the prisoners, general."

" Ha ! Now, young women, you say you are tho daughters of Webster Gayle ? Look at that man, and say if you know him."

The general pointed with his finger, and Stella following the direction, saw a man standing there in the darkest part of the tent.

She gazed incredulously for a while. Surely it could not be——

" Stella ! "

She could not mistake that voice. With a wild cry she ran forward, and threw herself into his arms. " Father, dear father !—alive and unhurt !—can I believe my eyes ? " Angela too, almost bewildered at first, soon understood that it was indeed her father, and she also clung around his neck.

The general and the officer looked on in silence. The scene—the joyful tears of the girls—tho old man's trembling voice—all were too real to be affected.

After a little time, the general said—

" So it seems that you are not a spy, sir, after all. But how does it happen that your daughters say you wero shot this morning ? "

" Yes, father," said Stella, raising her head from his shoulder, " how comes it you are alive and unhurt ! I myself saw that cowardly ruffian Darcy Leigh shoot—— "

" Stella, hush ! " said Webster, placing a hand on her mouth, " you know not what you say. Breathe not a word against Darcy Leigh. Rebel though he be, he is a noble-hearted young fellow. He it was who saved me from certain death. He whispered to me what to do ; he drew the bullets from his pistol, and but pretended to shoot me. Hence I am here safe."

A wail of anguish burst from Stella Gayle, and leaving her father, she held by the table, and hid her face in her hands.

" Coward—scoundrel—murderer ! " Those were the bitter words she had used at the very time when, against his duty and at his own peril, he had devised and carried out a scheme to save her father.

" Coward—scoundrel—murderer ! " Again it was she

who had insulted and reviled him, even at the moment
when she should rather have fallen down and worshipped
him. Was it to be always her fate to receive good for
evil from the man whom in her heart she loved, and who,
though she had professed to scorn, now scorned her?

These and other passionate thoughts swept over her
soul. She suddenly started to her feet, and forgetting the
presence of the officers, forgetting all but her own misery,
stood for a moment with clasped hands, and then cried
frantically—

"I wish I were dead! I pray that these words I now
utter may be my last!"

Her eyes glared fiercely, her face was ghastly pale, and
her dark hair, falling in confusion over her neck and
shoulders, gave the benefit of contrast to the picture.

"Stella, dear Stella," sobbed Angela, " what dreadful
words you are saying!"

"Leave me, Angela, leave me," she said, passionately,
"I am unworthy to live. I will go back to the rebel city,
and on my knees beg pardon for my base, unwomanly,
false words from him whom I have so bitterly wronged."

"Stella, my dear Stella, it is impossible!" said the
father, distractedly, trying to take her hand.

"It is not—it shall not be impossible. I will go—now
this very moment."

With these impetuous words, she made as though she
would go out; but at a nod from the general, who looked
on in wonder at this strange scene, the sentry within the
tent planted himself before the opening.

"These are your daughters, you say, sir," said the
officer. " I have reason to believe you speak the truth
You can have a pass to New York, or where you like.
North, but neither you nor they can be permitted to
approach the enemy's lines."

"Come, Stella, come—do you hear what the officer
says? You cannot be allowed to cross again, even if you
are mad enough to desire it."

"Stella, dear Stella, do come with us," murmured Angela.

By and by they soothed her into a sort of sullen apathy,
and she permitted them to lead her away.

But though she was quiet and silent, a great storm raged within her breast. "Scoundrel! coward! murderer!"—the memory of those bitter words was ever in her thoughts, nor could she drive it away.

---

## CHAPTER XXVI.

### RUNNING THE BLOCKADE.

WE will now for a space leave the Yankee camp, and return to that of the so-called rebels.

The news of the attempted escape of the prisoner, and his having been shot by Darcy Leigh in the attempt, was soon bruited abroad, and it was not long before Lupus Rock heard of it. That the girls had been suffered to cross into the Yankee lines was also known; and the two facts combined overwhelmed Lupus with consternation. Webster Gayle dead! and Stella gone! Where, then, was his power? Endless complications presented themselves to him. He could hardly realize the full extent of this disaster to his schemes. As to his uncle's property, he knew nothing; his claim lay in his power over the merchant—supposing the latter had willed it away, he could have no hold on the fresh possessors.

Certain of succeeding in this last attempt, he had even given back to Webster Gayle the assignment of the Yancey estate to him (Lupus), in order to disarm suspicion. This, of course, he intended to come back into his possession, as he meant his uncle to have been seized by a trusty emissary of his own. But now, as affairs stood, Webster was dead, and the papers found on him in the possession of Darcy Leigh, or whoever he had consigned them to. In this dilemma he knew not which way to turn —what to do.

What annoyed and infuriated him more than anything was the knowledge that Stella Gayle, whom he coveted as much as her father's wealth, should have escaped him.

It was useless for him longer to remain South—that he

fully determined on. His late uncle's affairs demanded his attention, and he doubted not that, with his knowledge and skill, he would be able to secure something worth his while. And, as for Stella Gayle—he ground his teeth as he swore that, though this time defeated, he would never relinquish the pursuit until he had gained her.

That night his company was told off on the same duty —to occupy a battery commanding an important bend in the river and also the road. Glaring, savage, and vindictive he went on the duty.

In the morning, when fresh troops were ordered up to relieve those in charge of the position, to their utter astonishment their own guns opened fire upon them, and they were awakened to the fact that the place was held by the enemy. It seemed incomprehensible. No firing had been heard during the night, and yet, when morning dawned, the Yankee flag floated over the redoubt; Yankee troops manned it, and the dead and wounded of the unsuspecting Confederates lay around, as again and again they rushed to recapture the position.

In vain. It was too strongly held, and during the night fresh guns had been brought up and mounted. Assault after assault was delivered against the betrayed positions without success. The assaulting parties were too weak, the place too strong; and before sunrise several hundred rebels had fallen in front. Meanwhile important movements were being executed along the road which the battery commanded. Large bodies of troops were marched along in close range of guns which, in an enemy's hands, must have done dreadful work.

About eleven o'clock in the forenoon a strong force of artillery and infantry was despatched by the Confederate general, with orders to retake the position at all hazards. The order was obeyed; and with great slaughter the Yankees were driven pell-mell from the place.

But the mischief had been done : a general action soon commenced. The Confederates advanced, and drove the Yankee army back. But for the temporary loss of the position commanding the road, retreat would have been impossible, and the Federals must have stood and fought it out, or have surrendered. The series of the terrible six days' battles commenced, which ended in the complete defeat of McClellan. But, though with frightful slaughter, he contrived to lead away the remnant of his army, and escaped utter annihilation.

Of Lupus Rock no more was seen or heard for a long time. He had deserted to the enemy with the whole of his own company, while stragglers from other companies of his regiment, to the extent of at least one-half, joined him. Many and bitter were the curses rained upon the traitor's head, and should he ever be captured, every one knew that his fate would be—five minutes' grace and then the halter.

Shortly after this, the whole Confederate army advanced, defeated all who opposed it, and triumphantly entered Maryland. Thence, after a series of desperate battles, ending with that of Antietam Creek, they again retreated, and again stood upon the defensive, inviting—defying the Northern hosts to make a third advance on Richmond. The 7th Carolinas suffered severely in the Maryland campaigns, but no regiment distinguished themselves more highly. The spirit of their patroness, the "Black Angel," pervaded all—men and officers; and though thinned in numbers, they came back with honours thick upon them.

Darcy Leigh had been again wounded, although not severely, and it was imperative he should retire for a time from active service.

Under these circumstances, Darcy once again turned his mind to his old profession—the naval one. The Spitfire had been repaired, altered, and coated with a defensive armour of iron plates and chain cables. She was now ready for sea, and Darcy applied to be appointed to the command.

Once more, then, we must transport ourselves back to Charleston, where Darcy was superintending the arming of the sloop.

Wharncliffe, some other old friends, with Darby Kelly and Jupiter, still followed his fortunes. Gerald Leigh and Captain George were detained with their regiment in the neighbourhood of Richmond, and the 7th Carolinas were still in the capital. Coralie St. Casse also remained in Richmond for the time, and for the present was forced to content herself with prayers for the safety of her hero, who was about to run out to sea, and prey on the Yankee commerce.

Darcy had thought long over the subject, and decided that his aim should be not only to burn, sink, and destroy, but, if possible, to make prizes, and take to a safe place all such vessels as he could overhaul.   Now it was one thing for a swift steamer like the Spitfire to run through the blockading fleet, but quite another for slow-sailing vessels, even when towed; therefore Darcy determined to establish a depôt somewhere up the coast, at a spot secure rom observation, and where there was no port.   After patient search he discovered a spot suited to his purpose.

Along a greater part of the shore of North and South Carolina there is a double coast, or an inner and outer one.   This rendered an effective blockade infinitely more difficult, while it afforded shelter for smaller craft plying along the shore.   This double coast is caused by long spits of land, mostly islands running parallel to the main land. Occasional breaks in these long islands give ingress to the narrow strip of water between them and the low, sandy mainland coast.

Passing from the sea through one of these inlets, distant about ninety miles in a north-easterly direction from Charleston, the coast of South Carolina comes into view beyond.   Sailing towards the south-west, the long island gradually approaches nearer to the mainland, till at one place the whole channel, from the island to the shore, is not more than two hundred yards wide.   At the very narrowest part there is a creek running into the shore of South Carolina for about half a mile.   This creek Darcy determined should be the head-quarters to which he could bring his spoil, and where he would collect a supply of ammunition and stores.

He had carefully explored the channel from end to end —going out day after day in a boat sounding the depth, and taking an accurate survey for future use.

The channel was narrow, tortuous, and full of shoals, so that while a vessel of light draught, commanded by one who knew the ground well, might with safety run down at full speed, larger vessels could not possibly pass ; while even the very smallest would be obliged to advance slowly and cautiously.   Thus, if the sloop were pursued, even in a crippled state, she could run down the channel, every foot of which he knew, and escape by the inlet at the other end, some three miles past the narrow part.

Accordingly, Darcy Leigh explained his views to the military commander of the district, and by his direction a sand fort was erected on one side of the creek, on which some ten guns were mounted, so as to effectually command the channel and the creek itself.   Around this fort some sheds were erected, and a good supply of ammunition, provisions, and coal collected.   A company of about seventy men were left in charge of this fort, and every measure taken, so that even if the retreat were discovered the place could not be taken by sudden assault.

Having made all his arrangements, Darcy wrote to Coralie informing her of what he had done, and of the place he had fixed on for the rendezvous.

A prompt reply came back.

" Dear Darcy,—I am glad to hear you speak so hopefully of your intended cruise, and doubt not you will make great havoc among the enemy's commerce.   I shall shortly leave Richmond and return to Charleston. If you can possibly, by any channel, let me know when you think of making your first run into the creek, I will, if possible, be there awaiting you.   I will gather a few irregular troops, and place them under the command of some officer I can trust.   That God may bless and guard you, my dear Darcy, is the earnest prayer of your loving

" CORALIE."

In a week from the receipt of this letter, Darcy stood on the deck of the sloop. She was no longer the Spitfire, but had been named by acclamation the Black Angel. She looked, as she lay alongside the quay as if she would not belie her name, but prove indeed a very destroying angel to the enemy's merchantmen, and with her iron-plated sides and ponderous guns, a formidable antagonist even to a war ship.

She had been *razeed*, that is cut down so that she floated very low in the water, offering but a small mark. In place of the long heavily sparred masts she before carried, she had now smaller and lighter ones, carrying nothing above the topsails. On each side were two large Parrot guns only, while at bow and stern was an enormous Dahlgren shell gun. This, with some half-dozen carronades on the quarter-deck, was all her armament.

But though she now carried fewer guns than formerly, she was infinitely more formidable, for their great size would enable her to lie off at such a distance, as by reason of her armour to place her nearly in safety, while she could pound away and destroy any wooden ship afloat.

At last the eventful night is come when this spiteful-looking little craft is to steam out and run through the squadron outside.

At eight o'clock in the evening the crew were all mustered and the articles of war read. Then each man was appointed to his station, and steam was got up.

As soon as it was dark the barges were cast off, and the Black Angel moved slowly and gracefully out into the bay amidst tremendous cheering.

Of course a moonless night was chosen, and what was even more favourable, towards ten o'clock a drizzling rain commenced to fall. Nothing could be more propitious. The wind rose slowly and low clouds swept across the sky, rendering it impossible to discern anything at more than a hundred yards distance.

The officers were all grouped on the quarter-deck, talking in low tones of the probability of success. The men were all at their quarters, lying down by the guns or about the decks, while the firemen were under the charge of Darby Kelly, Jupiter being king of the negro stokers. The engines were in perfect order, and worked easily and noiselessly as a lady's watch. At eleven o'clock precisely the anchor was taken up and the order given—

"Go ahead easy!"

Not a light was allowed on deck—not even in the binnacle, and the helmsman had to steer according to the starboard or port of an officer in the cabin who had before him a compass with a shaded lamp. This was the only light on board except the fires.

Slowly, silently, they steamed out of the bay in darkness and deadly silence. One might fancy her a phantom steamer manned by a ghostly crew. In the gloom the great guns can be distinguished on the decks, and around them the seamen, who mutter together in low tones.

And now the lights from the casemates of Fort Sumter are seen on the starboard bow. Darcy gives orders for her to be steered close under its frowning walls. They can even hear the sentry's measured tread as he paces up and down the ramparts.

Shortly more lights came in view, apparently far out to sea. These are the lights of the blockading squadron, and are continually flashing about, appearing and disappearing in a most mysterious manner. The vessels of the squadron are signalling one to another. Perhaps a vessel is suspected being in the offing. waiting an opportunity to run in ; perhaps even their intention to run out with the Black Angel is known. Who can tell ?

"Eleven," said Darcy, in a low voice, after counting the lights, to Wharncliffe, who stood by his side ; "a nice little nest of hornets to run through, certainly !"

"We must get through ; I don't see how we can fail. I believe we can outrun any vessel in the fleet; and even if discovered——"

"Why we will pitch a shell or two into them from those great iron champagne bottles, just in a playful manner, and show them our heels. Clad as we are, they can't do us much harm in the dark."

Onwards—still onwards—at a low rate of speed, but with a full head of steam, so that at a moment's notice the engines may be worked at their fastest. Gradually the lights of Charleston grew fainter and fainter, and the lights flashing from the enemy's ships more distinct.

"Silence, forward there !" said Darcy, hearing a low muttering among the men ; "let not a word be spoken.

19

In a quarter of an hour we shall be in the middle of the enemy's fleet. Stand by your guns, lads ; boys, ready with the battle lanterns.   At the word of command, light up, run out the guns—fire ; then douse all lights at once, and wait further orders."

It was desperately exciting.   The men peering over the low bulwarks could see, at barely a mile's distance, the lights on the yard arms and mastheads of the Federal war ships, right ahead—for such the channel compelled them to steer.

Darcy walked quietly round the decks, and again enjoined absolute silence.   " Not a word, men, but be ready to spring to your feet and blaze away."

As soon as the lights of the fleet were distant only about half a mile and right ahead, Darcy, who had been intently watching the bearings of a signal light on a point of land, signalled to the man at the wheel to heave the helm to starboard.   The vessel slowly came round, soon the lights, which had been right ahead, were broad on the starboard beam.

In silence and darkness the Black Angel steamed on, not a glimmer of light to be seen anywhere about her decks, not a sound, except the low rumbling of the engines, and the dash of the waves against her bows.   A man was now stationed in the chains with the hand-lead, but instead of cheerily singing forth the sounding—" By the mark, seven," he whispered to a boy, who forthwith repeated it to the young commander.

The water was rapidly shoaling—seven fathoms—six— five—four ; then Darcy sent word down to the engine- room still further to slacken speed, for the navigation was now perilous in the extreme.

On the one side stretched a dangerous shoal, while on the other moored, or hove-to, lay the blockading fleet. It was imperative to keep as near the edge of the shoal as possible, to avoid discovery—indeed, so close was the vessel running to the enemy's ships, that the bells could be distinctly heard as the half-hours were struck.

The tide was making dead against them—the engines were revolving at far less than half speed, so that the progress of the Black Angel along the edge of the shoal was very slow indeed.

They heard "two bells" struck by the various vessels on their starboard beam, then three bells—four bells. Four bells—two o'clock ! in another hour daylight would begin to appear in the east.

" Starboard, starboard easy," said Darcy, in a low voice, to the helmsman. "Wharncliffe, go and stand by the leadsman in the chains. We must absolutely skirt the shoal. What water does she draw forward and aft ?"

" Seventeen feet forward, eighteen aft."

" Three fathoms, ah ! we are now in four, only a fathom between us and the sand. We must run it yet finer ; let me know the instant the water shoals to less than three and a half."

Wharncliffe jumped into the main chains, and carefully scrutinised each heave of the lead.

In less than ten minutes he rejoined Darcy on the quarter-deck.

" Three fathoms and a half, barely, and steadily shoaling."

" Port your helm, easy aport."

The order was none too soon, for the next moment a dull bump was felt, followed by a dragging and grinding which told she had touched bottom.

" Hard aport ! over with your helm."

Darcy and Wharncliffe themselves lent a hand to heave the wheel over. The dragging and bumping continued for about half a minute, and then the vessel bore off from the shoal, and was again in comparatively deep water. Now, however, the lights, instead of being abeam, were again brought nearly ahead—the nearest was a point on the starboard bow, distant about three-quarters of a mile.

The course they were now steering would run her within less than a quarter of a mile of the outermost light, a dangerously short distance.

" Go round the decks, Wharncliffe, and see that all the men are at their posts ; enjoin silence and watchfulness. In ten minutes more we shall have run by in safety or shall have been discovered. Fill the space in the waist and between the guns with small-arms men."

Wharncliffe went to execute this order; and Darcy hastily descended into the engine-room, spoke a few words to the engineer, and then passed on into the stoke-hole. Here were Darby Kelly and Jupiter, stripped to the waist, shovelling coal on the furnace, and urging on the others.

Perspiration streamed from their bodies, and in the intense glare they looked like demons at work at Vulcan's forge. Darby and the other white men were as black as the niggers from the coal dust and smoke.

"That's right, my lads, keep the steam up; we shall want every pound of it."

"Say, massa Darcy, am it much hotter dan dis whar de debbil lib?" said Jupiter, with a broad grin.

"Go on wid ye, ye haythun! by jabers, you'll find that out soon enough."

"Sail, ho! right ahead! Port!—port!—hard aport!"

It was the man on the look-out who gave the alarm.

Darcy rushed up the ladder and on to the deck. All was excitement. The men who a minute before had been lying around the guns, now crowded the bulwarks and peered into the darkness. Darcy, running to the larboard side, looked over the bulwarks. Almost right ahead he could just discern a large black mass. Each moment brought it nearer, and he at once decided it was a ship lying-to without lights.

He wasted little time in staring, but ran first to the engine-room, and shouted, "Full speed ahead!" and then to the helm, which he himself took. Keeping his eyes on the dark mass, he steered the sloop till it lay about three points on the bow.

"Steady at that, my lad," he said, giving up the wheel; "keep her at that."

The engines now groaned and creaked heavily, and the vessel tore ahead at full speed, dashing up the spray and making a considerable noise. The lights of the enemy's vessels were now about a quarter of a mile on the starboard beam, while the ship without lights, which the look-out had discovered, was only about a hundred yards on the port bow.

Suddenly, lights flashed from this mysterious vessel ; a dozen lanterns gleamed and glistened in the darkness ; the roll of the drum and the whistle of the boatswain's pipe are heard, followed by the trampling of many feet.

" Ship ahoy ! what ship is that ?"

Darcy answered not a word, but merely motioned to the helms slightly to alter the course.

" Heave to, or I'll sink you."

" Wharncliffe, jump forward ; run out the guns, let the small-arms men be ready, and send some men to man the carronades."

Still the Black Angel steamed on, as if in sullen contempt. The men, in obedience to orders, flitted about her decks like shadows ; but not a light was shown.

But soon a bright light comes blazing over the sea. The stranger vessel is burning a blue light ; and by its intense livid flame the Black Angel is plainly seen as she steams swiftly on.

The next minute is heard the roar of cannon, the lurid flames from the muzzles of the guns streaming out into the darkness, and for a moment still further lighting up the scene. The shot whistles through the air ; the vessel is struck several times, the flying jib boom is shot away, and, a backstay being hit, the foretopgallant mast comes crashing down on deck. But the iron coating of the Black Angel fended off the greater part of the broadside. Some few men were wounded by splinters, but that was all.

" Starboard !—hard a starboard," cried Darcy, quietly ; " stand by your guns, men. We'll give her just a taste in return."

The vessel slowly wore round, until she passed under the bows of the stranger, distant only some twenty yards. In this position the enemy could not bring a gun to bear, while the guns of the other as well as the carronades would take full effect.

No sooner was the bow gun on the larboard side abreast of the enemy than Darcy gave the word—

"Gun No. 1 port side—fire !"

Instantly the loud report of the piece is heard, and the huge shell rushes through the air, and plunges slap into the bow of the Yankee man-of-war. Onward it goes—splintering, tearing, and carrying death and destruction with it, till, striking the mainmast, it bursts, scattering an iron storm of splinters on all sides.

"Small arms men—blaze away !"

The blue light is still burning in the poop of the enemy, rendering every object as visible as by daylight. Scarcely had the sputtering rattle of musketry commenced than the word is given to fire the other shell gun, which also takes effect on the enemy's hull. Then follows the feeble roar of the carronades, and the Black Angel has run by.

"Cease firing," is now the command.

The blue light on the enemy's deck has burned out, and once again all is comparative darkness ; comparative darkness only, however, for now a hundred lights flash from the other vessels, and it is evident, by the change in their position, that they are steaming up to the assistance of the unknown vessel.

"Port—port—hard aport," once again is the word, and the vessel's head is again brought round and headed out to sea. On board they can plainly hear the cries and groans of the enemy's wounded, which, however, gradually get fainter and fainter as, dashing at full speed ahead, the rebel vessel leaves her behind.

Another blue light is now burned, and this example is followed by all the other vessels, till the sea astern of the Black Angel is one blaze of light. Fortunately, however, the sloop is now at such a distance that, though the enemy's ships are plainly visible, she herself is shrouded in impenetrable darkness.

"Shall we give them a shot or two from our stern guns?" said Wharncliffe.

"No, I think not. It will only reveal our position."

"They seem to know it. See, every vessel is now steaming right upon us."

"Only guesswork. They know we shall run out and

make an offing. In an hour's time we shall have day-light, and I daresay they hope then to have us in sight."

Soon the blue lights burned out, and seeing the futility of it, the enemy burned no more, though the lights of the signal lamps showed that some, at least, of the squadron were in full pursuit. These lights gradually got fainter and fainter, proving that the rebel vessel was outrunning the others, till, in little over an hour, the grey morning light revealed seven vessels steaming in their wake, the foremost of which was over three miles distant.

Barring an unforeseen accident to the engines they were now safe, as each minute put a greater distance between them and their pursuers. Long before the sun rose five out of the seven vessels astern were hull down, the smoke from the funnels alone pointing out their position. This, too, soon disappeared; probably seeing the chase hopeless they had relinquished it and returned, leaving it to the only two vessels which appeared to have any chance at all.

At five o'clock Darcy Leigh, who had never quitted the quarter-deck, and continually surveyed the pursuing vessels through a glass, suddenly shut it up, and gave the order for the course of the vessel to be changed from E.S.E. to N.E.

No sooner was this order complied with than he said to Wharncliffe, who kept constantly by his side—" Go down to the engine-room and tell them to ease a few turns, so as to get about a knot an hour less out of her."

" They'll be near overhauling us in an hour or two, what with the change of course and slackening speed. That first steamer, whatever she is, is as fast as we are within a knot at the outside."

" So much the worse for her," replied Darcy, shortly. " If she catches us she'll catch a Tartar."

" You mean, then, to let them come up with us?"

" Yes, if they're fools enough, and sink them for their pains. Now let all the crew go below, and get an hour

or two's rest, keeping about twenty only on deck. You
yourself can turn in ; I am not sleepy, and will keep the
deck till those Yankees get up close."

The engines were now eased, and the vessel slackened
speed considerably. The alteration in the course brought
the Yankees in pursuit from being right astern to a
position about four points on the port-quarter. As soon
as the alteration in the course of the chase was discovered,
they also hauled up to the northward, and steered across
the bows of the Black Angel at such an angle as would,
in about four hours, bring the foremost of the two close
up, supposing the speed of all to be nearly equal.

The chase, in fact, was sailing along the perpendicular
of a right angled triangle, while the pursuing ships
traversed the hypothenuse.

As soon as the decks were cleared and the crew had
gone below, Darcy Leigh took his seat abaft the binnacle,
and ordered the steward to bring strong coffee with a
dash of brandy in it. He did not care to sleep, and yet
felt the necessity of feeling wakeful when the time for
action should arrive.

In this way the three vessels steamed on, the pursuers
gradually decreasing the distance, till, by five o'clock, not
more than three miles at most separated them.

## CHAPTER XXVII.

### THE YANKEES CATCH A TARTAR.

THE sun rose over a sea gently rippled by a topgallant
breeze from the west.

" Loose and set the courses, topsails, topgallant sails,
and jibs."

Such was the order which the young rebel captain now
gave. The topsails were first loosed and sheeted home ;
then the halyards were taken to the capstan, as there
were but few men on deck, and Darcy wished the others
to get as much repose as possible. The topsails hoisted,

the mainsail and foresail were next set, then the top-gallant sails and jibs. The Yankee steamers had set their sails some time previously, and now seeing the chase also make sail, they proceeded to clap on every inch of canvas. Topmast and topgallant stunsails, royals, staysails, and every available sail was set, till they heeled over considerably before the rising breeze.

At this time Darcy again paid a visit to the engine-room, the result of which was that the Black Angel slackened yet a little more in her speed—not much, but still more than sufficient to counteract the effect of the sails.

The crew on deck shook their heads, and muttered together as the hulls of the Yankee steamers rose yet higher and higher, till the main-deck guns of both were plainly visible. They thought that the ship was under full steam, and were nervous and excited at seeing the pursuers slowly but surely creep up. None but Wharncliffe were admitted into the secret, and even the lieutenant of the watch glanced uneasily and with sur-prise from the captain, calmly sipping his coffee, to the two Yankee steamers.

" They're overhauling us, sir, fast," he said presently to Darcy Leigh ; " there's a good breeze—shall we set the main-topgallant sail, and send another fore-topgallant mast aloft ?"

" No, Mr. Edwards, it's not worth while. See that the guns are ready for service, and get splinter nettings rigged ; then let the watch have their morning coffee, and call all hands to breakfast. In another hour that fellow in front will be in range of the Dahlgren guns."

" You mean to fight them, then, sir ?"

" Yes, if they're fools enough."

" They're heavier armed than we are, sir."

" No, not heavier ; they carry more guns, it's true, but I'm almost sure they have none heavier than our Dahlgrens ; besides, we are partly iron-plated."

" Yes, but not sufficiently to stand broadsiders of heavy metal at short range."

" No need ; they shall never get to short range. We

have the heels of the fastest of the two by at least a knot and a half."

" And yet they seem to gain on us."

" Because I have given orders to the engineer to slacken speed. Now, sir, get the splinter-nettings up. I expect they will soon begin to try the range ; at the first shot beat to quarters, and turn the crew up. I'll teach these fellows a lesson if they don't mind."

Darcy then lit a cigar, and the lieutenant of the watch proceeded to execute his orders, marvelling at, and admiring the coolness and forethought of the captain—but a boy in years, yet, as he thought, with a very old head upon his shoulders.

By some means or another it was not long before a whisper got abroad among the men that the captain meant to fight the Yankees, and felt certain of capturing or sinking them. They had all heard of his previous exploits, and, now that they knew it was part of his plan to be slowly overhauled by the enemy, they had the most boundless confidence in the result.

It was not long before the crew voluntarily turned out from their hammocks and crowded the decks. Darcy saw the eagerness and confidence of his crew with great joy, and felt doubly assured of success. At six o'clock coffee was ready for all hands, and a by no means unwelcome glass of grog was served out to all who were on deck.

The Yankee vessels could now be plainly made out. One, the foremost, was a steam frigate carrying twenty guns, while on the other, nearly a mile further astern, could be counted sixteen on each broadside. Both were fine vessels, well manned and well handled, and under other circumstances it would have been madness to have encountered either. But as it was, with the turn of speed certainly in his favour, probably carrying heavier guns, though so few in number, and with the additional safeguard of partial iron-plating, which, though comparatively imperfect, must be a great protection at any considerable distance, Darcy felt fully justified in the course he had determined on.

While the crew were taking their coffee, laughing and talking with all sailors' lightheartedness in face of danger, a puff of white smoke is seen to spout from the bow of the foremost steamer, and a round shot comes dancing and ricochetting over the waves, finally burying itself only some hundred yards astern of the Black Angel.

Almost immediately after the report is heard, the crew are summoned to quarters by drum and fife. For a few minutes nothing can be heard but the clatter of the coffee panikins, and the tramp of many feet hurrying below to lash their hammocks.

But in an incredibly short space of time, all this seeming chaos, the hurrying to and fro, the Babel of tongues, resolves itself into perfect order; the gunners are at their guns, the sail-trimmers at their posts, while the small-arms men crowd the waist and forecastle.

It was no part of Darcy's plan to let the enemy know he did not wish to escape; so, although likely to do harm rather than good, the sails were not taken in. Orders, however, were given to the engineer still further to slacken speed, so that the pursuing Yankee steamer might come within sure range.

Soon another jet, of smoke burst from the frigate. This time the shot howled through the air, and dashed through the main-topsail and fore-topsail, tearing a large hole in each.

"In all sail. Man the topsail clewlines and buntlines. Stand by, let go the topsail halyards. Away—aloft and furl—haul up the mainsail and foresail. Jib down haul, forecastle men. Let go the halyards—way aloft, men— pick 'em up cheerily."

And cheerily the order was executed; not, however, before two more shots from the bow gun of the Yankee steamer rushed through the air overhead, and splashed into the water some quarter of a mile ahead—proof positive that they were in easy range. In less than five minutes every rag of canvas was furled, and the men stood again on deck panting from exertion.

"Starboard!—hard a-starboard!"

Then the Black Angel slowly came round in obedience

to her helm, till her broadside was presented to the Yankee steamer. For a few minutes she was kept on in this new course, the enemy still keeping up his fire—the round shot dashing, splashing, and casting up the spray all around. Presently a shot struck her full amidships. There was a prodigious clang from the impact, but no harm was done—the iron plates proved of sufficient strength to prevent penetration.

"Stop her!"

Then the engines ceased working, and in a minute's time the rebel sloop lay almost still on the water, as though sullenly awaiting a foe she could not escape.

On came the Federal steamers, the foremost more than a mile ahead, each doubtless confident of an easy victory —perhaps anticipating that the audacious rebel, hopeless of escape, was about to surrender. If such was their opinion, it was soon doomed to be controverted by the stern logic of facts ; for a rapid and accurate fire was opened from the sloop.

First the two port guns were fired ; then the order was given to go ahead. She slowly wore round. When her stern was presented to the enemy, the big stern-chaser was fired, and then once more the engines were worked at full speed—nor was this slackened, till the distance gained had been in turn regained.

When Darcy judged this was the case, the Black Angel was again brought broadside on. Again the order was given to "stop her," and again the two port guns were loaded, and fired several times in succession.

Now the Federal steamer in turn wore round, presented her broadside, and delivered it. This was followed by the crash of falling spars, for it had taken effect in the rigging chiefly. Still, not a man was wounded, and the big guns were worked as rapidly as possible. The Yankee new began to find out his mistake, more especially when again the Black Angel presented her stern, and commenced pitching shells into him from the great Dahlgren stern-chaser.

All this time Darcy was careful to preserve the relative distances, convinced that his guns could play havoc with the enemy, though theirs in return did but little harm. Shell after shell was sent hurtling through the air, some falling short, some going overhead ; but every now and then one would plunge full into the hull of the enemy. On each of these occasions a considerable confusion might be observed, and, for a short time, the fire slackened, bearing witness to the damage done by the heavy shot. The Yankee commander was now alive to the danger, and, by no means relishing being made a target of, ceased firing, and steamed straight for the Black Angel ; but this by no means suited Darcy's purpose, so the vessel's head was brought round, and she also steamed straight away, keeping up a constant fire from her stern gun. After about a quarter of an hour of this fun, the distance between the two ships had been again so much increased that the rebel captain again brought her broadside on to the enemy, and let her remain thus, firing the broadside guns as rapidly as possible.

It now became apparent that the Federal steamer was much disabled—her fire was neither so rapid nor so accurate as formerly, and gangs of men could be distinguished working at the pumps.

The second steamer was now coming up to her assistance. Darcy, confident of the result, headed the Black Angel to meet this fresh combatant. To do this of course he had almost to retrace his steps, and pass within a few hundred yards of the first. As the rebel vessel steamed audaciously on, as it seemed, into the very jaws of the enemy, a most destructive fire was kept up by the bow gun, which again and again sent its heavy shell crashing into the hull of the Yankee.

So soon as the two vessels were broadside on, the Federal cruiser delivered her fire. At this close distance it did far more damage than heretofore—several men being wounded by the splinters which flew around. But if the Federal fire was more effective, that of the Black Angel proved absolutely disastrous to the enemy. One shot struck her on the water-line, tearing a large ragged hole impossible to plug. For a time her fire ceased, and it almost seemed that she would go down at once. A

signal of distress to her consort was run up, and, altogether, it was evident she was in a bad way.

"She will keep, I reckon," said Darcy. "Don't think
there's much fear of her running away. Leave her alone
till we come back, and blaze away with the bow gun at
the other steamer coming down on us."

After a few discharges the range was accurately got,
and the same game commenced with steamer No. 2 which
had proved so successful with steamer No. 1.

The Black Angel, after a few shots, steered to the
starboard, in such a direction as to prevent the second
steamer approaching closer. This latter was steaming
right down to the assistance of her consort; but when
the rebel vessel deliberately took up a position at about
half a mile distance, and commenced pounding away
with the heavy guns, she swerved from her course and
steered towards them.

After a few successful shots, Darcy gave the order to
go on ahead—not willing to allow the enemy to approach
to close quarters, where the superiority in number of
guns would tell in her favour.

The Yankee, apparently furious at being thus baffled,
steamed madly on—each moment separating her further
from her distressed consort. Like her, she got the worst
of it—the heavy shot of the rebel crashing into her,
while the latter was careful to keep at such a distance
as to render the protection of the plates sufficient.

Presently, Darcy, who had never ceased watching her
through the glass, determined to heave to and make a
short fight of it. He saw enough to convince him that
great damage had been done to the hull, and many men
killed and wounded. Indeed, he could, by the aid of the
glass, plainly distinguish the torn and splintered decks;
and also ascertained the fact that several guns were
deserted by the gunners, and ceased to return his own
slow, deliberate, but destructive fire. Accordingly, the
Black Angel was brought round and headed direct for
the enemy.

It was Darcy Leigh's intention to take her by board
when she had been sufficiently cut up by his fire. As he

steamed down towards her the bow gun was constantly fired. The third shot from this did terrible havoc; it threw its shell right into the between decks of the enemy, where it burst, creating dreadful confusion— direful slaughter.

The Black Angel was hit again and again; and if the enemy were not aware of her being partially plated, they must have felt considerable astonishment at the small effect of their fire.

Just at this juncture a slight accident happened to one of the engines, and Darcy was informed from the engine-room that it would be necessary to stop the engine for a few minutes. Before this was done, however, he brought her broadside to bear, being now just at a distance when their guns would tell most. Scarcely had this been done when the enemy's vessel slowly wore round, delivered her broadside, and then steamed right away.

A shout broke from the crew of the Black Angel! the men leaped on the bulwarks, in the rigging, and yelled forth derisive cheers at the enemy now in full flight.

"Run to the engine-room, and see how long before we can go ahead full speed. This fellow has had enough, and is going to escape if he can."

The midshipman sent on the errand returned, and reported that it would be five minutes yet before the engines could be safely worked. This brief space was occupied by firing with the bow gun at the retreating foe.

It was nearly ten minutes before the Black Angel again started in pursuit. When she did so, the enemy was at long range; so, for the time, Darcy judged it expedient to steam on in pursuit, without firing.

It is an old and usually true saying, "A stern chase is a long chase,' and on this occasion it seemed likely it would be verified. In a quarter of an hour the enemy, though brought nearer, was still at too great a distance to render the gunnery practice either sure or effective. But each minute lessened the distance, and it was evidently a question of time as to when the larger vessel would be overhauled by the smaller and swifter one.

While all on board were intently watching the chase as she steamed away for the shelter of the fleet off Charleston, leaving her consort to the enemy's mercy, the sound of a gun fired astern drew the attention of the crew of the rebel. This gun was followed by another and yet another, at regular intervals. The Yankee was firing minute guns in token of distress. In reply to these some signals were hoisted by the vessel they were chasing, which—not having the code, of course, on board the Black Angel—they could not decipher.

They were now so much nearer, that it was deemed advisable again to open fire on the chase, and once more the bow gun belched forth its mass of iron, and sent it shrieking over the sea in the direction of the enemy.

After the third discharge, and just as Darcy had watched the shot plunge into the sea a few yards only from the Yankee, an exclamation from Wharncliffe arrested his attention.

" Look !—see !—where is the other vessel ?"

Darcy did look at the place where she last had been, but nothing but sky and water met his eye.

" Escaped !" muttered Wharncliffe ; " impossible !"

" No—sunk," was the laconic reply.

Then Darcy jumped on the bulwarks and swept the sea with his glass. A few spars and fragments of wreck, with a few half-drowned men clinging thereto, were all he could discover of the ill-fated steamer.

" Hard-aport ! over with your helm, my man !" Then to Wharncliffe : " We must go and save some of those poor devils."

" We shall lose this other Yankee."

" Can't be helped ; mustn't let men drown like dogs, even if we lose a fleet of ships."

Half an hour brought the Black Angel up to the spot where the portions of wreck, spars, casks, hencoops, &c., marked where the ill-fated Yankee went down.

She had, indeed, caught a Tartar.

# CHAPTER XXVIII.

## FIXING A YANKEE CAPTAIN.

As soon as she was within a cable's length of the place where the Yankee had gone down the engines were stopped and a boat lowered.

Twelve men clung to pieces of wreck and spars. All the others had perished, for the vessel went down suddenly while the greater part of the crew were between decks. There was not time even to get the boats out, one of which was now floating about bottom upwards.

As there could be no fear of the twelve men rescued from drowning they were not confined or put in irons, but, having been provided with dry clothing, they were permitted to roam the decks at pleasure, examine the great guns and the iron plating, which had proved so disastrous to their own vessel.

The other steamer was now almost hull down, and though tempted for a moment to pursue and endeavour to capture her, yet, on second thoughts, Darcy concluded that she could not be overtaken till she had nearly reached the blockading fleet. Under these circumstances, then, the sloop's head was turned to the eastward. The fires were allowed to go down, to economize coal ; a new fore-top-gallant mast was sent aloft, the yards crossed, and, under topsails, coursers, jibs, and topgallant sails, the gallant little rebel sloop steamed away across the broad Atlantic.

The decks were cleared and washed, the wounded attended to, and the carpenters set to work to repair damages. Darcy, worn out and exhausted, retired to his cabin and his hammock, having given orders to be called at four in the afternoon, or earlier, if a sail appeared in sight.

It was a bright sunny day, a brisk breeze blowing from the north-west, just sufficient to give the vessel the least

possible cant as she danced merrily over the waves. A
universal calm reigned on board. The man at the wheel,
the man on the foretop-gallant yard, and the officer of the
watch above were vigilant. The watch below were in
their hammocks; and the watch on deck lay about in all
directions. Some spare sails were dragged up by permission of the officer, and spreading these, the tired sailors
indulged in sleep—that welcome solace to the wearied
body or the overwrought mind.

And so the Black Angel sailed quietly on, as though
she were a peaceful merchantman or a gentleman's yacht.

At four o'clock Darcy Leigh was awakened, and having
partaken of dinner in the cabin, he called all his officers
together to consult on what was to be done. A very
brief discussion ensued, and a course of action was agreed
upon which met the approval of all.

It was resolved that the vessel should be steered to the
south-east, until a spot about four degrees north of the
equator should be reached, which was in the track of all
homeward-bound Federal vessels from California and the
East Indies.

Although steam was not used, the fires were kept constantly in readiness for lighting, and orders were given
that instantly on the appearance of a sail on the horizon
they should be lighted and steam got up. The boilers
were constructed specially with a view to getting steam
up quickly; so that even on the approach of a fast ship,
the sloop might be under full steam before the other could
get within hail. Meanwhile, as she sailed merrily down
to the cruising ground, Darcy occupied the time in train-
ing his men at the guns and getting them into a state of
the utmost efficiency. In the course of ten days they
approached the spot indicated, and a vigilant look-out
was kept for the expected prey. As they got nearer the
line the steady north-east trade wind faded away, until
they lay amid the calms, the cats'-paws, the black rain-
squalls, and the waterspouts which prevail in those low
latitudes. "Sail ho!"

It is the cheery voice of the look-out from the foretop-
gallant yard, who at the first dawn of day has descried a

speck on the horizon. Darcy mounted to the maintop-gallant yard, and looked through his telescope at the stranger. She bore due south-west, but at present was at such a distance that only her royals and top-gallant sails could be seen. A light breeze was blowing from the south-east, just rippling the water, through which the sloop slowly progressed at the rate of scarce two knots an hour.

All was soon bustle and activity—the fires were lighted, and the ship's head brought to bear on the distant sail, which it was soon apparent was steering a northerly course. It appeared that the stranger was bringing up a fresh breeze with her—for while the Black Angel's sails flapped against the masts, the sails of the other could be seen fully distended by a rattling breeze. Thus, although the rebel sloop made but slow progress, the other rapidly approached, till in a couple of hours' time her hull began to appear above the horizon.

"A large, full-rigged ship," said Darcy, after a long look through the glass, which he then handed to Wharn-cliffe. "What do you make of her?"

"A Yankee," was the reply; "a Yankee, by her long mast-heads, stout topmasts, and white sails. A Britisher generally spreads hemp sails—that fellow's are cotton, I reckon."

"You're right, Wharncliffe," said Darcy, again looking through the glass; "she's a Yankee. I can now make out her wooden anchor stock. I never yet saw a Britisher with a wooden anchor stock; with them iron is cheaper than timber. Send the men to breakfast and splice the mainbrace. We shall be alongside in another hour. Our steam is up, and see, yonder comes the breeze."

And Darcy pointed to the sea in the direction of the strange sail. A long line of white-crested waves could be distinguished, which marked where a fresh breeze came tearing along.

"Hurry up, my lads—bear a hand with your break-fasts. Here comes Yankee Doodle right down upon us. Doubtless, he little thinks we rebels have got any cruisers afloat."

Darcy pointed towards the stranger as he spoke. A general rush was made for the bulwarks, and then, at scarcely four [miles' distance, a large ship might be seen, and from her peak floating the once well-loved—now the hated flag, the Stars and Stripes.

A ringing cheer broke from the rebel crew. The coffee pannikins were all hastily stowed away, the hammocks lashed and placed in the nettings, and the decks cleared for action.

This done, the word was given, "Splice the mainbrace;" then a huge tub filled with one-water grog was brought on the quarter-deck, and the steward proceeded to serve out to each man his whack.

By the time this was done the Yankee ship was not more than a mile and a half distant, and a shot from the bow gun might have reached her.

Although the decks had been cleared for action, it was almost an unnecessary act of precaution, for the stranger was obviously an unarmed merchantman, pursuing her way totally unsuspicious of danger, doubtless trusting in the number and vigilance of their own numerous cruisers to keep the highway of the sea clear of privateers.

All this time the Black Angel was steaming right down on her, without, however, hoisting any flag. The crew of the Yankee were gathered on the forecastle, about fifty in number, while from the quarter-deck the captain and officers regarded the strange sloop approaching. Probably they did not know what to make of the rebel steamer, now not more than half a mile from them.

" There are ladies on the poop, Wharncliffe; we'll take her, if possible, without bloodshed. I should hope they would never be mad enough to resist. Hoist the British flag, and fire a shot across her bows; the instant the gun is fired, run up the flag."

The next minute the Black Angel yawed in her course, so as to bring her broadside towards the Yankee; then a jet of smoke issued from the foremost gun, and a shot goes dancing and splashing along the sea some two hundred yards ahead of the merchantman; simultaneously up goes the British ensign, and floats proudly from the

A great commotion is seen on the quarter-deck of the Yankee. The captain is evidently in a furious rage, for he gesticulates violently, and paces furiously up and down.

"I can guess what he's saying, Wharncliffe; he's damning us for an insolent Britisher to dare to overhaul a ship belonging to 'the greatest country on airth—yes, sirree—by thunder !'"

The two vessels were now steaming along side by side, distant from each other about half a mile. The Yankee still defiantly kept on her course, refusing to obey the order conveyed by the shot across her bows,—to back her maintopsail and heave-to.

"Starboard your helm a little—steady so," said Darcy; "we must bring this fellow to his senses."

This alteration in the course rapidly brought the two vessels nearer. The Black Angel was on the starboard quarter of the Yankee, but under full steam rapidly overhauled her, going in such a direction as to pass close alongside and across her bows.

"Ready with the bow gun! Fire close under her stern when I give the word."

On steamed the supposed Britisher, till when only about a cable's length distant. Darcy gave the word.

"Be careful. Don't hit her, there are ladies on the poop, but let the shot go close enough to let them know we are in earnest. Fire !"

This time the shot splashed into the sea so close under the Yankee's stern, as to throw the spray on her decks, and the ladies' screams could be plainly heard.

Darcy took the speaking-trumpet, and jumping into the mizen-rigging, hailed—

"What ship is that ?"

"The American ship Polynesia, from Calcutta, bound to Boston. Who the blazes are you, who overhaul American ships on the high seas ?"

"Heave-to, or I'll sink you !" was the laconic reply.

Then was heard the roll of the drums as the crew were beat to quarters. The Yankee captain paced furiously up and down the quarter-deck; but as he again saw the guns run in and loaded, it is probable he came to the conclusion that the insolent Britisher meant to keep his word, so he sullenly gave the order to "back the maintopsail."

"Come on board in your boat, and bring your ship's papers!" was the next imperious command addressed to the merchantman. The captain swore and fumed, but ultimately the gig was lowered and quickly pulled alongside the steamer.

The Yankee captain jumped on deck, and after a hasty glance at the numerous crew, all at their posts, he walked quickly on to the quarterdeck.

"Who's the captain of this craft?"

"I am," said Darcy Leigh, who was quietly sitting on the rail, looking out at the merchantman as she lay motionless on the water, with her maintopsail to the mast.

"Starboard your helm! starboard!"

Then the young commander held up his hand to the officer on the bridge, and the engines stopped. This brought the steamer on the starboard bow, and nearly ahead of the other.

"And who the h—ll are you, sir, who overhaul an American ship on the high seas? Guess your d—d British Government 'll have to account for this hyar outrage."

"Guess they wont, captain," was the cool reply.

"The h—ll they wont! Then I reckon Uncle Sam 'll jest have to give yer a whipping, as he did in the last war, and in every other war since the day when Washington licked King George's hirelings at Bunker's Hill and Yorktown."

"Reckon you've quite enough on your hands, sir, without another war," replied Darcy, smiling. "Meanwhile, just hand me your papers."

"Here they are, sir; but remember, sir, I protest against this. I submit to this outrage, sir, from your superior force; but, by thunder, there 'll be a shine about this when I git to Boston."

"That may be some considerable time, sir. At all events, it is extremely unlikely your ship will ever see New England."

"H—ll and thunder! do you mean to say you'll stop an American ship on a peaceful voyage? There are my papers, sir, and they're all correct."

"Yes, so I see. Ship Polynesia, from Calcutta—cargo of indigo and sugar—bound to Boston—Captain Barton. Well, Captain Barton," said Darcy, rising, "you asked me what ship this was. Wharncliffe, run up our flag."

Then the British ensign was quickly hauled down, and in its place another run up to the peak—the Confederate flag—the starry cross.

"Captain Barton," said Darcy, laying his hand on his shoulder, "in reply to your interrogatory, I have the honour to inform you that this is the Confederate cruiser the Black Angel, and that you are my prisoner."

Amazement and horror sat on the face of the Yankee captain. He gazed from the flag at the peak to the rebel commander; then around the decks at the guns and the crew at quarters; then at his own ship as she lay tossing up and down on the waves.

"Je—rus—alem! is this hyar a rebel ship?"

"Exactly; and your vessel, the Polynesia, is the lawful prize of the Confederate Government."

"Snakes an' sawdust! hyar's a pretty go! And what the blazes made you hoist that cussed British flag?"

"Because I wished to take you without bloodshed. Now, sir, go back to your ship, and inform your crew and passengers that you have surrendered. I shall send a prize crew on board presently. Meanwhile, any attempt at treachery, and I will fire into and sink you as sure as fate. I care very little about the ship, and would as soon she were sunk as not, but I have no wish to kill and drown your crew and passengers."

The Yankee commander returned to his ship—now no longer his—looking woefully crest-fallen. He was met at the gangway by his first mate.

"Well, captain, what is it? What's the meaning of that flag? Shall I fill the maintopsail?"

"Reckon not, Mr. Smith. We're in for it, and no mistake. Yon vessel's a rebel privateer, and we're her prize; that's all."

"No chance of escaping?"

"Not a ghost. I should say she had a crew of two hundred men, and her heavy guns would sink us at the first fire."

In the course of a few minutes a prize crew, consisting of twenty men and two officers, was sent on board, and took possession of the ship. Some stores, all valuable portable property not belonging to passengers, and the ship's log and papers, were transhipped to the steamer. Then the crew of the merchantman were mustered aft, and were asked if any Southern men were present, and if so, whether they were willing to join the Confederates. About ten out of the fifty stepped forward in answer, and professed themselves willing to take the oath of allegiance. These ten were immediately sent on board the Black Angel with their traps, and ten men from the steamer were sent in their place.

This arrangement left forty Yankee seamen still on board. Thirty of these were sent on board the steamer as prisoners; also the captain, officers, and passengers. The remaining ten men were asked if they were willing to assist in working the vessel, in which case they would be well treated and no oath demanded of them; wisely preferring this to bread and water and handcuffs, they consented. This left thirty Confederate seamen on board, and ten Yankees. Ten of the former were sent back on board the Black Angel, leaving twenty Confederates and ten Yankees to work the prize. But as ten men had voluntarily joined the Confederates out of the crew of the merchantman, Darcy only lost ten men by the transaction, and this, of course, was a great object. The officer in command of the prize crew had received orders to sail for the coast of South Carolina, make the inlet, if possible, and run the vessel in. Should they be pursued, the vessel was to be run ashore, set fire to and abandoned, the crew taking to the boats and endeavouring to escape.

And now, once more, the maintopsail is filled; the Polynesia goes on her course, heeling over to the breeze, and going ahead as merrily as though she had not changed owners, leaving the Black Angel on the cruising-ground to look out for fresh prey.

A parting cheer from the rebel crew comes ringing over the sea, as the men thus celebrate this their first capture. In an hour's time the vessels are hull down to each other, and we will proceed to follow the fortunes of Darcy Leigh and his crew.

It is not our intention here to relate the exploits of the Black Angel in the way of pillaging, burning, and sinking the enemy's merchantmen. We prefer to proceed to incidents and adventures which bear more immediately on the personages of the story.

During a month's cruise, no less than twelve vessels had been captured by the rebel steamer, ten of which were despatched with prize crews with the design of evading the Federal cruisers, and running safe into port. In order to do this, however, Darcy Leigh had been compelled to part with so many of his crew as to leave his ship very short-handed.

Then, too, they had on board more than a hundred prisoners taken from the captured ships. Their coals began to run short, and, although they had plenty of provisions, it was deemed advisable to return to the rendezvous to refit, re-man, and get rid of the prisoners.

Accordingly the steamer was headed to the north-west, and their perilous homeward voyage commenced. Having ascertained by accurate observation the exact position of the ship on the chart, she was hove to till night should throw its veil over the ocean, and enable her to run in without chance of detection. There were no vessels in sight, and possibly she might have been safely brought in without being discovered, but it was considered so important that the rendezvous or depôt should remain utterly unknown, that it was determined to run no risk of discovery.

As soon as it was night steam was got up, and the ship steered straight for the inlet. There was no light or beacon to guide the way; so, of course, it was a ticklish affair; but, by care and skill, the long lowland was made, some miles to the southward; and then the ship was run along the coast, until the inlet was found.  All was then plain sailing, for every inch of the channel had been carefully explored and sounded; so that, shortly after daybreak, the masts of the captured vessels lying in the creek hove in sight, and by four bells the anchor was dropped in safety, amid the deafening cheers of their friends, who lined the shore to welcome the daring adventurer back to port.

Here, in storehouses, piled together, was an immense quantity of plundered goods, taken from the holds of the captured ships.  Silks, tea, and ivory from China; opium, coffee, indigo, jute, rice, spices, and all the various products of the East abounded; while safely stowed away in iron-bound chests were the gold, silver, and valuables.

The share of each sailor in this rich booty amounted in value to at least 5000 dollars, that of the officers being, of course, far greater.

No time was lost; but men were set to work at once, refitting, repairing damages, and hoisting in coal, ammunition, and provisions for another cruise.  The crew was made up once more to its full complement, the prisoners sent up the country, and all made ready for a fresh start.

Darcy had rather expected to see his brother, or the fair Coralie, his affianced, at the rendezvous; but as the first invasion of Maryland by the Confederates was then in progress, that sufficiently accounted for their absence.

Doubtless, at so critical a time, such splendid troops as his brother's cavalry and his own old regiment would be placed in the van.

On the evening fixed for the start of the Black Angel on her second cruise, Darcy stood with Wharncliffe on the quarterdeck, watching the sun go down behind the low sandy hills.  The evening was calm and beautiful, and calculated to give rise to a sad dreamy train of thought.  For a long time the two young officers stood in silence, each living in a world of his own far away from the somewhat dreary scene before them.

Eight bells struck, and Darcy awoke from his reverie. The steam up, the anchor hove short, and only the com-

mander's word was wanted to send the vessel forth on her
errand of destruction.

That word was at once given, and by midnight the
Black Angel was again ploughing the waves of the broad
Atlantic. Darcy Leigh gave the course as north-east, and
then again relapsed into deep thought. He felt sad and
lonely, and a sort of presentiment of coming evil over-
shadowed him, which with difficulty he kept down. At
midnight Wharncliffe came to take charge of the deck.

"Still the same course—north-east?" he asked.

"Still the same course—north-east?" answered Darcy,
dreamily.

"That wont run into the track of the homeward-
bounders; it will take us across the Gulf Stream, where
we are more likely to meet British and French vessels
than Yankees."

Darcy had a habit which, whether advisable or not,
gave his proceedings an air of mystery. He never
divulged his projects to any one, even to his most intimate friend Wharncliffe, till on the eve of execution.

Now, however, arousing from his fit of abstraction, he
thought it time to speak.

"Wharncliffe," said he, "it's monotonous work overhauling and capturing merchantmen, putting a prize crew
on board, and so on for weeks. I have a grand idea, and
mean to carry it out—a project which, if successful, will
send down our names to posterity—a project to which
everything we have yet done, either by land or by sea, is
but child's play."

Darcy spoke eagerly—with enthusiasm, and Wharncliffe asked, "What is it?"

"It is this: to wait for a dark, rainy night, then run
through the Narrows into New York Harbour, and
anchor just off the enormous warehouses and crowds of
shipping at the wharves. I know the harbour well, and
it can be done. Then we can either fire the town or send
and demand any ransom we like. It would burn like
tinder, and a few shells thrown to windward would
speedily lay the Empire City in ashes—guess that would
astonish the Yankee a few."

Wharncliffe was positively aghast at the audacity of the project, but did not reply for some time.

## CHAPTER XXIX.

### SEARCHING A LADY'S CABIN.

LEAVING the Confederate cruiser, the Black Angel, sailing to the north and east in a way which would soon bring her in the latitude of the Empire City, we will return for a while to some other characters in our story. The sisters, Stella and Angela Gayle, deserve our attention, as also their father and their amiable cousin, Lupus Rock, whom we last saw baffled, defeated, a deserter and traitor.

Webster Gayle was permitted to proceed to Washington, as soon as his identity was clearly made out, and his tale proved to be true. He had been there but a day or so, had taken possession of Holkar Hall, and had begun to put his business affairs in order, when who should again appear on the scene but Lupus Rock. After deserting his post, thereby causing infinite damage to the rebels, he had made his way into the Federal camp, and posted all haste to Washington, in order to secure all he could of Webster Gayle's property, whom he still believed to have been shot by Darcy Leigh.

Accordingly Lupus Rock, on his arrival at Washington, hastened to Holkar Hall, expecting to find all in confusion, though thinking it possible that his cousins, of whose whereabouts he was ignorant, might be there. He was, however, inclined to believe that they would at once go on to New York. What, then, was his amazement when on walking into Holkar Hall, he met the New York merchant on the threshold!

Lupus staggered as if struck, and gazed in doubt till he could doubt no longer. Webster regarded him sternly for a short time, and then said,—

" So, sir, you are here. A pretty scrape you got me

into.   By following your advice, listening to your serpent tongue, I had well nigh lost my life."

"I heard you had been captured and shot," stammered Lupus; "and yet I see you alive and well."

"I was saved, sir, by the courage and devotion of a brave man, rebel though he be.   Thanks to Darcy Leigh, and not to you, I am now alive."

"Darcy Leigh!"

The hated name brought back all Rock's self-possession and cunning.   He knew not the details of the affair, and did not stop to ask, but at once set to work to clear himself in his uncle's eyes.   He used all his art—spared no humiliation, no lies, no dissimulation, to persuade Webster that it was a fatal mistake.   The possession of the map which, being found on his uncle, so nearly proved his death warrant, he declared he could not account for.

It was his map certainly, and the only way by which he could possibly account for it was, that it had got mixed up with the account papers and the title deeds of the Yancey estate.

Still, though Webster Gayle's opinion as to his nephew's complicity was shaken, he was by no means convinced. Then Lupus pointed out to him in the most clear and masterly manner, that his uncle's death would, in a pecuniary sense, have been disastrous instead of advantageous to him, Lupus Rock.

Here he hit the right nail on the head.   His appeal to the "almighty dollar" was successful.   He pointed out to Webster that he, Lupus, had delivered up everything— the title deeds of the Yancey estate; also that he had but little hold on the heart of his cousin Stella, who seemed to have some unhappy prejudice against him, that her father's sanction to the engagement had always been his strong point, by means of which he hoped ultimately to win her heart.   That by the death of Webster his prospects would be ruined, for *he* would not inherit a cent of the property.

All this he showed so clearly, and made appear so unanswerable, that Webster Gayle's suspicions were scat-

tered to the four winds. He was still angry at his nephew
for having, by his carelessness, run him into such desperate peril, but that was all.

Not quite all, however. Beneath these was a tinge of
another feeling—one of relief—for be it known that
Webster Gayle, on looking into his affairs, found them
(thanks to Lupus Rock's skilful manipulation, though he
little expected as much) in such inextricable confusion as
to bewilder him. He had so long trusted in the clear,
cool head of his nephew and manager, that now he felt
the loss.

It was, then, with feelings of satisfaction and soreness
mingled, the latter predominating, that he accepted his
nephew's explanation, and at once asked him to go into
and explain the numerous complicated accounts and transactions, which his long absence had thrown apparently
into hopeless confusion.

Lupus' eyes gleamed with triumphant joy. Summon-
ing all his skill, he threw his whole energy into the task,
and in six hours had reduced to perfect order, what to
the bewildered merchant seemed chaos; and not only was
he able to account for every loss, but on the whole to
show a profit, notwithstanding all unfavourable circumstances, and even to hold forth good prospects of great
future profits.

When he had done, the merchant was, though he
knew it not, again his tool and slave. He looked up
with admiration, almost awe, at the hard-headed, cool
young man, whose business qualities were so splendid,
being alike able to grapple with the grandest speculation, and account for the smallest detail.

All this business was transacted at the office of
Webster Gayle's attorney in Washington. When they
left, it was arm-in-arm, and when Stella and Angela, who
had been out all day, returned in the evening, they
found their father and Lupus Rock discussing a bottle of
wine, and obviously on the best terms in the world.

Lupus greeted his cousins with perfect ease and cor-
diality, as though nothing had happened.

" Stella, my dear," said her father, " will you kindly

go down into the cellar and bring a bottle of the Bur-
gundy given me by the French ambassador ; we will
celebrate the safe arrival of us all on Northern soil."

"Cousin Stella," said Lupus, with a smile on his face,
"you remember the last bottle you brought up and the
trick you served me ?  It was too bad of you—but ' forgive and forget' is my motto."

"What was that, Lupus?" asked Webster.

"Oh, only a practical joke of Stella's, a long time back.
We will say no more about it now."

Lupus spoke so good-temperedly and lightly that his
uncle forbore to press the question, thinking it only some
trivial joke.

Stella left the room to do her father's bidding, while
Angela hurried to her own room to think over the reap-
pearance of her dreaded cousin.

As soon as she was gone, Stella leaned against the
wall of the corridor, and pressed her hand against her
heart.  What little colour remained now faded from her
cheek, and her face assumed that deadly pallor, that
look of utter helpless despair, which once before it had
worn.

"God!" she murmured to herself, "this man must be
Satan himself, or possessed with his bold, bad, all but
invincible spirit.  It was but yesterday that he betrayed
my father, almost to his death.  I feel, I know it must
be so ; and yet, now I find him once again—an honoured
guest, a well-prized adviser—nay, more—the master
spirit!"

Then she recovered herself, and, with slow steps, descended to the cellar to bring up the wine.

"It is my fate—my fate—that man is my fate—I
must marry him—loathing—hating—fearing! and yet I
must marry him.  I feel, I know it."

The wine was brought in, and Stella did not fail to
notice the expression of triumphant joy on her cousin's
handsome, though saturnine face.  He treated her with
the most faultless courtesy, the most profound respect,
and yet she knew him well enough to perceive that he
was gloating over a victory gained.  Even in his move

and smile, as he held open the door when she retired, she thought she could read the outward expression of that inward triumph which her own heart, her own fears told her he had gained.

In vain she tried to shake off the feeling of utter despair which possessed her. All courage and spirit seemed to have left her; she was as perfect a fatalist as ever fanatic Moslem. Where was the defiant, dauntless spirit she once possessed? Where the haughty mien—the proud words, and that commanding look which, in New York and Saratoga, had gained her the name of the " eagle-eyed."

It will readily be imagined that after Lupus Rock's experiences in the South, and more especially his desertion, he was by no means anxious to run any risks of recapture. After the disastrous retreat of M'Clellan's army from the Peninsula, the Confederates had been steadily advancing, and shortly again gave battle on the memorable field of Bull Run, inflicting yet another defeat on the arrogant Yankees. Then came indications of the approaching invasion of Virginia, and as many thought Washington by no means safe, Lupus was anxious to get further North.

He adopted a most wary and cautious mode of procedure with his uncle and cousins. While never crossing in any way, offending, or even exciting the suspicions of the former, he yet contrived day by day to worm himself deeper into his confidence (if indeed that were possible), and so to arrange matters as to make himself more than ever indispensable. Then, too, he advocated large speculations, contracts, &c. These, it is true, turned out usually very profitable, but involved enormous and complicated accounts of which he alone held the key.

As to his cousins, he treated them with unobtrusive kindness and respect, till Angela, by degrees, began to hate him less, merely from the fact that she saw less of him.

Lupus Rock was in no hurry; he bided his time, and having matured his plans—woven his net as it were—he waited for the right opportunity once more to throw it around his uncle, and once more hold his life in his hands. His influence was now as firmly established as ever, and he could at any moment commit Webster Gayle to a course of action which would be read by the Federal Government as rank treason—*the very least* penalty for which would be imprisonment and confiscation of all property. In fact, as affairs stood, Lupus had abundant proof of treasonous acts in the way of contracts to supply goods, arms, and munitions of war, which were obviously intended for the rebels. In those turbulent times, when every man suspected and hated his neighbour—the Republicans accusing the Democrats of treason to the Union, the Democrats accusing the Republicans of treason to the Constitution—it was easy to get any man —especially a prominent, wealthy man—into political hot water. Hard swearing, backed up by a little skilful manœuvring, would do a great deal. Lupus was great at manœuvring, and as for hard swearing, he could do a little himself, and find plenty of willing agents to aid him. Of that he had no fear. His immediate object was to remove further from the dangerous proximity to the Potomac and the rebels, who, if they caught him, he well knew would be his executioners. At present, then, his object was to leave Washington, and return to New York, where, in addition to his own private reasons, there was much business which required immediate attention. Accordingly, with but little difficulty, he arranged for the departure of himself, Webster Gayle, and his cousins. The original intention was to proceed by rail to Baltimore, and thence again by rail to New York, after resting one day in the former city.

But arrived at Baltimore, Lupus Rock had occasion to alter the programme. He discovered that which filled him with uneasiness—aye, which positively alarmed him. He found that he was followed, watched, and had reason to believe it was by members of a secret society. The members of this society call themselves "Knights of the Golden Circle." They have among themselves a private code of signals, as also a cipher intelligible only to the initiated. They are all either Southern men or Southern

sympathizers, and the ramifications of this brotherhood
are spread over all the Western, North-Western, and
Border States. It is but a short time back that some of
the members of this society were arrested in Ohio. A
man swore that, lying concealed under some hay in a
barn, he was an unseen witness of one of the meetings of
the Knights :—he swore that he heard a project discussed
for seizing on the persons of the President and his cabinet,
and either deporting them South or hanging them.

It is not surprising, then, that Lupus Rock felt alarmed,
knowing as he did that his every movement was closely
watched by vigilant eyes. He by no means felt himself
safe, even in Baltimore, which was full of Secessionists
and their sympathizers. He feared to walk the streets,
expecting each moment to feel the assassin's knife at his
back, or to be pistoled by an unknown hand from some
window. Such things were of daily occurrence, and the
perpetrators usually escaped with impunity.

Accordingly, Lupus Rock determined, for a time at
least, to go North, where as yet the Secessionists were
few in number, and powerless. He had but little difficulty in making the necessary arrangements with Webster,
and it was settled that the merchant should go first,
while Lupus should follow with his cousins. Webster
went by the Baltimore and New York railroad, it having
been arranged that Lupus should follow with the girls on
the following day ; but Mr. Rock had very urgent objec-
tions to going by rail. He knew he was a marked man
in Baltimore, and did not think it impossible that at a
convenient spot, the rails might be torn up and his person seized by his enemies, far from all Federal aid. Then
he well knew that terrible Judge Lynch would be called
into requisition, and his body hanging on a tree would
perhaps be the sole trace of the outrage.

So in view of this, Lupus booked the greater majority
of the luggage to New York, also himself and cousins,
paying the fare.

Then he telegraphed to Webster Gayle, that for very
important reasons it was unsafe for him to come by rail,
and he therefore asked permission to·come by steamboat,

which left Baltimore the same day. A telegram came back in reply, empowering him to act as his judgment dictated.

Armed with this, Lupus informed Stella and Angela of the change of plan. Stella, who had long since ceased to struggle, merely bowed her head; nor did Angela offer any serious objection. Then Lupus went and booked places in the passenger boat for New York in false names, and doubted not he would thus defeat the designs of his enemies, if they had any against him.

Most of the luggage was sent on by rail, and with merely a travelling bag apiece he drove in a fly to the pier, and went with the girls on board the steamboat which was lying alongside with steam up ready to start.

It was just eight days after the departure of the Black Angel from the creek, that the passenger steamboat Edwin Forest steamed down the Chesapeake Bay, bound for the Empire City.

The voyage passed pleasantly enough, and on the evening of the second day they were rapidly approaching New York, the captain expecting to make the light about ten or eleven o'clock.

As the sun went down, and night closed in, a drizzling rain and a dense haze perfectly obscured the horizon, so that great caution was needful in the navigation.

The captain had long been making the voyage backwards and forwards; so although the light could not be seen, he did not doubt he could take the steamer in safely by the soundings, as he had often done before. For this purpose a leadsman was kept constantly in the chains, while the steamer proceeded only at half speed.

But at this very time another vessel was approaching from the eastward under full steam. This was the Black Angel. Darcy Leigh had been keeping her lying off for several nights, waiting for a dark, rainy, boisterous one like the present. The wind had risen, and the falling barometer betokened rain and storm. For a desperate attempt such as the rebel commander contemplated, no night could be more favourable; and now the sloop was steaming straight for the narrows, of the position of which

Darcy had accurately informed himself by frequent observations. His plan was to dash on at full speed till shoal water was reached, and then to trust to his knowledge of the harbour to find and keep the channel.

＊　　＊　　＊　　＊　　＊　　＊

It is near midnight, and most of the passengers on board the Edwin Forest have retired to their cabins. The captain of the steamer is on the bridge, and has just made out the light through the thick haze of mist and rain which surround. The course is slightly altered, and the steamer goes ahead at three quarters speed.

The only other tenants of the deck are the officer of the watch, the men at the helm and the look-out, and Lupus Rock who, unable to sleep, is seated on a hencoop, wrapped in a large cloak, smoking a cigar. He can see down the skylight from where he is, and, himself unseen, can watch the figures of his cousins seated at the table.

Stella is writing, and Angela leaning over her shoulder, occasionally making a remark. Lupus regarded them as a tiger might his prey when all escape is hopeless. He could well afford to smile, and there was reason in the triumphant gleam of his eye. He knew his power and feared not the result. Often foiled, at last by dint of perseverance he had succeeded, and Stella Gayle had tacitly consented to accept him as her future husband.

And so he smoked on, and gloated over the thoughts of the possession of his glorious cousin. The steamer tore on through the gloom, and naught was heard save the dull beating of the paddles and the pattering of the rain. And now Stella having finished her writing, the two girls rose, and, each taking a candle from the sideboard in the saloon, retired to their cabin.

Angela at once undressed and retired to bed, the sleep of youth, health, and innocence soon closing her eyes. Stella also undressed, but did not at once seek her couch. She threw a wrapper over her bare white shoulders, and seating herself, leaned her head on her hand and plunged into a deep reverie.

She was aroused from her waking dream by the shouts of men on deck, and the hurried tramping of feet.

" Starboard, starboard ! hard a starboard !"

" Stop her ! stern all !"

Such were some of the shouts which greeted her ears. She opened the small bull's-eye deadlight, and looked out on the dark night. The fine drizzling rain beat in, but she heeded it not, for no sooner had she opened the deadlight, than the tones of a well-known voice fell on her ear.

" Port—port—port your helm and go ahead, or we shall run you down."

She could not be mistaken : it was the voice of Darcy Leigh. Wildly her heart beat, and she leaned forward drinking in every accent.

Then there was more confusion and shouting above.

" Port your helm—port—hard aport !" shouted the captain ; " go ahead with the engines."

But it was too late ; the helm had been hove to starboard, and the engines reversed.

There was an anxious pause of about half a minute, and then Stella could see through the port a black object looming on the sea. It was the hull of a vessel, and the next moment there was a dull crash—a shock—followed by the grinding of the two ships together.

The Edwin Forest heeled over from the force of the collision as though she would capsize. Shouts and cries now rent the air. All seemed in utter dismay and confusion. Then she heard the same well-known voice again from the other steamer—" Go ahead easy."

The two were now again some feet apart, and the strange steamer slowly forged ahead and once again was clear. But all was terror and confusion on board the Edwin Forest. Her bulwarks were stove in, her starboard paddle smashed, and all thought she was going down.

" We're sinking ! we're sinking !" a cry arose.

" Great heavens !" cried the captain, " are they going to leave us to sink ? What ship was it—a man-of-war ? I saw her guns—they surely must help us. Burn blue lights—send up rockets, and fire the signal gun."

All these orders were promptly obeyed by the panic-stricken crew.

Imagine the chagrin of Darcy Leigh on the quarter-deck of the Black Angel, as he saw the blue lights spread abroad their livid flames, the rockets shoot up in the air, and heard the boom of the gun signals of distress.

"Perdition seize this lubberly steamer!" he cried, angrily, to his lieutenant; "they have spoiled every-thing. The rockets will be seen, the guns heard by all the forts and war-ships in the harbour."

"Let us hope not," said Wharncliffe.

"The mischief is done—see!" and he pointed with his finger to where a rocket shot up in the air from the harbour. This was followed by another and another, evidently answering each other.

"All is lost now, so far as our scheme is concerned," he muttered; "it were madness to attempt it now. I suppose we had better send boats on board this steamer we have run into, in case she is sinking."

It was bitterly vexatious to be thus foiled in the very hour of success, for Darcy flattered himself that success was all but certain. There was no help for it, however; so the Black Angel was again ranged up alongside the passenger steamer, whose position was easily made out from the blue lights she kept burning. Then two boats filled with armed men were lowered. Darcy jumped into one, while a midshipman took command of the other, and both were soon alongside the Edwin Forest.

Strange to say, Angela slept through all the noise and turmoil. But Stella never ceased gazing through the open port, listening to every sound. She heard the boats row alongside, and knew that the steamer was boarded.

"What vessel is this?" she heard the voice of Darcy Leigh demand.

"The Edwin Forest from Baltimore to New York—and yours?"

"The Confederate cruiser Black Angel, commanded by me, Captain Darcy Leigh. Your vessel is my prize. Whether I take you, burn you, or let you go depends on circumstances. Now sir, bear a hand, and get me your cargo manifest; also a list of your passengers."

To say that the captain of the steamer was astonished would be very feebly expressing the truth. He was positively dumbfounded.

A rebel cruiser almost in New York Harbour !

"Come, sir—the manifest and a list of your passengers. I have no time to waste."

The armed crews of the two boats were now on the decks, and at some twenty yards' distance lay the rebel steamer, blowing off steam ; so the Baltimore captain knew this was no jest, incredible as it at first appeared.

The cargo manifest was brought, as also the list of passengers, and Darcy set about perusing them by the light of a lantern. Running down the list of the passengers' names, his eye was suddenly fixed by the words—

"Miss Gayle—

"Miss Angela Gayle."

"These two ladies are on board ?" he asked, pointing with his finger. "Who is with them ?"

"I am sure I don't know. I saw them talking with another of my passengers ; but don't know whether he has anything to do with them or not. They've paid their passage, that's all that concerns me."

"His name"—

"'Tis there on the list—Mr. Herbert Smithies."

"Herbert Smithies—never heard of him. Captain, I must search your cabins. I know not how true this list may be ; you may have half a dozen Yankee generals on board, for aught I know."

"Search away," replied the captain, sullenly. "I suppose ' might makes right.'"

Now Stella Gayle could hear every word of this conversation, for it took place on the quarter-deck, immediately above her cabin. Scarcely had it concluded when there came a hurried rap at her door.

"Who is there ?"

"Stella, open. It is I—your cousin Lupus."

"What do you require ?"

"Open, for Heaven's sake ! It is life or death."

" Impossible—I am undressed !"

" No matter—throw a shawl round you. Open, Stella; there is not a moment to spare."

Here she noticed that his voice trembled, and as he concluded he shook the door impatiently.

" At least I will see what he wants," she thought, and throwing a shawl over her, she opened the door.

Lupus instantly, before she could oppose him, hurried into the small cabin.

" What means this, sir ? What am I to understand ?" she cried, panting with indignation. " I will call for assistance."

" For Heaven's sake do nothing of the kind, Stella. My life is in your hands ; they are about to search the cabin. We have been boarded by a rebel—a pirate ; and if I am recognised, my fate is sealed."

" Your—life—is—in—my—hands ! Your—life—is—in—my—hands !" Twice she repeated the words, slowly and deliberately.

" Yes, Stella, you must conceal me ; they will not search your cabin. Am I not your cousin—the son of your father's sister——"

She interrupted him.

" So your life is in my hands, *cousin*—Lupus Rock ? And what favour have you ever shown me, that I should spare you now ? Have you not persecuted me, hunted me, traded on your influence with my father to gain your own ends ? Have you not rendered my life a curse ? And now you tell me your life is in my hands ? Lupus Rock, you have less spirit than I, woman though I am ! If I had wronged and persecuted any one as you have me, I would not only scorn to ask, but would scorn to accept life !"

" Stewardess, please request the ladies to dress themselves. I must enter all the cabins, and see what passengers are on board."

It was the voice of Darcy Leigh, and Lupus Rock grew ashy pale, and even trembled as he heard it.

" Stella, are you bent on betraying me ? The cabins

are about to be searched. It is that scoundrel Darcy Leigh!—he will recognise me!"

"Scoundrel yourself!" she cried, passionately. "Dare to say another word against that brave Southern gentleman, and I will throw open the door and have you cast forth. Wretch! dog!—how dare you?"

Stella was in her night-dress, with only an Indian shawl thrown around her; her hair fell loosely over her shoulders; her feet were bare, and as she hurled these words at her cousin, she stamped one foot vehemently on the ground. Lupus, despite his abject terror, could not but feel the power of her dazzling, angry beauty.

She stood for some seconds glaring on him with her large grey eyes. One by one he heard the cabin doors opened, and knew that in his search Darcy was but two doors from Stella's. And now he came next door.

"Stella, once again—do you wish to see me murdered?"

She gazed at him scornfully for a moment, and then, pointing with her finger beneath the bunk or couch, she said, "Get under there, you dog!"

Quick as thought he threw off his hat and cloak, and crawled beneath the bunk.

It was not without a desperate self-struggle that Stella had decided to conceal her cousin—and her enemy! Indeed, so far as it lay with her, the life of Lupus Rock did hang in the balance. Had her nature been less proud, less truly noble, she would have let him perish; but she did not, and that is all that can be said.

The next moment a knock came to the door.

"Enter!" she said, calmly, and Darcy entered. On seeing Stella not dressed, he was about withdrawing hastily, but she stopped him.

"Nay, Mr. Darcy Leigh, since such is your pleasure, enter. Since it is part of your duty to ransack ladies' cabins, pray do so."

He still stood on the threshold. "Come in, sir, I wish to speak to you. Send your followers out of hearing." Darcy did as he was bid.

"Well," he said coldly, for he had not forgotten the many insults she had heaped on him ; besides, he was angry, savage, at his scheme on New York being thus balked.

"When last I saw you—spoke to you—I did you an injustice."

"No matter," interrupted he ; "is your father well ?"

"He is, and is deeply grateful for your noble conduct."

"Noble conduct ! Ha, ha ! So Stella Gayle actually acknowledges a rebel can be capable of noble conduct? Wonderful !"

"Darcy Leigh, you mock me ; it is cruel of you."

She looked appealingly at him. What would she not have given for one word of kindness, of forgiveness ! That was all she could ever hope for. He was silent, so she again spoke.

"What are you doing now?—are you a privateer or pirate ?"

"If you please to term it so, I am. You ask what I am doing. Pillaging, burning, and destroying your Northern ships—that is what I am doing. I have already sent ten prizes safely into port, and burned as many more."

"Sent into port?—what port ? All the Southern ports are blockaded, and foreign ones are closed against you by the law of nations."

"You ask me what port—I will tell you—betray me if you choose. I have a port of my own ; it is situate——"

"Darcy, do not tell me."

She almost screamed, for she remembered Lupus Rock, and that he could hear every word.

Darcy knew not what possessed him. He was angry, and felt a fierce joy in taunting her.

"But I will tell you. Exactly seventy miles north of Charleston there is——"

"Darcy, hold ! If you love me, hold !"

"But I don't love you, and I will tell you."

She turned deadly pale at this rude answer to words

which escaped her by accident, and was silent. Then
Darcy Leigh went on, and minutely described to her the
situation of the inlet and the secret rendezvous.

She listened, and knowing who also listened, she felt
faint and sick with fear. Instinctively, almost, her eyes
turned to the lower part of the bunk, over which a curtain hung, concealing all beneath.

Darcy followed her eyes in some curiosity ; then, casting a glance around the cabin, his eye fell on the *cloak
and hat.*

Instantly he thought he comprehended the situation.
He jumped to a conclusion utterly unworthy of himself
and of her. Had he been less angry, or had he paused
to reason, he would not have acted as he did. As it was,
the memory of old slights, scorns and insults rushed
over his mind. His hour for revenge had come, and
ruthlessly he used the power.

"Stella Gayle," he said, slowly, deliberately, "you
once—nay, not once, but many times, called me a coward.
The last time you obligingly coupled it with the words
'scoundrel and murderer.' That which her virtue is to
a woman a man's courage is to him. Which is the more
contemptible, a cowardly man or a false woman, I
scarcely know—can you tell me?"

"Darcy Leigh, I do not understand you."

She drew herself up, and gazed in his face with somewhat of the old haughty look.

"No—then I will make haste and explain. I watched
your eye just now. Shall I lift yon curtain?"

He spoke mockingly, and every word was like a knife
in her heart. She clasped her hands pleadingly, but
could not answer.

"Is that your hat and cloak, Miss Stella Gayle?"

She gasped for breath. Slowly his meaning dawned
upon her. It was a terrible trial—a desperate thing to
hear and reply nothing.

"Now do you understand, Miss Stella Gayle? I know
you have a man concealed here. You called me coward
—I do not call you *wanton.* Adieu."

Then he went out, and closed the door behind him.

Stella fell on her knees by the side of the only chair in the room.

"Oh, God! that I should live to see this day—that I should hear such words pass the lips of Darcy Leigh and not die! To think how I have loved that man, and he called me wanton!"

Suddenly she started to her feet, remembering her cousin was concealed.

"Lupus, come forth."

He did as he was bid, and stood before her, pale, almost trembling.

"Stella, I thank you. It is more than I deserve."

"Do you wish to prove your thanks?"

"I do—tell me how."

"You heard what Darcy Leigh said just now?"

"I did."

"Lupus—kill him—find him out, no matter where he hides himself, and kill him. Do that, and I will be your wife to-morrow. Only avenge me, and wipe out in blood the bitter insults I have suffered."

"I will, Stella; trust me, I will. At present we are powerless, but I will see he shall be brought to book. I heard all that passed. He will doubtless before long make for the secret rendezvous. I will give information. A dozen ships of war shall be there awaiting him; he shall be allowed to go in, and then he shall perish like a rat in his trap."

"No, no, no, Lupus. Spare him, spare him! I did not mean it. Dare to use the information you overheard and I will kill you. Lupus, you dare not, you shall not! Swear you will not. Oh, God! I was mad to let him speak. I will never harm him—you shall never harm him—never—never."

Then she gave way to a fit of violent hysterics, crying and laughing, intreating, threatening by turns. By degrees she got calmer, and at last the wild weeping and wailing ceased.

Starting to her feet she cried, "Leave my cabin, you dog! It is you who have brought me to this."

Again she stamped her foot upon the ground, again her eyes, though red with weeping, flashed angrily.

The search was now concluded, and the rebel captain had returned to his ship; so Lupus Rock slunk away, leaving Stella to her thoughts and her misery.

---

## CHAPTER XXX.

### THE PURSUIT OF THE BLACK ANGEL.

THE brief pause in the tide of war following on the battle of Antietam, and the retreat of the Confederates back to Virginia, gave opportunity of absence to many officers who wished to visit their friends or attend to private affairs.

Among those to whom furlough was granted were Gerald Leigh and his friend the Englishman. They resolved to employ this time in visiting the spot which Darcy Leigh had selected as a harbour of refuge and rendezvous. The Seventh Carolina regiment was at this time ordered for duty at Charleston; Coralie St. Casse with Nina being also there.

On the arrival of Gerald and Captain George at Charleston they learned that the rebel sloop, the Black Angel, had last sailed from the creek on the South Carolina coast about a week or ten days before, and that she was expected to return very shortly. Coralie and Nina had gone on to the rendezvous, accompanied only by a few personal friends.

Although on furlough, Gerald occupied himself in recruiting his cavalry force with men and horses, and when they left Charleston his party numbered some thirty sabres. It was his intention on his arrival at the place where he hoped to see Darcy, to encamp with his force, and make the most of the opportunity by drilling and organizing the recruits.

On their arrival they noticed with surprise the pains

which had been taken to fortify and render the place secure against any sudden attack. On one promontory of the little creek a strong sand fort had been erected, and mounted with four heavy guns and twice as many of smaller calibre. The place was garrisoned by about two hundred regular troops, but in addition there were at least as many more irregulars or rangers : the Yankees called them guerillas. They were the inhabitants of the country, who had been attracted to the place by curiosity and a love of adventure. A small township was springing up at the head of the creek, which was named Palmetto-ville, after the Palmetto flag of South Carolina.

One morning, while Gerald Leigh was drilling his squadron of horse on the low sandy beach, the boom of guns was heard out at sea, and soon the smoke of several steamers could be seen. The excitement in the little fort was intense, as minute by minute the firing grew nearer and the vessels themselves came in sight. Soon the vessels could be made out, five steamers, one of which was apparently being chased by the other four.

Gerald, George, Coralie, and Nina stood on the highest eminence in the sand fort.

" It's Darcy's ship—no doubt of it," said Gerald. " I wonder is he going to run her in ? I should think not."

" Do you think it possible," asked Coralie, " that the enemy discovered this place, and lay in wait for him at the offing ?"

" It looks very like it. See, they are all steaming straight for the inlet."

The vessels were now only distant some three miles, and all doubt as to the chased steamer being the Black Angel was dissipated. She seemed to have been roughly handled, her rigging damaged, and the upper part of her funnel shot away. The foremost of the pursuing steamers was distant about half a mile, and kept up a constant fire from her heavy bow gun. The rebel steamer was evidently in a half-crippled state, and laboured but slowly along. Still, however, she passed through the inlet some distance in advance of the foremost of the Yankees ; and, having done so, at once rounded to the southward, so as for a time to place the low island between her and her pursuers. These latter now slackened speed. Doubtless the difficulties and dangers of the channel had been discovered.

They could see from their position in the fort that the crew of the Black Angel were working hard at the pumps. No doubt it was only a matter of urgent necessity which induced Darcy Leigh to run in—thus revealing the harbour and rendezvous.

An exclamation from Coralie drew the attention of Gerald Leigh. "See! look yonder on the island!"

Gerald followed the direction of her finger, and saw, on the long low island on the other side of the creek, a considerable body of men. These could not be seen from the sea, or, indeed, anywhere except the high ground at the rear of the fort.

"Yankees, by Jove! They've landed on the other side. What are they going to do?"

"They're dragging guns over to command the channel," said the Englishman, who was observing them through a glass.

It did not require a long survey to convince all that this was the fact.

"How did they land without our seeing them?" said Gerald, wonderingly.

"It's plain enough. They landed in the night."

"Then do you think they had information that Darcy's ship was expected to run in here?"

"I'm afraid there's no doubt of it. Those ships lay in the offing, while guns and troops landed on the island."

"What are they doing?" said Coralie, who had been anxiously watching the force on the island.

They now appeared to be busy throwing up an earthwork in such a way that guns mounted would quite command the narrowest part of the channel.

"They're getting their guns into position—heavy guns too, I'm afraid," remarked Gerald.

"Surely Darcy will never attempt to pass that narrow part, with the guns pouring out on him?"

" By Heavens! I'm afraid they can't see the guns from the ship—see, they are masking them."

This was indeed the fact, for numbers of the Yankee soldiers were now seen cutting down brushwood and branches of what few trees grew about, with which they carefully covered the breastwork and the muzzles of the guns, till the place presented the appearance of a thicket, somewhat more dense than that surrounding. All these manœuvres were hid from the rebel schooner, and were visible only to those on the high ground.

The Black Angel was now steaming down the inlet, keeping close to the mainland shore, followed more slowly by the Yankee vessels, who were compelled to act cautiously on account of the difficulty of the channel.

The sloop was quite low in the water, and from the desperate manner in which the men worked at the pumps, it was evident she was almost in a sinking state.

Her deck and sides were badly torn with shot, giving proof of a very severe engagement, in which the partial plating had not been effective.

Darcy's intention appeared to be to run her ashore further down the channel and under the guns of the fort. But to do this he would have to pass through the very narrowest part, and where the channel, such as it was, led close to the other side, right under the masked battery.

The sloop was now steaming slowly along at about thirty yards distance from the mainland shore. She could have been run ashore at any time, and all hands safely landed before the other steamers, now quite a mile astern, could come up. But probably Darcy wished to save the ship by running her under the protection of the guns in the fort. Of course he could not know what a trap was prepared for him and his brave crew, and so he steamed unsuspiciously on.

The fort and every available place was now crowded with rebel soldiers breathlessly watching the chase. Few knew of the Yankee battery established on the island, and most thought the escape of the sloop a certainty. She was now less than half a mile distant, the tide running strong against her, so that she made but slow progress. About half way, moored to the shore, were several boats, taken from the captured ships.

It would be an easy matter from these to walk along-side and give warning, or perhaps even a hail from the shore might be heard.

" Mount and ride down to where you see the boats, my man," Gerald said to one of his troopers; " attract attention on board the sloop—failing in that, get into one of the boats and row alongside. Tell Captain Leigh, or whoever is in command, to run his ship ashore at once, or he is lost. There is a masked battery of heavy guns in the thicket about three-quarters of a mile down."

The next moment the horseman was galloping along the sandy beach towards the boats. All watched his course with curiosity, though with no admixture of mis-giving, for no enemy was supposed to be near.

Scarcely, however, had he accomplished half the distance, when a volley was discharged from the woods on the mainland. The horse bounded forward furiously a few paces, then reared and fell back, crushing his rider beneath him.

" Confusion !" shouted Gerald Leigh. " They have landed troops and sent them into the woods. Mount, and away, men ! mount, and let us drive these sneaking curs from their ambush."

While Gerald's recruits were mounting and drawing up in line behind the fort, the guns were trained on the woods whence came the volley, and shells and grapeshot poured in. With what effect could not be ascertained, for they prudently forbore to answer the fire and reveal their position. It was impossible to say whether these woods were held by a company, a regiment, or only a few sharpshooters.

A ringing shout broke from Gerald's irregular cavalry, and, sabres flashing in the sun, they thundered over the plain and dashed into the thicket.

Meanwhile, the troops were thrown forward in open order, and as skirmishers to support the squadron of

22

horse. The shouts of the troopers in the woods and the clang of the sabres could be plainly heard, but not a shot was fired ; so it was impossible for the anxious spectators in the fort to know whether the enemy had retreated or still lay concealed.

Presently the horsemen re-appeared in much confusion, some quarter of a mile lower down. It was evident they had not succeeded in finding the foe, who, in all probability, had withdrawn further into the wood.

Gerald quickly re-formed his men, and then led them at gallop towards the fort, swerving, however, to the right, and again plunging among the trees and brush, which only formed a belt of forest along the shore, not more than a few hundred yards wide.

By riding right through and coming out on the other side he would very probably fall on the enemy, retreating in loose order, and quite unprepared to resist cavalry. Under such circumstances a very small number of horsemen could cut up a whole regiment.

Meanwhile, the officer in command of the little force of infantry threw his skirmishers into the wood, and proceeded to make way along the whole length. Those were moments of anxious suspense, while both Gerald, horsemen, and the infantry were hid from sight.

Suddenly a crashing volley is heard in the wood, followed by wild shouts. Then another volley.

After about five minutes' sharp firing, the rebel troops re-appear in the open—shattered and broken, and with many of their number missing. Coming suddenly on a superior force in ambush, they had suffered terribly, and had been forced to leave even their dead and wounded behind.

Hurriedly retreating to the shelter of the fort, they are re-formed by their officers, and their thinned ranks having been refilled by volunteers, they again advanced to drive the enemy from the wood.

The guns of the fort now continually rained shot and shell into the wood, so that it must have been rather warm for the Yankees.

But while this was being done, the Black Angel was

steaming slowly down the creek towards the masked battery, and was now nearly abreast of the fort.

Another messenger—this time, however, on foot—was despatched to the shore ; but long before he reached it, he, too, was laid low by the concealed sharpshooters.

Another, and yet another, shared his fate ; and soon five wounded men lay on the sand—all having fallen without accomplishing their object.

There is a limit to human bravery, as to everything else, and it is not strange that in view of their comrades helplessly shot down before their eyes, there should be no more willing to volunteer for so fatal a task.

" A thousand dollars to the man who will reach the shore, and either hail or go alongside the steamer !"

It was Coralie who spoke.

After a moment's pause, a man, tempted by the money, stepped forth.

He pulled off tunic, belt—even shoes, and then bounding over the parapet, ran swiftly towards the beach.

A perfect hail of bullets hissed around ; once he staggered—fell—and again rose and ran on, slowly, however, and limpingly. Then, when only twenty yards from the beach, he threw his arms above his head, and fell forward on his face—dead—pierced by half a dozen balls.

Coralie watched this tragedy with bitter anguish, not only for the fate of the poor soldier, but for the desperate peril the Black Angel was helplessly running into.

She conversed eagerly for a few moments with Nina, who stood by her side in vivandière costume.

" Yes, yes, Nina, it must be done. They will never fire on a woman. Your dress is well calculated for running rapidly, while my riding habit cumbers me. Come, quick, it must be done."

The two girls disappeared, and were gone for a few moments. Then all at once a woman is seen to leap over the earthwork, and commence running towards the rebel vessel, now steaming slowly along quite close to the shore.

A shout of approbation broke from the little party in

the fort, and even the gunners left their guns for a time, and climbing up on the parapet, watched the progress of the brave *vivandière*, as she ran swiftly on. No fire was opened on her till half the distance was accomplished ; but then, once again the sand is torn up, and the air alive with bullets.

Woman or no woman, she is not to reach the sea alive, if the enemy can help it.

The excitement is now intense. The soldiers are cheering frantically, and yelling defiance to the enemy hidden in the wood ; while the gunners ply the guns, and favour them with plenty of shot and shell.

All this is a mystery to Darcy Leigh on board the Black Angel. He has seen the fall of the mounted trooper, the six soldiers, and now sees with regret and pain a woman courting the same fate. Why such a risk should be run he cannot divine ; for safe within the fort, whose guns swept the whole ground, the defenders could successfully resist an attack by ten times their number. He knew not that on communication being opened from the shore depended the safety of himself, vessel, and crew—never dreaming that before he could run the ship ashore where he intended, he would have to pass within a few yards of a battery of heavy guns, which must inevitably sink the ship.

And now the devoted girl, running for dear life, is within twenty yards of the shore. She has passed so far unscathed. Behind lay the bodies of the dead and wounded, before her the beach—the waves gently rippling and washing it.

She staggers and falls.

A yell of rage bursts from the rebels who line the fort, answered by another yell from the crew of the sloop who crowd the bulwarks. All attention is riveted on the running figure, for she has again started to her feet, and even the guns of the fort cease their fire. Suddenly shouting and the clang of sabres is heard in the wood. Then a body of troops are seen hurrying out in great disorder. Before they can form, the terrible cavalry rush upon them and drive them before them in confusion.

But where is now the figure of the woman in the *vivandière* dress, who was not a moment ago running swiftly across the sand?

In the very moment of success and safety she is struck down by the ruthless bullets of the foe, and now lying bleeding, fainting, dying on the shore.

---

# CHAPTER XXXI.

## THE DEATH OF CORALIE.

THOUGH unable fully to understand the meaning of these repeated and disastrous attempts to reach the shore and communicate with the vessel, Darcy Leigh knew there must be some reason, and that a most urgent one, else six men and a woman would not have made so perilous an attempt. He gave orders for the engines to be stopped and the boats got out. In a very short time four of the boats were manned, and pulled rapidly towards the shore. Darcy himself was in the stern-sheets of the foremost gig, with about a dozen seamen, armed with cutlasses and pistols.

Meanwhile the remnant of the Yankees who had been driven from the wood by Gerald Leigh's cavalry, had again gained its shelter, and having apparently been reinforced, they re-opened fire. The guns from the fort opened in reply with grape and shell, while the Black Angel also took part in the engagement, thundering away with her heavy cannon. The small infantry force in the fort were deployed into line on the left, and thrown into the wood, with orders to drive out the enemy into the open, where the cavalry could act and the guns play on them, when they would be compelled to surrender at discretion.

A group of men surrounds the spot where Nina the *vivandière* fell; and Darcy Leigh, leaping from the gig the instant he touches the shore, also hastens towards the fallen girl.

Sweeping over the plain, making a wide curve, and cutting off here and there a straggler of the enemy ere he can reach the wood, the irregular horse, led by Gerald and the Englishman, dash up at a gallop. Gerald and George both leap from the saddle together, and throwing their bridles to a trooper, press on through the group.

"Who is it?" asks Gerald.

"It's the *vivandière* girl!—God rest her soul; for she's dying!" replied a soldier.

Gerald and George pressed on eagerly through the crowd, and soon stood by the side of the dying girl.

George knelt by her side.

"Nina! Nina!—where are you wounded, my dear girl?"

"Here, here," was the faint reply, as she pressed her hand to the spot where the neck joined the shoulder; "but it is not Nina—it is—Coralie!"

"Not Nina!" cried George, in amazement; "can it be possible?—Miss St. Casse?"

"Yes, yes; give me water—wine—I am faint. Where is Nina, and Darcy Leigh?—I would see them before I die."

The surgeon now pressed forward, and George rose to enable him to examine the poor girl's wounds.

He saw Darcy Leigh running up from the beach, and hastened to meet him.

"Darcy, did you see her shot down?"

"Yes, yes—I saw. It was therefore I got out the boats—the miserable cowards, to slay a woman."

"Do you know who it is—who lies wounded there?"

"Yes, Nina, the *vivandière.*"

"No, not Nina," replied George, sadly—"you must prepare yourself for terrible news, Darcy—I fear she is mortally wounded. There is that terrible ashen grey hue on her face by which I have never been deceived."

"Not Nina," faltered Darcy; "who then can it be? Not—George—not Coralie?"

"He grasped the other's arm, and looked earnestly

in his eyes. The only reply was an inclination of the head.

Darcy darted off, and pushing wildly through the crowd, was in a moment kneeling by the side of the wounded girl. Already the ashy hue of which George spoke had deepened. Already the bright lustre of the eyes had begun to fade away.

" Coralie !—Coralie—is it thus I see you ? "

A smile lit up her face—a smile of love and happiness. Her eyes sparkled brilliantly, and it seemed as though the flame of life were again about to burn bright and clear as ever.

" Ah, Darcy, you are here. Now I am happy—give me your hand."

" Doctor, is she seriously wounded ? " he asked, passionately ; " why do you stand there gaping—why do you not make haste to dress the wound ? See—it is on her neck—only a small wound, and it does not bleed much."

" The lady is in the hands of God, sir. Human skill can avail nothing."

" Is she, then, dangerously—mortally wounded ? " he asked, turning as pale as death.

" I fear so. It is almost certain that large vessels have been injured—that internal hæmorrhage is progressing at a fearful rate. I judge by the rapidly failing pulse."

" Wine—wine ! " she gasped. " Darcy, give me wine —I feel faint."

" Yes, give her wine," said the surgeon, sadly ; " it will feed the flame of life yet a few minutes more."

Wine was given, and Darcy raising her head, she took a long draught. All had fallen respectfully back, and stood in groups at some little distance watching the thicket where the enemy had disappeared, and the Yankee steamers, which had been stopped and were landing troops and marines in boats.

" Darcy—Darcy, come closer to me—kiss me, Darcy— let me put my arm around your neck—I shall soon be dead—I feel it creeping over me—it is dreadful to die,

Darcy, and leave you. Why did you not stop—why would you steam on after we had so many times tried to warn you ?"

"I don't understand you, Coralie. Why should I not? I meant to have run under the guns of the fort."

"Lift me up, Darcy, I will show you."

He raised her gently in a sitting position.

"The light is getting very dull, Darcy. Where is the ship ?"

Alas ! the noon-day sun was streaming in full splendour. He pointed the Black Angel out to her as she lay about fifty yards from the shore.

"Ah, yes ! look down the coast, Darcy—about half a mile—battery—heavy guns—island—masked——"

"Ha !" he exclaimed, suddenly, as, warned where to look, he discovered the treacherous masking of trees. "Now I understand why you risked your life. Oh, Coralie, my brave—my glorious—my beautiful Coralie, why did you not let me perish, rather than you should have suffered this ? But you will not die—see," he added, pressing a white handkerchief to the bullet wound in her neck, "the bleeding has almost ceased."

"Has it, Darcy ?" she said, with a smile. "I am growing fainter and fainter, colder and colder—dying—dying."

She slid from his arms, for he was holding her in a sitting posture, and lay at length on the sand, so still and motionless that for a moment he thought her dead.

Hastily raising her head, he found that at present, at least, it was not so.

"And Nina—where is Nina ? I should like to see her before I die. Nina—sister—Nina, where are you ?"

But no answer came to the plaintive cry.

"Was she not in the fort with you ?"

"Yes, something must have happened to her. She must be wounded, or she would be by my side. Darcy, you will see to Nina after I am gone. Sister Nina, dear Nina. I cannot tell you all. My time is short—my will, Darcy—Charleston—how dark it gets. Kiss me,

Darcy, dear—there, raise me once again, and let me look on our glorious flag."

He raised her up, and directed her dying eyes towards the flag which floated from the fort.

"Let me be buried in Charleston, dear Darcy, in the magnolia grove, by the chapel. Promise me you will not be unhappy."

"Great God! Coralie, how can I promise such a thing?" he replied, in a choking, gasping voice, for now, indeed, he knew that the hand of death was upon her.

"Darcy, if ever you love again, do not let my memory stand in your way. Promise me that."

"No, no, Coralie, I never shall."

"No matter—promise. I shall not die happy if I think my memory can ever stand in the way of your happiness."

"As you please, Coralie," he replied, kissing her pale lips.

"Place my arm round your neck again, Darcy; I cannot myself; I am too weak. Where is the flag, Darcy? I cannot see it now."

"There—there, dear Coralie; see how bravely it flutters in the breeze."

"Hark! what is that? is it distant thunder?"

Alas! it was the loud roar of the guns from the fort now opening on the wood, where the enemy had again begun to show themselves.

"Is it getting dark, Darcy?"

"No, darling; it is not long past noon."

"Ah! then, it is the night of death. Hold me tight, Darcy, dear; hold me close to you; they are dragging me away from you. I can't see you now. Where are you, Darcy?"

"Here, here, my darling!" he cried, passionately kissing her lips.

Then she laid her head back on his shoulder, her dim eyes gazing up unblinkingly at the noonday sun. She murmured sentences he could not understand—sentences in which his own name and that of Nina, Lupus Rock, Gerald, Stella Gayle, and many others, were all mixed up in strange confusion. The last delirium was upon her. He watched the dim eyes grow yet dimmer—noticed the ashen cheek of a dark leaden hue, while the features slowly assumed that anxious, frightened expression, the sure forerunner of death. He saw a grey film spread over the once bright eyes—eyes wont to beat with love for him. He felt her faint breathing grow fainter and fainter, and, placing his hand on her heart, he could detect no beating. Her arm was around his neck, her hand rested upon his cheek—it was icy cold. Suddenly he felt himself strained in a tight embrace.

"Darcy, dear Darcy! farewell——"

Then a low wail, a long though faint cry of anguish, burst from her lips ; her embrace relaxed, her head fell back, her eyes fixed in the stony stare of the dead, and Darcy knew that her spirit had fled for ever.

One more kiss he imprinted on her cold lips, then he rose, and laying her body gently down, he covered it tenderly with his cloak.

He then beckoned to some of his men, who quickly came up.

"Get a grating from the boat, and carry the body of this lady into the fort. Watch by it. I have other work to do."

Darcy walked straight up to where his brother and Captain George stood. They asked him no questions ; his pale sad face and gleaming eyes told them that all was over.

"Gerald, where are those accursed Yankees who fired on her ?"

Gerald pointed with his sword to the wood.

"Get me one of your trooper's horses. I will cleave some of their skulls for this morning's work."

He spoke in his quiet tones, but Gerald knew that to turn him from his purpose, were it to charge a thousand single-handed, would be utterly futile.

"Now, a heavy cavalry sabre—this plaything is useless."

He threw down the small, straight sword he wore, and selected a heavy, curved cavalry sabre.

" Ha, ha !" he muttered fiercely between his teeth, " this will split some of their cowardly skulls."

" What are you going to do, Darcy ?" asked Gerald, sadly, for he knew it was useless to oppose his brother in his mood ; " throw your life away ?"

"I care little, so long as I have vengeance for this morning's foul murder."

" See," said Captain George, pointing to the Yankee ships now lying nearly a mile off the creek, so as to be out of range of the guns of the fort; "see, they are landing marines and troops."

" Wait a little while, Darcy ; let us see what they are about to attempt."

This was soon apparent, for having landed about two hundred men, they formed them and marched towards the wood which skirted the strip of sandy plain, evidently intending to reinforce their comrades there.

At this moment a sharp firing was heard in the wood. The force sent from the fort had fallen in with the enemy, and the latter soon appeared at the edge of the wood, apparently being driven out.

" These are some of the scoundrels, are they not ? Bring me a horse, one of you fellows."

" Gently, Darcy, let them get clear of the wood first ; doubtless they mean to try and join their friends from the ship."

This was evidently their intention, for they formed in columns of subdivisions, and then marched rapidly across the sandy plain, the rearmost subdivision facing about every now and then to keep in check the rebels who followed them from the wood.

" To horse and away," cried Gerald, when they had gone about a hundred yards from the wood. In less than a minute every man was in the saddle, and the word was given to charge. The distance was not over a quarter of a mile, and at a furious gallop this was covered in little more than half a minute. But the Yankees, knowing there was a force of cavalry about, were all in readiness, and quickly and cleverly threw themselves into a square. They numbered about two hundred, and as they stood in this solid formation, presenting a *chevaux de frise* of bayonets, looked most formidable.

Darcy rode a couple of horses' lengths in front of either his brother or George, who had great difficulty in keeping up with him, so furiously did he spur forward, shouting all the while like a madman—a very unusual thing with him.

" Forward, boys ! follow me. Death to the murdering Yankees. Slaughter them, cut them down, give no quarter. A hundred dollars for every Yankee head. Hurrah !"

He was close to the bayonets of the enemy. They delivered one volley, which, though fortunately too high, emptied several saddles. The next moment Darcy Leigh, with a terrific shout, charged right on to the gleaming bayonets. The impetus of the horse carried him clear through and into the square, the poor animal receiving, however, two deep bayonet wounds in the chest.

George and Gerald were quickly after him—the former dashed through the same opening, while Gerald forced another. Then the troopers galloped after them, and for the Yankees all was lost. The square was broken.

Shouts, yells, and groans rent the air. The Yankees threw down their arms and scattered in every direction, most running to gain the shelter of the wood. But in this they were unsuccessful. Darcy Leigh, as soon as the square was fairly broken and dispersed, about half the Yankees lying dead or dying on the ground in the immediate neighbourhood, took with him ten men, and galloped off to the wood, so as to intercept any who might escape.

Thus sweeping up and down along the belt of open ground in front of the wood, Darcy allowed not one solitary straggler to reach its cover. Several, when they saw escape hopeless, and Darcy, his sabre dripping with blood, riding down upon them, fell on their knees and cried for quarter.

" No quarter to those who murder women," was the stern reply ; and usually the next moment the keen sabre descended on the wretch's head or body, in either case killing instantly. Sometimes, however, the fugitive would, hopeless of mercy, run to the last.

There was a fierce excitement in this which chimed in well with Darcy's present humour. To see them double and twist like hunted hares—gasping, panting, till at last the inevitable time came, and rising in his stirrups, the sabre would whistle through the air, gleam in the sunshine, and the next instant the running form would be a dark spot on the plain.

For two hours this lasted, and at the end of that time not a single man of the Yankee force who originally held the wood remained alive. The marines—half-drilled, and, as all fresh troops are, terribly afraid of cavalry—on seeing the solid square of the infantry broken, fired a volley and hastily retreated to their boats, leaving the field clear to the horsemen and their prey.

At the end of the two hours Darcy reined in his horse, and looking around, noticed with almost a sigh that there were no more to kill. The sandy plain for an area of about half a mile or rather more, was dotted with the dark forms of the dead, as they lay where they were cut down. Then the little force slowly returned to the fort, Darcy riding moodily in the rear, as though loth to leave off.

" At least," he muttered, as he replaced his sabre, dripping with blood, in the scabbard, " at least, Coralie, you are avenged. I wonder whether my hand cut down the ruffian who shot you?"

He did not immediately enter the fort, but dismounting, gave his horse to a trooper, and walked down to the shore, where the two boats' crews, who had taken no part in the fight, awaited him.

The men were talking as he came up, but when they saw him there was a dead silence. All had seen the fall of the lady, and now it was known who she was, there was not a man who did not share the grief of his captain.

" Mr. Johnstone," he said to the midshipman in command of the other boat, " go on board, and bring Mr. Wharncliffe to me."

The Black Angel lay off only some twenty or thirty yards, so in a very short space of time the boat had gone and returned with the first lieutenant.

" Wharncliffe," said Darcy, drawing him aside, " you must at once run the vessel ashore here. Then set to work ; get guns, stores, ammunition—everything out of her. Bring everything up to the fort ; then hoist our flag at every mast head and blow her up."

" Blow her up ! is there then no escape ?"

" By no possibility can we escape now. Had we gone about half a mile further, we ourselves should all have been made prisoners. There is a masked battery of heavy guns on the island. Doubtless even now they are expecting us to run by. It was in trying to warn us, that that noble girl lost her life. Of course you have heard ?"

Wharncliffe bowed his head. He had just heard from the boat's crew who had come to fetch him.

" At all events she is avenged," he said. " I watched the fight, and do not believe a man of the enemy escaped."

" Not a solitary one of the scoundrels," said Darcy, his eye gleaming savagely. " I believe I cut down twenty myself. Ha ! ha ! it was glorious to hear their pitiful screams for mercy, as I rode them down. Mercy ; what mercy did they show ? I gave them such mercy as quick, sudden death gives, and that is more than they deserved. See to dismantling and unloading the sloop, Wharncliffe, will you, there's a good fellow ? I am quite unfit my-self."

Wharncliffe promised to do so, and Darcy slowly walked up the sandy slope to the little fortress. The Yankee vessels hovered about at a little more than a mile's distance, but did not offer to approach within close range, nor apparently did they think it worth while wasting powder in long shots.

But what had become of Nina all this time ? Captain George was one of the last to enter the fort, and as he walked round the fosse or ditch which had been dug around it, he heard a faint cry, and going up to the spot from whence it came, he saw a female figure lying at the bottom. It required not a second glance to tell him it was Nina, although she was attired in Coralie's riding habit.

He jumped down, and hastened to raise her in his arms.

"What is it, Nina, my child? are you wounded?" he said, tenderly.

"No. I saw Mademoiselle fall as she ran along the sands—I started to go to her and save her, my foot slipping I fell into the ditch, and have sprained my ankle badly. But is she much hurt?"

George broke the sad news to her as gently and delicately as he could, but her grief was frantic. She sobbed and moaned as though her heart would break.

"Oh, why would she go on that mad errand!—I begged and prayed of her to allow me—but she would not. She even commanded me to change clothes with her, and remain in the fort. Oh that I had died for her!"

Poor girl! She had found but few friends during her troubled life, and now the best and kindest was taken from her.

"And now I am alone in the world," she said; "alone —without a friend."

"Not so, Nina. Am not I yet spared? and do you think you shall ever want a friend while I live?"

"Ah, sir, you are very kind—too kind."

Her dark eyes beamed on his face with a soft melting expression, and suffused with tears as they were, he thought them very beautiful.

"Lean your head on my shoulder, Nina; do not tire yourself by trying to sit upright;" and without a word she did as she was told.

Darcy Leigh gave a few necessary orders, and then left the execution of them to his brother and Wharncliffe.

By evening the Black Angel was totally dismantled from stores, everything having been taken from her and brought within the fort. The crew were also landed and employed in shifting the great bulk of plunder taken from the various Yankee prizes, and placing it on carts and waggons, to procure which, Gerald's horsemen were sent to scour the country. All through the night, the work went on, and by the afternoon of the next day a long train of waggons started for the interior in the direction of the Charleston railroad, distant about thirty miles. When the last of the waggons and escort had left, the prizes in the creek were set fire to, and a slow match applied to the magazine of the Black Angel. In a few minutes there was a great explosion, and when the smoke cleared away nothing was to be seen of the rebel cruiser but a few charred timbers.

A rude coffin had been made for the remains of Coralie, and, attended by a guard of honour, commanded by Darcy himself, they bore her body slowly along in the rear. The soldiers all carried their arms reversed, and Darcy had given orders that not a word should be spoken by any of the guard—threatening to shoot the man who should profane the solemn procession by laughter or con-versation. There was little need of the order. The heroism of Darcy Leigh, and his daring exploits, were well known to every Southern soldier; and as to the lady whose body they now bore, there was not a rebel in all the South who did not worship her very name.

The fort was not to be given up unless attacked by overwhelming numbers, a force of some fifty men being left to hold it. It was not likely, however, that the Yankees, now that the Black Angel had been blown up and all the prizes burned, would attack a sand fort on a barren coast, of no strategic importance whatever.

There is no need here to follow them in the march to the railway, and thence on. Suffice it that on the even-ing of the next day all the expedition safely arrived in Charleston.

There was a deep gloom in that city when the news of the untimely death of its pride and glory (Coralie, the Star of the South) was bruited abroad. The bells of all the churches pealed, and all the troops in the city were sent by the officer in command to do honour to the illus-trious dead, and escort her to her home, whence but a short time previous she had issued, all health, life, and enthusiasm—in the pride of her beauty, and the flower of her youth.

They buried her as she had requested, not in the city, but in a magnolia grove, belonging to the Roman Catholic chapel in the suburbs.

*Requiescat in pace.*

On her will being read, it was found that she had left one half of her great wealth to Darcy Leigh, the other to Nina, who was to assume the name of St. Casse.

Darcy, on his part, would not have accepted it, but enclosed in the will was a letter addressed to him, dated only three months back.

It ran thus :—

"MY OWN DARCY,—When you read this I shall be at rest in my grave. I have long had a feeling, almost a presentiment, that my days are numbered. I have forborne to speak of it to you, not wishing to grieve you or wound your noble heart. That you will not hesitate to accept the bequest I have made you is my earnest prayer. Remember, I make it as much for my own happiness as for yours. I know you too well to think you care for wealth, but still, for my sake, take and use at least the half of what was mine. It is possible that in the land of spirits I may be near you, even as you read this letter; need I tell you how it would grieve me were you to refuse this my last request? Darcy, it is the voice of the dead which now in writing speaks to you. To Nina, dear Nina, I leave the other half. Watch over her as a brother, Darcy, for my sake, and if need be, enjoin your brave brother Gerald to do so likewise. As I write this I know not what will be the manner of my death, or when the time will come. Let it be when it may, I die at peace with all men, even with my father's murderer, and freely forgive him who has been my greatest enemy —Lupus Rock. Now, Darcy, though when you read this I shall be gone from earth, I bid you adieu. If we can carry such feelings with us into another world, my love for you will be eternal.

"CORALIE ANDREE ST. CASSE."

23

After reading this letter Darcy declared with moist eyes that he would accept the bequest. Could he have done otherwise?

And now, burning for excitement to quench the grief gnawing at his heart, for his love for Coralie had grown from a little spark to a bright flame, he again sought service in the field. Once again without a ship, this was the only alternative, and it was one which chimed in well with his mood. Again he joined the 7th Carolina's, the regiment raised and equipped by his dear Coralie.

When, after a short stay at Charleston, this regiment again went to meet the enemy, it was up to its full strength of 1000 men, for Darcy had, from his own purse, filled up the gaps in the ranks which war and pestilence had made.

Every officer and private wore on his left arm a piece of crape, and the colours, torn as they were with many a bullet and sharp splinter, were furthermore draped in black.

As they marched through the streets of Richmond, they presented a somewhat lugubrious appearance, contrasting strangely to those who had seen them on the first occasion two years ago, when Coralie, in all the pride of her youthful beauty, her bright eyes sparkling with enthusiasm, had ridden at their head.

Again the tide of battle rolls over fair Virginia. This time the advance on the capital is by way of Fredericksburg, and while the rival armies are fiercely battling on the soil of the " Old Dominion," we will for a time leave them and return to New York, and see how things fare with the sisters, Stella and Angela Gayle, their father and Lupus Rock, by whose treachery it was, as the reader has doubtless guessed, that Darcy Leigh so nearly fell into the net, and which treachery, though failing to ensure his capture, yet brought about the tragic death of Coralie St. Casse.

# CHAPTER XXXII.

## SHOOTING A TRAITOR.

ONCE again Lupus Rock had to learn, that his attempt to compass the destruction of Darcy Leigh had failed. Immediately on arriving in New York he had given information to the Government of what he had heard, while lying hidden in Stella's cabin. He managed matters so carefully that she had no inkling of his intention, for, notwithstanding the cruel taunt of Darcy Leigh, now that she had time to think and reason, she would rather have suffered harm herself than that any should happen to him.

Lupus knew that immediately on the receipt of his information, several vessels had been sent to cruise off the spot he indicated, to lie in wait for the rebel cruiser. Anxiously he waited day after day for the news which should tell him that one, and perhaps the most hated, of his enemies was captured, and awaiting the sentence of death. At last news did come, but it confounded all his calculations.

The intelligence came first through the Richmond newspapers, and was afterwards confirmed by the official despatches of the Yankee commanders.

The Black Angel had been fallen in with as she was making her way to the secret rendezvous, bringing with her two prizes. A desperate running fight ensued, which lasted for more than twenty-four hours. The two prizes were abandoned and sunk, but in spite of all their efforts, the Black Angel, though terribly cut about, succeeded in getting ahead and entering the inlet.

Troops had been already landed, and a battery of heavy guns established, by which it was hoped that the rebel ship would be destroyed, and by the co-operation of the troops and marines her crew prevented from escaping.

23—2

How this was frustrated the reader knows. The Black Angel was blown up, but the whole of her crew escaped, while of the troops landed and sent into the woods to prevent the escape of the rebels, not one remained to tell the tale.

The accounts in the Southern papers wound up with the melancholy death of Coralie St. Casse, and the military honours paid at her funeral in Charleston.

This news was startling enough, but it was far from what Lupus Rock desired. He had, mingled with his hatred, an intense dread of Darcy Leigh, his brother, and their friend the Englishman. He felt—he could hardly account for the feeling—that so long as they lived there was no safety for him.

Even in the event of the rebellion being quelled and the Union being restored, he knew that still he would not be safe. They knew too much of his villanies—too much of his double treachery, and he was well aware that were peace restored at once between the Government and the rebels, there would be no peace between him and the Leighs.

The death of Coralie affected him little either one way or the other; his designs in that quarter had been hopelessly frustrated, and her death was even a matter of indifference; indeed, he rather regretted it, and feared the effect it might have on Darcy Leigh and Stella.

Lupus had long since divined that on the part of his cousin and destined wife there still lingered an attachment to the rebel officer, which even the last insult he had put upon her could not quench. Most of all then he dreaded a sudden peace, which might again throw them together and frustrate his plans on her fortune and person.

In view of this contingency, then, Lupus Rock strained every nerve to get the girl and her father completely in his power. It had long been tacitly understood that Stella was to be his wife, and by the end of the winter of 1862-63, he had wrung from her an unwilling consent to marry him during the ensuing summer. But though he gained his point it was not without a desperate struggle. Stella herself opposed but a faint, impassive resistance.

The idea had firmly taken root in her mind, that it was her destiny to be the wife of the man whom of all others in the world she perhaps most disliked.

Webster Gayle, who had been drawn by his crafty nephew slowly but surely into a vortex from which there was no escape, favoured his suit. He could not help it. Poor, avaricious man! the hard-headed schemer had not only got his business into such a state that no hand but his could arrange the vast mass of complicated details, so as to avoid tremendous losses, but again, despite the merchant's struggles and endeavours to keep himself clear, he had mixed himself up with schemes and treacherous transactions to a fatal extent. Lupus Rock held evidence enough of these dealings to hang a dozen men, and yet, although the prime mover, he had contrived to keep himself quite clear.

But if Lupus had little difficulty with Stella, and none with Webster Gayle, in Angela he found a most determined opponent. The gentle girl's whole nature seemed to be changed in her championship of her sister. Lupus Rock wondered at the energy and fierceness of his younger cousin, whom he had always been accustomed to look upon as a cipher. He had anticipated some trouble in vanquishing Stella's haughty spirit; but that Angela, usually so mild and gentle, should offer any opposition, was to him at once unexpected and confounding.

" Lupus Rock, you shall never marry my sister," she said to him even several times in a day.

" Angela, my dear child," he would reply, with assumed composure, " I shall marry your sister. Your father consents, and she consents ; it is not likely that you can prevent it."

" But I will prevent it. She loathes and fears you. She is not herself. The misery and anguish to which she has been subjected has affected her mind."

Once, when Lupus Rock, in reply to her passionate declarations, had quietly replied that, in spite of the whole world he would marry Stella, Angela goaded to fury, had said, "And the day you do so shall be your last, Lupus Rock."

" What ! my gentle cousin, do you threaten me ? do you think to frighten me by a threat of murder ?"

" No, not murder ; the just penalty of your crimes."

This threat of Angela's determined him to be doubly on his guard. He would make all his arrangements for marrying his cousin at a moment's notice, and would keep her sister ignorant of both time and place.

His plans were now so matured that he had but to put the screw on at any moment to gain his point. He signified to Webster Gayle his wish to marry his cousin during the summer, and be received as a partner in the firm of Gayle and Co., in place of dowry. The merchant made no objection, and so far as he was concerned, Lupus had but to name the day.

Towards the end of June, 1863, business of the greatest importance demanded his presence in Baltimore.

The merchant had considerable property inland, and houses in various parts of the State, and Lupus urged that this was a good occasion for visiting and seeing to it. Stella Gayle had lately been in indifferent health, and Lupus proposed that it would be an excellent plan for the merchant to take her with him, as the change must have a beneficial effect. It was accordingly so arranged. Webster Gayle and Stella started for Baltimore, leaving Lupus and Angela in New York.

Now, though Lupus had neglected no precautions to hide his real design from his cousin Angela, she, with a woman's quick perception, at once divined that it was his intention suddenly to leave her, and join Webster and Stella in Maryland.

Lupus knew that she had means of communication with Gerald Leigh in the South, but had not the least idea of the rapidity and safety with which these letters were conveyed. Nor did he know that Gerald's regiment was, with a large cavalry force under General Stuart, only a few miles south of the Potomac, and absolutely in the rear of Hooker's army. He thought, and indeed felt certain that both Gerald and Darcy were in Charleston the latter slowly recovering from desperate wounds received at the first battle of Fredericksburg.

At last Lupus thought that the time for action had come, that the fruit he had so long watched was ripe, and waited but to be plucked from the tree.

" Angela," he said, one day after dinner, " I am going over to Brooklyn on some business ; most likely I shall not be home to-night, as the boats do not run late. I shall take a small bag, and put up at the hotel."

" Really, Mr. Rock," she replied, " I don't know why you should tell me of your movements. I believe for your own reasons you are trying to mislead me. I am sure you have not told me the truth."

Lupus laughed scornfully, and left the room. No sooner had he gone than Angela sat down and indited a letter to Gerald Leigh.

As for Lupus, instead of going to Brooklyn, he walked straight to the railway station, and booked himself right through to Baltimore.

" When next you see your sister, Miss Angela," he muttered, " it will be as Mrs. Lupus Rock."

In the outskirts of the little town of Chambersburg, in the State of Pennsylvania, about twelve miles from the Maryland frontier, there is a little Episcopalian church, built of wood and roofed with pine shingles.

On a bright sunny morning in the last week of June, 1863, a fly containing three persons drives up. These three are Webster Gayle, Stella, his daughter, and Lupus Rock. It is evident they are expected, for an aged man standing at the door, who officiates as clerk and sexton, receives and ushers them in. Stella's face is pale, her expression passionless, resigned ; her air and manner indifferent, as though all hope having fled, she was prepared for the worst that fate might have in store. And cruel fate indeed was now about to wreak its worst vengeance, for she was about to kneel at the altar and receive as her husband Lupus Rock. His eyes gleamed with triumph, his step was light and buoyant, and in this moment of the accomplishment of the one great aim of his life, his manner towards his cousin was less cynical and overbearing. For in a few minutes she who had so often defied and scorned him would be his, both by the laws of God and man.

Stella retired for a few moments to the vestry-room, and waiting her readiness, Lupus and his uncle stood and conversed in low tones.

" God forgive me, Lupus," said the father, "if I am doing wrong ! How pale and languid my poor girl looks. Even at this last moment I have a mind to prevent this hurried marriage—at least, to postpone it till we return to New York. Then surrounded by friends, and with all the display and luxury which wealth can give, it may be, Stella might be awakened from this dismal apathy."

A blank angry expression came over the features of Lupus Rock.

" Postpone !—impossible, sir. I cannot submit to be thus fooled. Last night, and again this morning, in your hearing, Stella expressed herself willing to be my wife."

" Yes, yes—I know. Her fate !—she said it was her fate !"

" Yes, and it is her fate," replied Lupus, curtly. " Come ; here she is, and yonder stands the minister."

Then Lupus advanced and met Stella Gayle as she came out of the little vestry-room, and taking her by the hand, he led her to the altar. Passively, as one in a dream, she suffered herself to be thus led, and when Lupus arranged a stool for her, she knelt and silently bowed her head as might a condemned one, waiting for the stroke of the headsman's axe. Lupus knelt by her side, and Webster Gayle stood at some few paces distant, silently regarding this mockery of a marriage.

In slow, solemn tones, the minister commenced to read the impressive service which should bind these two together until death them part. Scarcely, however, had he commenced, than the clatter of a horse's hoofs is heard, and Stella turning her head—she scarce knew why,—saw a mounted dragoon ride by.

A wild, rough, and ragged-looking trooper he was, but he horse he bestrode was a fine one, the sabre he wore heavy, and his air and seat as worthy of admiration, as his uniform was dirty, dusty, and ragged. He bore a light staff or lance, on which fluttered in the breeze a small white flag.

The minister stopped for a moment reading the service—Lupus Rock, who looked round as he saw the strange soldier ride by the open door, wondered much what regiment he could belong to. The trooper galloped on into the town, and as the hoof-falls of the horse faded away, the minister again went on with the service.

He read very slowly, and omitted no part of the regular service, so that a full quarter of an hour had elapsed ere he came to the momentous question, "Wilt thou have this man to be thy wedded husband?" &c.

Lupus Rock had answered promptly and firmly, and then waited with bated breath for the words he had so longed to hear spoken by his cousin.

She, however, did not answer.

Pale as marble, lovely as a hewn statue, with fixed eyes, compressed lips, and heaving bosom, she at first appeared not to hear the question.

At that moment—the turning point of her fate—what a tempest of passion swept over her soul.

She was about to swear to "love, honour, and obey" the man whom of all others in the world she most feared and hated. No wonder her lips hesitated to pronounce the perjury—no wonder her hand shrunk from the ring which Lupus waited to place on her finger.

There was a dead solemn silence of nearly a minute, during which the minister gazed wonderingly from one to the other, while Lupus waited anxiously for the expected word. Then seeing she gave no signs, but gazed fixedly at the tablets over the altar-table, he touched her lightly on the shoulder.

"Come, Stella," he said, gently, for he was almost terrified at her singular manner, "do you not hear the minister?" She started as one rudely awaked from a dream. The minister then repeated the question, and after another long pause she heaved a deep sigh, and said the decisive words—"I will."

Scarcely were the words out of her mouth when again is heard the clatter of the galloping horse, and again the ragged trooper, bearing the flag, dashes by.

This time Lupus, in the pride and exultation of his heart, takes no notice of the solitary dusty soldier, and ere the sound of the galloping horse's hoofs has faded away, he has placed the ring on Stella's finger, and she is his wife.

When the ceremony was concluded they rose, and Lupus conducted her to the vestry to inscribe her name in the register. Webster Gayle, with a heavy heart, affixes his signature as witness, and kissing his daughter's brow, wishes her happiness. Happiness! She hears the word and smiles faintly in reply. Then her features resume the hard, inanimate, stony expression they had worn all along. But for the heaving of her bosom, and the occasional twitching of the clear cut, handsome lips, one might fancy her a girl of marble, petrified by the spell of some enchanter.

"Come, Stella, let us return to the hotel. Surely you are not cold?"

It was Webster Gayle who spoke. He had noticed with surprise that his daughter shivered slightly, although the weather was sultry and oppressive. Throwing a shawl over her shoulders he led her away, and consigned her to the care of her husband, who was settling the fees with the old clerk. Lupus placed her arm within his, and led her out into the open air and bright sunshine.

The fly in which they had come had gone some little distance up the road, the driver wishing to give the horse water. As they stood waiting his return they heard the clear blast of a bugle, some half mile away, apparently. Then succeeded the thunder of galloping hoofs, shouts, and cries.

The next moment a body of horse appears over the crest of the hill, and approaches down the road at a hard gallop. This is succeeded by another squadron, and yet another, till for quite a quarter of a mile the road is occupied by armed and mounted men. The foremost squadrons gallop quickly past, not taking the slightest notice of the party at the church door.

" Wonder what cavalry they can be," muttered Lupus. " Can't be Burford's ; it's not the uniform. What a ragged lot ; some of the Potomac army, I suppose." The colours were all faded, so that no clue was afforded by that means.

Five regiments, numbering at least two thousand men and horses, had galloped by, and as many more were behind. Stella, she knew not why, felt a strange interest in these unknown troops. Suddenly her eyes rested on a squadron descending the hill. The uniform tunic the men wore was dark grey, with butter-nut pants. A heavy curbed sabre and, unlike most of the others, holster pistols in place of carbines, were the arms carried by this regiment.

" Surely," she thought, " I know that uniform."

Scarcely had this thought flashed across her brain than her eye fell on an officer riding at the head of a company—a tall, handsome, fair young man, with his arm in a sling.

Stella gave vent to a sharp cry of recognition as he approached nearer—the officer's attention was attracted by this cry. With a rapid, sweeping glance he took in the group at the church door, then he suddenly shouted, " Halt !' and reined in his horse.

This sudden halt caused some little confusion, the companies in the rear riding close behind, becoming in some cases mixed up with that commanded by the young officer with the wounded arm.

For a moment or two he was lost to the view of Stella Gayle, but he quickly reappeared, spurred his horse close alongside of her, and reaching forth his right arm, seized Lupus Rock by the collar of his coat before he knew what was being done.

" Lupus Rock," cried the young officer, in a loud voice, " I arrest you as a 'deserter' and a traitor !"

So quick and sudden was the whole transaction that at first Lupus did not recognise his captor, but at the sound of his voice he turned deadly, ghastly pale.

"Dismount, two of you fellows, and hold this man. Blow his brains out if he attempts to escape. I must inform the general of the capture."

Two troopers instantly dismounted and rudely seized the bridegroom.

"What is it, Gerald?" asked another officer, riding up.

"What is it?" replied the other, in tones of triumph; "look, see," pointing to the prisoner, "I have captured the traitorous scoundrel. See to him, I must ride and overtake the general. A case of a drum-head court-martial, I reckon!"

Then he galloped off. The other officer gazed on Lupus Rock with no friendly glance, as he stood tightly held by the troopers at the church door. Webster Gayle and his daughter had retreated inside, so that the other officer had not seen them.

"So, Captain Rock," he said, "caught at last. I told you your day would come. I spared your life twice; now you will find a sterner judge."

Lupus Rock turned from white to lead colour, and his knees almost refused to support him. He gazed wildly around for help, or hope of escape.

No wonder his heart quailed and his brain reeled, for sudden as the lightning flash he had recognised the two officers. The one who had seized him was Gerald Leigh; the one who now addressed him, the Englishman, Captain George; and Lupus, to his mortal terror, knew that he was a prisoner in the hands of the rebel cavalry, who, in one of their raids, had swooped down upon Hagerstown.

The man with the white flag who had ridden past whilst the ceremony was going on, was sent to demand from the mayor the surrender of the town. With no means of resistance, that surrender, of course, was promptly made by the authorities, and Hagerstown was now in rebel hands.

In a very short time Gerald Leigh returned, with General Stuart in person. "That is the prisoner, general." he said, pointing to Lupus. "It is he who betrayed his post on the Chickahominy last year, and deserted with half his regiment to the enemy."

"Ho, ho! this is the arch-traitor, is it? Halt all the troops. Drum-head court-martial."

Then, turning in his saddle, he shouted,—

"Send the provost-marshal here."

When that dreaded functionary appeared, the general said, "We shall probably require your services in a few minutes, sir. Tell off a file of men, and be in readiness. Carbines—that will be quickest—don't see any trees about big enough. Now then, bring forward the prisoner and try him—ten captains—one lieutenant—I myself will be president—quick! no time to be lost. Prisoner, you are accused of treason and desertion; what do you say—guilty, or not guilty?"

"Not guilty. I protest against this proceeding, and demand to be treated as a prisoner of war."

"Protest away!" said Stuart, with a scornful laugh; "it won't serve your turn now. Prisoner pleads not guilty, gentlemen. What do you say—guilty or not guilty? I say guilty, myself."

The general was now surrounded by many more than the eleven officers he had called for, and from every mouth there issued a shout of—

"Guilty!"

"Prisoner, after a fair and patient trial," said the general, with a savage frown, "this court unanimously finds you guilty. Now we'll proceed to sentence. I will act as judge, and I sentence you to death. Pencil and paper, one of you gentlemen."

Gerald Leigh handed a pocket-book and pencil; and the general, hastily scribbling a few lines, tore out the leaf.

"Provost-marshal!"

"Yes, general!"

"Order for the execution of prisoner," said Stuart, with military brevity. "Report to me when sentence is carried out."

Lupus Rock was instantly dragged away towards the open ground in the rear of the church, and forced by

strong, relentless hands over the fence to a distance of
some fifty yards, when a halt was made. He struggled
fearfully, and so desperately, that it was with difficulty
three strong men held him. Not the faintest glimmer of
hope could he see, but he would not, could not give himself quietly up to his executioners' hands. Having lived
badly, he did not know how to die well.

"Will you be quiet, you wretch?" said the officer in
command of the firing party; "nothing can save you,
cease struggling, and you shall have three minutes for
prayer."

But Lupus only fought and wrestled the more desperately, his face ghastly white, his eyes blood-shot, his
hair wet with the perspiration of mortal terror. At
first he struggled in silence, but when he found his utmost
endeavours were futile, he cursed, swore, blasphemed,
threatened, and begged by turns.

Suddenly he ceased, and, panting with exertion said to
the officer, who stood scornfully looking on—

"Look here, sir, I require—I demand some short time
to set my affairs in order. I can give important information. I will betray the designs of the Federals."

"Will you?" was the contemptuous reply. "I don't
doubt you. You can if you like; I am ready to listen."

"But will my life be spared?"

"Ha! ha!—your life! No, not if you could betray
the whole Union army into our power."

"At least give me time to arrange my affairs and have
a clergyman," gasped the condemned wretch.

Lupus had, perhaps, some faint hopes that delay might
bring aid, that a Federal force might come up in time to
save him. Vain hope.

"Time to arrange your affairs," said the rebel officer—
"clergyman, no. Give you two minutes to make your
peace." He pulled out his watch as he spoke, and held it
in his hand.  ·

Again Lupus began struggling, yelling, and even
biting, in his frantic efforts to escape. The officer calmly
looked on, holding the watch in his hand. Second by
second passed on, and by the time the two minutes had

nearly expired he was almost exhausted. The hand pointed to the time, and the officer nodded his head as a signal.

"Kneel quietly, prisoner, and meet your fate like a man," he said. But when they attempted to force him to his knees he only redoubled his frantic struggles.

"Tie him to one of those small pine saplings," was the stern order; "he wont kneel and take his dose of lead quietly."

Then Lupus was dragged remorselessly along, and a cord being produced, he was bound with his back to a small tree. After seeing he was secure the troopers stepped back a few paces.

"See to your carbines, men, and when I give the word —fire!"

Then was heard the sharp click of the locks as the carbines were cocked. All this time Lupus was struggling fiercely, and had partly loosened his bonds so that he could sway his body to and fro.

"Go closer, men, close—five paces."

A moment's pause.

"Ready! Fire."

\* \* \* \* \* \* \*

As soon as Lupus was dragged away from the church door, Gerald Leigh, who had seen Stella Gayle, looked around for her, and then entered the church, where he found her near the altar with her father.

"Mr. Gayle," said he, hurriedly, "if you value your life and liberty, keep out of sight. Quick, into the vestry-room. If you are recognised, it will go hard with you." Webster, trembling and pale, quickly obeyed, leaving Gerald and Stella together.

"This is a strange meeting Stella," said Gerald.

"Strange, indeed. I cannot understand it," she answered in passionless tones. "Is Northern soil again to be invaded by the rebels?"

"Just so, Stella, and if we fail this time, we will at least give your people some idea of the miseries of war at your homes. Again and again we rebels will show you that, if you can invade the South and get back in safety, we can invade the North and get back when we please. This is but a cavalry raid, or reconnaissance. The main l ody of the army is now crossing the Potomac. My friend George and I return to Richmond at once with despatches. Let us come into the open air. A church is no place for idle talk."

Stella followed him as one in a dream ; events followed each other in such rapid succession, that she could with difficulty persuade herself it was all real.

"And now, Stella, what are you doing here ?"

"Hark ! what is that noise of shouting and yelling ?" she asked suddenly ; "is it not the voice of Lupus ?"

"Probably so," said Gerald, "he is a prisoner."

He did not like to shock her so far as to tell her he was about to be shot, for although he knew not that they were married, yet he remembered she was the cousin of the condemned traitor.

"What of your brother Darcy ?" she asked next.

Gerald looked sad and answered slowly,—"Darcy ! ah, poor Darcy ! It is, I fear, all over with him."

"Great Heavens ! is he dying ?"

"It is feared he cannot recover. He has been many times wounded during the war. At the battle of Chancellorsville he was again hit, a ball struck him in the chest, wounding the lungs ; it has been extracted, but he is not expected to survive—indeed, Stella, to tell the sad truth, he is sinking fast. Sometimes he is delirious, and then he often asks for you."

"Ah ! wretch that I am ! " she cried passionately, clasping her hands. "I will see him, Gerald, I will see him. Take me to him. Let me hear from his lips before he dies that he forgives me."

"Impossible, Stella, he is in Richmond."

"No, no, not impossible ; take me with you, Gerald," she said, imploringly.

"Stella, we go with despatches at full speed. The railroads are torn up for full fifty miles. You could not keep up with us nor stand the fatigue."

"Yes, yes, I can—I will," she replied, earnestly. ' Get me a swift horse and a side-saddle."

Gerald hesitated.

" But what of your father, Stella ? "

"Oh, he will return North with Lupus Rock ; and I can afterwards rejoin them and Angela."

" Angela ; ah !—I heard from her a few days back. She told me what I could scarcely believe—that you were about to consent to be the wife of that villain,—I must say so although he is your cousin—Lupus Rock. She begged me to save you, and even informed me you would be somewhere in Maryland or Pennsylvania. She implored me to prevent it if possible, saying that you were being forced into this match."

" Save me ? Oh, Gerald ! it is too late. Accursed be the hour I spoke the words."

" What words ? I don't understand you, Stella."

"Ah ! I forgot—you do not know." She paused for a moment, then added,—" Gerald, an hour ago—at this church—I was married to Lupus Rock."

" Great Heavens ! can it be possible ?" Then Gerald remained as if bewildered—thunderstruck.

" Unhappy girl ! "

At that moment there was a discharge of firearms, followed by a fearful yell.

" Ha ! what was that ?" cried Stella. " Are the Federal troops coming up ?"

Gerald moved a few paces so as to command a view of the ground at the back, and then returned.

" What was that discharge and that cry, Gerald ?"

" Stella, you just now said that an hour ago you were made the wife of Lupus Rock."

"Yes," she said, breathlessly

" Well, that discharge, that death cry, means that you are now his widow. Lupus Rock has been shot for his crimes. So, Stella, in the space of an hour you have been maid, wife, and widow."

She made no reply. The sudden shock deprived her of speech. The colour forsook her cheeks, she gasped for breath, her limbs failed her, and she might have fallen had not Gerald supported her into the church, and placed her on a seat.

24

Then she buried her face in her hands, and in the sacred building humbly put up a prayer to the Almighty. Her greatest enemy, her most relentless persecutor in this world, he had now gone to answer for his crimes before the great tribunal, and from the depth of her soul she forgave him.

## CHAPTER XXXIII.

### STELLA GAYLE'S RIDE TO RICHMOND.

LEAVING her alone for a short time, Gerald walked up to the rear of the church. The troopers were just leaving, after having performed their duty. The body of Lupus Rock was still bound to the tree. It was horribly disfigured, for every bullet of the ten fired had pierced either the chest, neck, or lower part of the face. Captain George joined him, and the two remained gazing on the mutilated corpse.

" A dreadful fate," said the Englishman, " but if ever a man deserved it, Lupus Rock was that man. Come, Gerald, let us mount and away."

Gerald rejoined Stella in the church. Pale and frightened, she was awaiting him.

" Gerald, this is terrible—horrible—with all his sins upon his head."

Gerald merely bowed his head, and said he must be going, as duty called him.

" No, Gerald, you shall not go thus—you shall take me to Richmond. Indeed, indeed—do not refuse me this."

She was so earnest and persistent in her appeal, that Gerald was induced to consider it. He remembered that his brother, in his delirium, frequently called on her name, and the thought struck him that the sight of her might soothe him, and perhaps even save his life ; so he decided to grant her request, if possible.

" Stella, do you persist in your intention ?"

" Yes, yes ; let me look on his face before he dies."

"In one hour I must return with the despatches. Can you be ready?"

"Yes, yes,—now—this instant."

Gerald smiled at her vehemence.

"Well, Stella, I will provide you horse and side-saddle. Have you a riding-habit?"

"Yes, yes; I will go into the town and put it on."

"Come, then, I also must go into the town for my despatches." Then he offered her his arm, and leading his horse they walked slowly on.

"Do not look to the left, Stella," he said, suddenly remembering they would pass within sight of the dead body.

"Ah!" she said, "are they burying him?"

"No," said Gerald, "let the crows have his body—a fitting doom for such a man."

"Gerald," she said, suddenly halting and grasping his arm, "do not let this be—do not show resentment after death. It is not for us to judge him—let him, then, at least be decently buried. Remember, Gerald, he was my cousin, and——" but she could not pronounce the word.

"You are right, Stella. With his life human justice should be satisfied. I will take the responsibility on myself."

Then he gave orders to four troopers to dig a grave and bury the remains of Lupus Rock.

An hour later, Gerald, George, and Stella Gayle were galloping along the road towards the Potomac, on their way to Richmond.

Webster Gayle in vain attempted to dissuade his daughter. Indeed, he was too much horrified and prostrated by the terrible fate of Lupus Rock, to offer much opposition; so he returned North, inwardly resolved never again to trust himself so far South, and in no cas to incur again the vengeance of the rebels.

Darcy Leigh lay in a hopeless state, suffering from low fever, in addition to his wounds. Thin and wasted, with hollow cheek and glittering, though sunken eye, too weak even to raise his hand—the doctors shook their heads, and said the end must soon come. Day by day he grew weaker and weaker, and latterly he had been unable to partake of any food. Occasional sips of port wine, procured at great cost and trouble, alone seemed capable of adding a little fuel to the expiring furnace of life.

Jupiter, the negro, was constantly by the side of his couch, fanning him, and brushing away the flies from his face, for he himself was incapable of even the slightest exertion. Few would have recognised in that wasted form and pale face, the dashing rebel who two years and a half ago had run away with the Spitfire, and had done so much in the service of the rebel cause.

Occasionally he fainted right away, and many times the faithful negro would say with a sigh,—

" Poor Massa Darcy, him dead now, him no play snakes an' glory wid de Yankees no more."

But strange to say, still he lingered on, and at the date of the arrival of Gerald, George, and Stella Gayle in Richmond, he was still alive.

They stood by his bedside, and though unable to move, he signified by a faint smile that he recognised them.

" Darcy," said Gerald, " some one has come to see you."

" Yes—yes," he whispered, faintly, " you and old George. God bless you, Gerald—it will soon be all over, I think."

" No—some one else—a lady Would you like to see her?"

" Who ?" he asked mutely with his eyes, for the exertion of speaking made him faint.

" Stella Gayle."

" Ah!"

A slight faint cry broke from his lips, his eyes glittered with unwonted light.—" Mine—mine! " he murmured— " yes, I will see her."

They gave him wine, and having taken a draught, he seemed to recover strength and asked to be lifted upon the couch.

Stella, almost as pale as the wounded man, was brought in by Gerald. She gazed for a moment at the now pale face and shrunken form of Darcy, and then falling on her knees by his side, seized his hand and kissed it. Gerald and George withdrew a little way.

"Darcy—Darcy, you are not going to die—you will recover, I know you will."

"I am afraid not, Stella—the sand has almost run out —I fear my hand will never hold a sword again."

"No—no, Darcy, you are better now—I am sure you are. There is quite a colour on your cheek."

"Is there, Stella? that is more than I can say for you. You look pale enough, my girl. This is kind of you, Stella—I can die happier now. Do you know, Stella— I don't mind telling you now—I always loved you, through all, and ever, notwithstanding slights, scorn, and insult."

"Oh, Darcy, Darcy, forgive me. How could I have been so unkind, so cruel?" she murmured, weeping. "Could I but live the last three years again! Darcy, I loved you, I did love—I do—I never loved any one else— I always shall love you."

A brighter flush came to his cheek, and his eyes shone brighter as he pressed her hand.

"Stella," said Gerald, touching her gently on the shoulder, for she remained in utter forgetfulness of every-thing, his hand pressed to her lips, " you had better come now. It is not safe to excite him too much."

Then she rose, and imprinting a kiss on his forehead, she suffered Gerald to lead her away.

" By golly !" said Jupiter, "I tink dat's de physic, Massa Darcy. Better dan all de bark and pison dey bin gibbin' you."

It was now evening, and Darcy soon fell asleep, and passed a better night. The next morning Jupiter waited on Stella Gayle soon after sunrise.

" Well, Jupiter, how is he?" she asked eagerly.

"Tink he's better, missa. He ate some chicken soup dis morning. It's all dat physic you gib him."

" Physic I gave him?"

" Yes, missa," said Jupiter, grinning from ear to ear " you know dat you done jist 'fore you go 'way."

Stella blushed, and said, —

"Don't be foolish, Jupiter. Can I see him?"

"Yes, missa ; dis chile reckon you may. Tink another dose of dat physic do him good."

When Gerald and George came to visit him, they found Stella by his bedside. The fever had left him, and he was stronger. But this had happened so often before and had been followed by a relapse, that they scarcely dared to hope. But the day passed and the next came without the dreaded fever reappearing, and it was certain he was stronger.

The surgeons now pronounced it as their opinion, that if he were removed to where he could enjoy sea air, or if possible, a sea voyage, he might recover ; but that if the fever again returned, all hope would be over. He could not possibly resist another attack.

After waiting seven days they thought it possible to remove him to Charleston, and this was resolved on. The journey was slowly performed, Gerald, Stella, George, and Jupiter accompanying him.

Arrived safely in Charleston, a brisk sea breeze which prevailed still further revived him. But the irritation caused by the bullet-wound in the chest never ceased, accompanied by incessant spitting of blood. The doctors were of opinion that the only chance of ultimate recovery lay in a sea voyage, and his removal to a colder climate, the oppressive heat of Charleston offering a fatal barrier.

It was finally decided that as it was quite hopeless that he would be able to serve in the field again, he should be placed on board a swift steamer, and run the blockade. Madeira—the climate of which was thought most suitable—was fixed upon, and preparations were quickly completed.

"Darcy," said Stella, when the time had almost come, "only a few more days, and then we must lose you. The thought is dreadful."

Darcy looked in her beautiful face, and smiling, said—
"Leave me, Stella!—must you, indeed—that is very cruel."

"Oh, Darcy," she said, colouring and casting down her eyes, "you know I must."

"Stella, dear, won't you come with me?" he said taking her hand.

She was silent; if she had answered, it would only have been as her heart prompted.

"Come, Stella—you will not leave me, will you? If you do I shall die."

She burst into tears, and keeping by his side, she said in a faltering voice—"Darcy, as you please—you have but to command, and I to obey."

"What, Stella!—will you leave all?—friends, home, sister, father?"

"All, Darcy, and cling to you."

A week afterwards they carried him down to the wharf in a sort of palanquin, and took him on board a swift steamer about to run the blockade. After landing him and Stella at Madeira, the steamer was to proceed to England for a cargo, call again at Madeira to inquire for his health, and run the blockade in again to Charleston.

Of course it was arranged, that when sufficiently recovered, Stella should be his wife.

Jupiter and Darby Kelly were to accompany them. The latter the day before asked to see him, and was shown into the room where he lay on a sofa, with Stella watching by him.

"Arrah now, Masther Darcy! would ye be after lavin me behind you? Sure after all the hard knocks and scrimmages we've had together, ye wouldn't desert me?"

"Why what can you do, Darby, except fight?" said Stella, smiling; "and there is no fighting where we are going."

"'Deed an' there's lots I can do, miss. Sure don't his honour want a *valet*?"

"But Jupiter occupies that post, Darby."

"Bad luck to his black skull! An' it's myself has a good mind to break it for him, the haythen nager, to stand in the way of any Oirish gintleman. Well, just list a bit, yer honner. Ain't yer honner goin' to be married?"

"Well, what of that?" Darcy replied, with a twinkle in his eye.

"May be yer honner 'll be afther wantin' a leddy's maid?"

Both laughed at this; but it was agreed that Darby Kelly, in reward for his faithful services, should go.

And so Darcy Leigh, in the cool of the evening, was carried on board the Greyhound, the little steamer which was to run the blockade and bear him away.

"Stella," he said, as he lay on a couch on the quarter-deck, just as twilight was deepening into night, "I feel hot, and my wound pains me again."

Stella in deep alarm felt his hand and brow; decidedly he was hot and feverish.

At the last moment, and while the vessel was lying alongside the wharf, moored only by a single warp and with steam up, the medical men were again brought to see him.

They looked grave, and said that it might arise from fatigue at being moved.

"Do you think the fever is coming back?" asked Stella, anxiously.

"We must hope not."

"But supposing it does?"

"We are all in the hands of Providence, Miss Gayle."

Stella felt alarmed and uneasy, as did Gerald and George. Was the terrible fever coming back in all its fury, to prey on his still weak frame, and the wound still inflamed and painful?

Fervently she prayed that it might not be so; but remembering the previous words of the doctors, that in that case there was no hope—her heart sank within her.

---

# CHAPTER XXXIV.

### THE CONCLUSION.

THE hour for the last farewell has come, when Gerald and the Englishman must bid a long, perhaps eternal farewell to their companion in arms.

But they are not the only ones who come to catch a last glimpse—exchange a last pressure of the hand with the wounded man. There are Wharncliffe, and Grey, and Winston, Trent, and others, whose acquaintance has been either old and of long standing, or had been made and cemented on the battlefield. It seems, indeed, that Charleston has poured out all her beautiful daughters to bid adieu to the wounded man. Many glances of admiring pity are cast on the pale face of Darcy, and some, too, of envy on Stella, as she bends tenderly over him.

But soon it is night, and as the run out is to be attempted after dark, the hawsers are cast off, and she steams slowly away. The night passed quietly, and when morning broke the Yankee ships could be made out in the offing, but no sign of the Greyhound. She had, in the darkness, run safely through.

"Thank God for this at least!" said Gerald Leigh, heaving a sigh of relief. "Safe through those bloodhounds—the sea-breezes on the voyage, and the mild balmy air of Madeira will soon put him right. Come, George, up to the office, and let's see what telegrams came down the line to-night. I long to be with Lee on the soil of the Old Dominion once more, to fight yet another battle for the 'Stars and Bars.'"

"More battles, more blood, more misery; when will all this end? Are you not yet tired, Captain Leigh, of this desperate war?"

The voice proceeded from a lady, dressed in deep mourning, as, alas! were too many in Charleston, for near relatives slain or struck down by disease.

"Tired, yes; as a man might be who is forced to defend his home against thieves and murderers, but by no means inclined to give up. No! if it is to be, let it be; let us fight the fight out to the bitter end; let it come to a war of extermination, as it will sooner or later, when no quarter will be given, no prisoners taken—a war to the death. So long as we are united among ourselves, Nina, they can never conquer us. Shall we despond because they have starved out two strongholds on the Mississippi, and just succeeded in keeping our armies from their

capital? Our cause is lost when our men's hearts fail
them, and that, please God, will never be."

Nina only sighed, and turning to Captain George, said,
" And why should you thus continue to risk your life?
Have *you* not had fighting enough? You are an English-
man, and as such can now honourably retire."

"If I do may I be ——; well, never mind, Nina, I
only mean to say that, as Gerald and I began this business
together, I mean to see it through."

" Ah, well," she said, sadly, " you will get killed or
wounded to death, like Captain Darcy, and then I shall
be without a friend in the world."

" Nina, you are rich; money will find you many
friends."

She turned away in silence, but seeing that she was
hurt at his words, he moved closer to her.

" Don't be angry, Nina. I didn't mean to make you
so when I spoke of money."

" Much you care," she replied, pouting.

" What! for money?"

" No, for me."

" You know I do care for you, Nina."

" I do not know it. I don't believe it," she replied,
but her voice trembled, and the rich brown of her cheek
deepened to crimson.

" Do you wish me to mean it?" he said, smiling, and
taking her hand. There was no answer. " Come, Nina,
I shall think your wealth has made you proud, if you
treat me thus."

" Again you taunt me, again you throw this wealth in
my face; but for the memory of her who left it, I would
cast it from me, and be again Nina the *vivandière.*

" And were you so indeed, without a cent or a name,
I would still be as I now am—yours; so, Nina, doubt me
no more."

" And you mean to say——"

" That I love you; but you knew that long ago. Come,
one kiss, and let us talk of other things. I have much
to do yet."

A grateful, loving glance, with eyes suffused with tears,

her frame trembling with joy, and flushed face held up to his for the kiss he asked, was his answer.

The end of July, 1863, and the beginning of August witnessed a succession of desperate attacks on the defences of Charleston by the Federals. Foiled in their attempts to force an entrance into the harbour by their iron-clads, these latter now drew off to a safe distance, and joined in the continued and terrible bombardment kept up on Fort Wagner by batteries on the island.

Shortly before twelve o'clock on a day in the beginning of August the fire, which had been unusually severe, gradually died away, and to the prolonged thunder of the great guns a deep silence succeeded.

The next morning, before daylight, the thunder of guns is again heard, and hastily dressing they hurry to a position on a battery commanding a view of the harbour.

The firing seemed to be a considerable distance in the offing, and was evidently confined to the ships of the squadron. Gradually it approached nearer, as though caused by the blockading ships pursuing some audacious vessel attempting to run in. Presently the fire grew slacker and then ceased, as though the vessel had either escaped or had been captured.

A heavy morning mist hid the harbour from sight, so that it was impossible for the lookers-on to tell the result.

In vain Gerald and many others strained their eyes in the endeavour to make out a steamer running in. The battery was on high ground and above the mist, but all beneath lay shrouded in a veil.

Suddenly and unexpectedly is heard the boom of a gun. It is quite close—in the part of the harbour leading to the Cooper River.

A murmur of surprise runs round among the officers on the battery. "What can it mean, firing in the harbour right under the batteries!"

Men gaze in each others' faces in blank astonishment, and a superior officer presently gives orders for a boat to be manned, and the meaning of this firing discovered.

Again the guns peal forth; and, at the sound, Gerald Leigh, who is looking in another direction, turns and sees above the mist, which is rapidly drifting away, the masts and funnel of a small steamer, carrying only two small guns, one of which is being loaded, while at the other stands a man ready to fire.

At a signal from an officer on the quarter-deck this gun is discharged, and quickly following the flash and smoke, the report is heard.

Then it is noted that all the flags on the steamer are half-mast. Minute guns, too! Can she be in distress? Impossible; for she is within a cable's length of the shore.

On the skylight on the quarter-deck there is an object covered by a flag. A sentry stands beside it with reversed arms.

Kneeling by the side, with her face hidden in her hands, the form of a female may be discerned, and at a little distance a negro and another man, whose features cannot be recognised, lean against the mizen-mast, and seem to be looking sadly on. Again is heard the report of the gun.

"George," said Gerald, pale as death, while tears rolled down his face, "it is poor Darcy.'

\*     \*     \*     \*     \*     \*     \*

The vessel which had run the blockade inwards was the same which a week previously had run out.

Stella Gayle's fears had been too well founded. The fierce fever had again set in, and in three days Darcy Leigh—the brave, the gallant—had given up his soul to his Maker. There was no need now to proceed to Madeira, so the steamer once again run into Charleston.

Like wildfire the news spread that the young hero was dead. The bells of all the churches tolled, and a vast crowd followed the coffin to the grave.

And so, after a short but brilliant career, perished one of the many brave hearts who in this desperate conflict perilled and lost their lives for their country.

And now that the principal actors are removed from the scene, it is time to drop the curtain on this our drama.